KNIGHTS O

THE FORGOTTEN PROPHECY

Book 1: In Search of the Great Dragon

MYLES ALEXANDER

© Copyright 2021 Myles Alexander

Cover art by Jamie Noble

Dear Ines,
I really hope you enjoy it!
[signature] 9-6-2021
Edinburgh
SCOTLAND

IN SEARCH OF THE GREAT DRAGON

CHAPTERS

1. THE ANCIENT SCROLLS
2. THE MESSENGER
3. BATTLE OF DRAGON'S PASS
4. THE RIDE HOME
5. ENTERING ETERNITY
6. ETERNIAN HIGH COUNCIL
7. THE SEVEN KNIGHTS
8. TEMPLE GARDENS
9. ETERNIAN THEATRE
10. JOURNEY TO THE ORACLE
11. INSIGHTS OF WISDOM
12. ANCIENT DELPHOESIA
13. PATH TO THE BUVARIOUS
14. EYE OF THE STORM
15. MEETING OF DESTINY
16. FOLLOWING ONE'S HEART
17. UNDER THE STARS
18. DREAMING OF DRAGONS
19. THE JOURNEY ONWARDS

20. BRIDGE OF LEGENDS

21. INTO LANDS UNCHARTED

22. VALLEY OF THE GODS

23. THE ANCIENT CASTLE

24. TWIN SUNS

25. A NEW ACQUINTANCE

26. AGE OF LORDS

27. REIACUS LEGEND

28. AGE OF HEROES

29. ACHTREIAS: GREAT HERO OF ETERNITY

30. AGE OF REASON

31. SKOLASTROS' PAST

32. VALLEY TEMPLE

33. TOWARD THE GREAT MOUNTAINS

34. SERENDIPIDOUS ENCOUNTER

35. INTO THE BUVARIOUS

36. SNOWSTORM

37. THE FINAL STRETCH

38. ICE CAVES

39. THE GREAT ONE

40. REIACTUS AND THE KING

41. THE PEAK

42. IN SEARCH OF THE FORESTMAN

43. THE HIDDEN VILLAGE

THE ANCIENT SCROLLS

When the earth shakes like thunder,
The Great Dragon will soar;
and a once vast empire shall fall

The veteran archaeologist chipped away frantically at the small wooden chest, his sense of anticipation growing by the instant, wondering what priceless treasures he might discover within: would there be gold coins, lavish jewels or perhaps a map leading to riches in uncharted lands? Whatever the case, they must have been here for countless eons, he excitedly thought, harking all the way back to an age when men of supreme courage, fearless devotion and unbridled ambition roamed these ancient lands, seeking the immortality of glory. He wondered if those brave souls had once possessed this mysterious chest and their hands caressed its invaluable contents, before imagining their adventures into distant lands and struggles with many a foe over countless eons of history.

While lost in thoughts of suns long past, Brachaeis unwittingly managed to prise the silver-plated chest wide open. He gasped, carefully reached inside and removed what appeared to be a set of parchment scrolls, with elaborate inscriptions and rough, weathered edges. There were simply no words to describe his sense of utter bewilderment. Composing himself, Brachaeis carefully unravelled the mysterious documents and was quickly immersed in their intricate writings and long, captivating stanzas.

"By the gods above, could they *really* be... the scrolls of the Ancient Prophecy?" he wondered, reading the first page from top to bottom in sheer astonishment. It was without question, a discovery unequalled since the Age of Heroes itself, and something he could have never conceivably imagined in a thousand passing suns. As Brachaeis' wise old eyes examined the mysterious writings, he came to the unequivocal realisation it could mean only thus: the great dragon's return would soon be upon them. Indeed, it had been said just prior to this happening, writings pertaining to it would be discovered in a most unexpected way.

For countless eons of Eternian history, kings, seekers and adventurers alike had sought the glory, prestige and honour of this unheralded discovery, only to have their dreams of immortality scuppered by the merciless hands of the gods. After all those who had come before it was to be he, Brachaeis, a humble servant of his majesty who would hold them in his hands. It was an unearthing beyond all imaginable compare and of proportions quite unsurpassed, with the potential to change not only his nation, but very course of history itself.

"Remarkable, this is *truly remarkable*," he gasped in disbelief, caressing the fine edges of the delicate parchment leaves, as though trying to authenticate their primordial beginnings. "By the hand of the ancients themselves," he added with incredulity, thanking the gods profusely it be upon *he* that a boon of such unparalleled magnificence bestowed.

Intuitively, Brachaeis cast a glance to the other side of the long, dark cave, where his young apprentice was sifting through a pile of golden artefacts.

"Protoeous, come quickly!" he barked, beckoning wildly to his enthusiastic pupil. Brachaeis had come to the realisation of what it all meant, adamant *nothing* could now halt the great changes that had been yearned for so many suns. With those all-too-familiar sparks in Protoeous' eyes, Brachaeis saw a thousand words unspoken: it was in that moment he knew it *would be so.*

The apprentice scurried over from the mound of valuable objects and knelt beside his captivated superior on the rocky cave floor. Protoeous was equally incredulous as he clenched his hands together, his eyes widening in sheer disbelief.

"Whatever have you found, master?" he asked, peering dreamily at the intriguing discovery. Protoeous had quickly forgotten the bounty of ornate jewels, gold pieces and other valuables strewn throughout the cave, so instantly beguiled was he. The surrounding treasures were of an age long past in their nation's illustrious history: their value, however, incomparable to these most sacred documents.

"You would not in a thousand suns believe it," managed a shocked Brachaeis, falling hard against the rough cave wall as he struggled to grasp the significance of it all. The apprentice moved ever closer, equally curious as to the nature of this unexpected finding.

"A set of scrolls!" Protoeous cried, breathless with shock. "And of *many eons* past; but, how could they have survived for so long?" he continued, realising the depths of a cave not the most intelligent place to store items of such intricate delicacy.

The apprentice gazed intensely at the mysterious writings, which were now considerably faded. Brachaeis was equally bewildered, scratching his head in confusion.

"Only the gods could possibly know, my young companion," he responded, shaking his head, likewise wishing to know how they had come to be in this most unsuspecting of places. "Please, have a look for yourself!" Brachaeis handed the parchment to his impish, bright-eyed apprentice, who reached over with palms outstretched. "But be cautious. They are *extremely* fragile: from the Age of Heroes itself, if I am not mistaken!"

Protoeous took the unravelled scrolls carefully within his grasp, all too aware of their significance and enormous potential held: it truly was a moment of historical proportions. The world began to fade away mystically into the cavernous background as Protoeous stared into the script, his eyes flickering deliriously across the countless lines of cryptic text.

"I simply cannot believe it!" he whispered, turning to his wise master.

Brachaeis gestured enthusiastically, willing him on. "Keep reading, Protoeous: there is more, *so very much* more," he said, motioning anxiously with his slender, educated fingers.

The apprentice promptly shifted his eyes back to the mysterious writings, curious what ancient secrets might soon be revealed. As Protoeous slowly read, Brachaeis lay back against the jagged cave wall, rubbed a thin layer of sweat from his forehead and took a deep reflective breath. He clenched his hands together in contemplation, realising the profound implications for not only Eternity, but the *entire* known world…

The city-state of Eternity had a rich tapestry of myths and legends, reaching long before her recorded history and much-revered Age of Heroes. Of particular fascination was the legendary Reiactus: a grandiose being that, many eons ago saved Eternity from a fate quite uncertain during *that* great heroic age. The story goes that the ancients had been locked in mortal combat with the First Empire for many moons, their number falling rapidly with every passing sun. With loyal allies by their side, the Eternian army was forced to retreat behind their city walls, defeat almost certain against this overwhelming malevolent force. When all hope for victory seemed lost, a dragon of immense physical proportions appeared from the skies above and swept into the titanic battle ensuing, far below. The being attacked enemy lines without mercy, thwarting their unrelenting advance. Providing the allies a chance to regroup, they bravely fought back to claim a dramatic rearguard victory, bringing an end to the First Empire and its ambition for *total* control over the known world.

The mysterious dragon was instantly hailed a hero and had been remembered ever since as Eternity's great saviour. The massive creature was badly wounded in action, however, having sustained many wounds from the relentless barrage of imperial artillery. At the king's behest, the dragon stayed in Eternity until the final setting of the suns, revealing amongst many other things his *true* identity and purpose. The giant imparted that he had been sent from the Higher Realms as a protector of the known world, with the ability to intervene in circumstances of an exceptional nature. Despite attempts to assist the wounded titan, Reiactus explained that only by returning to his faraway home could his wounds of battle ever be healed. Promising one sun to return, the dragon took off into the Buvarious Mountains, never to be seen again. His departure was as dramatic as his arrival, with immortality in Eternian history, myth and legend assured, forevermore.

It was a story that had captured the imaginations of bards, kings and adventurers alike, inspiring many a daring soul over the eons to embark on the perilous quest in search of their enigmatic hero. Many had set out, with few ever returning to tell the enthralling tale. There was an ancient prophecy foretelling the mighty dragon's return and that he would once more light Eternity's darkest moment: it had long been anticipated, but there was little indication until now, that it would ever come to pass. Brachaeis for one had always been a firm believer, never questioning that one sun the dragon *would finally* return and fulfill the prophecy.

The esteemed and noble King of Eternity, Alectorious the 2nd, was a passionate student of his nation's illustrious history, having left not a stone unturned in search for the truth of his people's origins and to where they were ultimately destined: anything that might shed light on Eternity's mysterious beginnings was thoroughly examined. Little did his majesty realise how close they were to answering those many questions that had for eons troubled the minds of great thinkers and philosophers alike. When King Alectorious learned of a cave uncovered by the recent earthquake, he had hesitated not a moment in despatching his chief archaeologist and historian, Brachaeis Mesirius Soearias. The earth thunder had ravaged much of the lands, causing widespread damage throughout the seven city states. Although it had exposed numerous sites of significance, this particular cave had been of greatest interest due to its proximity to the fabled Dragon's Pass and a castle ruin from a now-long-past age.

It was a moment Brachaeis had all his life dreamed: he firmly believed that not only was the dragon's return imminent, but the dawn of a grandiose new era for Eternity and the wider known world was finally upon them. The archaeologist rested his head gently against the rock wall, taking several breaths to relax his fretting nerves. With eyes firmly shut, he allowed his imagination to drift briefly into the realms of Astrala: the place one's spirit travelled to in their dreams. When they finally passed on from this ephemeral world of matter into the realms of the non-physical, Eternians believed their souls would travel to the mystical lands of Athepothesia, where the gods themselves were said reside. Those who had defied the will of the gods were sent to The Netherworld: a dark, formless place of endless nothingness where all manner of sinister beings were said to exist.

As the chief archaeologist came to his senses, he further contemplated the permutations of this startling discovery and all it entailed: magnificent as it was unexpected, dramatic as it was unbelievable, wondering if it would prove to be all he had ever hoped and dreamed. It was a thought that but a few suns ago seemed impossible: now Brachaeis could almost touch the air of change with own his bare hands. Meanwhile, his young apprentice was reading frenziedly through the scrolls, whose inscriptions were faded from countless eons hidden deep in the cave. He was careful not to damage the ancient parchment, the profound importance of which could only be imagined by one of such humble beginnings. Protoeous could hardly believe his eyes as he reached the second page of the curious writings: that which had been prophesised, for so many suns.

"By the gods above, Brachaeis, did you see this?" he asked, preparing to read a particularly striking passage. "Master, listen!"

Brachaeis did exactly this, leaning over intently as his apprentice read out loud, much in the way one would when reading a story by oneself.

In the final suns of the last great king's reign,
a mighty dragon shall fall like a blinding light from the skies above
and forever vanquish the forces of darkness from these once-benevolent lands.
Unbeknownst to the world of men, the great one has long awaited in
the heights of majestic mountains unnamed, until his moment of destiny.

"It speaks of the great Reiactus *and* his imminent return!" Protoeous gasped, unable to restrain his feelings of sheer elation. The archaeologist was bleary-eyed with shock as he tried to come to terms with what he had just heard. He struggled for a moment to respond before finally managing to focus on the mysterious writings.

"That it does, my young companion! In all my suns I could have never imagined - quite unbelievable indeed," Brachaeis beamed, with his eyes lighting up like proverbial stars in the night sky.

There was now a single question on Protoeous' euphoric mind.

"I wonder, master: what do you think it means?"

"I believe it signals the beginning, Protoeous, of the end of *all* that is not of the light. It shall be the dawn of the final age: greater even, than the Age of Heroes! This, our known world is on the verge of tremendous change, my young apprentice!" Brachaeis exclaimed, rubbing his hands together in sheer delight. The excitement of this magnificent destiny felt almost tangible to Protoeous, such was the passion with which his master spoke.

"I can hardly believe it!" he incredulously gasped. As he realised the implications of their find, Protoeous visualised that promised land of freedom and prosperity that had hitherto been a figment of his wild imagination. Brachaeis had no doubts at all, wholly convinced of the scrolls' meaning that he was.

"Now you *must* believe, Protoeous; with all of your heart and every fragment of your soul," he said, speaking now in a far more serious tone.

The archaeologist paused and took a deep breath, allowing for a moment of mutual reflection.

"If what you speak of *is* true, master, these may well be the scrolls of the Ancient Prophecy!" Protoeous elated, with the promise of great change inspiring him beyond belief. He stood suddenly, bumping his head on the roof of the cave. Rubbing the subsequent lump, the apprentice continued, unconcerned. "It was said the scrolls would be discovered not long before Reiacus' return…"

Brachaeis nodded in tacit agreement. "…Indeed, and if it really *is* them, Protoeous, it is a *very* exciting moment to be alive!" he exclaimed, with an exuberance not felt in countless eons. "We are tremendously fortunate, for the gods have *truly* blessed us!" he added.

Casting his attention back to the scrolls, the archaeologist hoped it would signal the changes so desperately needed for these beleaguered lands. It was said Reiactus' return would herald an age of unparalleled transformation beyond anything that had come before. Brachaeis had studied the Ancient Prophecy in great depth, hoping for many eons it would *finally* come to pass. He could hardly believe it might be so soon, and in his very own life.

Protoeous continued to examine the antique documents, frantically searching for signs of their origin. He turned eagerly to the following page, desperate for an answer.

"What of this script here, master? It is quite unlike *anything* I have ever seen – I can read not a single word!" he gasped, pointing to an unintelligible passage in the bottom right-hand corner of the parchment.

"It is an ancient Eternian dialect: almost certainly from the Age of Heroes!" Brachaeis replied, having quickly recognised the series of uniquely-shaped pictograms.

"Whatever does it say?" Protoeous impatiently asked, lightly pressing his fingers against the worn parchment.

His master moved a bit closer, squinting in an attempt to decipher the complex series of characters.

"I am not *entirely* sure - I shall most certainly have to translate it when we return to Eternity," he conceded, struggling to make out any detail in the dimly-lit environment of the caves. "But first, they *must* be delivered to his majesty, and without delay! These scrolls *must not* under any circumstances whatsoever be allowed to fall into the hands of The Empire, Protoeous. Mark my words: the very fate of our entire civilisation is at stake!"

"But master!" the apprentice said, casting a suggestive glance to the swathes of invaluable articles scattered across the rough cave floor. Brachaeis knew exactly what Protoeous was thinking but showed due restraint, emotionlessly cutting his sentence short.

"Come now - gather your things - we return at once to camp!" he coolly ordered, hastily grabbing the precious documents.

Brachaeis moved swiftly to the entrance of the bounty-laden cavern as Protoeous was hesitant, peering back longingly at the countless valuables.

"What of all this treasure, Brachaeis? By the gods, we cannot simply abandon it all - there must be an untold fortune - and of great value to Eternity!" he protested, motioning to the gold, ornate jewelry and elegant weaponry strewn throughout, secretly wishing for a share of the spoils.

Brachaeis turned and looked Protoeous straight in the eye.

"My young apprentice, the words I hold now in my hands are worth more than all the gold you could *possibly* imagine - believe me in this," he said, waving the delicate scrolls steadfastly in the air. As the apprentice dropped his head, disheartened, the veteran changed his tone, smiling sympathetically. "Look. Perhaps if the king allows it, we can return once more - if that is what you *truly* wish," Brachaeis said, knowing *well* the feeling of discovering such bountiful treasure, yet so soon having to abandon it.

Protoeous wished to argue but knew he had little choice in the matter.

"I trust in your wise judgment, master," he conceded despondently, literally and metaphorically dragging his feet along the rocky cave floor.

"There *will* be another chance, Protoeous, I promise," Brachaeis warmly encouraged, turning before moving to the light at the end of the narrow passageway. Protoeous followed reluctantly, leaving behind the many gold, silver and diamond-emblazoned artefacts. Discovering such treasures had been a dream come true for the apprentice, as much as it was heartbreaking to leave them behind; perhaps *never* to be seen again.

The two spritely archaeologists hastily made their way out through the narrow stone corridor, out into the open air and bright blue skies - a welcome relief from the claustrophobic nature of the caves. The apprentice took a breath of fresh air and relaxed, absorbing the beauty of the surrounding rolling green hills and meandering streams, deep into his body and soul. Protoeous could truly feel something special in the air: that after all these eons living in fear, change would *finally* be upon these troubled lands.

Nearby, Brachaeis had carefully wrapped the scrolls in a soft blue cloth to protect them from the powerful rays of the binary suns shining from high above. He signalled to Protoeous, and the two moved briskly to their fine steeds, which were closely guarded by a mounted squad of Elite Eternian Guards. The king had insisted only his very best warriors accompany them, such was the importance placed upon archaeological discoveries. The king had had a strong intuitive feeling something *very* special lay hidden in this cave: it was not the first instance his acute senses had duly been vindicated.

"Rhiedous, we depart immediately for camp - we have a discovery of tremendous importance for his majesty!" Brachaeis ordered with force reverence, grasping the reins of his noble white equine. He pulled himself swiftly onto the saddle as his apprentice did likewise. They had to move quickly, for there was no knowing who might be taking an interest in their handiwork.

In moments, the commanding lieutenant was spurred into action.

"At the speed of the gods, sire!" Rhiedous humbly acknowledged.

He signalled his fellow guardsmen, who moved rapidly into formation around Brachaeis and Protoeous. Instants later, the two archaeologists sped off with the group of mounted warriors in the direction of the temporary Eternian camp, not knowing what fate awaited. Protoeous cast one long last glance back to the cave as they rode over a small hill, saddened to leave such bountiful treasures behind yet enlivened by the possibilities ahead. Brachaeis thought more about their discovery, its tremendous implications and if the known world was finally, after so many eons on the verge of great change.

He could have never in his wildest dreams imagined what was soon to transpire…

THE MESSENGER

Stegalos firmly closed his eyes as the winds howled with a high-pitched whistle, over the rolling hills and valleys afar, blowing swathes of hair over his youthful face. Brushing his light-brown locks aside, the intelligent messenger and scout turned his horse round from whence he had been, as if guided by an inexplicable, otherworldly force. He intuitively looked up to a small rocky outcrop not more than a few spears wide, with the strangest tingling sensation running deep into his very bones. As the powerful winds subsided for the briefest of moments, Stegalos swore he had heard something or *someone* echo from over what was presumably a cliff's edge. The attentive messenger sat upright in his saddle, focusing on the outcrop with his discerning blue eyes. Upon seeing nothing suspicious, he initially dismissed it as nothing more than wild imagination, as his mighty steed trotted in a near-perfect circle.

All seemed otherwise quiet and calm on the grassy hills surrounding the fabled Dragon's Pass: but something just was not right. Stegalos had a feeling in the furthest depths of his body, right to his very soul - it was something indescribable - something he had never, in all his suns felt before. A mysterious voice from deep within was telling, almost forcing him to further investigate. Only moments ago he had dismissed the small rocky hill to the south-west as a fleeting thought, but as one of Eternity's most trusted riders, it was *imperative* he follow even the smallest intuitive impulse that the enemy might be close at hand. It was, after all, a great honour and responsibility to be in direct service to the king himself. It was a duty he was immensely proud to fulfill and cherished every moment as if it his last. Stegalos had promised there would be not a stone left unturned to ensure the safety of his nation - and this sun would be no different.

Situated north-west of Dragon's Pass on the foothills of the great Buvarious Mountains, the city-state of Eternity had long been anticipating an attack from the empire, and it was one which could arrive any sun now. Such were heightened tensions in the region, the army led by King Alectorious himself was stationed in a nearby temporary camp in anticipation of hostile incursions into Eternian territory. There had been whispers of heavy imperial activity by informants in the occupied city states but there was little evidence to substantiate these outlandish claims. The king had insisted on leaving nothing to chance and that any possible threat, no matter how small, had to be treated most seriously.

Stegalos was long overdue back at camp but knew it would not take long to investigate. The brazen young scout turned his trusted steed back toward the rocky outcrop and rode a few gallops before dismounting onto the soft grass.

"Await your master patiently, Phelious. I shall not be long," Stegalos promised, stroking his equine affectionately on its thick brown mane. Phelious shook his head profusely, neighing in acknowledgement of his thoughtful master. The messenger then turned and advanced toward the mystifying hill. Silently and slowly at first he went, following that mysterious, inexplicable impulse. Step by step, his heartbeat grew faster, bit by bit, that intuitive feeling stronger. As Stegalos began up the grassy, rocky hill, his anxiety intensified as all the permutations of what it might be flashed through his translucent mind. As the hill steepened, he used his hands to steady himself, with his breaths becoming deeper with each and every step.

After much exertion, Stegalos finally reached the top of the rocky outcrop before collapsing to the ground in exhaustion. He slowly stood with hands placed firmly upon both knees to catch his breath. The messenger's eyes were quite firmly shut, as if he wanted to avoid that which he sensed he would wish not see. Dramatically slowing his breathing, Stegalos could hear the echoes of a thousand voices reverberating throughout the sweeping valley, far below. The greater part of him was in denial, yet the other knew the only thing it could possibly be. As the Eternian rider nervously opened his eyes, his entire body froze in shock at the unbelievable sight before him.

"By the gods above!" was all he could manage, as the realisation of a thousand nightmares struck him in a moment that felt like forever. All Stegalos' worst fears were realised in that one chilling instant: as if the gods of thunder had hit him with their unrestrained wrath.

"How could this be?" he whispered in utter bewilderment, trying to come to terms with the enormity of what he saw. In the valley before him, a vast army of heavily armed soldiers stood in formation, wearing shining black-and-gold armour; fully equipped with sword, spear and shield, ready at a moment's notice for action. It was the most terrifying thing Stegalos had ever seen: endless rows of dark warriors standing to attention, as if awaiting their final orders for battle. There were others nearby busy practising their swordsmanship, while yet others, much smaller in number, were engaged in some sort of meeting. They were quite probably the commanding officers, judging by their long black capes and elaborate golden-crested helmets. The messenger's heart raced out of control as he scanned the endless hordes, feeling utterly helpless to act. Countless thoughts raced through his mind but there was only one conclusion he could possibly draw as to their intentions.

"By The Great Spirit - it was ever so lucky I followed that intuitive feeling!" he whispered. "They *must* be preparing for invasion! I had best warn the king, at the very speed of the gods!"

In his shock, Stegalos had forgotten he was in direct view of the entire gathered force, with it only being only a matter of moments before he would be seen. But it was too late: his position on the rocky outcrop had already been given away to observant enemy eyes.

"Intruder!!!" screamed a member of the infantry, before pointing in Stegalos' direction. A bowman instantly responded, unleashing an arrow at tremendous velocity. Before he could react, the arrow hit the stunned messenger directly in the right leg, tearing through tender muscle fibre and ligament. Stegalos fell to the ground, screaming in sheer agony. He managed to compose himself just long enough to snap the arrow and draw the barb from his thigh. Stegalos was now barely able to stand, but managed to roll down the grassy hill to his waiting steed. Arrows continued to rain down, with one almost piercing the wounded messenger's shining blue-and-gold armour. In moments, yet another volley of arrows punctured the grass around him, but again failed to hit their elusive target.

Panic quickly began to reverberate throughout the gathered army, as the soldiers knew failure to halt the intruder would have truly fatal consequences. It was soon relayed to the commanding officers, who frantically tried to take control of the escalating situation.

"Stop, you blithering imbeciles!" screamed a Gomercian officer, running furiously to his archers. "*Do not kill him*, fools!" he wrathfully screamed, clipping the nearest marksman on the head with his open hand. "Do you not see? He will lead us *straight* to the Eternian camp!" he fumed, pointing in Stegalos' direction near the cliff's edge. The officer clenched fists as he raged with frustration, realising the entire operation was now in serious jeopardy. "You!" he shouted, turning to a nearby mounted warrior. "Follow him to the enemy camp - as soon as you know their location and number - return! *Do not* fail me again!" he spat.

"Yes, My Lord Valatrox!" the rider replied, readying his imposing mount before taking off swiftly in pursuit of the Eternian messenger.

Stegalos had meanwhile managed to drag himself onto his trusted steed, trying his best to ignore the agonizing pain and focus on his duty. All Eternity now relied upon him: he dare not let them down, no matter what the personal cost. The messenger took one final look at the outcrop, praying to the gods above he would not be followed by the enemy multitudes.

"To camp, Phelious. Ya!" he cried, pulling hard on the reins of his loyal stallion.

Phelious took off at lightning speed, as if having read his master's thoughts. In his exhausted pain, Stegalos was barely able to hang on, unable to erase the memory of what he had just witnessed. "Eternity is in great danger - we *cannot* - we *must not* let them catch us, Phelious! The king must be warned at all costs; if it means even our lives!"

The messenger held on tight as Phelious galloped with all his strength to the safety of camp. The two gallant beings traversed several hills and streams, pausing for not a moment until he sighted trusted companions. Just as the Eternian position came into view, Stegalos began to fall into semi-consciousness. Located not far from the edge of the fabled Dragon's Pass, the temporary camp was surrounded on all sides by thick green pine forest, with its location well hidden and until this moment, entirely unknown to the enemy.

The duty sentry, watching from a distance in the makeshift observation tower, caught sight of Stegalos' rapid approach and realised all was not well. He immediately sounded the alarm to his fellow watchman.

"Haelious - rider returning at great speed - and he looks to be wounded. Warn the king at once!" Seihresious bellowed, relaying from the watchtower to his alarmed companion standing on the ground beneath.

Haelious swiftly made his way not ten spears distant to the king's tent, which was emblazoned with two shining gold stars and a large blue dragon: the mark of Eternian royalty. Regally perched on top of a small grassy hill, the tent was surrounded by his majesty's finest Elite Guardsmen, all donning shimmering blue-and-gold armour and distinctive plume helmets.

"At once!" Haelious replied, moving swiftly to the king's tent.

As the soldier reached the entrance, he reluctantly edged inside, hoping not to interrupt anything of great importance. King Alectorious had been hitherto discussing the recently discovered set of scrolls with a number of his most trusted knights and companions: Rapacosis, Jalectrious, Thelosious and Gavastros. There had been much impassioned debate as to their true meaning and purpose but all were in thorough agreement the ancient scrolls would have a profound impact upon the future of their nation and most certainly, the wider known world. Haelious stepped forth, promptly clearing his throat to speak.

"My lord, pardon the interruption!" he exclaimed, as all heads turned to the sentry. The young watchman stepped hastily forth, removed his helmet and bowed in accordance with Eternian custom.

"Ah! What have you to report, my good man Haelious?" the king gleefully demanded, carefully handing the scrolls to his nearby squire, Synctrious, for safekeeping.

"It appears we have a wounded rider, sire: he returns in great haste!"

All present could immediately feel the change in atmosphere as they turned their focus to the young but vulnerable sentry standing before their king, Alectorious.

"By the gods, who is it?" he demanded anxiously. Moving a step closer, the king looked into Haelious' eyes with deep concern, immediately fearing the worst.

Trying to compose himself as tension in the tent increased by the instant, he knew something of tremendous consequence had just transpired. Before Alectorious' question could be answered, an exhausted figure burst in and collapsed in front of the king and his knights. Desperately short of breath and greatly distressed, the poor weary soul could barely utter a word. The king was in utter shock, reacting quickly.

"Stegalos!" he cried.

Alectorious leapt to his loyal messenger's assistance and the other knights hastily gathered round as medics were called in to attend the gaping wound in Stegalos' leg. The king knelt, placing his hand on the messenger's shoulders. Alectorious could only imagine the pain his chief rider was experiencing. He spoke to him in a quiet, soft voice.

"My trusted companion, whoever did this to you?" he demanded, furious at the fate Stegalos had suffered.

Trembling, the frightened messenger slowly raised his head, with a look in his eyes that told a thousand terrifying tales.

"It was they, my noble king - the ones of which you have spoken, dressed in black-and-gold armour they were - untold warriors preparing for battle."

The king froze in disbelief as he looked up and locked eyes with his respected general, Rapacosis. In one chilling instant, they both knew *exactly* of what Stegalos spoke.

"This was most certainly not the work of bandits, sire; these were trained soldiers. The Black Knights of Gomercia: of that, there can be no question," concluded the king's chief warrior in his trademark guttural timbre. A veteran of countless campaigns against Eternity's arch nemesis, Rapacosis would be ready for anything the enemy could throw at them.

After coming to his senses, the king finally managed to articulate a cohesive response.

"By the gods in Athepothesia, we scanned the area three times this morn! *How* could this be possible!?" he gasped in frustration, his palms wide open with incredulity.

The general kept his nerve, as ever ice cool, knowing it was the only way to overcome the adversity faced and see this testing moment through to the end.

"They are a highly mobile force, sire. Perhaps not as much as ourselves; nonetheless, they could well have arrived after our last riders departed. It is a vast area, Alectorious - we could not possibly have covered it all." Rapacosis insisted, as the other knights nodded in agreement. The general was a veteran of many battles with the Gomercian Empire - in his experience, they cared little for the welfare of their fellow man - their only desire was for conquest, gold and all that the spoils of war entailed. Rapacosis turned his attention to the trembling Stegalos, who was still greatly distressed from his perilous ordeal. The immense pain had begun to subside, however, and his leg patched up by the skilful Eternian medics. The general knelt, looking the messenger squarely in the eye, unwilling to accept anything but the undeniable truth.

"Stegalos! By the gods and The Great Spirit willing, listen *very* carefully and tell me now: how many warriors did you see?" he demanded, in a deeply serious tone. "It is imperative we know this army's size - our nation and people are in tremendous danger - do you understand the words I speak unto you?"

Stegalos shook his head in confusion, struggling to provide a clear answer to the imposing figure towering right above him. The knights waited as the king grew increasingly nervous, knowing they had not much longer to act.

"I cannot be sure, my lord - there were many - so very many," Stegalos answered, as he struggled to recall the intimate details of his petrifying ordeal. Perhaps subconsciously he wished not to alarm the gathered knights, but the general would have none of it: he grabbed the messenger firmly by the shoulders and questioned him again more forcefully.

"Stegalos, how many? In the name of the gods, we *must* know - for the sake of your fellow countrymen, if nothing else!" Rapacosis aggressively demanded.

The pressure was almost too much for Stegalos to bear as the other knights anxiously looked on.

The messenger of middlehood eons closed his weary eyes and cast his mind back to that single terrifying moment on the now-infamous rocky hill. It had happened all so quickly, he thought; the blink of an eye having felt like many moons, indeed. Delving deep into his memory, Stegalos managed to recollect some of the finer details of his traumatic ordeal. It would certainly not be what the king or his knights wished to hear, but hear it they must.

Stegalos finally opened his eyes to face the imposing figure of the general, knowing he was *not* the bearer of good tidings.

"I would say the equivalent… of at least… three… full divisions… general," he most reluctantly announced, gulping nervously in anticipation of the knights' reaction.

Rapacosis' eyes widened in disbelief as he realised it could mean only one thing…

"It must be an invasion force, sire: no army of this size would come here for any other reason," he promptly concluded, before standing upright to face the king.

Alectorious was utterly lost for words as his greatest fear had been realised in one chilling instant. Not all amongst the knights were as perplexed, however, with it being the perfect opportunity to prove their mettle on the field of battle.

"I say we fight them here and now, and end this once and for all!" exclaimed Gavastros, willing and eager as always for combat. Arguably the greatest living swordsman in all Eternity, the brash young knight was yet to test his guile and sublime skills on the field of battle. The others were quick to placate the prodigy's insatiable desire for conflict, well knowing the harsh reality of what lay ahead.

"Gavastros, use your head for once, man - this army is threefold our number - you will not live long with that cavalier attitude of yours!" warned the more pragmatic Jalectrious, one of the king's more experienced knights. As a veteran of several battles, he had the responsibility to ensure his more inexperienced counterpart restrain from any rash or unruly behaviour.

"It might well be the only way, Jalectrious," conceded the general, with a great sigh.

Placing his hands on his head, Rapacosis momentarily turned away to gather his thoughts as a high degree of tension began to permeate the tent and conflicting opinions were duly voiced and exchanged.

Whatever the knights' differences, a course of action would have to be decided upon, very soon. Thelosious, the more cerebral of the knights, felt a more cautious approach would be best as he clasped his hands together in thought.

"Their number is great indeed, my king - perhaps returning to Eternity and seeking reinforcements would be the wisest choice…" he reasoned.

The king was in seeming agreement, judging by the brief spark in his blue-green eyes.

The general expressed serious reservations as he turned to his fellow knights, realising their forces would be left greatly vulnerable by such a manoeuvre.

"It is far too risky, Thelosious. Our rearguard would be badly exposed to the pursuing enemy and we would lead them straight to the gates of Eternity: this *cannot* be allowed to happen!" he warned sternly, as the others signalled their agreement. In his thirty-seven eons on this beleaguered known world, the general had never taken such unnecessary risks.

The king acknowledged this, but was unable to conjure a suitable solution. Turning to his majesty, Rapacosis called for immediate and decisive action.

"It will not be long before the Gomercian legions pour in through the pass - we *must* act now - what are your orders, sire?" he powerfully demanded, with every moment now crucial to success.

All eyes then shifted to Alectorious, who had never in his reign as king experienced anything quite like this. He was unmoving and speechless, with the countless permutations of their startling predicament running mercilessly through his head. Retreat, and it would look like an act of weakness, or worse yet, they may even be chased straight back to Eternity. Face the Gomercians this sun, and the Eternian army could be overwhelmed. If only the future could be seen, he thought in tremendous frustration. The king wished for the briefest moments he could be whisked away to the mystical lands of Athepothesia, as if he had never been. As the weight of the known world fell upon his noble shoulders, Alectorious realised the fate of Eternity now rested in his hands. A trickle of sweat poured down the king's face as his heart began to pound out of control, with his mind unable to think in any way cohesively. The general could wait not a moment longer: they simply *had* to act.

"MY KING!" he barked in trepidation, as the other knights looked on with equal unease. They felt powerless as the situation became too much for their young and impressionable leader to bear. He sensed there was little other option. Drawing a deep breath to calm his volatile nerves, King Alectorious looked the Eternian legend directly in the eye.

"General Rapacosis, there is not one amongst us with the experience and knowledge of battle as you. I hereby empower *you* with this decision, and trust you will decide upon the best course of action for our nation. I am king, yes, but am young, with very much to learn."

Rapacosis stared deep into the king's eyes and nodded in acceptance of this tremendous honour. The general knew that he alone now carried the burden of many Eternian lives upon his broad, powerful shoulders.

"Very well, my king; as you so wish," he replied, calm and steadfast.

All eyes fixed upon the imposing figure of the general, who was as cool as ever and quite unperturbed by the gravity of the situation at hand. Drawing on his vast experience of service to king and country, Rapacosis knew it was the perfect opportunity to strike, and if successful, it would be a thunderous blow to the empire's ambition for total control of the known world.

The general stood several paces back from the other knights, readying to speak of his audacious plan.

"This is indeed, a formidable army we now face: they outnumber us by a great number and will be heavily armed. In spite of what it seems, my fellow knights, I do believe they are at a *considerable* disadvantage," he suggested, quite to the amazement of all. The king was especially perplexed, unable to fathom how it would be possible to defeat this, numerically at least, much greater force.

"The Gomercians, at a disadvantage? By the gods, Rapacosis, are you raving mad? They are some *threefold* our number!" he said, unable to believe what he was hearing.

The other knights reacted with equal expressions of astonishment, realising the enormity of what they were up against.

"Alectorious is right, Rapacosis - this is a massive force - against such overwhelming numbers, we would be taking an *enormous* risk," Thelosious agreed, but the general was completely undisturbed by the dangers of what lay ahead.

Rapacosis raised the palms of his hands, trying to restore calm amongst his fellow knights. "That may be so, my companions. However, there is little question of the Gomercians' intentions: by taking the path through Dragon's Pass, they would avoid detection on the open plains and march *straight* to Eternity with little warning. As ingenious a strategy as it may be, it is one Nerosis should know is *extremely* dangerous. He appears, however, blinded in his lust for conquest," the general calmly concluded.

The king was still very much disbelieving, suitably voicing his concerns.

"Dangerous, you say; for the Gomercians? This is lunacy, Rapacosis!" he protested, shaking his head in much confusion as the others did much the same.

A wry, cunning smile appeared on Rapacosis' battle-hardened face, knowing *exactly* what was required to thwart the enemy's advance.

The general knelt down and removed his dagger from its elegant blue-and-gold sheath, drawing a diagram of the legendary pass on a patch of dusty ground, illustrating its narrow walls and winding passageways as best he possibly could.

"Exactly, my king!" he exclaimed, pointing his dagger at the other knights. "For in Dragon's Pass, numerical advantage means little, perhaps nothing at all! Even at its widest point *here*, it allows for only one division at a moment to march through. At the tail of the pass, here, only *a third* of that number!" he explained, pointing to the relevant points on his rough diagram.

The king's eyes lit up as the general continued and the others quickly became excited. The knights realised the truth of what Rapacosis spoke and that they *might just* have a chance of thwarting the inevitable Gomercian attack. The Eternians huddled round as the general explained the finer details of his daring, but ingenious plan of attack.

"I say we take our best warriors and place them in a tight phalanx formation here, at the tail of the pass, and we hold that line with all that we have, my fellow knights - it is our only hope of thwarting the imperial advance and achieving victory for Eternity," the general proclaimed, before replacing his dagger in its brightly-decorated sheath. Rapacosis slowly stood and looked at each of his companions as a wave of confidence flowed through the group. Their eyes began to sparkle with more than just a glimmer of hope: the Eternians now genuinely believed they could achieve what moments ago had seemed impossible. "We can only pray that Guerris fights by our side," Rapacosis added with a disgruntled sigh. Guerris was the god of war to whom they would pay homage in suns of conflict. He was especially popular with young Eternian warriors, who often prayed to him on the eve of battle.

"Do you truly believe we can hold this line, Rapacosis?" Thelosious questioned, deeply concerned at the tremendous risk they were taking.

"We *can* hold that line, for Guerris *will be with us*!" the belligerent Gavastros interceded. Unable to restrain his hunger for action, the prodigy simply could not wait to face his mortal foes in combat, as confidence emanated from his aura, greater by the instant.

Rapacosis and the other knights looked to their noble king, whose expression of despair had suddenly changed to one of courage and hope. Alectorious' eyes brightened at the prospect of a famous victory, with there being little doubt of the path ahead.

"And the remaining divisions?" he questioned, in a tone that was all but a subtle seal of approval; the positioning of the warriors being a mere formality. Rapacosis raised his head with a pride in his eyes that only a great warrior could have, knowing this was perhaps his final call to arms. Beside him Gavastros raised his chin, unable to hide a little smile in the knowledge that *finally*, he would fight for his country. Thelosious was as always cautious, prepared for the reality of the colossal task ahead. The other cool-headed veteran, Jalectrious, knew exactly what was required on this great sun of reckoning, drawing on memories of countless battles past.

The general turned to the king and explained his daring plan of attack.

"The remaining divisions will stay back in the narrow channel, well out of sight. Upon seeing only one division, the Gomercians will think the battle won before it has even begun. When the moment is of the essence, my king, you charge in with the Elite Guard and hit them on the flanks as hard and fast as you can: they will *never* know what hit them." The sense of anticipation continued to grow amongst the gathered knights.

Rapacosis spoke in such a direct and powerful manner that his speech alone could scare away the entire Gomercian army, thought the king, as he visualised how the battle might unfold. This strategy was so typical of Rapacosis and indeed, many of the great Eternian generals: draw them in, hit them hard, fast and with *all* that you have.

"One must learn to fight with one's mind as well as one's sword, Alectorious," he added, before tapping the side of his head. The king felt truly inspired by this iconic figure, so revered throughout these mysterious lands was he.

An electrifying energy permeated the tent as the realms of reality and fantasy began to blur before their eyes. The knights realised that soon they would be on the field of battle fighting for not only their nation, but their very own lives. It would be a moment long-remembered in Eternian history, thought the king, as he nodded to the general.

"And so it shall be, my fellow knights. Upon this high sun, the noble army of Eternity will engage the Gomercian Empire at Dragon's Pass. Relay the commands, Rapacosis."

The general wasted not a moment in calling on his most senior hoplite, Hephaesious. The king and his knights, meanwhile, fixed their gold-plated swords to their elegantly decorated belts before collecting their large, round bright blue shields in preparation for battle: it would be like nothing they had ever experienced.

"Yes, sire!" replied Hephaesious, rushing inside the tent with shield and sword at the ready. His blue-gold armour had been well polished in the early morn and shone proudly in the small amount of light beaming in through the roof. Rapacosis swiftly delivered his orders.

"The enemy approach: all hoplites to be armed and ready for battle!"

The senior hoplite bowed. "Immediately, sire! And the Elite Guard?" he asked, knowing their importance to success in any military engagement.

"They will see battle, I promise, but shall wait in reserve for when the moment arrives," the general authoritatively answered.

Hephaesious nodded. "Understood, sire!" he replied, and scurried out of the tent to deliver the orders. Rapacosis turned to his fellow knights, whose skill, intelligence and leadership would be paramount to victory on this historical sun.

"Gavastros, Thelosious," he said, with a brief silence ensuing.

"General," they simultaneously responded, nervously awaiting his command.

"You will be required at the front with myself and the hoplites," he announced.

Thelosious nodded reluctantly but the overzealous Gavastros was considerably more enthusiastic, relishing the chance to *finally* face up to his nation's arch nemesis: the tyrannical Gomercian Empire. Gavastros was an immensely gifted swordsman and warrior, having won many a tournament in his relatively short eons as an Eternian knight. Despite his complete lack of battle experience, he had no shortage of courage or indeed, determination.

"It will be the greatest of pleasures," he replied with single-minded ambition. Fixing his sword to his bright golden-blue belt, the prodigy moved toward the narrow tent entrance, unable to contain his sheer sense of elation. Thelosious' reaction was quite in contrast to that of his younger, rather impetuous companion. At twenty-nine eons, the cerebral knight was certainly one of the most experienced of the group.

"As you wish," he sombrely added. Despite his deep commitment to the Eternian cause, Thelosious believed in war as only a last resort. When pushed against the proverbial wall, however, the most philosophical of knights would fight with all the might the gods allowed. The general turned once again to his noble king, whose nerves were already beginning to incessantly shred.

"Alectorious, I strongly advise that you to remain behind in the reserve division with Jalectrious. When you charge in, the Elite Guard shall be with you, every step of the way. I promise, they will *never* leave your side. Fear not, my lord, for you will be surrounded by the very finest of warriors," he assured, knowing protection of the king was paramount.

"I fear not for my safety, General, only that of my nation and people."

Rapacosis nodded with a warm smile before delivering the last of his orders.

"Rhoedos - send riders back to Eternity to report the situation and request reinforcements - although I fear the battle will be over by then," he said to the nearby auxiliary, who was also a member of the Elite Guard.

"At once, sire!" Rhoedos responded, immediately racing outside of the large tent.

As the knights departed to fulfil their duty, the Eternian camp quickly became a hive of activity, with soldiers and young squires alike running back and forth, gathering weapons, shields and helmets as the situation was explained and orders duly issued. The feeling in the air was of great anticipation, for the moment had finally come to face their perennial arch-nemesis. It was one the Eternians had long awaited, but had not imagined would come so soon. Despite the enormity of the task ahead, one could sense the course of history was about to change and that *Eternity* would celebrate a tremendous victory. It would be not long before the lands would be rid of the oppressive empire, once and forevermore.

"Division Eight, fall in with me!" screamed Rapacosis, taking up position in the centre of the Eternian camp. Before he could finish, almost half his men had gathered, with the others not far behind with sword, shield and spear gripped firmly in hand. A living legend of his era, General Rapacosis was a figure of great inspiration to the young Eternian soldiers: not one amongst them would ever dream of defying him.

Donning their legendary blue-and-gold armour, the hoplites would do all in their power to ensure they returned to their city as nothing less than heroes. It was a tremendous honour to serve in the ranks of the Eternian divisions, and one that each and every man would sacrifice their lives to uphold. Indeed, many were in a state of shock as the reality of their situation sank in, unprepared for the fact they would soon be in the heat of battle against their perennial arch-nemesis. Others were simply relishing the chance to fight for their country, with their own lives being very much of secondary concern.

The hoplites were soon lined up row by row in perfect formation with shields and spears at the ready, waiting for the much-revered general to speak.

"If I am to fall this sun, Ehrious, it will be a good passing - an honourable one," said one hoplite to another as they hastily moved into their positions in the line.

"It will be that, Rhiedos - but fear not, for the gods shall be with us - I *know* that they will," Ehrious replied with unwavering confidence.

"Aye, it will be a great sun for our nation!" Rhiedos agreed, as the last members of the Eighth Division fell into line.

Rapacosis tightly gripped his shield and spear, readying to address the sea of valorous souls standing there before him.

"Brave and noble warriors of Eternity - hear me now! Upon this bright sun, we boldly march into the jaws of our most formidable foe. Their number may be great, but will never in a thousand eons equal the courage I see in each and every one of your eyes. Fear not what shall soon transpire, my noble companions, for The Great Spirit shall *always* be with us *and* our Eternal nation. And if you are to fall, know the gods will catch you safely and bring you to your *true* home in the heavens above!" he roared, igniting a desire to fight hitherto unseen. The gathered warriors cheered passionately in response, prepared for anything fate may bring. The general looked to Thelosious and Gavastros, who nodded to each other without a word being said: they were ready for the battle of their lives.

"Eternians!!!" shouted the veteran general. "Forward, into the breach! May the gods be with us all!" he screamed. Each line of the hoplite division began to peel off one by one, making their way swiftly into Dragon's Pass as the reserve divisions, led by Alectorious, followed close behind, onwards to their glorious destiny.

THE BATTLE OF DRAGON'S PASS

Before long, the Eternian divisions reached the mouth of the legendary Dragon's Pass, whose narrow, winding walls of rock had been a source of both wonder and intrigue for scholars and citizens alike for countless eons of history. As they rumbled down, tension became almost unbearable for many of the young hoplite warriors. Such that it was, in even the most hardened of souls a sense of unease could be felt: for never in all their suns had they experienced an environment as harsh and unforgiving as was this. Many were beset with terror at the enormity of the task ahead, naturally questioning if they would ever see the light of their beloved nation again. If they *were* to survive, it would leave an indelible mark upon each and every last one of their lives, and deep scars that might never truly heal. Indeed, the coming battle would be the ultimate test of these valiant warriors and their ability to overcome the seemingly impossible, but a challenge the Eternian army was more than capable of rising to. If their existence as a free nation was to remain unchallenged, no quarter could be given to their Gomercian foes. King Alectorious knew it would be a defining moment in his nation's history: nothing but a resounding victory would suffice.

As he walked forward, Alectorious looked up in awe to the sheer faces of rock surrounding, realising the dangers of which Rapacosis had previously spoken - even in the wider parts, the high, narrow winding walls were barely wide enough for a single division to pass through - never mind an entire invasion force! It seemed the empire was, as the general had intimated, taking an enormous risk - and one it would come to deeply regret. Alectorious could hardly believe that so soon, they would encounter their age-old rivals here.

Marching further ahead of the king and the Elite Guard, General Rapacosis looked around in equal astonishment at the imposing walls of rock staring down upon them from either side, wondering what manner of being could have created such a menacing place. It was as if the cliffs were alive and breathing, threatening like jaws of a monster, readying to pounce and mercilessly devour its prey. The slightest mistake by the two approaching titans and it could all be over: like a bolt of lightning from the proverbial heavens above. It only added to the intense pressure Rapacosis and for that matter, every warrior now felt. The general was confident, however, with total faith in his men and their ability to rise to any challenge the gods might bestow upon their path. Rapacosis firmly believed the Eternian army would, upon this sun, etch another page into the illustrious history books of their nation, and edge them ever closer to the freedom that had been yearned now for so many eons. Eternity would *finally* stand up to the might of the Gomercian Empire - and emerge victorious.

Flanked by his trusted lieutenants Thelosious and Gavastros, General Rapacosis led the Eighth Division front and centre through the winding path towards The Tail of the Dragon. It was the narrowest part of the legendary pass, where the tactically astute Eternians would try and block the imperial army's advance. By placing their lethal phalanx in the middle of the tight passageway, they would effectively nullify the benefit of greater numbers, thus enabling the Eternians to take full advantage of their highly-trained hoplite foot soldiers. The king continued to follow out of sight with his Elite Guardsmen and reserves, ready to enter the fray when called upon. He was feeling greatly apprehensive about the battle ahead despite Eternity's perceived tactical advantage. Alectorious realised it was of paramount importance their phalanx held strong; for if it were to falter, his forces would be quickly enveloped by the larger number of Gomercians. The king, however, trusted the general and that his wise judgement would safely deliver *Eternity* to victory this sun.

The Eternian hoplites threw up clouds of dust from the desert-like ground below as they marched through the perilous winding pass, overshadowed as it was by those imposing walls of stone. Indeed, very little direct sunlight could find its way through, with little chance for anything to survive: a fitting place perhaps for a battle between these two ancient titans.

After several twists and turns through the meandering rocky passageway, the Eternians, led from the front by General Rapacosis, finally arrived at the fabled Tail of the Dragon: a slender channel joining the two halves of Dragon's Pass. The pensive veteran looked at the jagged walls of rock narrow dramatically before his eyes, smiling in the knowledge that only the wrath of the gods themselves could break Eternity's impregnable phalanx. After not more than thirty spears, The Tail opened up into a large rocky amphitheatre. From there, the enemy would inevitably soon gather and attempt to push their way through to the other side, and on to Eternity. It was something Rapacosis could never allow to happen and would, with his courageous men, do *all* in his power to prevent. The general wasted not a moment in preparing his troops, knowing it was critical they stopped the Gomercians from breaking through that ever-so-slender rocky channel.

"ETERNIANS, FORM UP!!!" he roared at the very top of his lungs.

The hoplites reacted instantly, effortlessly forming a perfect phalanx around the three commanding officers, Rapacosis, Thelosious and Gavastros, ready for anything the gods might throw in their path. The general's authoritative voice was never to be questioned and commanded the greatest respect from every last one of his faithful subordinates. Standing in total silence, the soldiers patiently waited for their orders.

"Hoplites, FORWARD!!!" Rapacosis cried.

The Eternian phalanx marched on as one unbreakable unit, coming to a halt in the centre of the narrow channel. There, they would attempt to draw the enemy into their ingenious trap. It was a strategy used many hundreds of eons ago during the Age of Heroes, and Rapacosis was certain it would succeed again. The hoplite warriors stood proudly in the Dragon's Tail with spear and shield in hand, their muscular bodies protected by that famous blue-gold ornate shining armour: the colours of their glorious nation. Emblazoned upon their breastplates and shields was the mark of Eternity: a great dragon and magnificent binary star, which shone so brightly upon them this sun. On each of their gold-coloured belts was attached a sheathed short sword, ready for when the moment *finally* arrived. Side by side in formation they stood - silent, motionless and seemingly emotionless - fearless of whatever they might face. It would be the ultimate trial of skill and gallantry, and would test the collective Eternian resolve to stand up to and thwart the advance of the formidable imperial army.

Before long, the thunderous footsteps of enemy soldiers began to echo throughout the intimidating pass, with tension growing within the Eternian ranks as they rapidly moved into view. The Eternians' breaths became deeper as their hearts beat faster, their focus now only greater as they drew ever nearer to confrontation. Two great titans would clash upon this sun: one would be victorious and one would fall.

Standing in the centre of the front line, General Rapacosis was flanked on either side by his ranking lieutenants: the perennially cool-headed Thelosious and prodigal Gavastros. Both were skilled warriors but only Thelosious *truly* understood the reality of what lay ahead. The more inexperienced Gavastros was, however, willing and eager as ever to fight and test the skills he had spent his life perfecting. The prodigy looked ahead to the Gomercians, noting them unsurprised by the sight of an Eternian division blocking their path. It was something that deeply concerned the exceptional young knight.

"Rapacosis, they seem quite unmoved by our presence - they must have known all along we would be here!" he remarked in astonishment, turning anxiously to the general.

"They have eyes everywhere, Gavastros," replied the physically robust general. "They were probably alerted to our presence as we were theirs. Let it not worry you: we have a strong position and they know not yet of our reserves. The Gomercians think they shall but walk all over us: little do they know what awaits them! Fear not, for their hubris will be their downfall, my hasty young companion!" Gavastros responded with a nervous nod, yet was still eager to engage the enemy and prove his valour this fine sun.

Row upon row of imperial soldiers began lining up not fifty spears distant from the Eternians in the open space in front of The Tail, awaiting their commander's order to engage.

With confrontation imminent, the general realised the moment had come to address his loyal troops. Rapacosis was well aware of what lay ahead, wishing to prepare his men accordingly for what would undoubtedly be a colossal encounter. He was a realist on the best of suns, knowing that many Eternian would perish - perhaps even himself. It was a tremendous responsibility that for even him could be overwhelming. If it were to be so, Rapacosis wished the last words heard by his soldiers would be of nothing but inspiration, hope and fortitude. It was of the utmost importance that each and every man understood the reasons they fought: for the greater good of not only Eternity but *all* the known world. It was so much more than the gold and riches that besotted the minds of their Gomercian adversaries, who could never truly understand the knightly virtues for which Eternians so willingly sacrificed their lives.

Suddenly, Rapacosis broke rank from the robust phalanx and stepped out to face his courageous soldiers.

"Knights and warriors of Eternity - hear me now!" boomed the general in a voice of thunderous proportions.

Rapacosis walked slowly along the front line, thrusting his mighty sword to the heavens as all eyes were enchanted by his tall, imposing frame. "Know that upon this sun we have come not to wage war, but to defend all that we love and hold dear: our nation, families and the word of the gods themselves!" he shouted, his eyes sparkling like diamonds.

The hoplites cheered voraciously in unison as Rapacosis gazed into the eyes of his entranced men, attempting to draw out every last ounce of strength hidden deep within them. The general truly knew how to inspire an army. "Wherever your soul travels from this sun forth, be it to the heavenly ethers amongst the gods or your homes in our great nation, forget never who you are or where you came from; for your actions of valour shall never be forgotten!" he cried, as the hoplites cheered again uncontrollably. The general continued unremittingly as he felt their spirits lift. "Since the Age of Heroes hitherto, Eternians have fought to defend their country and freedoms we hold so dear, and many brave souls have sacrificed themselves in the fight against the tyranny of imperialism that threatens our nation. I challenge you *now* to rise up and emulate those heroes, and remind the forces of darkness they shall never in a thousand eons hold sway over this world. You come from an ancient, proud nation, my men: honour it this sun! For I promise, if you are to fall, Eternity will never forget, and your names shall forever be etched in history!" screamed the general, punching the air with his all-mighty sword.

The hoplites went into uncontrollable hysterics: chanting, screaming and shouting like madmen. Rapacosis' words had hit a raw nerve in these impressionable young patriots, who would happily sacrifice their lives for their country. The general was far from finished as he searched for all the words of inspiration he could muster: it was essential morale be as high as possible just prior to battle.

"Show the Gomercians who you are and that we shall *never* surrender - in this life or the next - ETERNITY FOREVER!!! Atlantiea Kublairah Ramabara!" he screamed in a deafening roar, as he held his shield and spear aloft.

The hoplites burst into a chorus of cheers, clanging their swords on their shields as the bright sunlight reflected off their shining blue and gold armour. They chanted the names of their leader and nation, confident that victory *would* be theirs.

"For Eternity!"

"For the king!"

"Eternity forevermore!" they yelled in unified elation.

The general looked upon his soldiers, knowing the moment had come to fight for their country. Gavastros and Thelosious flashed a glance to one another, knowing without a word spoken this army was ready for anything the gods could throw at them.

Rapacosis began to draw a line in the sand with his sword from one wall of The Tail to another. It was much to the curiosity of Gavastros, who was quite unsure of what to make of it all. The general turned to face his men and stared with a fire in his eyes Gavastros had never before seen. Was this it, he thought: *the* legendary speech so many had spoken of?

Rapacosis stood frozen, still paces in front of the line he had just drawn. His eyes were hypnotically fixed upon the gathered hoplites, from whom he commanded full attention and respect. The men anxiously awaited the general's final words. Rapacosis readied himself, firmly grasping the handle of his shield and sword, and addressed his men with a passion unlike anything Gavastros had ever heard before.

"Warriors of Eternity! Do you see this line in the sand?" he yelled, pointing with his sword at the line crossing the narrow dusty channel. "Look and remember it very well: for as warriors, it is all you will *ever* have! Defend it like there is no morrow and hold it like *all existence* depends on it! Fight for it with every fragment of your soul and every ounce of your strength! Fight for your nation this sun, noble warriors of Eternity!" cried the general.

The hoplites went into an uncontrollable hysterical delirium, screaming and chanting louder than ever. Gavastros looked around in astonishment at his compatriots, having never witnessed such a raw display of national pride: he knew they would be unstoppable.

Rapacosis duly took up position amongst his men in the front line, with their will to overcome the enemy unbreakable, their spirit indestructible and belief, simply unmatchable.

Gavastros was ready for confrontation, which was now moments away. He gripped his sword and shield tightly in anticipation, knowing it would be a battle of colossal proportions.

The Gomercian army opposite was standing in broken formation, with their rectangular shields and lethal short swords poised very much at the ready. Their shining black armor outlined by thin streaks of gold was an equally menacing sight to behold. The Gomercian Legion uncharacteristically stalled for a split moment, as if their collective consciousness questioned the wisdom of engaging souls of such unrestrained passion. Soon, a fragment of the legion started to mobilise. It was an intimidating sight: their black-and-gold armor contrasting starkly with the Eternity's bright blue. With the enemy almost thrice in number, it would be a *true* test of Eternian strength and resolve. As the Gomercians rapidly closed in, Rapacosis attempted to cool his army's collective nerves.

"Hold fast, men and remember all you have learned - fear not, for the gods *will* be with you this sun!" he cried, concentrating on the rapidly approaching enemy hordes.

The Eternian ranks stood shoulder to shoulder, man to man – motionless, again emotionless as the Gomercian legion quickly gained speed and a quiet confidence, sensing it would be *they* who emerge victorious. The Eternians, however, had other ideas, believing *their* nation was favoured by the divine.

Gavastros looked ahead to the rapidly advancing Gomercian units with nerves calm, readying himself. As the enemy broke into a full charge, the prodigy's life flashed before his eyes: his childhood, middlehood and training for knighthood gone in but an instant as he wondered if all he had learned would see him through to the end of the battle. It could happen so quickly, he thought: one false move and it would all be over in the blink of an eye.

I cannot fall this sun, he thought, as tears began to well in his eyes. *For all that I have ever learned and been would be wasted – and all those I ever loved, lost to me forever.* He glanced once more to the twin suns shining so brightly above, in search of that one last spark of divine inspiration. Gavastros quickly returned his focus to the advancing enemy, pondering if he would ever set eyes upon those brilliant celestial twins, ever again.

The Gomercians were now moving in at full speed, the very ground trembling as they approached, the air ringing with deafening screams as the enemy drew their swords. It would not be long to contact as the Eternian division huddled in tight formation - their nerves ice cool, determination unbreakable and their focus, utterly unshakable.

Moments later, General Rapacosis raised his mighty sword to the heavens and delivered the final call to arms.

"ETERNIANS, NOW!!!!!" he screamed with dramatic effect.

In perfect unison, the hoplites fell to the ground and grabbed their cleverly-concealed spears. They quickly rose, aiming the lethal steel-tipped weapons at the approaching enemy. The Gomercian hordes were taken utterly by surprise, unable to slow enough to avoid them. With a thunderous clash, the Gomercians ran straight into the Eternian shield-and-spear wall, with many instantly falling or badly wounded. Their ranks were sent into complete disarray as the Gomercian commanding officers began to panic, having expected nothing but a decisive victory. It was the perfect start to the battle as Gavastros flashed a nod of agreement to Rapacosis: their audacious plan was coming together *exactly* as hoped.

"Hold the line!" yelled Rapacosis.

The Gomercians began to pile up on the front line of Eternian shields, trying to push them down to the other side of The Tail.

"DRIVE!!!" ordered Rapacosis, realising it was *exactly* their plan.

In perfect unison, the hoplites responded with an all-mighty shove, pushing the enemy hordes back down The Tail and out into the open pass. There, they would be far more exposed, allowing the reserve Eternians to charge through on the flanks. The Gomercians regrouped, trying moment and again to push through the impenetrable barrier of warriors –

but to no avail. To and fro the enemy swung their swords, desperately trying to break the Eternian lines. The shield wall held fast and strong, however, with not a single life yet lost to the incoherent attacks of the inexperienced imperial forces. The Eternians were simply far too organised and disciplined for the relatively untrained mercenary force that was the Gomercian army, who fought for gold, riches and that alone. The Eternians fought for something that could never be bought, valued nor ever traded: their freedom.

"Watch the flanks!" screamed Rapacosis, noticing the Gomercians trying to pass through the widening gaps at the side of their phalanx. Several hoplites broke off the rear in response and ruthlessly cut down any enemy that dare attempt to pass through. The imperial soldiers continued to try and break down the seemingly impenetrable wall of shield and spear but the Eternians held firm and strong.

Without thinking, the shell-shocked Gomercian commander ordered his second legion into battle, leaving one more in reserve. He realised victory was now far from certain, having failed to accept the enormous gulf in class between the two rival armies. They were losing far more warriors than had been anticipated: something his leader, Nerosis, would be most displeased about. If this continued, they would have no choice but to retreat and return to fight another sun – but surely it would not come to that? Defeat now at the hands of their arch-rivals would be a most devastating blow to their invasion plans.

A second legion of the enemy charged fearlessly into battle as their cohorts continued to throw themselves mindlessly at their Eternian adversaries. As the Gomercian number grew, the general realised the phalanx had done all it could and would not hold for much longer.

"Eternians, ready to break rank!" he screamed. Rapacosis knew that even though they were outnumbered, the Gomercian army would prove no match for his highly trained hoplite warriors. With shield wall still very much intact, the hoplites drew their swords in readiness to engage the enemy man to man.

"Ready, General!" screamed his commanding hoplite, Hephaesious, from the centre of the phalanx.

Rapacosis paused for a few moments before delivering the order. "BREAK NOW!!!" he cried with a deafening roar.

The Eternians suddenly broke formation, pouring out of The Tail into the open pass with their shining swords at the ready. The hoplites zealously engaged the stunned Gomercians, with each warrior picking off the nearest enemy in sight with aplomb. A countless number of duels ensued as the Eternians quickly stamped their authority on the battle, taking not a single step backwards. They were clearly the superior warriors but the Gomercian number began to swell, threatening their commanding position. The Eternians were soon fighting for their very lives as wave after wave of auxiliary Gomercians came literally out of nowhere, desperately trying to re-establish a foothold on the battle.

Meanwhile, King Alectorious had moved within sight of the duelling armies with his reserve hoplites and Elite Guard in anticipation of entering the fray. As he observed, the king began to panic at the sight of his army being surrounded, and knew they had to act fast if Eternity was to be victorious this sun.

"Jalectrious, surely it must be *now* - our men will be overwhelmed before long!" he anxiously cried, motioning to the duelling titans beyond the narrow channel of rock.

"I see it, my king, but should we not await the general's signal?"

The king began to lose patience. "If we wait any longer it might well be too late!"

As if on cue, Rapacosis started to frantically wave his sword.

"Sire, look - the general's signal!" cried Sephoelious, one of the Elite Guardsmen, also known as shock troops for the dramatic manner they entered battle.

The king looked ahead beyond The Tail to his struggling companions and, with an exhilarating surge of national pride, drew aloft his mighty sword from its bright golden sheath. Walking several paces ahead, he turned to face his men.

"Knights and warriors of Eternity, defend your country and *all* that you ever loved: FOR THE GREAT SPIRIT AND ETERNITY!!!" Alectorious raised his shining blade to the skies as his men replied in kind, drawing their mighty blades aloft with unbridled zest.

With weapon gripped tightly, the king advanced fearlessly into the breach as his Elite Guard and hoplite warriors followed close behind.

"Protect your king!" yelled Jalectrious. The Elite Guard rapidly formed a perimeter around his majesty as they charged at the clashing armies. Like a shock of lightning, Alectorious' Seventh Division thundered into battle, smashing through enemy lines and throwing them into complete disarray. The commanding Gomercian looked on helplessly as more Eternians came out of nowhere, instantly turning the tide of battle in his rival's favour. He glanced back to his own reserves, knowing he would have little chance of victory without them. The Gomercian was faced with a pendulum decision: should he gamble, use every last man and hope the battle swung once more in his favour, or swallow his immense pride and flee to fight another sun? The outclassed Gomercians continued to sustain heavy casualties as their commander pondered, with every moment now crucial to the final outcome.

The Eternians continued their relentless ascendancy, driving the enemy further and further back. The battle had clearly swung in the Eternians' favour as the Gomercians fell one by one; their commander horrified by the extent to which they had been outclassed. The Eternians fought with a passion, conviction and skill he could only dream of: utterly fearless in the face of all adversity. The Eternian king threw himself into the fray, despite that at any moment, his life or that of his soldiers could be over. It seemed against all logical sense to risk so much, but fight on he did in the name of something much greater than himself.

As the battle raged on, the Eternians continued to dominate, and the general was confident victory would soon be theirs. Suddenly, a wave of Gomercians charged into the fracas from the opposite side of the pass, with the Eternians having to quickly regroup to thwart their advance. In the flurry of confusion, the king was knocked from his feet by a charging Gomercian soldier: he fell with a nasty thud to the ground and lost grip of his sword. With the Elite Guard heavily engaged in combat, only Gavastros saw his noble leader fall. The prodigy reacted quickly, knowing it would be over in moments.

"ALECTORIOUS!!!" he screamed. Without thinking, he flung his body over the king's for protection as several Elite Guardsmen realised what had transpired and moved quickly in support. The Gomercian meanwhile needed no second invitation, attempting to finish off his defenceless regal prey. He held his sword upward, thrusting it into the pile of bodies with all his might. Gavastros received a nasty wound to his shoulder, but a brace of Elite Guardsmen arrived instants later, mercilessly hacking down the Gomercian. Others soon followed, rapidly forming a protective perimeter around the king and Gavastros. The prodigy was suffering greatly from his gaping wound: his act of selflessness had almost cost him everything; but he had saved the life of the king. The Eternian hoplites, meanwhile, had managed to push the remaining enemy back into the pass from whence they had come, having outclassed their opponents in every conceivable facet of hand-to-hand combat.

The Gomercian commander conceded there was little hope for victory as he observed his men capitulate to the mighty Eternians. He reluctantly raised his hand and finally gave the signal for his army to retreat. It was a humiliation hitherto unimaginable and would not be forgotten by Gomercian and Eternian alike for many moons to come. It would only serve to strengthen Eternian resolve, thought the enemy commander, knowing they would be more prepared than ever to resist their arch-rival's ambitions for total control of the northern known lands. The Gomercian soldiers were quick to follow their orders and flee down The

Tail, as if having never wished to be fighting at all. The Eternians were, by contrast, ecstatic they had managed to defeat their bitter enemy of countless eons past.

"They retreat!!!" cried Hephaesious. He raised his sword to the bright blue skies above as his subordinate hoplites went into sudden and delirious raptures.

"Victory for Eternity!!!" screamed one, as he raised his hands theatrically to the air.

"Praise the gods!!!" another shouted, as countless hoplites raised their swords jubilantly to the heavens.

It had been a remarkable victory against the odds, of which the ancient heroes would have been truly proud. The gods had smiled upon Eternity this sun, thought the king, as he observed the scenes of euphoria all around. He wondered if this would be the turning point: the beginning of the end of the empire and a return to the path of peace, harmony and a love of all things. Deep down, he knew it *would* be so.

As the last of the Gomercian soldiers scurried away, Rapacosis fell to his knees on the dusty ground. His heart pounded as he took several deep breaths to cool his ever-so-fractured nerves. In any battle one could fall in but an instant: he knew this only too well. Again, Rapacosis had defied what he believed to be his destiny, and for another fight against his old rivals he would live. The general had survived many battles in his eons of service, but this he had least expected to. Rapacosis sat back and looked up to the beaming suns in the skies above, expressing his gratitude to the higher powers that be.

"Thank you, oh Great Spirit, for delivering victory this sun, and for sparing a life that does not deserve to be," he whispered, unable to believe he still lived.

Rapacosis took another deep breath before collapsing in sheer exhaustion. The Eternians believed The Great Spirit to be the force that existed throughout all things, creating all there is, was or would ever be. It had the power to do anything it wished, including deciding the victors of battle. On this sun, it had clearly favoured *the Eternian* cause.

As the dust began to settle, attention quickly turned to the king and Gavastros, who was struggling for consciousness on the dusty ground of the pass. Alectorious and the other knights were deeply concerned for their brave companion as scores of hoplites gathered round in an attempt to help. Indeed, Gavastros was a part of folklore and was looked up to as a hero by young Eternian warriors: with his unmatched swordsmanship, deft skills and courage, most could only dream of emulating the prodigious one.

"Gavastros!" whispered the king. "Leave us not this sun, my dear companion: it is not yet your moment!" he pleaded, shaking him by the armoured collar.

The prodigy struggled to open his eyes as the wound continued to sap his vitality.

"Worry not of me, my noble king, it is but a scratch - tell me, did we achieve victory?" he asked, his voice slightly quivering.

The king smiled warmly, motioning to the scenes of elation all around.

"That we did, my companion, listen: can you not hear the cries of our men? The gods fought with us!" Gavastros managed but a faint glow. "You fought with tremendous courage - inspired us to great things this sun, Gavastros - Eternity shall never forget. You will forever be honoured amongst our greatest heroes, I promise!" the king encouraged, as several medics gathered round to treat Gavastros' gaping wound.

"History destined us for victory, Alectorious - I only hope I live long enough to see its glory remembered," the prodigy muttered proudly as he reached to touch his noble king on the shoulder.

Alectorious could only agree with his loyal servant of many eons.

"I pray to the gods above you shall, Gavastros, as every last Eternian alive this sun."

THE RIDE HOME

The Eternian army marched their way homewards with spirits high and a heightened sense of invincibility following their dramatic rear-guard victory at Dragon's Pass. For some of the group, it felt like nothing could ever defeat them; for others, it was simply a relief to have survived this most perilous of ordeals. The knight's reactions were greatly contrasting: Gavastros exuded a tremendous sense of pride, while Thelosious hoped it would be the last of such epic encounters. Rapacosis was in a rather sombre mood, with his true feelings as always very much an unknown quantity. King Alectorious was meanwhile deep in thought as he trotted along the path on his mighty steed, pondering the magnitude of their achievement and its implications for the wider known world. He realised it would be a triumph remembered for many moons to come, retold by writers and poets alike in Eternity's illustrious Book of Heroes a thousand eons from now.

Two by two the brave hoplites lined the stony road: a relic of an era long forgotten in the history of these ancient lands. Many were wounded and battle-weary from the titanic confrontation but none questioned the virtues of their noble sacrifice for king and country. Alectorious and his commanding officers proudly headed the front of a huge caravan of warriors which stretched as far as the eye could see across the vast Marathosian Plains.

The king felt a great sense of relief having overwhelmed such a vast number of the enemy, and although there was still a long way to go, he knew deep down that the tide of fortune was *finally* beginning to swing in his nation's favour. He turned to his loyal rider in readiness to deliver a message home, with it being customary to inform the people of a battle's result immediately following its conclusion.

"Straloctrious: ride ahead to Eternity and send word of our great victory! Let the people know our men fought with valour against tremendous odds!" the king ordered. A deep feeling of pride emanated from his voice, knowing the sacrifices made by each and every one of his brave warriors this sun. He truly appreciated the significance of this titanic confrontation, which had surely changed the course of Eternian history. Straloctrious was quick to react, adjusting his golden stirrups as he pulled alongside his noble leader.

"At once, Sire! And what of the High Council?" he asked, knowing it customary for them to assemble directly following any battle.

"We gather as soon as possible - the morrow at mid-sun."

"As you wish, my Lord!" Straloctrious jubilantly exclaimed, before saluting his king.

"May the gods hasten your return!" Alectorious replied, with eyes gleaming in the bright rays of the twin suns that shone from high above. The messenger nodded once more and readied his steed for departure. "Ya!" he shouted, pulling tightly on his horses' reigns. Straloctrious quickly broke rank from the long line of battle-weary soldiers, riding ahead on the rocky path to the magnificent hilltop city in the distance.

Countless souls had fallen in defence of their nation this sun, with many having had their first ever taste of battle. Despite being trained from a young age, nothing could have prepared these courageous hoplites for the frightening reality of war and all it entailed. Many lived for the thrill of being so close to that fine line of life and Athepothesia, managing ever so slightly to defy the merciless hands of the gods by surviving battle. Some thrived on such an existence and were eager for more, while others questioned why they had chosen this path; so dominated as it was by such meaningless, senseless violence. The sight of companions and foes alike falling before their eyes had proven an experience for which they could have never been truly prepared, shattering the innocent notions of chivalry, devotion and humbleness they had long come to associate with service in the Eternian army. The veterans by contrast marched on with an emotionless, aimless gaze, oblivious to the madness they had not only been witness to, but an integral part of. For them it had been just another sun in their life as an Eternian warrior: there was a duty to perform for their nation and perform it they did, living in the knowledge their actions on the field would be for the greater good of all the known world. Now they would return to the safety and comfort of those closest to them within Eternity's impregnable defensive walls. A small number of hoplites struggling to keep up with the march were overwhelmed with emotion: the sight of companions falling before their eyes having proved to be a deeply traumatic experience.

Even the emotionally rock-hard Rapacosis questioned the sense in all this insanity, wondering if the Gomercian soldiers *also* felt these things. He cast a thoughtful glance to his men - those innocent faces - souls so scarred by the countless perils of war. As the unofficial head of the Eternian army, Chief General Rapacosis had seen all these things and so much more in his long service: the sight of companions passing in one's arms had occurred so often he had almost become immune to it. The general gazed sorrowfully at those young soldiers; those unmistakable expressions seen on so many suns before. Nothing but the experience itself could have prepared these men for what they had witnessed: a life taken so meaninglessly, callously and in the very blink of an eye. But this was the way of war and indeed, very nature of the warrior. Rapacosis observed his men before casting an evocative glance to the young Eternian king, who even for he was unusually quiet. It had been Alectorious' first taste of battle and was something that had clearly, deeply affected him. Sensing all was not well, the general approached in an effort to console his troubled leader. Rapacosis drew his horse alongside before speaking in a calm, sensitive tone.

"My great king Alectorious, you fought with tremendous courage this sun, as a true warrior and King of Eternity. You inspired us to great victory: of this, you must be immensely proud!" he offered, with a telling wink and nod of the head. The king was quickly dismissive of the veteran's overt praise, turning to face his imposing frame.

"You know it is not so, Rapacosis, I was protected by many brave young warriors - countless of whom fell in my stead - men to whose families I owe an incredible debt," he downheartedly countered, feeling responsible for those who had so courageously given their lives. Rapacosis would have none of this talk, and reacted in a stern but composed manner. He turned to look the Eternian leader directly in his enigmatic blue-green eyes.

"These men fell to defend their king, Alectorious *and* their nation. For them, there could have been no greater honour," the general maintained, shaking his head. "They fought like soldiers, as brave warriors. They fell for *you*, like *true* Eternians, defending all that was ever dear to them. How long will it be before you accept your place in this world? You are everything a king should be - if only you would believe it," Rapacosis lamented, perennially vexed by the king's inability to accept this rather obvious truth. Alectorious' philosophical mind had always been unconvinced of the necessity of such war-like ways, firmly believing any conflict could easily be resolved by simple negotiation and dialogue. Regretfully, it seemed battle was the only thing that could bring an end to Gomercian rule of these once peaceful lands.

"So much violence, pain and agony, you can feel it on the field long after the dust of battle has settled. Why must it be this way, Rapacosis? If indeed they *are* merciful and all powerful, why ever do the gods allow such suffering, pain and torment?" Alectorious quite rightfully questioned. The general looked out evocatively to the snow-capped mountains of the Buvarious Mountains in reflective thought, searching for words of inspiration.

"Only the gods and The Great Spirit know the answer to this, my king: I am but a humble warrior. What I *do* know is that they test us in many ways, and we must fight to overcome these obstacles with all that we have and *all* that we are," Rapacosis expounded, pausing for a moment of mutual reflection. He continued, relaxing his powerful shoulders.

"If we had *not* fought this battle, the Gomercians might have gone on to breach the gates of our beloved city, and many more innocent Eternians would have most certainly lost their lives - we could have never allowed this to happen, Alectorious - you must understand," Rapacosis firmly warned, all too aware of the terrible consequences of inaction.

"Of that, I have not question or doubt," conceded the king, humbled as he cast a proud glance to the sea of blue and gold shining armour following behind.

"Make no mistake, Alectorious, this is the first of many battles to come against the Gomercians - you must be strong for your nation and those heroes who have fallen before you - let their sacrifice *never* be in vain," Rapacosis counselled, as he stared intently into the king's eyes. Alectorious was thoughtful as the two men continued, turning briefly again to the long line of loyal warriors as he searched within for an appropriate response. The king knew well of what the general spoke and was not particularly relishing his next encounter with their arch nemesis. Indeed, he felt fortunate to have survived this particular battle, but feared he might not be so lucky again. Alectorious turned to the general, raising his head with meaningful intent.

"From this sun henceforth, no Eternian shall *ever* fall without good reason, Rapacosis. Many fell for their nation this sun and those they love dear: we shall honour their sacrifice by winning this war," promised the king. He smiled proudly as his bright blue-gold helmet flickered tellingly in the light of the late-noon suns, and a bird of prey swept down from high in the skies above.

"That they did, my liege, and that, we most certainly shall," the general wholeheartedly agreed. Rapacosis began to ride ahead upon his mighty steed before turning back briefly to his noble leader.

"Alectorious..."

"Yes general?"

"*Now*, you are a king."

ENTERING ETERNITY

After an emotionally-charged ride along the ancient Road of Heroes, Alectorious and his mighty army finally reached the gates of their elegant home: The Kingdom of Eternity. Nestled on the rolling foothills of the great Buvarious Mountains, there was not a more awe-inspiring sight to behold in the entire known world. A fortified city of some seventy-three thousand souls, Eternity was surrounded by seemingly unbreakable walls, with turrets rising to heights unequalled throughout the lands. Enchanting woodland thrived not far away and the crystal-clear River Glasovia flowed from the mountains in the northwest, bisecting the edge of the forests with that of the city walls. The tranquil waters of the river eventually wound their way out to the sweeping plains of Marathosia, forming a natural barrier of protection across the northern known lands.

In the distant northeast, the majestic snowcapped peaks of the Buvarious Mountains reached high into the skies above, almost touching the abode of the gods themselves. These captivating summits were of indescribable beauty and incredible power, beguiling mystery as well as intrigue, and of immensely sacred importance to this profoundly spiritual nation. There was, many would say, not a more spectacular sight in all the known world: the majesty of this striking fortress and splendour of the mountains together as one, like twin beacons of hope for these most troubled lands. Eternity was a place of a thousand legends and countless many dreams: so ancient that no man alive could remember its birth, nor would breathe long enough to see its end. It was said Eternity would live on in spirit long after it had disappeared from this enchanting world, serving always as a reminder for those who had passed into the ethers.

The forests surrounding Eternity only added to its mystique, filled as they were with all manner of creatures including deer, foxes, eagles, hawks, badgers and squirrels, amongst many other curious entities, and the vast grassy fields to the south provided arable land from which to grow crops or warn of approaching invaders. It truly was a perfect location for this remarkable fortress nation.

The curtain walls surrounding Eternity were some five hoplites in height and several spears thick, with each section conjoined by large conical-shaped white towers that reached skyward like small mountains. There, defenders were well-placed to see approaching enemies and respond accordingly with their powerful longbows. From the tiled blue cones crowning each tower, the Eternian flag flew proudly in the wind: a golden twin-star back-dropped by a bright blue. It was forever a reminder of who they were, where they came from and all they had ever lived and fought for.

Countless sentries patrolled the walls both sun and night to warn of impending danger, with their number greater than ever due to recent heightened tensions with The Gomercian Empire. There was no telling when the enemy might attack: Eternity *had* to be prepared for any eventuality. The city's defences were as spectacular to the visitor as they were intimidating to invaders, with a magnificence equaled only by their sheer size. Indeed, it was widely believed to be impossible to lay siege, such was the menacing nature of Eternity's fortifications. In the event of such an attempt, the inhabitants would be more than ready to respond.

As the king and his men reached the main gate of the outer city walls, trumpets sounded to signal the arrival of the victorious army: the sense of excitement quickly reached boiling point as lines of mesmerised soldiers marched inside and the many citizens crowding along the towering stone ramparts began to cheer voraciously for their heroes.

"It is good to *finally* be home," whispered Alectorious, drawing a sigh of relief as they neared the inner gatehouse. As the mighty drawbridge fell and portcullis rose, the noise reached almost deafening levels: it was a sense of excitement he had never felt before. As they approached the drawbridge, others caught their first glimpse of the triumphant army. Beside themselves with excitement, they cheered and whistled away. As he crossed, Alectorious looked up with a smile as he saw the Eternian coat of arms, which depicted two blue dragons directly facing one another; each with a crown on its head and together holding a single Eternian flag. It was a relief to *finally* see that again, the king thought as he moved forward, flanked closely by his companions Gavastros and Thelosious.

The three knights trotted through the massive stone gatehouse, astonished by the magnitude of welcome waiting them: the city's cobblestone streets were lined with countless adoring citizens hoping to catch even the briefest glimpse of their noble king and his men, shouting and screaming as if those of myth and legend were returning from the mystical realms of Athepothesia. Never in all his suns had Alectorious witnessed a display of such raw, unrestrained patriotism: the number of citizens was so great that guards had to physically push them back to make way for the advancing ranks of soldiers, many of whom were overwhelmed by the sheer sense of occasion.

Indeed, stories of the army's heroics at Dragon's Pass had spread quickly throughout the city, with none wishing to miss the chance to pay homage to the brave victors. Passionately waving blue and gold flags; cheering, dancing and singing melodic songs, the citizens were unable to restrain their ecstatic jubilation that triumph had *finally* been achieved. Eternity had stood up to her arch nemesis - Nerosis and the tyrannical Gomercian Empire - and emerged triumphant. They had waited many eons for this sun, and would savour every last moment.

"Hail, great King Alectorious!"

"Mighty Rapacosis and Gavastros, we salute you!"

"Long live our noble king!" hailed various members of the crowd. They waved and cheered in adoration of the seemingly endless procession of warriors, with even the battle-weary amongst them alive with excitement. Women and children of all ages threw petals of their nation's colours: blue, yellow and purple from the edge of the street into the path of the men, many of whom were simply overawed by emotion. It would be a sun long remembered by soldier and citizen alike thought Alectorious as he looked on in gratitude to the countless souls enjoying the occasion. People from all walks of life were uniting in celebration of this stunning victory that would surely be recorded in their illustrious "Book of Heroes". The king was astounded by the overwhelming level of support despite having lost many a brave warrior on the field. He turned to his trusted companion to express as such.

"It makes me so very proud to be Eternian, Gavastros," he remarked, waving to the ecstatic crowd as he trotted along the ancient cobblestone road. Alectorious' distinct purple plume made him clearly stand out: there was never any question who the Eternian leader was.

"My noble king, I could live a thousand lives and yet a thousand more in this, our gallant nation!" the prodigy proudly replied, before theatrically saluting the crowd. Cheering avidly in response, many a female admirer was left utterly breathless. There could not have been a greater sun in all existence to be alive, thought Gavastros: enjoying, absorbing and living every moment as though there were no morrow.

"My feelings *exactly*," Alectorious smiled in agreement, likewise waving to the awe-inspired citizens. The Eternian people absolutely adored their king, for Alectorious was unlike any that had come before: deeply philosophical in thought, spiritual in his outlook on life and genuinely cared for the welfare of his subjects, no matter what their station in life. Now that, at least in the eyes of the citizenry, he had proved himself as a military leader also, Alectorious the 2nd would surely be remembered amongst the greatest kings in history: most certainly if he could inspire *total* victory over the Gomercian Empire.

The path to the castle led the king and his knights through the main city streets, lined with many trees from which crisp autumn leaves of countless colours and hues were beginning to fall. The soldiers were swarmed by yet more adoring citizens as they passed through several neighborhoods, attracting multitudinous admirers as they went.

Soon they reached the majestic city gardens, which were awash with fountains, streams and all manner of plants and animals, including numerous deer and squirrels - favourites of the king. Shortly after, they passed the famed Eternian Temples, where citizens would venture in search of wisdom from the Higher Realms. The Temples were considered to be the home of the gods and were thus, greatly revered as such. The path then wound up a small hill to the King's Castle: a magnificent structure towering high above the inner and outer city walls. The beguiling fortification was a stunning array of conical blue and white towers, adorned with gold-emblazoned designs and various statues in homage to Eternian heroes of eons past. It was the permanent residence of the king and his seven knights, and others fortunate enough to be his direct service. It was also the seat of the High Council, who in the morrow would meet to discuss Eternity's current predicament, and an appropriate course of action to thwart the empire. In suns of crises, the castle was, in combination with secret caverns below, capable of holding large numbers of the populace.

As the king and his knights trotted closer, a small drawbridge was lowered from the gatehouse, inviting them into the castle's alluring interior. The group trotted into the lush courtyard one by one to yet more pomp and ceremony as trumpets sounded to welcome their arrival. The hoplites and Elite Guard had already made their way to the barracks before they returned to their homes and those most cared for.

Alectorious and his knights slowly approached the castle entrance, which was decorated with elaborate sculptures of dragons and knights from the Age of Heroes hitherto. On the main door was a particularly striking carving of a sword and dragon which had always caught the king's eye. Waiting to greet the victors were several high councilmen, who had been patiently waiting in their long blue robes.

"All hail, King Alectorious! Eternity salutes the heroics of his noble majesty and courageous knights!" a young courtier announced, as the king swiftly dismounted from his steed. He removed his helmet to reveal his short brown-blonde hair, and fittingly saluted. A beaming man in illustrious golden-blue robes soon approached, adding his personal words of congratulations before making a theatrical bow.

"A tremendous victory sire: truly befitting the Age of Heroes!" lauded Abraiyias, one of the senior councilmen sure to be present at the morrow's gathering.

"Justly humbling words, my councilman; but thank instead the many unsung heroes that bled for their nation, and the families who will not see their sons this night."
The councilman lowered his head, dramatically changing to a more mournful tone. As much as it had been glorious, victory had come at a tremendous cost.

"Aye my Lord - many a brave young warrior fell this sun - and for their bravery on the field will *never* be forgotten." Alectorious could only nod in agreement. The king's personal servant Hulious was close at hand, sensing the tumultuous events had been a little too much for all involved. Approaching, he calmly offered his thoughts.

"Some rest would do his majesty unimaginable wonders; may I humbly suggest a warm bath and healthy banquet to heal those nasty wounds?" The others were very much in agreement, with Gavastros especially partial to a healthy feast. The king acknowledged in kind, raising his palms with a distinct change of disposition.

"Well, why not a celebratory banquet for all? I am not the only soul to have suffered the scars of battle! This sun shall be one of rest for *all* Eternians; for in the morrow, there is much to discuss in the High Council," he candidly admitted, with silent nods of agreement all round. "Splendid! It shall be so, my king," Abraiyias agreed, gleefully clapping his hands. With that, each of the knights retired to recover from all the sun's excitement, drama and for many, enormous personal loss. It would be remembered for countless eons to come, in the great "Book of Heroes" and annals of Eternian history. Acting on intuitive impulse, the king decided to speak briefly with councilman Abraiyias before returning to his castle chambers.

"Abraiyias, a word if you please," the king insisted, pulling him gently aside.

"Yes, my king." he responded, sensing a matter of great importance.

"What of the councilmen - have there been any whispers?" he nervously asked.

"Well, most are elated by our victory, as you can imagine - but in equal measure, many rightly fear this is only the beginning of a much larger offensive into Eternian territory. They worry his majesty does not have a cohesive strategy to thwart the enemy and that without meaningful and decisive action, our great city will soon fall. Indeed, the suns are short, my king - and their passing will wait for no man," Abraiyias forthrightly stated, leaving the king in momentary silence. Alectorious had only one response to this.

"That, they *never* will, Abraiyias," he replied, before bidding farewell. Alectorious promptly returned his steed, Sephalos to the stables before heading to his chamber in the imposing towers of his lofty castle home. After such a tumultuous sun, Alectorious needed to be alone to deeply contemplate the path ahead for not only himself, but the nation of Eternity.

ETERNIAN HIGH COUNCIL

Victory at Dragon's pass had sent shockwaves of euphoria throughout the Eternian Kingdom, with the elated populace sensing that great change was finally upon them after all those eons of hardship, struggle and toil. Alectorious and his knights were, however, well aware the Gomercians would inevitably return to exact their belligerent revenge - and in far greater numbers than ever before. The king had duly summoned the Eternian High Council in the hope a suitable course of action could be agreed upon to thwart the impending threat. For many moons the council had voraciously debated how best to respond to the ever-encroaching imperial menace in the northern lands and their ambition to consume the entire known world into their rapidly growing sphere of power and influence. The differences in opinion were many but the city of Eternity could no longer wait for the hand of fate to decide her destiny: the moment to act had *finally* arrived.

The High Council was held in the main tower of the King's Castle: a large, domed assembly room with inspiring views of the Eternian Kingdom in all her magnificent glory. The interior of the brightly-lit chamber was adorned with all manner of striking wall paintings, carvings and designs, which appropriately reflected the richness of Eternian culture and the great minds that had graced this nation over her seven hundred eons of existence.

The sophisticated councilmen soon began to file inside with much vigorous ado, taking their respective seats on either side of the king and his knights, who would traditionally arrive last. The chairman was by convention always the first to speak, sitting as always he would directly opposite his majesty. Holding a diamond-emblazoned gold sceptre, he stood to open what would be the seventy-third session of the Eternian High Council.

"Praised be the gods and Great Spirit! The worthy Knights of Eternity have succeeded in vanquishing the heathen, yet again saving our glorious city from the most perilous of dangers! The nation of Eternity will long remember and celebrate this tremendous victory for many eons to come and I, Abraiyias, on behalf of the Eternian High Council, wish to express all due feelings of humble gratitude to your most heroic of deeds! It must be bestowed upon these fearless seven knights: our noble King Alectorious the 2nd, the long serving veteran chief-general Rapacosis, Jalectrious the brave, the young prodigy Gavastros, Maxious the stronger, Thelosious the philosophical one - and let us never forget the legendary master tactician, Stratos. For countless eons our city walls have been unbreached and our army undefeated in battle, much to the envy of the rest of the known world! It is a proud history and tradition you have so courageously upheld and will no doubt continue to do so for many eons to come. Like our forefathers before us and courageous warriors in the Age of Heroes, your names will forever be etched in Eternian history!" a beaming Abraiyias announced, as he raised his arms theatrically to the air. The council rose to a stirring round of applause, expressing due words of appreciation to the gallant king and his knights: it was a truly euphoric moment for all.

"The gods have spoken in our favour with their wrath of thunder!" one councilman boldly proclaimed, as many others cheered loudly in agreement.

"Eternity forevermore!" shouted another with confidence, as the noise level grew.

"Long live the king!" said yet another with pride, with all clapping rapaciously. Abraiyias was as always in a hyperbolic state, wishing to laud any and all plaudits on the seven knights he could possibly muster. Indeed, it was customary for the opening speaker to express such words of gratitude to uplift the spirits of the all gathered.

As the excitement in the ornately-fashioned chamber began to quell, the ever-vigilant Brotoeas was quick to bring everyone crashing back to reality.

"My fellow Eternians and councilmen, in as much as we relish basking in the glory of this magnificent victory, I do ask, how long will it be before an *even greater* force sent against us? A mighty triumph at Dragon's Pass it was indeed: but know it was a mere fraction of the entire Gomercian armed forces! The ambitions of Nerosis are boundless and shall consume all in his path until the greatest prize is captured, my dear companions: The City of Eternity. Make no mistake, it is *our* lands he lusts for more than any other - with walls unbreached in seven hundred eons, this mighty fortress overlooking the great Buvarious Mountains and Marathosian Plains - it would be a cherished prize to any conqueror, and without question, the Gomercian Empire!" he starkly warned, with many unable to argue with the pragmatic councilman's logic. Murmurs of agreement began to reverberate throughout the chamber as several others voiced their opinions.

As tension grew, the astute councilman Diwalos cleverly took his cue, sensing many would favour him. He spoke with great vigour, strongly expressing his point of view.

"Brotoeas speaks words of many truths, my king; the megalomaniacal ways of Nerosis will stop at *nothing* until his despotic empire complete! This latest attempt, granted, a follied one, clearly signals his intentions! It is my, as well as many of my constituents' belief that it is his intention to launch a full-scale invasion of Eternity - and I move that we prepare accordingly!" he demanded, in no uncertain terms. One of the most thoughtful of the thirty-seven councilmen, Diwalos was well known for his boundless dedication to the people. Murmurs turned to loud disagreements as a clear split began to emerge. One councilman suddenly jumped out from his smooth, decorated marble bench in heated response.

"It is *we* who should take advantage of the tremendous opportunity the gods have bestowed upon us! They spoke once in our favour with their wrath of thunder, and blessed us yet again with victory at Dragon's Pass! Can you not see the signs, my fellow Eternians? We must strike while the gods still favour us - at the very heart of the Gomercian Empire!" insisted the pugnacious Periclosis, undoubtedly the most hawkish member of the council.

The chamber erupted into an animated chorus of chatter as conflicting opinions were passionately exchanged; the energy in the room became increasingly intense as the collective conscience was confronted with the very realistic possibility of invasion. As the discussion began to veer out of control, King Alectorious took his opportunity.

"Gentlemen, please if you may; listen to my words!" he pleaded, raising his hands to signal his intention to speak. The noise level fell dramatically as all eyes shifted to their honourable leader. Dressed in his impressive shining blue and gold ceremonial armour, the king's position was *never* in question.

"Gentlemen of the council, your fears and anxieties are well grounded, shared very much by my fellow knights and I. Indeed it *is* true that in our long and proud history we have never been invaded, but know that Nerosis' desire to subjugate us under his oppressive rule is stronger now than ever before. Without doubt, a course of action must be decided upon. However, I neither wish nor condone any rash decisions be made simply to appease the populace. There are many lives at stake, my fellow Eternians: our citizens, soldiers, allies… and each and every one of ourselves." the king evocatively warned, looking around the gathered circle of souls. Silence fell upon the bright decorative chamber as the gravity of the situation truly began to sink in. As the councilmen quietly contemplated, a lone soul had the courage enough to speak his mind. Forward he stepped, very much to the bewilderment of all.

"If I may be so bold, my king," he insisted, requesting permission to speak.

"Go ahead Scotaeous," nodded Alectorious, as all eyes shifted their attention.

"One possibility that has long been spoken of would be to launch a campaign to liberate the city-state of Saphoeria. Long ago it was our closest ally, if indeed any are able to remember, before the truculent Gomercians swept ruthlessly across these once-benevolent lands. I have not a doubt in my mind the Saphoerians would rally behind us *if* we were to free them from imperial rule. With the Gomercian army having just suffered such a crushing defeat, perhaps *now* might be the moment to take those first steps, my companions, towards liberating the known world," he suggested, with many subtle voices of agreement heard throughout the chamber. There was sound logic to his idea, as many in Saphoeria still held deep sympathies for this eons-long alliance. The king did not seem to share this enthusiasm, harbouring serious reservations about any realistic chance of success. He rose from his throne and began pacing around the elaborate marble floor, quietly contemplating with arms firmly behind his back. Stopping suddenly, he finally addressed the gathered councilman.

"There is no knowing if the Saphoerians would be willing or indeed able to support us in such an ambitious venture: we simply cannot afford to underestimate the extent of Nerosis' corruption, my dear councilmen. The influence garnered from his gold discoveries is unmatched, allowing him to bribe any and all in positions of power. Might I also add, the Gomercians pay handsome sums to mercenaries, whose only loyalty is to their sword, shield and fortune it may bring. Furthermore, any Eternian support in Saphoeria would be quickly suppressed and many lives unnecessarily lost. Even if we *did attack* Saphoeria, the empire would still be able to call upon reinforcements from the other occupied cities. Not to mention the cost of such an endeavour! I am unwilling to sacrifice Eternian lives unless *total victory* can be assured. Can anyone guarantee of this?" the king solemnly demanded, looking around to a sea of veritable silence. The Eternian standing army, excluding reserves, numbered some three-thousand seven-hundred souls. It was highly skilled, trained and well-equipped but relatively small in comparison to its Gomercian counterpart. The combined imperial forces were some six-fold the Eternian number, meaning success in pitched battle would be a near impossible task. Councilman Brotoeas was somewhat more optimistic in his views.

"Nothing is guaranteed nor assured, my king, but we have few other options than to take the empire head on - dismantle it from the inside-out and liberate the occupied city states one by one - it is the *only* way," he definitively argued, as mutters of agreement reverberated throughout the ornate council chamber.

In total, there were seven city-states located throughout the known world; each unique with its own culture, characteristics and idiosyncrasies. Eternity was located in the far-north, while slightly to the south-east was its old ally, the river city of Saphoeria. The nation of Calgoria was situated in the heavily-forested area to the south-west, while another traditional ally, Brasovia, was positioned almost directly south atop a small mountain in the middle of the vast Marathosian Plains. Further to the south-west was the lake-city of Trakoesia; and in the deep south-east laid the remote clandestine mountain nation of Bactrosia. In the most southern extremity was Eternity's arch-nemesis and greatest foe: the city-state of Gomercia and capital of the so-called Gomercian Empire.

Alectorious was not at all convinced of a costly full-frontal assault on Saphoeria. The empire had been weakened by the earth thunder and dramatic loss at Dragon's Pass, but if anything, it would only serve to strengthen its famously steely resolve. For certain, the Gomercians would not yield without a monumental fight. Alectorious was utterly convinced there *had* to be another way: something so audacious *even Nerosis* would not dream of…

"An attack on Saphoeria: is that not what Nerosis and his generals would most expect?" he posed, pacing around the lavish chamber with meaningful intent. "Predictability would be our downfall, my dear councilmen, most especially in war. Nerosis knows only too well of our once close relationship with the Saphoerians and will, without any shadow of doubt be protecting it accordingly," the king warned. The stony-faced expressions of the councilmen were a stark vindication their worst fears could come to pass, if that was indeed the path Eternity chose to follow.

Alectorious paused for a moment, readying to voice his bold suggestion. He knew it would not be widely accepted, yet in spite of its audaciousness, was in his eyes at least the only feasible option remaining. The Eternian leader raised his head daunted, looking around the sea of wilful faces staring right back into his blue-green eyes.

"Well, what of Brasovia?" he unexpectedly posed. The king's words elicited gasps of shocked revulsion at the mere thought. Nonetheless, he boldly carried on. "The Gomercians would *never* expect an attack there. Strategically, there could be no better place to strike - at the very heart of the empire! Nerosis might control much of the known world but Brasovia is the key, my fellow Eternians: without it, he would lose control of Saphoeria, Calgoria and the rest of the northern lands. *If* we can take *and* hold Brasovia, it would be only a matter of moons before the other occupied cities rebelled - and the Gomercian Empire crumbles before our very eyes." Before the king could finish, strong voices of derision could be heard throughout the chamber. Alectorious was already beginning to regret his suggestion, having not expected such passionate opposition to his idea.

A mountaintop fortress not a sun's ride away, Brasovia was, after Eternity, the most impregnable city in the known world. The Gomercians had taken Brasovia by ruthlessly starving the population before bombarding it with powerful siege weaponry. With their walls crumbling and supply lines cut off, the Brasovians had little choice but to surrender and submit to Gomercian rule. It had been as much an indignity for the Brasovians as a crowning moment for the empire, for whom there was only one more jewel left to capture…

"The strategic value of Brasovia is undoubted, my lord. Nevertheless, it would be virtually *impossible* to launch a successful invasion: high in the mountains, one road in and out *and* surrounded by vertical cliffs on all sides! Even a successful invasion force would be completely isolated - a surely suicidal venture!" an incredulous Brotoeas presaged. Councilman Diwalos also expressed his feelings on the matter, but with a degree of doubt.

"Aye, he speaks the truth, my king - it would be an *enormous* risk. Success would not be guaranteed as you wish it and many brave souls would surely be lost." he vexed.

Murmurs of disapproval continued to echo throughout the chamber as the king felt increasingly isolated, his eyes darting around the room searching for answers. In his desperation, he turned to his ever-reliable master tactician. It was a dramatic break from council protocol, which stated the king *always* spoke on behalf of the seven knights. It was a bold but shrewd decision.

"General Stratos, your thoughts, if you please!" he demanded, in a tone of considerable anxiety. The most tactically astute of the knights calmly offered his insights.

"My great king, Alectorious, we have been assessing the possibility of a full-assault on Brasovia for many suns now, with it being of the immense strategic value that it is; but as councilman Brotoeas has alluded, it is a *tremendously* risky proposition. With only one narrow road in, our troops would be badly exposed to the Gomercian artillery, *even if we were* to reach the gates. I would be reluctant to support any such attack, my king. In the absence of a viable strategy, it would result in almost certain defeat. Saphoeria, if anywhere, would be our best chance of success; but even *that* would involve considerable risk, *especially* if the Gomercians were to redirect their forces from other cities."

Alectorious felt he was in an even worse predicament than before. As if guided by a mysterious force, the king looked to the elaborate wall decorations depicting countless battles from across the ages. An idea suddenly dawned: certain it was of divine inspiration.

"What if we were to send a small army to Saphoeria as a decoy and attack Brasovia with our main force?" It seemed the king had found an answer as many reacted positively and began chattering excitedly amongst themselves, but Stratos did not share their enthusiasm.

"A fine plan sire, but any decoy army would be at great risk if the Gomercians were quick to respond: the imperial communication networks are unmatched and they could send for re-enforcements in the blink of an eye. Furthermore, we would need a large number of troops to not only take, but hold Brasovia," the master tactician warned. The king and others were despondent, realising the idea would not go ahead without the support of their most experienced knight. Indeed, the Gomercians had developed an efficient method of communication through highly-trained riders and fire-signals, allowing Nerosis to be rapidly alerted of any Eternian incursions into his territory. The only way around this would be if the sky gods became angry and inundated the lands with rain and thunder. The king decided to hold back on his idea for now, praying that another option would soon present itself.

"Alright, let us keep the Brasovian and Saphoerian possibilities open for now. There *must* be an alternative to open warfare - I simply do not wish to unnecessarily risk any one life. Perhaps we could simply draw the Gomercians to Eternity and wear down their army - they well know the strength of our defences and would commit a massive number of troops - and it would leave the occupied cities under-protected and greatly vulnerable. The Gomercian's overwhelming ambition could be their very undoing," Alectorious claimed, alluding to a more clandestine plan of attack. Stratos was still *far* from convinced.

"With an army of that size, it would only be a matter of suns before our walls breached, my king. It would not be wise to provoke attack, even when confident of victory," he wisely remarked, with murmurs of agreement echoing throughout the fine dome-roofed chamber. The tactical mastermind continued, with all eyes focused on him.
"Quite simply, we need another option, my lord. Whatever course of action we eventually decide upon, it will involve considerable risk and loss of life: that simply *cannot* be avoided," he starkly added, as Alectorious lamented his lack of viable options.

"If only we had an invisible army, we could hit them when they *least* expect it," he dreamed. The king sat back, looking to the elaborate blue and gold coloured ceiling as if searching for a sign from the heavens. The council was again silent until another soul found the courage to suggest his idea, despite the many that would surely oppose.

"May I be so bold, my king, as to mention the forestmen of Catharia?" councilman Scotaeous bravely suggested. A strong chorus of derision immediately rang throughout the chamber; such were the feelings of mistrust toward these secretive nature-dwellers. "Please, let me speak!" he demanded, wildly waving his arms. The king promptly stood to intervene, raising his voice to the unruly.

"Quiet all - Scotaeous will be heard!" he thundered, as the noise quickly dissipated. Alectorious had secretly hoped the Catharians would be mentioned, having always been secretly fascinated with these mysterious forest peoples. He could never publicly bring himself to talk of it though, fearing ridicule or loss of favour, especially with some of the more conservative members of the High Council.

"Scotaeous; please continue!" he insisted, impatient to hear the councillor's thoughts.

"My king, we may not have the most cordial of relations with the forestmen, but they are no companions of the empire - of this we can be most certain! Experts in guerrilla warfare, hit and run in small numbers on any sun or night - and I hear they have been causing Nerosis considerable problems of late! The Catharians could be *very* suitable allies, my king, and fight that secret war of which you speak!" Many were in disbelief the Catharians even mentioned, never mind an alliance with them proposed. Councilman Brotoeas was one of the more astonished, expressing this sentiment.

"The Catharians!?" he ridiculed. Many others shook their heads in equal bewilderment as the defiant Scotaeous continued, confident he could sway opinion. "Companions not of Nerosis, sure, but I hasten to add, equalled only by their dislike of ourselves! They believe us to be impure for separating ourselves from the natural world, high in our lofty castle, away from the heart of The Great Spirit: the forests, animals, mountains and rivers alike!" he argued, as others began to come to his defence.

"I heard they swear to have no council with anyone who does not share their beliefs!" added the hawkish Periclosis, however inaccurate that he was. How can we possibly form an alliance with those who would have no word with us?" he asked, as many mumbled in agreement. Scotaeous quickly dismissed their prejudiced opinions, continuing unashamedly in his defence of the forest peoples.

"They are proud of their culture and their beliefs, as we Eternians are ours! I have no doubt they share the same desire to preserve all that they hold true, but it is no reason to dismiss the possibility of closer ties completely out of hand - *especially* if it means an end to the empire! *If* we were to form an alliance - mark my very words, fellow Eternians - their guile and our strength combined would form a devastating combination!"

The king sensed an opportunity as many expressed a sudden change of heart: the logic in Scotaeous' argument was undeniable. Alectorious began to lose himself in his thoughts as his imagination drifted into the mystical realms of Astrala.

"It reminds me of the Ancient Prophecy," he dreamily remarked, freezing suddenly and delving deep into thought. The chamber and all that surrounded blurred mysteriously into the background as the king began to recall The Prophecy of the Great Dragon. It was something Alectorious had been reluctant to mention, for fear of ridicule more than anything else. Many had come to believe it was a story of pure fantasy: the delusional ramblings of ancient scribes and mystics. The king was finally ready to defy his own doubts, sensing something out there was asking… inviting him to do exactly thus…

"Have no fear," whispered a quiet, soothing voice emanating from deep within his soul. "The gods are with you," it continued. Alectorious felt the most unusual tingling sensation throughout his body as the gathered council grew increasingly anxious. They watched with great perplexity, sensing all was not well.

"My king?"

"Whatever is wrong?"

"King Alectorious!" their concerned words came, unable to comprehend *what* was happening. The king finally snapped out of his trance-like state and looked up, gazing at the chamber in acute realisation of its grandiose magnificence. The dome-shaped room was filled with beautifully-mastered paintings and mosaics depicting Eternity's rich history of heroes, legends and victories throughout the myriad of ages. Feeling truly inspired, the king turned to face the council, who were watching with mesmerised curiosity, simply unable to understand. Taking a deep breath, Alectorious finally spoke, and with words of great profundity.

"There was a sun long ago in the ancient Age of Heroes when a being of tremendous strength, courage and honour saved these lands from almost certain defeat from forces that were not of the light. We were fighting a long protracted war against The First Empire, in league with our auld allies, the Saphoerians and Brasovians, but all was not progressing as had been planned. We were surrounded on all sides, outnumbered and outflanked - people had given up all hope of victory, believing it would only be a matter of suns before Eternity collapsed under the immense pressure and The First Empire had its way over the entire known world - something unthinkable but moons previously. There was a defining battle when Eternity and her allies were fighting an overwhelming enemy number, with the tide turning rapidly against them. When all seemed lost, a powerful dragon came from deep within the Buvarious Mountains, helping them to claim a dramatic victory. The mighty being fell to his wounds, and was from that moment on immortalised in Eternian history and legend. He is none other than our greatest hero, most inspirational legend and now only hope: Reiactus."

The council sat mesmerised with jaws wide open and eyes transfixed on their noble leader. The king's retelling of this tale provided such inspiration in these suns of struggle. He spoke with such emotion and pride in his nation's history: from Eternity's beginnings in the

Age of Heroes and many struggles thenceforth to the rise of his own kingship. He was well known for his fondness of classical Eternian history, seizing upon any opportunity to use its vibrant stories to uplift his people through the spirits of the ancients. The council had listened intently in this knowing, absorbing every word with great intrigue. Alectorious continued with unrelenting fervour, hoping it would have the desired effect.

"There is an Ancient Prophecy that speaks of when Reiactus will return to aid Eternity once again in her moment of greatest need. It is written that when all hope again seems lost, the mighty dragon will swoop down like a blinding light from the skies above, vanquishing the forces of darkness, once and forevermore. Soon after this glorious victory, the righteous will ascend to the Higher Worlds to be as one with the gods and The Great Spirit: a place of indescribable beauty and bliss that knows not the suffering, pain nor conflict of this beleaguered world. Eternity will be free - and peace will reign on these lands, once and forevermore. For many eons have we awaited this sun, my fellow Eternians: I believe now, it has *finally* arrived."

The sound of silence was so deafening it seemed to almost echo throughout the beautiful chamber. The story of Reiactus had been long-revered throughout Eternity but forgotten over the eons as memories faded and the few who still believed gradually passed into Athepothesia. Most had lost hope Reiactus would *ever* return, but there were many who still adamantly believed.

As the councilmen sat in silence, a wise prophet named Pythaeious boldly came forth, walking straight to the centre of the shining marble floor. He raised his hands to the air as gasps of incredulity rang throughout the chamber.

"Ah yes, great King Alectorious, The Prophecy of Reactus and his return: such did it captivate hearts and minds in ancient suns yet faded into obscurity with the passing of eons.

It is truly sad, my fellow councilmen, that in as much as we revel in our own magnificence, those defining moments of our glorious history are so easily neglected. We forget the tremendous bravery of our valiant ancestors, the sacrifices they made and why it is we still live and breathe here this sun. It was prophesised that Reiactus *would* return - and I for one have no doubt of this," Pythaeious announced, with the council completely absorbed. The king was especially beguiled, perennially impatient to know more.

"But from *where,* I do ask, Pythaeious? There is not a man alive who could tell us this!" The council nodded in unison, whispering in agreement with their noble leader. The prophet smiled as he paced around the bright council chamber, looking to the ceiling as if in search of response.

"Some say Reiactus' soul comes from the stars in the night sky, where his kind, along with the gods themselves watch over and protect us. Yet others that he comes from deep below the surface of these lands, where enormous caves exist and the suns pass as they do not here. Undoubtedly, one of our most famous legends says that upon his passing, Reiactus' body was taken deep into the Buvarious Mountains by luminous beings from a distant star. Bringing him miraculously back to life, Reiactus promised, in exchange for their good deed, to watch over and protect the known world until he was once more called upon to serve the will of The Great Spirit. Throughout the ages, all manner of men: knights, seekers, mystics and scholars alike would make the perilous journey into the Buvarious Mountains in the hope of finding the long-lost dragon. Seeking personal glory, deep spiritual insight or the secrets of our mysterious past, these brave souls believed there could be no greater achievement than to discover this enigmatic being. Many ventured there but to this sun, none are known to have accomplished this gallant feat. It became the holiest of quests, from which those who returned would be treated as the gods themselves."

The collective imaginations of the councilmen were now lost in a faraway land, utterly captivated by Pythaeious' mesmerising speech. The prophet continued as he paced frantically around the chamber, with all absorbing his every last word. "It is said only the purest of hearts have eyes to see him: some even suggest only those of royalty can do so, but thus-far, no king has attempted to seek him out, fearing they might never return. It is written an Eternian king *would* one sun make that perilous journey… yet we still await…" he suggestively added, casting a subtle glance to his majesty. As he finished, Pythaeious stood back to invite response. Brotoeas was quick to voice his opinion, standing dramatically from his marble seat.

"We all appreciate the importance of Reiactus to our nation - indeed, many revere him as a hero, drawing much strength and fortitude from his legend, which has inspired profound works of art, writing, painting, sculpture - and even song! Some worship him as the gods themselves - such is his stature in Eternian lore. But that is all it is - a legend, my king and fellow councilmen - and nothing more," he boldly asserted. Brotoeas continued unabated. "As surprising as it may seem, we have little historical evidence to support Reiactus' very existence! It was, might I add, not long ago he was prophesised to return to prevent the very rise of the empire! Needless to say, this did not occur and indeed, we have nothing other than ancient wall carvings and vaguely-worded scrolls as proof of his existence. And talk of our world merging with the gods; well, this has been considered at length by many reputable scholars and philosophers, who have an almost unanimous disagreement of such possibility. Well, I say it is fantasy at best - we could never dare *even think* we are as one with the gods," he argued, rather seriously distorting the facts. There were still many firm believers of Reiactus' legend; perhaps the king most of all. Brotoeas' outburst prompted a mixed reaction as Diwalos spoke.

"A great hero of our history is Reiactus, my fellow councilmen; but to put *all* our faith in him saving us again would, well, simply not be wise at all," he warned. Councilman Abraiyias was quick to add to his vocal counterpart's claims.

"I for one strongly believe in the legend of Reiactus *and* that he *will* return, but even I would not put all my trust in something for which we have no solid proof. My great King Alectorious, do you have reason to believe it is soon to transpire? Have the gods spoken unto you - given a sign perhaps?" he impatiently questioned, with a strong sense of anticipation.

Alectorious paused and glanced to his knights, who nodded without a word spoken. The moment had finally arrived. The king stood dramatically from his throne, removed a set of scrolls from under his tunic and raised them above his head.

"I wish to present to you, my dear councilmen, a set of scrolls discovered just prior to engaging the Gomercian forces at Dragon's Pass. They *not only* mention Reiactus, but his return!" Collective gasps of astonishment echoed throughout the chamber, so taken were they. An air of excitement swept throughout the council, followed by an uncontrollable chatter as several stood and approached, hoping for a closer look.

"This is unprecedented! Please my king, read them to us!" demanded Brotoeas, with others demanding the same. Anticipation grew as the king carefully unrolled the ancient documents; the gathered councilmen were barely able to control their delirium.

"They speak thus," he announced, preparing to read a segment of the scrolls.

> **"When the earth shakes like thunder,**
> **The Great Dragon will soar,**
> **And a once vast empire shall fall…"**

A gasp was heard like a gust of wind sweeping across the distant mountains - or a deep subconscious memory had suddenly been triggered - one could not tell which.

"Unbelievable!" "Astounding!" "This is unprecedented!" came the numerous reactions. Sensing opinion swaying in his favour, the king continued in earnest.

"The earth has shaken my companions - now will the great one follow?" he asked. The stunned councilmen simply had no reply but Abraiyias soon broke the silence.

"Is there no more, my king?" he despairingly asked.

"Far from it, my companion! I found this part somewhat more intriguing," Alectorious replied, turning his eyes to the light-brown coloured parchment.

> **"Before the suns set on the Age of Kings,**
> **A great awakening shall transpire;**
> **And the lands of man and the gods will be again as one."**

"Does this spell the end of Eternity, or are we destined for a better world? I truly wish to know!" the king insisted, as he held aloft the mysterious writings.

Many of the councilmen were in shock while others were deep in contemplation; yet others were lost as if caught in a fantastical dream. Pythaeious stood from his chair and edged towards the king to see for himself. Others gathered as the king handed the scrolls to the prophet, who was greatly impressed by their quality. Pythaeious handled them delicately.

"They are almost perfectly preserved!" he exclaimed, caressing the fine edges of the ancient parchment. The king could only agree with a meaningful nod.

"And very much authentic, too - from the era of King Alectorious the 1st according to our scholars!" he assured, as excitement in the chamber continued to grow.

"This script, I cannot read it!" exclaimed Abraiyias, pointing to an unrecognisable section.

"By the gods; it is classical Eternian!" added Pythaeious. The king nodded.

"It is yet to be fully translated but seems to substantiate theories of the dragon's return," he confirmed, as many of the councilmen began to contemplate the meaning of the scrolls and their discovery's wider implications.

"In light of this revelation, upon what destined path does this lead our nation, my king?" Abraiyias questioned, with the other councilmen wondering likewise.

"This, only The Great Spirit can answer, my dear companion. I move that until the scrolls are properly translated, no further decisions be made. Meanwhile, I shall travel to the ancient sanctuary of Delphoesia in contemplation of the path ahead. Upon my return, we shall decide upon a final course of action," he announced, eliciting a more positive response from the councilmen. Delphoesia was a complex of ruins in the north-east on the path to the Buvarious Mountains: a place of sacred importance to Eternians where kings had had wise insight imparted to them throughout the eons. It was also not far from the Oracle of Dabouge, with whom Alectorious would often consult whenever the path ahead unclear.

"Would it truly be wise to leave *now*? There is no knowing *when* the Gomercians might attempt invasion. My noble Alectorious, Eternity *cannot* afford to lose you in these most desperate of suns," warned a concerned Abraiyias. There were murmurs of agreement but the king was completely unperturbed, responding in a calm reassuring manner.

"That is *precisely* why I must go, my dear companion: *all* avenues *must* be pursued. Delphoesia has long provided wise insight and brought great fortune to Eternity. General Rapacosis will rule in my absence; Stratos, as his deputy, will further explore our military options with the knights in the war council. For now, we prepare all contingencies for invasion: triple the wall-guard, call up the first reserves and warn the citizens to brace for the very worst, for it may soon be upon us." the Eternian leader starkly warned.

"Very well, my king, but what of the Catharians - do we pursue them?" Abraiyias asked, with several others nodding curiously. The king was coy in response.

"Any enemy of the empire would be a powerful ally, indeed. However, I ask that no contact be made until my return," he indifferently replied, fleecing his *true* affections for the enigmatic forest dwellers. "Are there any objections?" Alectorious then asked. Glancing around the bright decorative chamber, there was total silence.

Although a conservative strategy, it was the only realistic option at this point - the Eternians would do as they had for many eons - hold their position fast and defend with all that they had. It was a plan no-one could find reason to dispute in the absence of a viable alternative. Abraiyias looked around, replying in line with his duty as speaker.

"There are none, my king," he duly observed, shaking his head. Alectorious breathed a sigh of relief, knowing he had bought himself at the very least, a few suns.

"Very well!" the king announced, standing theatrically from his throne. "Upon the morrow, I shall journey to Delphoesia! Two suns from now, the council shall reconvene. All agree?" he asked, with secretly, very contrasting intentions. The response was unanimous.

"Aye!!!" they shouted, in a final seal of approval. The king returned to his place as the councilmen slowly filed out, chattering amongst themselves of the uncertainties ahead.

Alectorious turned his thoughts to his imminent journey, hoping The Temples of Delphoesia would provide answers to his many pressing questions. Although not mentioned, it was the king's every intention to also seek out the Oracle. She was unpopular with many in the High Council, who believed she unlawfully intervened in the affairs of the Eternian state. Alectorious had no such qualms, having sought her wise insight on many occasions: her accuracy was always unwavering. If The Great Spirit willed it, he would be imparted all he required and the noble King of Eternity would go on to fulfil his bright destiny.

THE SEVEN KNIGHTS

There was not a greater honour in all the known lands than for a young hoplite to join that prestigious group of warriors: the Knights of Eternity. There were seven knights including the king himself, with each having proved beyond all questionable doubt their valour, courage and fortitude above and beyond their regal call of duty. The king traditionally hand-picked each of the knights making up the group, selecting only those he *truly believed* would serve their nation's greatest good. In veterans Rapacosis and Jalectrious, Alectorious had seen strong leadership and powerful charisma; in Stratos, tactical and strategic genius; in Gavastros and Maxious, sublime combat skills and physical prowess, and in the knight closest of all to the king, Thelosious, the ability see beyond what his eyes could see and all reasonable logic comprehend. With Alectorious as their head, the knights spearheaded a vanguard of formidably courageous warriors, ready to lead Eternity through any imaginable challenge the gods might throw in their path.

As was the custom following the High Council, the seven met in the Knight's Chamber, which was located in the pinnacle of the main castle tower. It was a secretive place of much fascination to the common populace and where few out-with this exclusive inner circle had ever the privilege to venture. It was a perfect opportunity for the knights to voice their opinions on Eternity's current state of affairs and was this sun, surely to be most forthright. The Knight's Chamber was naturally smaller in size to that of the High Council but in no less measure important. Its smooth, coloured walls were decorated with intricate mosaics and paintings from famous battles and glorious triumphs from Eternity's long and vibrant history; from the legendary Age of Heroes and Alectorious the 1st right through to more recent battles with the Gomercian Empire. Soon it would surely include that now famous victory: "The Battle of Dragon's Pass".

The chamber was roofed by a perfectly-shaped light blue, gold and purple coloured dome from where sunlight streamed in through to the gathered knights below. The circular chamber was dominated in the centre by an unusual triangle shaped table, with a place each for the king and his men to be seated. There was intriguingly, one seat left spare, heralding back to those ancient suns when not one but *two* kings would rule Eternity, side by side. Ancient legend had spoken of an eighth knight who would one sun rise to take that much foreshadowed place, but in the many generations that had passed, none had proven equal to this tremendous honour. The surface of the central table was decorated with an elaborate blue and gold image of Eternity's greatest hero: the legendary dragon Reiactus, in all his magnificent glory.

The seven knights quietly entered the bright chamber with mixed feelings; some excited, while others anxious as to what would soon be discussed. All duly took their places around the table, with Alectorious at the head and three knights sitting on either side.

The king relaxed on his unexpectedly spartan throne, making himself comfortable in a way he could not in the High Council. If there was anything he dreaded about the kingship, it was the eyes of a score of statesmen watching his every muscle, move and gesture, waiting for a chance to pounce on any conceivable fallibility. The knight's chamber was a refreshing departure from the often politically-motivated intentions of the councilmen and was thus, a perfect opportunity for honest opinions to be voiced. The king would speak for all during the High Council, but in this clandestine little abode, Alectorious expected nothing but honest, forthright views from each and every one of his knights.

Alectorious peered round meaningfully into the eyes of his companions, as if trying to reach into their very minds and souls. He hoped they would speak the truth of their feelings, fears and doubts: not what they believed their king *wished* to hear. Alectorious rose from his throne and placed his hands firmly on the smooth marble table, suitably addressing the gathered band of warriors. They all duly sat up, listening to their noble leader intently.

"My brave and noble knights, we achieved victory beyond imagination at Dragon's Pass, which will indeed be remembered in poem, writing and song, long after we pass into Athepothesia. Without doubt, it was a triumph for the spirit of the Eternian people as it was equally, a blow to Nerosis and his tyrannical empire," the king announced, looking meaningfully into the eyes of his knights, who were quick to express their feelings.

"To Eternity!" Gavastros exclaimed, rising from his seat, drawing his shining sword melodramatically and thrusting it into the air. The other knights were quick to concur, standing to reveal their blades of valour.

"To Eternity!" they bellowed, as the king echoed their electric sentiment.

"To Eternity!" he concurred, also lifting his sword aloft. In moments, they returned to their seats as Alectorious continued to address the perilous situation at hand.

"As tremendous a victory that it was, we all know the Gomercians will return, and in much greater numbers. I know not when or how, only that it will be thus. My spirit is torn and foresight weak, I only pray we find the solution that we seek. I ask that you speak freely, my companions, for there are no secrets within these divine walls," he suitably invited, knowing they would not disappoint. The king's loyal followers were initially silent, trying to articulate their thoughts and feelings on the matter. Gavastros was first to speak: opinionated as he was skilled with a sword, the prodigy never hesitated to offer his most intimate thoughts. With typical exuberance, he vented his frustrations in one fell swoop.

"Alectorious, my great king, why we ever bother with the council I am quite unable to fathom. They talk and talk - and we simply listen - and listen more. Now here we all are, with nothing decided or changed! We need action sire, not this idle chatter! When will something be done? Let us go out and fight some Gomercians, at least! Or if there is a chance Reiactus *is* in the Buvarious, I say we go *now* before it too late! My word, I shall do it by myself, if need be!" he insisted. Thelosious and Maxious could not resist a quiet chuckle at their companion's refreshing directness, but the king held a quite different view.

"I realise the High Council seems aimless some suns, Gavastros, but know there are many within it with much wisdom and knowledge to impart, and guidance when the path ahead unclear. We are not tyrants as are the Gomercians: the High Council is the voice of the Eternian people and *they* matter. Their thoughts *must* be heard if we are to be true to ourselves as a free nation, please never forget that," he scolded. Although the king in theory had absolute power, the opinions of the citizens were always carefully considered. Gavastros immediately backtracked, replying in a far more reserved tone.

"I do apologise, my king: it is not my place to question the council's purpose, nor importance to our nation, as much as they *do* irritate me. I merely wish to express my frustration at our lack of progress - as the suns pass quickly, with no sign of change," he stressed, worried of Eternity's fate, which now hung precariously in the balance. There was a general consensus amongst the knights, with Maxious offering his unwavering support.

"I am with Gavastros, to the final setting of the suns: I say we move *now* against the Gomercians, before it too late!" he exclaimed, with his companion nodding in agreement. Maxious was only moons ago ordained into this elite circle of knights; like Gavastros, by virtue of his excellent swordsmanship and leadership of hoplites. Now was the chance to prove his mettle amongst the very best of Eternity. At just twenty eons, Maxious was by far the youngest of the group. Rapacosis was naturally cautious of his overzealous attitude.

"Maxious, your gallantry is to be admired but there is more than swordsmanship and bravado to the Eternian knighthood: there are suns for fighting and those more wisely spent studying the enemy, coming to the realisation of not only how but *why* we fight. You have yet to fully understand the *true* nature of the Eternian warrior, but your sun shall duly arrive," he warned, trying his best to temper the youngest of knights. The master tactician Stratos offered a rather more pragmatic idea.

"Gavastros *does* have a point, Alectorious; the suns do grow short and eventually, a strategy of engagement *must* be decided upon. We have bought ourselves some suns with victory at Dragon's Pass; not forever I say, but enough to re-group for the inevitable Gomercian response. An attack on Saphoeria or Brasovia would stretch Eternity's capabilities to the limit and put our army at great risk. Any other options, no matter how implausible, have to be explored. My king, *you* ultimately must make a decision - and very soon," The others nodded in agreement as their sense of direction became much clearer.

"By the gods Stratos, what exactly are you suggesting?" Alectorious asked with a nervous gasp. Stratos cleared his throat and clenched his fingers together tightly as if about to reveal the answer to something of profound importance.

"I concede my fellow knights that, while from a tactician's point of view the king's intuition might seem somewhat unorthodox, in this particular instance, it might in fact provide greater insight than even *my* vast knowledge could offer," he cryptically responded. The knights all seemed baffled, so used were they to Stratos' normally direct nature. Alectorious began to drift into a dreamlike trance as an image of a great blue dragon and sweeping mountains ranges flashed through his mind.

"I shall tell you my companions, all I have thought of since touching those ancient scrolls has been to venture into the Buvarious Mountains, to see with my own eyes those majestic snowy peaks, and discover once and for all if the great Reactus lives on. It is an attraction quite inexplicable - almost as if the gods themselves are beckoning me to fulfil an ancient mystical quest - never in all my suns have I felt so strongly about something so intangible," he expressed, but as though still holding something back. Thelosious knew exactly of what his regal companion spoke and did not hesitate to offer his support.

"It has been written the dragon would await his sun of return in those great peaks - perhaps he *is* summoning us - and we should seek him out," encouraged the philosophical knight, as the king expressed his unequivocal agreement.

"I truly believe it be so, Thelosious," Alectorious concurred, with his blue-green eyes sparkling. The others did not all share this disposition, with Jalectrious particularly vocal.

"I wish no disrespect to my king or our great hero, but there is no conclusive evidence, written or otherwise, that Reiactus is even there at all!" Jalectrious was suspicious of any mention of the dragon, knowing how easily Alectorious was swayed by such talk. Gavastros by contrast would look for any excuse to embark on a bold mountain adventure.

"It is a sign from the gods, my companions - can you not see this? I say we go *now* and see for ourselves!" he exclaimed, mesmerised, as Maxious needed no second invitation.

"And I!" he vigorously proclaimed. Thelosious nodded subtly as even Stratos appeared convinced but Rapacosis maintained his stoic disposition. The king listened as his knights exchanged conflicting views, allowing things to take their natural course. Thelosious added his thoughts to the growing disquiet amongst the band of valiant companions.

"All these eons we have waited for this moment, Jalectrious; can you not see? The Prophecy is coming to fruition before our very eyes - the gods have spoken!" he proclaimed, excited by the prospect of magnificent adventure. Rapacosis was concerned by the king's silence, trying to draw him into the absorbing discussion.

"Alectorious, what more have you to say of this?" he asked, looking meaningfully to the Eternian leader, who was brought back to the moment with an abrupt jolt. Looking around at his companions with evocative intent, the king spoke.

"My fellow knights; you know I have *always* been a firm believer in The Prophecy of Reiactus' return: it has given me hope when all I felt was despair, guidance whenever the path unclear and inspiration, when I needed it more than ever. Until the scrolls' discovery at

Dragon's pass, it had in many ways felt like a fantastical dream - something I believed in deep down yet consciously, felt would never actually transpire. All that has changed - I truly believe that *not only* has Reiactus returned, but he awaits us in the great Buvarious Mountains - *and* that it is our destiny to find him," he forthrightly expressed. It was an enormous leap of faith for the king to invest so much in something for which there was so little tangible evidence. Such was his passion for this enigmatic tale however, the boundaries of fantasy and reality all too often seemed to blur into one. Alectorious waited patiently, trying to gauge the feelings of his knights, who were naturally rather taken aback. Thelosious had a sense of where this was all leading, further probing his eons-long companion.

"Alectorious, what *precisely* are you suggesting?" he asked, somewhat confused.

"I have always been taught to follow the signs of the gods, Thelosious, whenever they have spoken. I believe they now summon us to embark on a noble quest high into the Buvarious, to discover once and for all if Reiactus still lives." There were mixed feelings amongst the knights as Rapacosis was quick to spell doubt. He sat upright with his powerful forearms calmly resting on the smooth marble table, his thick dark beard evocative.

"You know I have always held our legends in the highest esteem and that any Eternian brave enough to emulate them afforded all conceivable plaudits. Indeed, it would be a chivalrous quest into those great mountains, befitting the ancient heroes themselves. But consider the dangers, my king: remember the fate of those who have travelled that path and the obstacles, perils and foes you might face," warned the veteran warrior, expressing his grave reservations. Thelosious was quick to temper the overly wary general's thoughts.

"With every great endeavour come inevitable risks, Rapacosis - you know this more than anyone. As Stratos rightly said, all options, no matter how unreasonable *have* to be considered. What if it *does* hold to be true - that Reiactus lives - and that he shall come to our aid?" he reasoned, in a somewhat provocative tone. Rapacosis was equally so, offering a stark warning in reply as the other companions watched on intently.

"And if he is not - and the life of the king and many others lost?" he dramatically retorted, widening his eyes fiercely. A veteran of countless military campaigns, the general was always one to throw caution to the wind. Alectorious entered the debate again, re-enforcing his belief that travelling to the Great Buvarious was the only way.

"I deeply appreciate your concern for my wellbeing, Rapacosis; but as king, the decision is ultimately mine. As such, it is a risk I am more than willing to take," he interjected, turning to face the general. "I truly believe the gods *are* guiding us, and that it is our destiny to journey into the Buvarious Mountains," he categorically added. His loyal companion Thelosious nodded in agreement as Rapacosis finally conceded, such was the king's determination to follow his heart's path. The general knew he was powerless to do anything and would respect his decision. "I cannot argue with the calling of the gods, my king. If it is that you must go, take only our very best warriors; for there is no knowing what lurks in those mountains," he advised, warning of the perils that lay in uncharted lands.

"I shall take only the finest Elite Guardsmen, I assure you, Rapacosis," the king promised, as his mood brightened. The general acknowledged with an appreciative nod.

"Very well," he flatly answered, with nothing more to say.

"Well, what are your orders, my king?" Gavastros subsequently asked, as the others nervously waited. The king replied as his eyes shone with a star-like sparkle.

"I shall travel as planned to Delphoesia after consulting the Oracle, and if the meeting is favourable, then on to the great Buvarious," he answered, eliciting smiles of agreement from several companions. Rapacosis knew he could not stop the king but continued to voice his concerns. "I respect your decision, my lord, but if the Gomercians attack in your absence…" he began, but the king was quick to dispel any fears.

"It is why I have chosen *you*, Rapacosis, in co-operation with Stratos to rule in my stead: Eternity could be in no finer hands," he incisively replied. It was a flattering show of confidence from the king as both Rapacosis and Stratos nodded in exultant compliance.

"Thelosious, Gavastros and Jalectrious will accompany me to Delphoesia, along with a small detachment of Elite Guards. Maxious, I ask that you stay in Eternity with the general and Stratos," the king ordered, with all except one satisfied with their forthcoming duties.

"You know I can fight as well as any here - why must I of all stay?" demanded a bewildered Maxious. The king was sympathetic but straightforward in his answer.

"You have yet much to learn, dear Maxious: your opportunity to shine will arrive one sun but for now, the gods have other plans," he hearteningly answered. Maxious nodded reluctantly, knowing he could not argue with the will of the Eternian king. Jalectrious was already looking ahead, concerned the people would be unduly alerted to their plans.

"This is a sizeable enough force, Alectorious and could quickly raise suspicions *if* you gather my meaning," he suggestively remarked. Knowing secrecy was of paramount importance, the king had already thought this through well.

"Indeed. That is why we shall depart early in the morn from the northern gates. None shall know, I promise. Any further questions?" he asked. Looking into the eyes of his companions, the path now seemed so clear; as if it had always meant to be.

"Only one, my noble king - when do we leave?" the prodigy asked, greatly excited.

"We depart in the morrow, Gavastros." Looking to his companions with meaningful intent, the king continued. "Rest well, my fellow knights, for we have a tremendous journey ahead. Before long, we shall know once and for all if The Prophecy holds true - and the great dragon lives on." With that, the Eternians retired for the evening, with their fate now firmly in the hands of the gods.

TEMPLE GARDENS

Before setting out for Ancient Delphoesia, Alectorious sought some quiet solace in the tranquility of the Eternian Temples; to abscond however briefly from the turmoil that so beset his nation and likewise, most of the known world at this present moment. Located not far from his opulent castle residence, the king would often venture there in suns of great uncertainty, seeking wise guidance and council from one of his most trusted companions, Plasos: teacher, mystic and dedicated follower of the inner path. A visit to the temples was also a chance for Alectorious to connect with those profound spiritual energies that were acutely present throughout this deeply sacred abode.

The temples were surrounded by elaborately-fashioned gardens of the most exquisite beauty; with fountains, streams and a vast array of exotic flowers, plants and vegetation abounding. Small animals including squirrels and cats roamed freely, running and chasing each other around the expansive greenery with joyous aplomb, while strikingly colourful birds chirped constantly from tree branches as if to express their deep appreciation of this beautiful dwelling they called their very own. It was truly a terrestrial paradise to behold and one that Alectorious cherished more than any other. Citizens were free to venture to the temple gardens at any moment of their choosing but were bound by a strict code of silence; for it was the very sanctuary of The Great Spirit they were entering. Eternians believed it was to here the spirits of the gods and their ancient ancestors visited, and was to communicate with these revered beings they ventured, in the hope of gaining deep insight into their lives and unknown paths ahead.

There were three temples located within the gardens - a main and two smaller ones. They were simple yet elegant in structure, painted in a bluish-white and gold, with each reaching a little more than two hoplites in height. With slightly slanted blue tiled roofs, the temples were encompassed by beautifully-fashioned blue and gold coloured columns that were decorated with all manner of intricate designs such as dragons, mythical animals and many creatures from the vast and vibrant animal kingdom.

As the king approached the main temple, he immediately felt a soothing, benevolent energy reaching out and engulfing his kindred spirit, as if beckoning him within. Alectorious took a gentle breath of fresh air before stepping towards the entrance, feeling a powerful sense of upliftment the closer he approached. At the top of the temple steps, a familiar figure awaited in the shape of a temple priest - or minestros as they were commonly referred to across much of the known world. Dressed in a blue and gold coloured robe and with hands firmly clasped, he patiently waited for the king to arrive.

"Greetings, noble Alectorious," announced the elderly man in a soft, welcoming voice. "It is a pleasure as it is *always* an honour to welcome his honorable majesty to The Temples of the Gods and Great Spirit," he added, as he opened his arms and motioned to the spectacular surroundings. The king was humble - and his response direct.

"As it is equally a pleasure for I, Plasos, wise minestros of Eternity," he fittingly replied. Slightly bowing his head, it was a show of respect for the mentor Alectorious had known since childhood suns. The king was slightly anxious: uncertain perhaps of what insights their meeting would soon bring. Sensing this, Plasos relaxed his disposition, inviting the king forward as pleasantries were duly dispensed with.

"Well make haste, Alectorious, we have not all sun!" he quipped, clapping his hands together again as they managed a light-hearted smile together. Plasos was one of great knowledge and wisdom, revered throughout the known lands for his deep insights into life and the existence of all things. An author of many texts on spirituality and the gods, there was not a higher authority in the kingdom on such matters. The king looked up to Plasos in a way he did no other, feeling privileged to have a soul of such heightened awareness with whom to seek council. He would often consult Plasos on a variety of matters before making a personal visit to the temples in an attempt to connect with the essence of The Great Spirit. Plasos was as always in a jovial mood; perhaps unexpected from one in such an esteemed position.

"So what brings you here this fine sun, Alectorious; something in particular, or is his majesty simply in need of some fine conversation?" he cheerily remarked, as the king smiled. Plasos was one of not only great wisdom, but of good humor and excellent company.

"I think a bit of both, my old companion!" he chirpily replied, knowing it would prove a most insightful encounter.

"Please, after you, my king," Plasos motioned, already sensing a matter of tremendous urgency. The two made their way swiftly around the main temple entrance to a quieter part of the gardens, thus maintaining the privacy of their conversation. Plasos and the king found their way into a small enclosed garden populated with colourful exotic flowers and shrubs: the perfect location for the secret matters of state soon to be discussed. The minestros motioned to one of two well-polished white marble benches in the middle of the fine garden. "Please, be seated," he kindly offered, with a swift wave of his hand. The king duly obliged, sitting and relaxing as best he possibly could. Plasos did likewise opposite in eager anticipation of what would soon be spoken. Alectorious began in a low voice, ever wary of who might be eavesdropping on their conversation. He looked around briefly before speaking.

"By now, you must have heard of our momentous discovery; indeed, it seems the entire city has erupted into a state of euphoric chaos," he remarked, quite unsure how his mentor would respond. Plasos was remarkably calm, as though having expected exactly thus.

"Ah yes indeed, the scrolls of The Great Prophecy; exciting suns we now find ourselves in, Alectorious! It is something one could not have foreseen but is to be rejoiced without question. I had thought as countless others that The Prophecy's fulfillment was long lost to us. Many believed it simply a myth - nothing but the ramblings of ancient romantics such as myself - it seems as though they have finally been proven otherwise!" he replied with a light chuckle and tellingly mischievous grin. The king's enthusiasm reflected this; he continued, leaning over with hands tightly clasped.

"The scrolls speak of Reiactus, and that he shall soon return to aid our noble struggle: it seems to be an undeniable sign The Prophecy will finally come to pass!" he elated, before probing his mentor. "What are your thoughts - do you believe it *will* be so, Plasos?"

The wise man was philosophical as he also clasped his hands together.

"Know Alectorious, that nothing in this world is ever an absolute; but truth be told, for I, like so many others, there could be no greater thing than to witness Reiactus' return. I do admit; the larger part of me can and *will only* believe when I see it transpire before my very eyes. For many eons have I waited, hoped and prayed for change, Alectorious, for a world free of the struggle, pain and torment we have known now for too many suns. Throughout my younger eons, I was utterly *convinced* Reiactus and his brethren would return and restore order to these troubled lands - yet, we still wait. It suitably inspired me ponder at length, The Prophecy and the nature of its' *true* meaning," he acknowledged, eliciting a powerful response from the Eternian leader. Alectorious sat upright, utterly fascinated to know more.

"What do you believe it *is* then, Plasos: The Prophecy's *true* meaning?" he asked with unbridled intrigue. The wise old minestros sat back, taking a deep breath of fresh air into his lungs before expressing his thoughts on this most contentious of matters.

"After many eons of contemplation, I came to the realisation that The Prophecy was far more cryptic than we had at first been led to believe. I concluded it was a tool of the gods, compelling the people of Eternity to awaken the spirit of the dragon that exists deep within us all: that indomitable bravery, defiance and willingness to never give up under *any* circumstances. By rousing this dormant strength, the world would rise up together and defeat the forces of darkness not only without but *inside* of ourselves. When this is achieved, I believe it will be *then* that the great one shall *finally* return." Despite the controversial nature of his suggestion, he knew of Alectorious' openness to such ideas. The king was intrigued by his mentor's insights, leaning forward before probing.

"If that *is* so Plasos, what would be that one thing to compel us to awaken that great power inside?" Plasos was guarded as he leaned back in careful thought.

"Only together with your brave knights can that question be ever answered, my king; I am but a humble minestros who interprets the signs of the gods. As much as I wish it be so, I cannot answer *all* the mysteries of life and the universe," he maintained with a deep sigh.

Plasos impulsively looked up to a small bird chirping on a hedge, feeling almost envious of the creature's simple but divine existence. It was inspiring to think such a tiny being could live in such harmony with itself and all that surrounded: something that few *people* had seemingly the ability to do.

The minestros returned his attention to the king to express his thoughts. Gripping the sides of the smooth marble bench, he tellingly spoke. "We Eternians are an advanced people, my king - *that* is without question. We built this great civilisation and brought order to what had once been a deeply fractured land and yet, there is still so much to learn of this mysterious world of ours and the ways of The Great Spirit. I have lived a long life, Alectorious and experienced many wondrous, mysterious things, but I shall never fully understand the nature of this bountiful creation in which we live. As you, I still have many questions. I fear however, they shall not be answered before my *own* sun sets into the distance," Plasos admitted, with more than a hint of sadness. The king was sympathetic to his companion's plight but decided to first address more pressing concerns of state.

"I very much share these sentiments, Plasos, but what dominates my thoughts now more than anything else is the path ahead for Eternity: the current crisis has been discussed at great length in the High Council but with no definitive conclusion. It all seems to keep returning to the same thing: the legend of Reactus and his prophesised return. As you know, a number of prominent scholars believe the great one retreated into the Buvarious Mountains following the First Eternian War and that he still lays there in wait. Ever since the discovery of the scrolls, I have felt this inexplicable pull to those majestic peaks. And, it is after much consternation I have decided to venture there, to know once and for all if the dragon lives on," Alectorious dramatically announced. Plasos reacted with surprising calm as he nodded and squinted his wise old eyes, carefully choosing his words.

"Every man has a way of interpreting the signs of the gods, but always question your *true* motives for such bold adventures, Alectorious. Those mountains have a powerful allure that could consume your entire life before you realise a single sun has passed - and sweep you dramatically away as if you never were - I of *all* should know this…" he sheepishly admitted, and with a deep melancholy sigh. The king curiously sat up, wholly unclear as to what his loyal companion was alluding.

"You mean you have *been* to the great Buvarious?" he skillfully deduced, and quite in shock. Plasos confirmed as his eyes began to sparkle like clear diamonds.

"Once, long ago in more peaceful suns, towards those enchanting peaks I did venture. Oh, I came so very close, Alectorious, I could almost *touch* them with my own bare hands," he nostalgically recalled. The king was almost lost for words, sitting up with a look of bewilderment as he probed his mentor further.

"But you had never mentioned this before, Plasos - why ever not?" he asked in disbelief, shaking his head in complete confusion.

"There is a moment for everything, Alectorious… and it is *now* that I shall finally impart..." The king was utterly mesmerised, impatient as he clenched his fingers together.

"I truly do wish to know more of these adventures, Plasos!" Alectorious insisted. The old man obliged, casting his mind back as though it were only the previous sun.

"So much has changed since those long past eons…" he sighed, pausing for a moment of reflection. "…As a young soul, I was fascinated as you are now by tales of Reiactus and a mysterious world said to exist beyond the great Buvarious Mountains, and was steadfastly determined to find this elusive abode. It all happened in the late autumn of my thirty-third eon upon a sun that is now long lost to me. Having decided to find out once and for all what lay beyond, I gathered all that I needed and at the end of that very moon, I ventured out toward those mystical mountains, expecting never to return. The path was long and arduous but the beauty and tranquility I experienced out there was a fitting aphrodisiac. The natural surroundings were enchanting beyond description: the power of The Great Spirit itself flowed freely throughout the endless forests and valleys, up to the enchanting mountains and into my very heart and soul. If the gods were to have chosen an abode in this world, I was sure it would be there, high in those lofty peaks. It was an experience I shall never forget for the remainder of my suns, Alectorious, and a peace I have never in all my endeavors been able to recapture," Plasos lamented, wishing he could be whisked away instantly back to those suns so memorable. Alectorious was quite taken by his mentor's tales of this swashbuckling mountain adventure, desperately wishing to emulate him.

"Truly astonishing, Plasos - after all these eons, I had no idea!" the king gasped. "How far did you manage to travel?" he asked, with his attention now quite undivided. Plasos focused, intuitively re-connecting to the experience through his vivid memories.

"After many suns journeying up through winding forests and braving the elements, I finally reached a magnificent valley high in the mountain passes, which was of such captivating beauty I could have honestly stayed for the rest of my eons," the veteran adventurer began, as a clear picture formed in his head. "Oh yes Alectorious, the Great Buvarious Mountains - they will capture your heart and take you on the most wondrous imaginable adventure - and before you know it, steal your dreams like a cunning thief in the night," he added, with the slightest hint of bitterness. The king was rather mystified by this forthright admission, expressing as such a he cast a brief glance away.

"I do not understand, Plasos - I thought the great Buvarious was a place of one's dreams…" he remarked bewilderedly, recalling all he had read of this majestic place.

"Perhaps only if the gods will it," Plasos despondently replied. Oblivious to his mentor's painful memories, the king continued impatiently.

"What happened in the valley - did you continue no further?" he pressed, enchanted as he was inspired by this spellbinding story of adventure. Plasos seemed reluctant at first but knew he could not turn back now from revealing the truth.

"Well, the night I reached the valley, a great storm set in, the likes of which I had never seen before in all my eons. It raged fiercely, relentlessly for three suns and nights long, with thunder, lightning and rain falling irrepressibly from the merciless heavens above - as if the skies were possessed by the unrestrained fury of the thunder gods. I was fortunate to find refuge in an old castle ruin on the edge of the valley, with its old stone walls sheltering me from the lashing elements and warming me from near-freezing temperatures. I thought I would never leave the valley alive. On my third night, I had a mysterious dream warning of great danger if I dared continue. Having almost run out of supplies, I had no other choice but to return. I always regret not venturing further - so very close was I - yet so far…" the brave minestros reflected, visibly downhearted.

"But you had no choice, Plasos - had you continued, you might not have survived - and gone on to help so many in Eternity as you have!" the king reasoned, but Plasos was momentarily inconsolable as he cast his mind back to those long lost eons.

"That it is purely conjecture, Alectorious; perhaps I would have made it *if* I had tried."

"But surely you could have returned another sun?" reasoned the king.

"Well, I had been planning to the following spring, but with the rise of the empire and various other bandit tribes and mercenary groups, such travel became far too dangerous, especially for a lone unarmed soul such as myself. I imagine there was a reason the gods wished me not to continue that autumn… something they did not want to be discovered… until now, that is…" Plasos intimated, as the king's eyes lit up intensely.

"Do you mean Reiactus?" he cleverly deduced. Plasos nodded subtly as his mood shifted to a distinctly more positive tone.

"Maybe so..." he replied, but as if withholding a thought.

"Then it is a sign I *should* go," the king divulged, as Plasos sounded warning.

"It could well be he awaits your arrival, Alectorious; but be mindful always of the dangers those enigmatic mountains pose, for their beauty can be very misleading. Know also that The Gomercian Empire has long been fascinated by the great Buvarious and mysterious power they wield. Now more than ever they yearn to know its secrets - you had best exercise the greatest of caution." The king however, was confident that all would be well.

"I am well aware of the dangers, Plasos: I have prepared accordingly and shall travel with my *finest* of warriors. If it is truly meant to be, I have faith the gods and Great Spirit will protect us." The wise mentor was still very wary, hinting with a clear tone of disapproval.

"If that is your decision, I am as your humble subject obliged to support you, my king; but from one man to another, I can only pray for your safe passage." Alectorious nodded in recognition before hastily changing the topic to something of a more cordial nature.

"What interests me more than anything is the other prophecy written in the scrolls: it speaks of a sun when the lands of men and the gods become one. What know you of this, Plasos - would this be possible in our lifespan - if indeed at all?" the king asked with great curiosity, knowing it was something that would equally fascinate his mentor. Plasos sat back in silence, awkwardly rubbing his chin in realisation of the subject's sensitivity.

"Ah yes, this is, as some have referred it "The Forgotten Prophecy", quietly debated by philosophers and scholars alike for many eons. It has unfortunately, long since disappeared from the consciousness of the Eternian populace and *largely* dismissed by those who claim to be learned as "scientifically impossible" - or by others who deem it blasphemy to *even suggest* we could stand as equals to the gods. I and others of more open minds realised *exactly* what this meant: it created too much of an inconvenience, asking too many important questions about our world that could not easily be answered. Long ago, it was suppressed by a small number of conspiring councilmen and subsequently forgotten. We of the spiritual path however, have always had a far more open mind to such possibilities: things that might otherwise threaten the political powers that be." A distraught expression appeared upon the king's face as he tried to articulate his feelings of frustration.

"How, by the gods could such treasonous acts be possible in Eternity - a supposedly free nation? It is every soul's right, not privilege to know of this great transparence! I can only imagine what I shall do if I find those responsible," he furiously reacted. Plasos did his best to restore calm but was as much sympathetic to the king's ire.

"I wholehearted agree with you, Alectorious; but remember this was many eons ago, when people were not of the understanding they are now. Those responsible have long passed into the afterlife, where they will no doubt answer for all they have done. As individuals and a society, we must learn to forgive, forget and let go, before we can ever move forward and create the world we *all* deserve to live in," Plasos gently explained. The king finally conceded, though he was still greatly vexed.

"You are not wrong, Plasos - but it just is so difficult some suns, it really is…"

"To forgive?" asked the minestros.

"Perhaps more to forget…" the king admitted, as he glanced to the blue skies above. "You are not alone in this, Alectorious; you are most certainly not," assured Plasos, dramatically changing his tone as his face became rather serious. "For now, your chief concern must surely be to rally your citizens, as conflict with the Gomercian Empire seems to be all but a foregone conclusion," he observed, worried his king's preoccupation with dragons and prophecies was causing too much distraction from the task at hand.

"I can assure you, Plasos everything possible is being done to protect the people and ensure Eternity's safety." The wise old minestros nodded in tacit approval, realising nothing more need be said for now on this. Alectorious paused and took a deep breath of fresh air to calm his volatile nerves as he looked to the birds playing cheerfully in the nearby hedges.

"You know, I had always believed Eternity to be a place of such perfection: free of the corruption and trickery that now so plagues these lands." Plasos found it difficult to argue with the king's assertion as he also focused on the delightful winged creatures.

"While we are a *relatively* advanced society, it is not *quite* as much as people would have themselves believe; for there are many things we cannot explain about this world, and will not, for many eons to come. The stars in the night sky, for example; we know not their *true* nature or what beings may live there even! Some say they are worlds as our own; others that they are heavenly bodies where the gods themselves reside; yet others, that it is to where we shall travel after our passing from this world! There is still to be any sort of *unanimous* agreement on this most perplexing of issues. In light of all that, I *truly* believe it possible that we as a people can rise up to a much better place than we now find ourselves..." It was a response not expected but warmly received as the king felt a surge of delirium.

"You mean to say it *will* come to pass: that the worlds of men and the gods shall become one?" he asked, ever more impatiently. Plasos was understandably reserved, wishing not to build up the king's hopes too much. Both knew deep within that it *would* be so.

"I do sense great change in the air, Alectorious; whether such a mergence shall transpire, only the passing suns can tell," he inconclusively replied, as the king pressed.

"But you believe it *is* possible?" he asked, sensing Plasos holding something back.

"I believe that in this world and universe *anything* is possible - *if* you believe it strongly enough in your heart and soul," the cryptic minestros answered, before continuing in a more serious tone. "I believe you *were* given this prophecy as a test, Alectorious; of courage, fortitude and the ability to look deep within and trust that hidden voice of inspiration and hope," he emotively stirred. The king had only one answer to this.

"That voice tells me only one thing, Plasos; that I must travel to the great Buvarious Mountains." His mentor nodded respectfully, knowing his pupil had found his chosen path.

"If you *truly* believe that is your destiny, then it is your heart's calling you must follow, Alectorious," the minestros insisted. There was nothing holding the king back now: even the wrath of the thunder gods themselves could not hinder his fated path. Alectorious narrowed his eyes, looking meaningfully into his old companion's.

"I was born for this journey, Plasos: it is the only path left for me to walk. I give thanks for your council and shall always cherish it."

"And it will *always* be here for you, my king," his mentor warmly assured, bowing his head in kind. Alectorious smiled before rising to his feet and taking a deep breath, already thinking of the many challenges that lay ahead.

"I shall seek further guidance in the temples before returning to the castle - there is much I have to prepare for my quest." Plasos likewise rose, offering due words of support.

"May the gods and The Great Spirit *always* be with you, Alectorious, and guide you to a safe return," he hoped, bowing his head. The king did likewise, bidding farewell before making his way up to the main Eternian temple. There, he would seek a more personal connection to The Great Spirit, and seek divine guidance for the path ahead.

The Eternian temples were located at the very centre of the opulent gardens: a fitting place perhaps for this most revered abode of the gods. They were the most beautifully enchanting creations one could possibly imagine, with ornately-decorated columns and walls as captivating as they were enticing to any visitor fortunate enough to encounter them.

The temples were of deep spiritual importance to this ancient nation, serving not only as a place of worship but for citizens to sooth their weary souls and receive appropriate guidance. There were three temples all told: The Temple of The Great Spirit and two smaller ones, which were designated for the various Pantheon of Eternian gods. It was possible to worship any combination of gods in any given temple, but the effect was believed to be far more powerful if a particular god were chosen for a specific purpose. The Great Spirit was the all-encompassing, all-powerful force in the universe that presided over *all* the gods, and to whom one would *ultimately* communicate. The temples truly were the most sacred of places, where only those of the purest intentions could venture.

The king approached The Temple of The Great Spirit with a sense of enormous anticipation as he felt a mystical otherworldly force flowing throughout his body and soul: a sensation so powerful he had to pause momentarily before edging closer to the impressive row of blue and gold fashioned columns. Alectorious felt an overwhelming sense of peace as he arrived at the small but impressionable entranceway, knowing words of great wisdom would be imparted within. He looked admiringly at the exterior before taking a deep breath and moving through the enchanting entranceway.

As the king passed inside, a mystical energy began to enshroud the king, permeating every part of his noble being and very soul. Walking further within the ancient structure, he marvelled at the somewhat rough yet natural-looking walls. Alectorious had always been enchanted by their humble but striking simplicity, the very nature of which sent a powerful message from this great dwelling of the divine.

There were a number of small torches placed at equal distance along the whitish-coloured walls, illuminating the temple with a mysterious golden glow. Between each torch was an elegantly-fashioned coloured crystal, with each colour representing one of the Pantheon of Eternian Gods. At the foot of the temple was one large golden crystal representing The Great Spirit: the all-encompassing universal force to which all souls, including the gods themselves, were ultimately answerable. Indeed, people would often consult this divine power before an appropriate god came forth. There were a countless number of gods believed to exist beyond the realms of physical matter; watching over, protecting and guiding the people of the known world throughout life's tumultuous journey.

There were seven main Eternian gods: Aphroedisia, the goddess of love, beauty and good fortune; Guerris, god of victory and war; Arturious, the god of mountains and adventure; Caledoesious, god of forests, animals and the earth; there was Siriosious, the god of the skies and unknown realms of existence; Kairos, the god of wind and change; Poenessia, goddess of water and fluidity; Athesia, the goddess of knowledge and wisdom; Hephaesious, god of art and creativity - also a popular first name. Finally, there was Promaestious, the god of all hopes and dreams, and of the entire pantheon of gods.

There were a number of lesser gods to whom Eternians would also pray; some imported from other cities or fashioned by their own imagination, even. The people would pray to any number of these deities or if they so wished, directly to The Great Spirit itself. For many, speaking to one of the gods was a far more personal experience. The king was particularly fond of Arturious and Caledoesious, having since childhood suns felt a very strong affinity with the mountains, forests and natural world. Although they were gods of a particular realms of existence, all were knowledgeable about a great many things.

The king knelt in the middle of the sacred temple with eyelids firmly shut, taking several deep breaths before speaking in a soft but meaningful whisper.

"Oh Great Spirit, guide me upon the highest path of my humble soul's calling; allow me to serve my nation of Eternity in the best possible way to restore peace to these once benevolent lands and bring glory once more to your name," he attentively prayed.

Alectorious waited patiently, knowing an answer was not always certain to follow. It was with hope rather than expectation one would consult The Great Spirit, with any form of guidance imparted *always* deeply appreciated. The king suddenly sensed a soothing presence surrounding his aura, as if a kindred soul from Athepothesia was telling him that all would be well. He could not see with his own eyes, but deep in his heart he knew that someone or something otherworldly was out there, guiding and protecting him onto his highest path. The mysterious being dramatically spoke in a mature, poised voice.

"Noble King Alectorious of Eternity… it is within the depths of your soul that the answers to all that you seek will *ultimately* be found… but it is to the mountains high that your path now leads, for it will be in those heavenly abodes you shall discover the key to that which you have sought for so many eons. Go now, humble, gracious and valiant one, for a great destiny awaits." As the mysterious voice faded away, the Eternian king opened his eyes with an inspired sense of awe. Now more than ever before, Alectorious was determined to fulfil his bright destiny and the dream of a better world for all.

ETERNIAN THEATRE

After all the commotion of recent suns, Alectorious needed nothing more than to enjoy some of the finer things in life and forget he was the leader of a powerful nation-state. As King of Eternity, such opportunities were few and far between: certainly from the perspective of the average citizen who knew little about the workings of his majesty's inner sanctum. There were, contrary to what one might have believed, ample opportunities for the king to indulge in such worldly pleasures: a healthy banquet with companions by his side exchanging stories of ancient heroes and myths was one of Alectorious' favourites.

Perhaps more than anything else, the king enjoyed a visit to the theatre, where re-enactments of long-past battles, adventures and contemporary events were played out with great vigour by actors and actresses trained in the classical arts. There were serious as well as humorous retellings; the former very much a salute to the brave deeds of their ancient ancestors, while the latter were more playful jibes at their age-old adversaries, the Gomercians. It was fitting that on this particular sun, a long-anticipated series of plays would take place. It was the perfect chance for the king to lose himself in the vibrant stories soon to be re-told to a grandiose audience in the recently refurbished Eternian Theatre, which was located on the boundaries of the opulent city gardens. Upon this fine night, the stars and moons shone brightly upon the great walled city, providing the perfect background for what would be a truly captivating evening.

Thelosious rushed up the winding stone staircase to the king's regal chamber, frantically searching for his eons-long companion. Knocking on the large mahogany door, he quietly let himself in. The king, however, was very much lost in a world of his own.

"Alectorious, are you not yet ready? The entire theatre is waiting for you - Gavastros and the others are already there!" he enthused, with his sense of anticipation abundantly clear.

The king's cerebral companion was an even more devoted patron of the theatre, never missing a chance to lose himself in the excitement, humour and sheer unpredictability of this most favourite of pursuits. Alectorious had been enjoying the clear night sky and countless stars shimmering in the untouchable distance, dreaming of an unknowable future. The king would often gaze up from his chamber balcony to this vast creation of light, in wonderment of those enigmatic stellar bodies as they danced gracefully in the skies.

"I do apologise, my companion; it really is easy to lose oneself out there," he pensively remarked, as he looked out to the myriad of shining beacons above. Thelosious neared his companion before leaning over the balcony.

"Indeed it is; but do not lose yourself too much, Alectorious, for your people are expecting you!" Shaking his head, Alectorious snapped out of his trance-like state.

"Of course - let us make haste!" the king exclaimed, returning inside to fetch his warm coat. Flinging the thick covering over his shoulder, the king and Thelosious made their way down the spiralling staircase through to the main hall. There, they were met by a detachment of Elite Guard, who would safely escort them through the city streets, all the way to the bustling Eternian theatre.

"Evening sire!" greeted Thespious, the leader of the seven waiting warriors. Dressed in typical light-blue and gold armour, he truly was a model Eternian soldier.

"Thespious! It has been too long, my companion; however has the known world been treating you?" the king asked, genuinely pleased to see one of his favourite guardsmen again.

"Well, my wife is expecting her first child, so blessed be the gods for that!" he replied elatedly. Alectorious expressed due congratulations as he clasped his hands together.

"Be that indeed, Thespious; I wish you all the very best together," he said, while ever so briefly imagining such a life for himself. He knew that for now, his regal duty had a much higher calling.

"Oh, thank you, my lord," Thespious replied, tipping his shining blue helmet.

The group followed the winding city streets before eventually finding themselves at a secret entrance to the theatre which was reserved exclusively for the king and other important dignitaries. Alectorious could immediately sense the atmosphere as he passed inside, feeling that warmth and companionship usually associated with a gathering of those like-minded. The Eternian theatre had long been an arena of learned, thoughtful souls - a world away from the terrifying perils of battle. The theatre itself was a semi-circular shape, with three main seating areas rising up gradually from a small stage and two staircases dividing them. There was a large reserved space for the king about halfway up - distinct with its special elegantly-carved wooden seats, comfortable cushions and bowls of tasty-looking fruit. On a clear sun there was a perfect view of the snow-capped mountains in the background, which would only add to the drama onstage. Alectorious gazed from his standpoint at the top of the theatre to the crowds of joyous citizens chattering below as the air of anticipation steadily grew. It was always a special occasion for the king, having from childhood suns greatly enjoyed his visits to this luminous entertaining abode.

"Thank you, Thespious; I shall be fine from here," the king insisted, signalling the burly flanking sentry, who took a respectful bow in kind.

"Very well, my lord; enjoy the performance," replied the robust Elite soldier, remaining on guard where he was. The king and Thelosious made their way down the right-hand steps toward the middle of the seating area, with the people quite unperturbed by the presence of royalty. The king was known for his love of theatre, so it was to be quite expected. Indeed, it was considered unsightly amongst the more educated populace to make a fuss; just as Alectorious himself would have it. As the two arrived at the row of their reserved seats, Thelosious grabbed his companion on the shoulder, holding him slightly back.

"Whatever is it, Thelosious?" the king asked, looking around, somewhat disconcerted.

"Alectorious, there is someone I would like you to meet," he insisted, motioning to a pretty, dark-haired elegant young woman seated not a handful of spears distant. The king looked over, feeling a shudder of embarrassment and the briefest sensation of fear.

"Oh Thelosious, why do you always do this to me – and when I least expect it!" he grumbled. Thelosious had for long attempted to play Cupid, trying many a sun in vain to help his companion find a suitable mate. Would it be this sun?

"Come now, Alectorious, she is *exactly* your sort!" he fervently insisted. After much consternation, the king finally conceded to his stubborn compatriot.

"Well, who is she?" the king asked, curiously glancing over. With a firm shape, long dark hair, hazel-brown coloured eyes and olive skin, Alectorious was unable to deny interest.

"It is senator Diwalos' daughter; her name is Sephia," Thelosious said, as he mischievously raised his eyebrows.

"That… is Sephia? My, has she ever grown. Well, she is most definitely *the* type," the king incredulously gasped, with eyes widening and heart beginning to palpitate.

"What is but idle chatter, Alectorious, really?" Thelosious continued, hopeful.

"I have little choice, do I?" the king good-naturedly chuckled. Thelosious shook his head before casting a glance towards Sephia.

"That you do not, my dear old companion - go ahead - she *is* expecting you!" he encouraged, giving Alectorious a playful push in the back. The king sheepishly made his way along the row of seats to the seated lady of some twenty-one eons, who was quick to see his approach. She nervously stood and turned to face him, bowing in recognition of his noble presence.

"Oh, your majesty; it is the greatest honour!" she squealed, before bowing in kind. The king was immediately taken by her innocent demeanour, sighing likewise in relief that she was of the sensitive sort.

"Please, call me Alectorious; there is no need of ceremony here," he insisted, calmly raising his palms in an attempt to relax her nerves.

"Oh… Alectorious…" she gasped, almost lost for words and blushing profusely.

"Well, you must be Sephia - it is a most wondrous pleasure to meet you."

"And you, *Alectorious*," she replied, letting out a childish giggle.

"Shall we be seated?" he asked, motioning to the plush cushioned seats.

"Of course!" she said, with a broad smile. Both the king and Sephia took their positions as the crowd continued their incessant chatter. Alectorious was lost for words, petrified of saying anything that would make him look the fool. Sephia was equally nervous, and was desperate to make a good first impression. Her father hoped it equally; perhaps for reasons somewhat more ulterior, however. The king tried his best to relax and be natural, speaking for now only matters of the moment.

"You know, since childhood suns I have adored the theatre - the thrill of not knowing what would happen next - it has always captivated my imagination," he remarked. Sephia was very much in agreement, turning to the king with a sparkle in her hazel-brown eyes.

"Oh, I know; my father would often bring me here when I was younger. I would dream of one sun standing out there performing to a great audience… but alas, it was never to be…" she bemoaned with a great sigh. Alectorious was rather taken aback by this admission.

"Really? Well I never…" he managed, expressing his surprise.

"Expected it…?" she responded, as Alectorious quickly tried to backtrack.

"I am sorry; no, not at all - in fact, I am sure you would make a fine actress! I just…" he offered in vain. Sephia dismissively waved her hand.

"It is alright, really… not many do. Daughters of Senators are not deemed suitable for such devotions, but that is another *long* story…" she replied despondently. Alectorious sensed he should push no further as an awkward silence ensued. Sephia felt it her turn to speak; realising her king's obvious discomfort, she dramatically changed her tone.

"Well enough of me; I can only imagine how it would be to be King of Eternity! By the gods, you have the *entire* city to pamper your every need, wish and want!" Sephia exclaimed, trying to imagine such a privileged existence.

"I could only dream of such a life, high in a lofty castle tower," she wistfully added. Alectorious was quick to bring her thoughts of grandeur back to reality.

"It is not all you might imagine, Sephia - really. There is tremendous expectation on my shoulders to fulfil the wishes of our people and to honour the memories of our ancestors. The excitement lasts a while, but it all soon fades away to the stark reality of the Eternian kingship," he bluntly explained, while secretly yearning for far more personal freedom.

"Come now, there must be *something* you enjoy about it, Alectorious!" Sephia insisted, brushing her long hair back as she looked at him with her piercing eyes.

"Well, I have a nice view from my balcony!" he admitted good-naturedly. Sephia's eyes lit up, barely able to contain her delirium.

"I would love to see that, one sun!" she intimated, wondering what it might be like.

"It would be an honour!" the king replied, sensing an opportunity as his thoughts were interrupted by all the commotion on the stage.

"Oh look, the play is about to begin!" Sephia exclaimed with juvenile excitement. The audience was silent as a flamboyantly dressed man walked to the centre of the stage to announce the beginning of the evening's show. The theatre would always consist of at least two plays: on this particular evening a re-enactment of an ancient mythology followed by a more light-hearted comedy. It would be quite a feast for the eyes.

"I bid you all welcome to his majesties' royal theatre, in honour of the great Promaestious!" he announced, in reference to the highest of Eternian gods. The man continued with zest, waving his arms around profusely for theatrical effect.

"And so it is without further ado, I invite the esteemed three main actors to the stage, who will present to you the latest work by our great playwright, Alexious the bold: "The Great Journey"!" The crowd erupted in applause as the three famed actors took to the stage, waving and blowing kisses to the enchanted audience. The crowd replied in kind as all the ladies present threw coloured petals of blue, yellow and purple to their favoured actor, with some of them shrieking hysterically.

"First, I present Aeischylious: the latest talent in a long line of Eternian performers, ready to dazzle you with his sublime acting skills! Tonight, Aeischylious will play Graos, one of three Eternian heroes to be represented this night!" The crowd cheered as Aeischylious bowed and waved in appreciation. The presenter continued. "Next, I present to you Sophoxious, who will play none other than the indomitable Achtreias!" he exclaimed.

Again, the crowd cheered wildly as Sophoxious acknowledged his many admirers, with bright blue eyes gleaming.

"And finally... who all you ladies have been waiting veritable moons to see - and soon to take his place amongst the greatest of Eternian actors, I present, Euriphidious!" The noise levels reached almost deafening levels as the indomitable Euriphidious stepped forward, removing his tunic to reveal a well-toned muscular body. Sephia put her head in her hands in utter disbelief.

"I cannot believe that man, his hubris is beyond reproach, really!" she disbelievingly scowled. Alectorious by contrast took it all in rather good humour.

"I have to agree, very un-Eternian; none-the-less, a fine actor, indeed," he countered with a cheeky smirk, perhaps if only to wind Sephia up a little bit. Euriphidious was one of the king's favourite actors, now a theatre veteran of some twelve eons.

"This fine night, Euriphidious will play no less than our legendary King Alectorious the 1st!" announced the presenter, as the crowd went wild. "Revel in the enjoyment, my fellow Eternians!" he fervently encouraged, before making a swift exit from the stage. The actors suddenly disappeared behind a dark curtain at the rear of the stage as evocative music began to play in the background. A narrator began to speak, ushering the beginning...

"Many eons ago, a valourous band of young warriors from deep in the mountains came, pursuing their dream of discovering another world, just as their own. In their long journey through perilous passes and icy rock walls, many dangers did they face, but undeterred by even the gods themselves were they in pursuit of glory..." As the narrator finished speaking, the three main characters dramatically re-entered the stage. In accordance with tradition, they spoke in Middle Eternian, a dialect not used for hundreds of eons. The audience watched intently, spellbound by the majesty of the moment as the play duly began to unfold.

"Many suns hast we traversed great mountains, my liege; but for how many more must it be?" asked Graos, as "Alectorious", he and Achtreias strutted with chests puffed out, moving confidently about the stage.

"For *countless* more if it must, brave Graos; for it the only station now left to us! Dost thou not agree, fine Achtreias?" asked Alectorious the 1st - the crowd's eyes now transfixed.

"Aye, mine treasured Lord Alectorious - for there is much glory to be had, beyond those great snowy peaks! Other lands to name but ours, fair maiden to comfort our weary figure and, the bounty of many treasures, no less!" he said. Aeischylious' character countered with a dramatic sweep of his arm as he reached to the sky.

"Fine boons they been indeed, lusty Achtreias, as any who hast toiled as ye. But would it fill thy soul as thy purse - or open thy weary eyes from the slumber of all that is carnal?" The king was incredulous at such a suggestion, reacting likewise.

"Would thou not revel in such fine adventures, my just and noble Graos? Or would there be another grace thou seek, to fill thy hole of which thou speak?" asked Alectorious the 1st. Achtreias very much agreed, trying to come to terms with what Graos was suggesting.

"Thy liege axe thee fine question; is there not game thou wish to brighten thy weary suns?" he asked his noble companion.

"If it fell upon me by happenstance, valiant Achtreias, they would be free gifts the gods bestow, indeed; though been such things pursuits of worthy men?" wondered Graos.

"All be that carnal, been they not the wish of every kind? Thy life without game would be most foul, think I. Must thy coy existence be without imperfections, brave Graos?"

"Think I, that all kinds must suffer hardship, hasty Achtreias; be it fro the graces of one's imperfections or will of gods themselves. Fare as thee will, great lusty one, but know the consequence of thy rash actions..." warned Graos, as Achtreias incredulously baulked.

"Thy words surprise! Thou deem me not a worthy man, companion Graos? Be it not that I fulfil thy lofty ambition?" he said, moving closer to his deeply principled counterpart.

"I say thou are not lewed, Achtreias; indeed, a worthy man hast many just positions." explained Graos. Achtreias however, was yet further bewildered.

"What mean thou of such talk? A worthy man is just thus! Am I not he, I demand?"

"Thou been indeed, noble Achtreias - but by virtue of not just sword alone, there been many of thy kind - he who enquires the ways of The Spirit, world and mind, indeed." explained Graos, as the audience watched in sheer captivation.

"Baffled am I by thy talk, fellow warrior. Aghast, thought of worlds with no sword! What is thy sentence, noble liege? Believe thee, he speaks truth?" asked a clearly repulsed Achtreias. With hands on hips and a serious expression, "Alectorious" spoke.

"Believe I, there are many paths of worthy men: we now walk but ours. Indeed; one must shape their destiny as him lest, for only he can answer for his own actions."

"Most wise council, great king! Alas, the gods shall suffer me to follow my *own* path." Achtreias concluded. Graos seemed distressed, pointing dramatically to the east.

"What be thus, I say!" he exclaimed, as the audience gasped in unison.

"A dragon, no less, companions!" exclaimed Achtreias. Graos was visibly worried of its intentions as he looked in trepidation.

"Be it hostile, I wonder?" he petrified. There was no question as the king concurred.

"It be indeed, worthy Graos! Draw thy swords, companions; for this moment we fight!" he exclaimed. From the side of the stage came a large, bright red dragon, "piloted" by two skilled operators. It circled the stage before running up the stairs between the enchanted audiences, with all gasping in wonderment. The dragon suddenly turned back in readiness to attack the exposed adventurers, who drew their swords in unison for combat.

"Be gone from whence thou came, hideous beast!" exclaimed Alectorious the 1st. Achtreias was far more antagonistic, beckoning the creature forth.

"Come hither, thou vile fiend: I shall cast thee yonder with but a swift of my blade!" he confidently proclaimed. Graos tried to sound warning but it was to no avail.

"Thou fair us no grace, pugnacious Achtreias, with such hubris as thus!" he said, as "the king's" eyes widened in trepidation.

"The brute attacks - ready, my brave cavaliers!" he warned, as the menacing dragon came running down the stairs toward the three knights. The being cast a stream of imaginary flames upon its first pass, with the Eternians just managing to evade them. It passed again as the king and Graos managed a hefty strike. The dragon squealed in pure agony.

"Take this, villainous swine!" yelled Alectorious the 1st, as a mixture of cheers and laughter emanated from the captivated audience. The dragon was hurt but quite unperturbed, readying for yet another assault on the beleaguered band of adventurers.

"Let I, brave companions!" insisted Achtreias, hastily brushing Graos and the king aside. He held his sword with both hands, confidently awaiting the looming dragon's approach. When the creature was but a spear's distance away, Achtreias took a mighty swing of his blade, slicing it cleanly in two. The actors playing the dragon fell theatrically to the floor of the stage as the audience jumped from their seats with cheers of mesmerised elation.

"Bravo!" they yelled.

"Well done, you all!"

"Magnificent performance!" sounded their various cries. Swathes of coloured petals were thrown dramatically from the crowd to the three actors; Aeischylious, Sophoxious and Euriphidious, who all bowed together in gratitude. They then fittingly departed the stage as the narrator brought the enthralling play to a formal close.

"And so the three knights travelled onto much greater adventures - and a world they could have only imagined in their wildest of dreams." The audience cheered again as a rather plain looking man took the stage to make a casual announcement.

"I thank you all dearly for attending this fine evening; our actors have worked so terribly hard to make it as memorable an occasion as possible. There will be a brief intermission with light refreshments before our final play of the night: a comedy entitled "Nerosis the Haughty"." he proclaimed, rubbing his hands together with a humorous glee. His announcement was met with much laughter from the audience, who were clearly relishing the chance to see their "arch-nemesis" on stage. As all stood to take a break, Alectorious turned his attention to his companion for the evening, Sephia.

"A fine performance indeed; those three actors together could never disappoint." he remarked, clearly impressed, but Sephia was of a very different opinion.

"I would have much rathered a good drama, to be perfectly honest. Do you not ever tire of such virile entertainment, king Alectorious?" she asked teasingly, with hand on her finely shaped chin as she looked dreamily into his blue-green coloured eyes.

"I admit, it is only the beginning for me…" the king replied. Sephia was very intelligent and quick to discern exactly what he was intimating.

"It sounds *almost as though* you were about to leave on an adventure yourself!" she light-heartedly remarked, before casting her head downwards, knowing it *was* so.

"Indeed; for in the morrow, I shall embark on a secret journey with my knights," the king accidently divulged. Alectorious immediately regretted his actions, having usually been very careful not to let things of that nature slip. "But you must tell no-one of this," he added sternly, in a vain attempt to backtrack. Sephia was oblivious to the sensitive nature of the information and was simply unable restrain herself.

"Of course; but where will you go, Alectorious, and for how long will it be?" The king was reluctant to divulge more but knew he could not hide the truth forever.

"If the gods will it, not more than seven suns," Alectorious continued, just as the next performance began. "I shall tell you more afterwards," he added, wondering how he could possibly evade the topic again. Sephia nodded as they returned their attention to the stage.

The crowd became silent as the three actors took again to the stage, dressed in what appeared to be typical Gomercian attire of black and gold. The audience responded with a playful hostility, heckling and booing in great amusement.

"Boo!!!" "Hiss!" "Down with Nerosis!" they came, as the "Gomercians" retaliated.

"Oh be quiet, you cretinous vermin! We Gomercians shall crush you like insects!" was the impromptu response from one of the costumed actors, much to the good-natured hysterics of the crowd. Unperturbed, the narrator began introduce the play.

"The inner sanctum of the Gomercian Empire was both dark and scrupulous, engulfed by hubris, moral decay and all those things begotten by dishonest men. Only they could not see this in their blindness to all that was right and just. Nerosis and his men talked and squabbled, certain that they were destined to rule over all." With that, the three "Gomercians" took to the middle of the stage, gloating with a menacing gaze. The first of them spoke with a humorous high pitched voice, as was common for plays of this kind.

"I say, lord Nerosis; it pleases to see so many squirm under our thumb!"

"It does indeed, but it is not enough, lowly Valatrox!" the Gomercian leader replied.

"But my lord, you have much of the known world under your control!"

"Much? I do not wish for much! Did I say I wanted much, you despicable fiend?"

"Oh no, no my lord; you did not!" his subordinate replied, as the audience chuckled.

"I did not, do you understand me?" Nerosis screamed, looking out to the gathering.

"Yes, my lord, I… I do. But, if I may, whatever has this to do with Promaestious?" Valatrox inexplicably asked, as the crowd took their cue.

"It has nothing to do with Promaestious!" they shouted in unison. It was a popular inside joke amongst regular theatre goers, referring to the Eternian god for whom plays were always performed.

"What are you all on about, you blithering idiots!" blurted Nerosis, approaching the edge of the seating area. The crowd merely booed, heckled and hissed in response, greatly enjoying the performance thus far. The atmosphere was almost palpable, such was the intensity with which the audience were transfixed.

"Oh, forget you lot! I shall vanquish you all one sun, I swear! As I was saying, I do not want much, I want more… no, I want it all! Do you hear me?" continued "Nerosis".

"I do, my lord; but how will we achieve this great aim?" his frightened follower asked, stepping slightly backwards.

"It matters not how, do you hear me? Only that it is done! By *our* gods, do you listen to nothing I say?" Nerosis retorted, slapping his subordinate across the face.

"Yes I do, lord; sorry, my lord," Valatrox replied, as "Nerosis" continued.

"Indeed… more than anything at all, I wish to see those wretched Eternians suffer the fate they *all* deserve!" he controversially said. The writers of the play seemed to have gone too far on this occasion, with the script prompting some rather hostile responses among the crowd: some took it more personally than had been intended.

"Blasphemy!" was one evocative shout, as a crazed member of the audience charged the stage with hostile intent. He ran across to the actor playing Nerosis and tackled him heftily to the ground as the crowd went wild. Several others followed to join the action as a huge melee broke out on stage, with punches flying left, right and centre. The three actors managed to escape the fracas as the duty Elite Guardsmen rushed in to break up the offending citizens. It was much to the surprise of the king, who was watching in a dazed awe, but it was all over before he could even blink.

"Well, that was an unexpected surprise - enough drama for you, Sephia?" he playfully asked from his safe vantage point in the crowd, as he leaned over to his attractive companion.

"A little too much for my liking, my king!" she responded, as the worried-looking stage manager, Astarious, approached. Alectorious exchanged some serious words as Astarious nodded in compliance, before eventually returning to the centre of the stage to make an important announcement.

"In light of this evening's unexpected events, the actors, I and the king himself have decided that, due to the tense nature of recent suns, this evening's play shall continue no longer. Any who wish for a partial refund shall be reimbursed by the royal treasury. I thank you all for attending and we hope to see you all at the next moon's performance." The crowd responded predictably with collective but harmless boos and sighs of despondency, before filing reluctantly out of the theatre, having otherwise enjoyed the lively presentation. Alectorious remained seated with Sephia as Thelosious passed for a quick chat.

"A little surprise, my king; I hope you enjoyed the dramatic climax!" he rather suggestively remarked. Alectorious was quick to read between the proverbial lines.

"By the gods, Thelosious - you mean to say that was choreographed?" he asked disbelievingly. His cerebral companion moved closer, so as not to be heard by eavesdroppers.

"A little bird whispered it *might* have been so: apparently the scriptwriter had run out of ideas and decided it was the only way he could end it! But of course, I cannot be certain..." Thelosious sheepishly explained, and with small a wink, unable to resist a hearty chuckle.

"Of all the gall - they could have just been honest. Well, it is done now. I much preferred the mythology, anyway. It was a somewhat historically inaccurate interpretation of Achtreias, mind you - nonetheless, most enjoyable. It reminded me somewhat of Gavastros, yourself and I - only on the best of suns, of course," the king humorously remarked, winking. His cerebral companion was very much in agreement.

"But of course!" he laughed. "It seems as though history has repeated itself!"

"Is that not what history is, Thelosious - but the story of life constantly re-inventing itself in countless shapes and forms over the eons?"

"Few would see that, but I think it is very much so," agreed the cerebral one.

"Tell me, where has Gavastros got to this fine evening?" Alectorious queried, looking curiously around the theatre as Thelosious glanced to a group of people ten spears away.

"He seems to be busy entertaining some young maidens over there: the gods only know of his intentions," Thelosious replied, raising his eyebrows as he pointed to the corner of the theatre, but the king was rather indifferent.

"Well, we shall leave him be," he insisted, with nothing more to say on the matter.

"Indeed - and I shall leave *you*. Enjoy the evening, Alectorious - Sephia," acknowledged Thelosious, patting his companion on the shoulder before disappearing up the theatre steps. Alectorious relaxed on the plush colourful cushions, trying to forget all his troubles as Sephia pressed the king on word of his adventure.

"So you will leave Eternity; but to where, Alectorious?" she asked in trepidation. Grabbing him tightly by the hand, Sephia had already become rather attached. The king really should have kept quiet, but alas, it was too late to turn back now.

"I see you will not give in," he sighed, feeling in somewhat of a bind. Sephia shook her head with a light smile, her eyes beaming into the king's.

"You must not tell a soul, Sephia," he insisted, as Sephia shook her head again.

"Not a soul," she promised adamantly, with ears acutely poised. The king continued in but a whisper, knowing that anyone could be listening.

"There was a discovery of some ancient scrolls that spoke of the great Reiacus' return…" he tellingly began. Sephia gasped, covering her mouth before looking around. She then returned her focus to the king before moving in closer with great intrigue.

"Really? I… do not…" she responded, before the king finished her sentence.

"Believe it?" he said, as Sephia nodded. "We suspect he might now be in the Great Buvarious, and it is to there we soon plan to travel." Sephia was beside herself with excitement, bouncing up and down as if a child.

"Oh!!! I so wish I could go with you - it sounds to be such fun!!!" she exclaimed, as the king's expression suddenly became very serious. He squinted his eyes as he spoke.

"It will be no banquet, Sephia: there are many dangers high in the Buvarious and there is every chance I or any one of my men shall *never* return." Sephia was utterly befuddled, unable to fathom what compelled men to do such things.

"Then why do you take such risks, Alectorious? In any case, the dragon is supposed to come to *us*, is he not?" she quizzed, vaguely remembering something about The Prophecy she had read a few eons ago with her private tutor.

"That was written, indeed. But the gods have spoken in my dreams, Sephia - they are calling me there - of that I am sure. I have had an inexplicable pull to those mountains all my life - one that I simply cannot explain," the king revealed. Sephia was clearly unable to share his viewpoint, shaking her head in not more than disgust.

"So you will risk your life all because of a dream?" she hissed, clearly unhappy about Alectorious' immanent departure. He was quite taken aback - at first speechless before he could gather his thoughts. The king leaned closer, speaking with passion.

"It is so much more that, Sephia: it is a calling from a higher place, for a purpose that cannot yet be fully understood. There are some who follow it, even when to all others, such a path seems like madness. But therein lays the true test - of whether we have the courage enough stand on our own two feet and *truly* be a free nation again," Alectorious explained, as Sephia sat with arms folded. She grudgingly accepted the king's wise sentiment, knowing deep down what he had said made perfect logical sense.

"Go if you must, Alectorious, but know I will be awaiting your return." The king was quite taken aback by her refreshing directness, and took several moments to muster a meaningful response to his new found beau.

"And I very much look forward to it, dear Sephia."

JOURNEY TO THE ORACLE

The king awoke with a sense of anticipation not felt since his long-past childhood eons, wondering of the many experiences that were soon to be had. He knew it would be an adventure unlike any that had gone before, and would most certainly be the ultimate test of resolve, courage and the very kingship itself. Alectorious would, along with his knights, travel further than any Eternian in recent memory, deep into uncharted lands and the great Buvarious Mountains. Few had attempted such an audacious voyage in their nation's long and proud history and yet fewer chivalrous souls had returned to tell their enthralling tales.

As Alectorious lay in quiet reflection, he momentarily questioned the wisdom of departing Eternity in this period of great crises. He naturally worried what might befall the kingdom in his absence, with the ever-encroaching threat of Gomercian invasion looming on the horizon. These doubts quickly dissipated as the king remembered it had been the calling of his heart that had led to this decision: he truly believed the divine had spoken and that he was being guided to his highest calling.

Alectorious eased slowly out of bed before walking out to the south balcony of his splendid regal quarters, with emotions growing powerfully within. He rested his hands gently on the smooth marble railing, taking a deep breath of fresh air before glancing out to the bright blue skies, then to his beloved Eternity, in all her illustrious beauty. He gazed longingly at the tree-lined boulevards, elegant gardens, mystical temples and countless citizens going peacefully about their affairs in the bustling city streets, far below: he would *never* forget his much-treasured home no matter how many suns he was absent. Alectorious then peered further out, beyond the city walls and across the wide open plains, wondering if this troubled world would *ever* see the elusive peace its people had yearned for so many eons. For the briefest of moments he pondered what lay beyond the known lands and if there was a better place, somewhere out there in the distance. Casting his eyes back to Eternity, the king knew it might be many suns before he again laid eyes upon his cherished city. Alectorious took several deep breaths as if to absorb the surrounding beauty before casting a glance northwards to the dramatic snow-capped peaks in the distance, piercing the skies like bright heavenly jewels. Alectorious knew without question or doubt that a great adventure awaited. The king took one last meaningful look out to the city before returning to his regal chamber in preparation for the momentous sun ahead.

"A pleasant dorm, sire?" asked a polite, unexpected voice. It was Alectorious' personal helper, who usually assisted in putting on the king's shining blue and gold armour.

"Thank you, Hulious, it was very much so, indeed," Alectorious courteously replied, while trying to fasten his breastplate firmly to his chest as his helper moved in closer to assist.

"Here, my liege; let me help you with that," Hulious insisted, tightening the straps. "You will need every last ounce of energy, my king; for you have a strenuous journey ahead," he continued, somewhat overstating the difficulty of the ride to Delphoesia. The king did his best to hide the truth, knowing it would be very much more than this.

"One can never foresee what obstacles the gods might bestow upon one's path, Hulious," he suggestively replied. Hulious did not quite manage to grasp the subtlety of the king's message as he continued to assist.

"Right you are, sire: you never know *when* the Gomercians might rear their ugly heads!" he naïvely quipped, the king relieved Hulious had not read too much into his words.

"So very true, my old companion!" replied Alectorious, with an overly-lively chuckle, followed by a more subtle sigh of relief. Silence fell as the king fastened his greaves and forearm protectors and Hulious helped assemble the more intricate pieces of body armour. Soon enough they had finished, and Alectorious stood up for one final inspection.

"Well, that just about does it, my king - fit and ready for battle!" his helper jovially concluded as he made some finer adjustments. Alectorious felt a slight sense of guilt as he readied to depart, for Hulious was completely unaware of what was soon to transpire.

"You have always been loyal, Hulious, and for that I shall never forget you," he admitted quite out of the blue, while somewhat risking exposing his secret plans. His assistant was quite taken aback, yet was all the same flattered by this unexpected praise.

"Well, thank you, my king! It has always been a great honour to serve his majesty!" he unknowingly replied, bowing respectfully in kind.

"And it is an honour to be *your king,* Hulious: goodbye, my companion," Alectorious said, with a hint of sadness in his eyes. The king left his chamber without looking back, making his way down the spiralling tower staircase to the main dining hall, which dominated much of the castle's ground floor. Many a banquet had been held here throughout the eons, celebrating victories, birth-suns and various other cultural occasions. It had been the scene of much revelling following the dramatic victory at Dragon's Pass but two nights previously, where the convivial Gavastros had no-doubt played an indomitable role.

Alectorious sat at his ornate dining table alone, as for him, the morn was for moments of solitude and quiet contemplation of the sun ahead. He was feeling a distinct sense of sadness, having never in all his eons been away from his beloved city for more than a sun. Soon the morning meal was served, with his servant making sure the king's gastronomic needs were fully met. With plates firmly in hand, he carefully approached the table.

"Here you are, my king, your favourite as requested: Chilusian stew, dry oats and freshly-baked Eternian bread," he kindly offered, placing several small plates on the hard wooden table. Alectorious felt a deep sense of gratitude for all these small pleasures: things he could otherwise so easily take for granted.

"It looks absolutely sumptuous, Aelious; I shall enjoy every last morsel," he replied, with stomach rumbling like never before. It would be a hearty meal, indeed.

"It truly brightens my sun to hear that, my king," Aelious wholeheartedly replied, reaching for a large silver vessel. "Some juice, perhaps?" he asked, as the king began to eat.

"Oh yes please; that would be perfect," Alectorious agreed, as he consumed every last morsel with joyous aplomb.

The king quickly finished his morning meal, thanking Aelious once more before making his way to the royal stables in the southern part of the main castle grounds. There, a grandiose collection of the finest steeds in all Eternity could be found, ready to fulfil their duty for king and country. Alectorious entered the stables with an elated sense of adventure, admiring the many gallant steeds standing proudly before him as they neighed, stamped their hooves and tossed their manes, impatiently waiting for their customary morning run. The king peered through the stable to the courtyard far on the other side, seeing his loyal knights and companions waiting in formation: Gavastros, Thelosious and Jalectrious, along with the city's finest Elite Guardsmen. Fully armed with swords and shields by their side, these fearless warriors were prepared for anything fate might throw in their path.

"A fine sun for a ride, my king, and for it, you have the very finest of equines," came a cheery youthful voice, as the king turned to see a familiar face.

"That it is indeed, Busafious!" he acknowledged with a warm smile. As chief stableman, Busafious took great pride in this honoured position, having carefully groomed Alectorious' personal steed, Sephalos, for the sun's journey.

"And a fine animal for a great journey," he quietly added. The king was very much in agreement. He gently stroked Sephalos' smooth brown coat, feeling a tremendous strength emanate from this beautiful animal's aura. The king's trusted steed neighed quietly in fitting appreciation of his master's affectionate gestures.

"I have included the extra supplies you requested: all you require is here," Busafious assured, pointing to the leather satchels attached to either side of the saddle. Alectorious nodded in recognition as Busafious pulled them tightly shut. The stableman's eyes were suspicious for the briefest of moments, realising there was far more than required for a single sun's expedition. He realised it must have been for good reason and was in any case, in no position to question the orders of the king himself. Alectorious sensed this but kept his cool.

"Absolutely splendid, Busafious; as always, a job marvellously well done," he commended. The king tactically handed the stableman a small golden coin - a most unexpected gift. Busafious was beside himself with joy, expressing as such.

"Oh thank you, my lord - it really is too much!" he gasped, wide eyed with joy.

"Enough! You have always done your duty, Busafious, to the utmost of your ability. Return home, for you may rest this sun!" Alectorious insisted. The stableman was speechless.

"Oh thank you, my great king!" he gasped. Bowing in respect, Busafious was quick to disappear from sight, no doubt to enjoy his superfluous earnings.

•

"I hope I did not arise too much suspicion with those extra supplies, Sephalos," the king whispered, affectionately stroking his steed's soft mane. "In any event, it will be a fine sun for a ride," he added, smiling in the knowing he could always trust Busafious: a loyal servant now of seven and a half eons. All those in direct service to his majesty had sworn a strict oath of secrecy and were trained to follow orders on any sun or night, without question. Their loyalty could never be in doubt: for Eternity could ill-afford knowledge of the king's movements to reach beyond the city walls.

Alectorious cast his lingering doubts aside as he shifted focus back to the task at hand. He grabbed the saddle of his horse, placed his right foot inside the stirrup and proudly mounted, ready for anything the gods could throw upon his valiant path.

Sephalos began trotting in circles, neighing as he adjusted to his master's presence before returning to a stationary position and awaiting further instructions. Alectorious took a deep breath and rode out to his men, who were waiting in perfect formation in the stable courtyard. The Elite Guardsmen were aligned in two equal rows, with the three knights waiting at the end. Alectorious trotted slowly through the rows of warriors, with each man nodding in quiet acknowledgement as their leader passed them by.

"My lord"

"My king"

"Your majesty" they whispered, careful not to arouse any suspicion beyond the castle walls. Alectorious nodded respectfully, raising his hand in acknowledgement of each of his soldiers as he moved to the end of the line. There, he was greeted by his loyal knights and companions: Gavastros, Jalectrious and Thelosious, who were all in a rather buoyant mood.

"A splendid sun for a ride, my king!" Jalectrious cheerfully remarked.

"That it is, my companion," Alectorious coyly acknowledged, with the others in equally high spirits. Gavastros was his usual self, speaking exactly what was on his mind.

"Fear not the Gomercians; for we shall crush them without mercy if they dare near us!" the truculent prodigy exclaimed, hoisting his shining shield into the crisp morning air.

"Gavastros, it is good to have you with us," Alectorious responded, nodding in due recognition. Thelosious was next to honour his majesty, but in a quite contrasting tone.

"I come in humble service to king and country, my lord," he unpretentiously offered, and with a slight bow, showing off the impressive golden plume swaying atop his helmet. Alectorious was appreciative of his companion's ever modest disposition.

"And it is in equal humility I serve thee as king, Thelosious." The king, his knights and Elite Guard manoeuvred their fine horses into a near perfect circle in readiness for departure. It was an ancient custom followed since the Age of Heroes, no matter how small or large the task might be - an expression of solidarity amongst Eternian warriors, as well as a perfect opportunity for the king to address his gallant band of followers.

"Gentlemen soldiers of Eternity! Upon this fine sun we depart to fulfil a task small in nature, but know it could be more than you ever imagined: the Gomercian Empire edges ever closer to our gates and we must be ready for *any* eventuality," he warned, looking deeply into the eyes of his brave men. Only the three knights had any idea of the king's *true* plans, with the Elite Guards having been told only what was required. "In light of this, know that some of you might never return: are there any unwilling to ride with me and risk all for their nation?" the king asked, looking into the steely, battle-hardened eyes of his men. It was a customary question before any journey but the answer was always a foregone conclusion. Alectorious looked around the circle of valiant souls, with not even a whisper in response. The only audible noise was the heavy breathing and neighing of horses and their stamping hooves on the dusty ground, showing their eagerness to do their duty. It was abundantly clear all were equal to the task as the king nodded proudly in conclusion.

"Then forward we venture, Eternians: may the gods and The Great Spirit be with us!"

The knights and Elite Guard duly broke rank, trotting two by two out of the stable courtyard towards a secret city entrance behind the main castle walls. As they approached, a tremendous sense of excitement began to infuse the group, wondering excitedly what lay ahead. The adventurers eagerly made their way through the large stone gatehouse, down a narrow tree-lined winding path to the forests surrounding the city, and onwards to their destiny. The king took one last glance back at his illustrious towering castle home as he trotted peacefully along, pondering for the briefest of moments if he would ever see it again.

"We'll be back before you know it, Alectorious," Thelosious encouraged, as if having read the king's thoughts. Alectorious was not entirely convinced of his bold proclamation.

"You never know when your final sun might set, my old companion; you really do not," he admitted with a sigh. Thelosious did his best to be reassuring, raising his right hand.

"We embark on this quest by the will of the gods, my king; you must trust they will watch over and protect us." Alectorious knew deep down that he spoke the truth, and all would be well. He acknowledged with a nod before returning his attention to the path.

Before long, the group of warriors found themselves deep in a thick pine forest: a veritable world away from the elegantly-fashioned buildings and orderly ways of Eternity. Alectorious looked around at the countless trees, plants and shrubs, feeling a sense of calm he could not fathom elsewhere: surely nothing could befall them in such a divine place.

As the Eternians rode along the narrow, winding wooded path, they very much enjoyed the quiet tranquillity of the forest - an opportunity rarely afforded in recent suns. Even Gavastros was taken by his placid new surrounds, having seldom ever ventured outside his formidable castle home for a purpose other than to do battle.

"I could never imagine the Gomercians in such a place - do you really think they would have the gall to come thus far?" the prodigy mulled, pulling up alongside the king, who was very much lost in a world of his own.

"Nor I, Gavastros, but we must *never* underestimate our enemy; for as Knights of Eternity, we must be ready for any eventuality," he starkly warned, casting a serious glance to his loyal companion. Gavastros was quick to offer his reassurance.

"That we must, my king, at every waking moment; but if we *do* encounter them, know that *I will* be ready," the prodigy proclaimed, with his bright red plume wavering in the breeze: a fitting reflection perhaps of his burning desire for combat.

"As *always* you are, Gavastros - as always you are," Alectorious responded with a heartfelt smile as the prodigy fell back into line. After negotiating the winding forest path, the king and his men eventually reached a large clearing, at the centre of which lay a striking ancient well. Gavastros was truly astonished, expressing his feelings as such.

"What is this, Sire? I have never seen it before!" The king was only too happy to explain as he cast his mind back to studies of history in his middlehood suns.

"It is understood that Eternians in eons long past would stop here before a long journey. There are no written records of the well's beginnings but it is widely believed to be in recognition of Ishoesia: an ancient goddess of good fortune that was worshipped long before The Age of Heroes." Gavastros imagined the ancients gathering around, tossing coins inside and making many a wish. As the Eternians approached the aged structure, the king signalled his men to stay back as he dismounted his steed. As Alectorious approached, he felt a most unusual sensation: a wave of inexplicable, powerful energy sweeping throughout his body and soul. He moved closer, walking round the perimeter with great curiosity before stopping at its mysterious, inviting stony edge.

The king leaned over and looked into the bottomless depths, wondering if it had an end. He reached into his pouch for a small golden coin and tossed it into the abyss: it fell for what seemed like an age before finally splashing into the invisible waters, far below. Alectorious closed his eyes firmly and made a wish, praying to the gods above it *would* be so. For several moments he stood in silent contemplation before returning to his noble equine. The king mounted his steed and the Eternians continued without a word being said. Soon they were deep in the forests, revelling once more in their splendid surroundings.

"I hope the gods grant your wish, Alectorious. Whatever it might be, I am sure it would make a difference in this struggling world," Thelosious encouraged, knowing his companion's selfless nature well. The king was inspired by these kind words of support.

"If only all good wishes were to be thus, Thelosious: imagine a world where one could but think, and it would be so," he intuitively expressed. It was a profound notion, and promptly elicited the more philosophical side of his cerebral companion.

"It would be as living the sweetest dream, Alectorious. Perhaps such a world *does* exist, somewhere out there in the vast creation of The Great Spirit; and perhaps one sun, we shall discover it," he reflectively offered. Alectorious was very much intrigued by this notion.

"I hope it *is* to where we are destined; for there could be no greater place imaginable," the king replied, knowing it would be idyllic. With that, the Eternians continued along the tranquil path as they enjoyed the rolling hills, majestic forests and crystal clear streams of the absorbing countryside. Before long, the Delphoesian temples came dramatically into view: the king's spirits immediately lifted, knowing his old companion's home was not far away.

"Sire, is it not the dwelling of the Oracle?" Gavastros asked, pointing to a small, thatched wooden house nearby a gently flowing, crystal-clear blue stream.

"Indeed it is," the king cheerily answered, as excitement grew within each of the knights. They realised the knowledge and wisdom soon to be imparted would not only help in their gallant quest, but determine a more positive course for all the known world.

"Does she know of our arrival?" the prodigy wondered, concerned that she might be absent. Alectorious had no question at all, firmly believing it was destiny.

"The Oracle has powers of foresight we could only in our wildest dreams imagine, Gavastros. She can see the unseen and know the unknown; trust, for this sun was *always* meant to be."

INSIGHTS OF WISDOM

It was about half a sun's ride to the home of the Oracle, with the journey taking the king and his men through some truly breath-taking countryside - from rolling green hills and winding forest paths to the most beautifully splendid fields of coloured wild flowers and curious animal species - a world away from the city they had left behind but half a sun ago. Further on from the great seer's home were The Temples of Ancient Delphoesia: remnants of a long-past era in Eternian history where kings would visit for inspired messages from the divine. It was also where Alectorious would travel after his consultation with the Oracle to pay homage to *that* glorious bye-gone era.

As the group of travellers neared the small, thatched-roof cottage, an overwhelming feeling of calm washed over Alectorious; it was a sensation quite indescribable but a fitting aphrodisiac to his countless sunly worries as King of Eternity. The Oracle's abode was a humble dwelling: built of thick wooden logs and covered with tightly-bound twigs and surrounded by exquisite gardens of multitudinous flowers, shrubs and exotic plants. A beautiful crystal-clear stream flowed past the side of her small home and a peaceful meadow populated by various species of flora and fauna was located not seven spears away.

In the distant north, the great Buvarious Mountains jutted out spectacularly from the majestic forests, reaching high into the blue skies above with evocative intent. Their snowy peaks were surrounded with spectacular patterns of white cloud that formed all manner of curious shapes and signs like dragons, lions and other such mythical creatures. Indeed, Eternians would often look up to the skies in search of messages from the gods, whom they believed spoke to them in many different ways. The gentle singing of birds and clear flowing waters of the stream further illuminated this magnificent habitat: the most idyllic the king could possibly imagine. Only in the lands of Athepothesia could a place of such magnificence exist, he thought, while gazing around reflectively at his tranquil surroundings.

It was a truly dream-like existence the Oracle lived; a state of near-perfection in comparison to the cramped nature of the seven city-states. Of course, proximity to the natural world enabled her to better communicate with The Great Spirit and receive any messages of wisdom it so wished to impart. The Oracle was famed throughout the lands, being one of the few souls in the northern known world to see things with such foresight, clarity and understanding. The seer took enormous pride in her position, knowing the great responsibility she held to the people of these troubled lands. In more peaceful eons, many would travel from afar to receive guidance on countless things; but in more recent suns, the rising threat of Gomercia meant the risk had become far too great. Despite her small dwelling's vulnerability, the very thought of attacking an oracle was believed to be most barbaric, and would bestow tremendous misfortune on one who was to do so. It was something even the Gomercians would not consider - at least for now - but one could never underestimate the audacity of Eternity's perennial arch nemesis.

The Oracle often provided great insight to the king and it was a companionship he valued perhaps more than any other. Indeed, his presence was an honour she had not had for many moons and it was always most deeply appreciated. Although visiting unannounced, the Oracle awaited patiently by her small thatched-roof cottage as if expecting the king's arrival. She was clothed in a long blue dress with a sparkling golden trim and wore a striking gold amulet around her neck with a number of purple coloured crystals embedded within it.

"King Alectorious the 2nd of Eternity, it has been far too long - and in such haste you arrive!" she suitably exclaimed, stroking an amicable feline creature held softly in her arms. Alectorious was content as he was relieved to see his companion since childhood suns, well aware that he was of the increasing threats in the area.

"It has been thus, dearest Megalia!" the king replied, embracing her tightly as one would expect an old confidant. The Oracle's youthful looks, long, flowing blonde hair and deep blue eyes were more reminiscent of a fair maiden than great seer; but as with much in these mysterious lands, all was not as it first seemed. Megalia was characteristically swift to express her thoughts, so concerned was she for the current plight of Eternity. Born of the great city, she had spent most suns since her twentieth eon outwith. The twentieth eon in one's life was considered most significant, for it was the age that middlehood would end and the journey of adulthood and indeed, life finally began; however, it was not until the twenty-eighth eon that *true* adulthood was reached.

"I sense much trouble brewing in these lands," she chillingly remarked, recalling several disquieting dreams she had had in recent suns. The king fittingly lowered his head.

"Alas, I think it has *always* been so, Megalia; but without doubt, now more than ever before..." he sighed, looking despondently to the heavens. The Oracle realised there was not a moment more to wait, promptly inviting the king inside her cosy little dwelling.

"I sense we have much to discuss this fine sun - please, my king," the Oracle hastily motioned. She cast a long glance around the surrounding area, then to the waiting Eternian soldiers before making her way briskly inside. Alectorious followed, ordering his men to keep an eye out for any suspicious activity.

"Eyes sharp, my companions; alert me immediately if you see anything!"

"Yes, Sire!" the soldiers replied, as the king disappeared into the Oracle's little abode. The interior was like something out of a dream, with its brightly-coloured decorations and ornaments indiscriminately scattered throughout: quite in contrast to the elegantly-fashioned rooms of the king's castle. Alectorious entered and immediately relaxed, feeling very much at home amongst the many curious paraphernalia.

"So, whatever busies you these suns of late, my dear companion?" he queried, looking in fascination to the many books, precious coloured stones and unusual ornaments spread throughout the small dwelling. In the middle of the room there was a round-shaped wooden table draped in a blue, purple and gold cloth, with two very comfortable looking chairs facing one another. The Oracle was frank in her response as she hastily cleared a space.

"Many things busy me, yet of late, there is more that troubles… than ever before. Please Alectorious, be seated," she kindly invited, with all the pomp and ceremony of Eternity refreshingly absent. Megalia duly pulled a chair out from the table, motioning to the king with that all-too familiar delicate smile. Alectorious fittingly sat, making himself comfortable on the soft, padded chair as the Oracle began to rummage through an assortment of bottles, plates and items in a small chest located close to the thick wooden wall.

"May I offer you one of my special brews, perhaps?" she asked, knowing it the king's favourite. Alectorious unknowingly licked his lips in anticipation as he politely replied.

"Oh yes indeed, if you would be so kind," he enthused. The king sat back and relaxed as he could not normally, as the pressure of the kingship had always made it difficult to express his softer side. The Oracle handed him a glass of her finest brew before sitting directly opposite in an equally comfortable position. Alectorious took a sip of the potent beverage before looking up at the mysterious array of crystals and dream-catchers hanging from the old wooden rafters as they swayed to and fro in the gentle breeze blowing in through a small window in the corner of the cottage.

"We shall now begin," she said without warning. The king braced for what could be an enormous revelation as Megalia relaxed, breathing in and out with meaningful intent. She was suddenly deep in concentration, gazing into the mysterious purple-blue crystal ball located in the middle of the table. The Oracle sat perfectly still with eyes firmly shut, her delicate hands suspended close to the mystical crystal as she waited for the right words… and inspiration to find her. After concentrating deeply for some moments, she finally spoke in that familiar enigmatic voice of profound insight.

"I see the never-ending winds of change blowing towards a better world, great king Alectorious: one of hope, brightness and fortitude for *all*. You have the power within to lead your nation to this enchanted place - if only you have the courage enough to follow the pathway of your heart… and very soul..." she dramatically revealed. The king was instantly beguiled by her poetic words of wisdom, silent as if to signal his desire to know more. The Oracle squinted her cat-like deep blue eyes, concentrating more deeply than ever as Alectorious felt an intense, other worldly-energy permeate the room.

"Your greatest nemesis… the one thing standing between you and this glorious place are the armies of the Gomercian Empire. Indeed they are strong - but are weakening - and will become weaker still…" the Oracle emphatically proclaimed. It conjured a strong response from the king, who saw there was more than just a glimmer of hope for the future. Her prophetic words caused Alectorious to sit straight up in his chair: his eyes and ears were absolutely fixated as the Oracle continued, unabated in every way.

She began to raise her voice slightly as a subtle chill ran up the king's spine. "Nerosis´ unquenchable thirst for power and glory will be his eternal undoing, as it has been for all those who have walked upon this path - of that, there can be no question or any doubt in the worlds at all. The thirst for power is one that can never be quenched nor a hunger ever satisfied; there is a part of him and his followers, however small that realise this undeniable truth. In this knowledge, he tightens his merciless grip ever more upon the lands he rules, trying ever more desperately to conquer those… who will not be. This senseless desire to rule over the people of the known world will be his ultimate downfall: know this above all else. But complacent you must not be, King Alectorious - for before you is an opportunity to starve Nerosis of that which he desires most of all - and for you to lead the world once and forevermore, *back* into the light. Know always that Eternity is immensely strong, Alectorious, but the power within each and every one of us is *far greater* than any nation could ever hope to be. Heed these words well and you shall be one step closer to victory and the light we *all* seek." The Oracle finished speaking, snapping dramatically out of her trance-like state, breathing heavily and sweating as if having witnessed a great calamity. Megalia dramatically rose from her seat and grabbed a cup of water, gulping it down as fast as was possible. She finally managed to calm down, remembering that she was in the safety of her cosy wooden hut and dear companion of many eons.

"By the gods, are you alright, Megalia?" the king asked in great trepidation.

"I am fine; give me but a moment," she insisted, before slowly returning to her chair. Alectorious had listened intently to her foretelling words, knowing they could well hold the key to his nation's salvation. The king waited patiently for the Oracle to recover before burdening her with the countless questions now besieging his mind. He took it slowly at first, realising she was under a considerable amount of stress.

"You speak words of great wisdom and insight, dear Megalia - they hearten my soul and give much hope to our beleaguered nation - yet, I feel no closer to answering the one question that has troubled me for so many suns…" the king admitted, with yet more to say. The Oracle was relaxed once again, listening intently as the king went on. "…I wish to know what action must be taken to free our lands, once and forevermore from this despotic empire." Megalia looked thoughtful as she bowed her head and took several deep breaths, knowing the great importance of what they now spoke.

"Only within yourself can this question ever be answered, my king," she flatly replied. Alectorious was naturally disappointed, frustratingly probing further.

"Can you see nothing at all?" he asked, with palms wide open. The Oracle was at first hesitant but finally yielded. Megalia concentrated deeply into her mysterious crystal ball, summoning the spirits of the gods themselves. The king felt a very unusual presence in the room as the Oracle continued to divulge all that she knew.

"I see companions from a long past age uniting... mysterious forest dwellers – they shall come to your aid... men of the caves and mountains will support you in these most desperate suns. This world is not as it seems, Alectorious. Many are those who watch over and protect you, awaiting your moment of greatest need. Indeed, there are many forces of good, unknown to Nerosis and his dark sorcerers: heed this well. That which they cannot see, embrace Alectorious! ...With all of your heart and soul..." she fervently encouraged.

The king's mind was buzzing incessantly as countless more questions arose. Who are the forestmen, he thought - the Catharians perhaps? And men of the caves - he had never heard of such peoples - how could they possibly help? He questioned, knowing the divisive nature of the topic within the High Council. Alectorious sat up with intent, his back straight.

"You speak of the forest men - I know well of their dislike of Nerosis but would they stand side by side with Eternity? And these men of the caves, I know nothing of - do they dwell somewhere we know not yet of?" he asked, questioning the validity of her predictions.

"I realise your doubts and fears, Alectorious - the how and why of their assistance is not for you to be in worry of - only that you believe in these words I speak on the gods' behalf... and that you have faith in The Great Spirit that, at the right moment and place, all that you need will find *you*," she explained. The king had doubts but found it hard to argue.

"I shall trust in you, my companion, as *always* I have," he acknowledged. Megalia hastily continued, with much more to speak of this eventful sun.

"The weakness you perceive in the men of the forests and mountains will be their greatest strength - embrace it! - For they will help deliver the decisive blow to Nerosis' seemingly impenetrable grip on the known world. Believe in what I reveal to you, Alectorious; for I have only ever spoken the truth..." she assured. The king was convinced of what he must do. As the Oracle finished speaking, silence fell upon the room. Alectorious sat quietly in deep reflection of all that had been imparted before suddenly, he had a thought.

"I must tell you of something, Megalia," he dramatically revealed.

"What might that be?" the Oracle asked, as she sat up with intrigue. The king continued hesitantly, unsure what her reaction might be.

"There was a discovery made just prior to the Battle of Dragon's Pass: a set of ancient scrolls..." he began. The Oracle's head tilted slightly, her eyes narrowing with curiosity as the king continued. "...They spoke of the return of Reiactus... and that a vast empire would soon fall..." The Oracle sensed there was more, remaining silent until she heard all he had to say. "...It spoke *also* of an age soon after that our world would become as one with that of the gods. What know you of this prophecy, Megalia?" the king questioned. "Why had I not heard it before?" The Oracle sat up straight in her chair, surprised she had not also.

"Alas! The gods have spoken - unusual that I did not foresee this but not *entirely* unexpected - they work in mysterious ways, indeed," she tellingly revealed. Megalia leaned closer to the king before speaking in a quiet, whispering tone.

"Tell me, Alectorious - what are your thoughts - *your* feelings on this matter? Forget all that the scrolls, I, or *anybody* else has ever told you. Go deep within your heart and soul and *trust* in what it speaks to you... I then ask... do you *truly* believe the dragon *is* to return?" she questioned, in a serious but rather soothing voice. The king remained silent as he looked within for an answer and swiftly came to a conclusion.

"If I were to speak through my heart and soul - yes, but..."

"No! No buts!" replied the Oracle, dramatically striking her hand on the table as if to convey the importance of her message. "Trust Alectorious - you must show *trust*. When you leave this world, all that is left is your soul - believe in it," she dramatically inspired. Alectorious nodded silently, unable to argue with her divine words of insight.

"There is more to this, Megalia…"

"Please, do go on..." she encouraged, as the king relaxed in his plush chair.

"I had a dream of a mysterious dragon: it was several moons ago but I remember well… it was so very real… almost more than reality itself… something I have never experienced *anything* quite like," he admitted. The Oracle knew well of these types of dreams: it was usually when the gods wished to impart something of great importance.

"Tell me more of this dream…" she insisted, clasping her delicate hands together.

"Well, I was travelling through the clearest blue skies imaginable towards a distant mountain pass. When I arrived, I found myself in an enormous cavern lit by a mysterious golden hue. Out of nowhere, an enormous blue dragon suddenly appeared then vanished before my eyes. In the titan's place, a magnificent bejewelled crown appeared upon a large boulder; much like The Destiny Stone of the ancient Eternians. It was so very real: as if I was actually there," he divulged elatedly. The Destiny Stone was where kings since the Age of Heroes had been crowned upon but was now long lost. It was the first the king had mentioned of his dream, knowing it would almost certainly invite ridicule; especially from certain members of the High Council. For the Oracle and others of such foresight, dreams provided much guidance for the path ahead.

"This is most interesting, Alectorious; a sign from the gods, without question. What do *you* believe they wish to tell you?" she asked. The king was pensive before responding.

"It seems I am being summoned, for reasons unbeknownst to the great Buvarious Mountains," Alectorious concluded, unable to see any other plausible explanation. The Oracle was plain in response, raising her voice for emphasis. In her twenty-five eons on these known lands, she had always been forthright in all that she ever said or did.

"Then to the Buvarious Mountains you must go!!!" she exclaimed, motioning in the direction of those famous icy peaks. Alectorious had his doubts, expressing as such.

"My heart's desire *is* clear Megalia; but would it be wise to abandon my kingdom for a mountain adventure based purely on a dream? Eternity is on the verge of invasion: it is a great deal to risk in these most uncertain suns." The Oracle was completely unrepentant as she bent forward, looking straight into the blue-green eyes of the king.

"Alectorious, listen to me: you have *always* been a firm believer in dreams, yet you *still* question. Answer me this: in all your suns have your dreams ever *not* spoken the truth?" she demanded, as the king reflected momentarily.

"Well, not that I remember…" he began, but the Oracle gave him no chance to finish.

"A true follower of the path knows his dreams speak only *that*, Alectorious. Know that they are the sacred doorway through which the gods and The Great Spirit offer their guidance, protection, inspiration *and* hope when the path ahead unclear. It is not your imagination, my king - believe me in this." Alectorious still harboured serious doubts, greatly worried about what other's opinions might be of him.

"The High Council will think I am mad for leaving Eternity leaderless in such crises!" he exclaimed, then was suddenly quiet. "Yet, it also seems to be the only way forward…" the king candidly added. The Oracle was sympathetic and quick to allay his fears.

"Worry not of that, Alectorious; know that many are those who can act in your stead! You must heed the word of the gods! They are helping, guiding and directing you towards your highest calling! Listen not to the words of men or your mind, for they will *always* deceive you. Only through the dreams of your heart and soul will you discover all that you ever seek: trust, believe and know the gods speak *only* the truth," she heart-fully encouraged. Clasping the king's hands, she looked deep into his eyes: his spirit immediately lifted in the knowing all would be well. There was something else that greatly vexed him, however. Alectorious had never spoken of it with his companion and was unsure how she would react.

"What of this other prophecy, Megalia - that our world will become one with that of the gods - what know you of this?" he asked in great curiosity. There had been many whispers in the Eternian spiritual community, with the wider populace remaining largely ignorant of this foretold monumental happening. The Oracle's face suddenly became guarded and serious, as if she knew far more than she had thus-far revealed. There was much that Megalia withheld from her closest of companions, knowing there were things even the spiritually adept Alectorious would find trouble accepting. This was not one of them, however. She bowed her head as if in shame before looking the king straight in the eye.

"I know of this prophecy," she bluntly replied. Alectorious was frozen and speechless, demanding immediate answers from his closest of confidants.

"Why ever... I... I do not understand. Why have you never mentioned this before?" he incredulously asked. The Oracle knew she had no choice, and explained herself clearly.

"Everything happens when it is meant to, Alectorious - I felt you were not yet ready until now - and so it has proven. Indeed it *is* that our world can lift up to this higher place; perhaps even to be amongst the gods, one sun. But before this can *ever* occur, the people of this world must see the error in their ways, and that war and domination can no longer hold sway. They must *not only* realise this, but take responsibility for their part in it, unite as one and together slay the forces of darkness that now cloud these once-benevolent lands. When this happening transpires, the gods will stand by Eternity's side and the empire will fall, once and forevermore," the Oracle boldly proclaimed. Alectorious' reaction was that of surprise.

"We as Eternians see this! We wish for no war or conflict in this world: all we have ever desired has been peace!" he exclaimed. The Oracle nodded in agreement, expanding.

"Indeed it is, Alectorious, but *not only* Eternity - *all* the known world must see this, including those of good hearts within the empire that is Gomercia, and act with all the strength the gods allow - you are to help achieve this great end. Remember, you are as one with those imprisoned souls: it is as one you have fallen and as one you must now rise to defeat the forces of darkness." Pausing briefly to allow a moment of mutual reflection, the Oracle gently stroked her feline companion which had playfully jumped on her lap.

"It will be so - I promise. We *will* stand together and defeat Nerosis' empire, once and forevermore." the king insisted. The Oracle nodded with a total belief in his words, realising nothing more needed be said on the matter. Megalia felt the intuitive urge to look once more into her mysterious crystal, sensing there was yet more to impart the intrepid Eternian king.

"I have something else to tell you, Alectorious," the Oracle revealed, entranced as she gazed deep within the enchanting purple-coloured sphere. The king wondered what it might be - something about Reiactus' whereabouts - or The Prophecy, even? He listened intently.

"Upon your journey to the mountains, I envisage you shall meet one like no other: with a strength and purity of soul unequalled by any that has come before. Where, I do not know; when, I cannot say… but only those of pure heart will recognise his virtue, while others will seek only to destroy him… as his power is so great, it alone could turn the tide of this war..." she dramatically announced.

The king wondered who it could possibly be: an unknown Eternian, Catharian or Brasovian, perhaps? Megalia went further. "There shall be one from up high to guide you to the path of the light… trust in him." The king immediately thought of the great dragon, Reiactus. "If you are patient, Alectorious, one sun there shall be another to warm your heart… embrace her… and your path will be illuminated like never before," she promised. There was a long pause as the king absorbed these unexpected revelations, before the Oracle spoke once more.

"If you believe in *anything* I have said, you will go to the Buvarious Mountains, my great and noble king - and meet your glorious destiny." The king intuitively knew the truth in all that she spoke, answering in no uncertain terms.

"If it is the last thing I ever do, Megalia, it will be to scale those lofty peaks."
The Oracle was content, knowing Alectorious was to follow the calling of his heart. The path ahead now seemed clear but the king was concerned for the safety of his dearest companion. "In this current state of affairs, I very much fear for your life, Megalia; to remain here would not be wise. I urge you to return to Eternity where you will be safe," the king pleaded, knowing he would *never* forgive himself if anything untoward were to befall her.

"I sense also, the imminent danger in these lands; so be it, we shall meet again in Eternity!" she heartily agreed, excited to return to her beloved city not seen in many suns.

"Splendid; and I shall trust in you to inform the council of my decision to travel to the Buvarious Mountains," the king insisted, knowing the Oracle would not let him down.

"Of course, it will be done, Alectorious." With that, the king rose from his seat, bowing in gratitude for all that had been revealed to him.

"As always a pleasure and *always* your companion, dear Megalia," he said, embracing her once more. As he departed the cottage, they exchanged one last meaningful glance.

"And I always *yours*, Alectorious," was Megalia's heart-felt reply. The king reluctantly walked outside as tears welled in his eyes, before making his way out to his waiting knights and Elite Guard. The Oracle meanwhile returned inside to gather her things for the journey to back Eternity, knowing it might be many suns before she saw her beloved cottage again. Alectorious tried his best to calm himself; he took a deep breath of fresh air, feeling that powerful sense of vitality he had always felt after receiving his companion's insights of wisdom. It would however, take several suns to fully integrate these revelations into his being that were so necessary for the path ahead. The king looked around to find the Elite Guards, led by none other than Gavastros, busy practising their swordsmanship.

"Knights, gather round!" Thelosious, Gavastros and Jalectrious all looked up animatedly, stopped what they were doing and walked briskly to the king. Thelosious ordered the Elite Guard to continue their exercises as they huddled round their noble leader.

"My companions, I have come to a decision," the king announced, as his knights responded with looks of expectancy. Alectorious hesitated slightly, taking a deep breath before finally revealing his plans. "It is my decision that we shall travel to the Buvarious Mountains, to discover once and for all if the great dragon lives on." It drew a mixed reaction from the three knights but Gavastros was quick to lend his support, being always partial for daring adventure that he was.

"Excellent decision, my king!" he agreed, zealously nodding his head. Thelosious was also in favour, having always been a firm believer in the dragon prophecy. Although the idea was audacious, in his mind, it was the only viable course of action remaining.

"A wise choice my lord - when would you have us leave?" queried the more thoughtful of knights. Alectorious stared into his companion's eyes without a word said, as if to convey the answer. "You could not mean…" Thelosious added.

"I do indeed - we depart immediately!" Alectorious concurred. It was too good to be true for the prodigy, for soon they would follow in the footsteps of their ancient ancestors.

"That's the spirit, my lord!" he enthused, excitedly clenching his fists. Not all were in agreement, though, with Jalectrious standing alone in his objections.

"What of the council, my liege? We are expected to meet again in but a number of suns: they will not approve of what will be surely seen as an arbitrary and indeed, foolhardy course of action!" he protested, casting doubt on what he believed to be an overly rash decision. Jalectrious knew well of his companion's enthusiasm for Eternian myth and legend, and was concerned it all too often clouded his better judgement.

"Indeed, Jalectrious - it is for this very reason the Oracle will return in my stead to inform the council of my decision," Alectorious explained. Before Jalectrious could counter, Gavastros leapt swiftly to his king's defence.

"The council will only try and stop us, Jalectrious, as always they have! They do not believe in, nor do they care for the dragon, or any of our history or legends, for that matter. Their only concern is the power and prestige afforded by their elated positions!" he scathingly proclaimed. The others expressed subtle nods of agreement but uttered not a word. This view of the High Council was commonly held amongst Eternian warriors but was something perhaps only the forthright Gavastros was brave enough to express.

"Gavastros is right, Jalectrious," Thelosious agreed. "They will surely try and hold us back. If we are to go, it must be *now*. We have the finest Elite Guardsmen to ride with us - their number equal to *at least* three Gomercians each. We have nothing to fear of the path ahead but the shadows of fear itself," he enthused. The king added his thoughts.

"There are simply not enough suns to double back - it must as Thelosious says, be *now* - or never at all," he insisted, as Jalectrious thought of the worst-case scenario.

"Eternity with an absent king - if word of this travels to Gomercia…" he chillingly began. The king sympathised with his concerns but was quickly dismissive.

"Eternity is in safe hands, Jalectrious: Rapacosis and Stratos are more than capable of ruling in my stead. They are well-versed in the workings of the Eternian state, as you all are, and know *exactly* what is expected of them in my absence," he assured. Jalectrious realised it was futile to argue as the sense of excitement grew quickly within the others.

"How long shall we be gone?" asked Thelosious, with Gavastros equally enthused.

"I envisage not more than seven suns; by the gods and The Great Spirit willing, our return will be *long* before any attempted invasion. Some might say I am mad, but I truly believe with every fibre of my being that this is the path we have been called upon to follow," the king proclaimed. His two more adventurous knights were unequivocal in agreement.

"And I!" agreed Thelosious, nodding his head.

"So think I!" added Gavastros. Jalectrious was expectedly more hesitant.

"I might have my reservations, my king, but if this is your most sincere wish, I can but only wholeheartedly support you," he diplomatically offered. Alectorious nodded to his men in gratitude, knowing he would require every ounce of their strength for the journey.

As the knights broke rank, orders were quickly relayed to the Elite Guardsmen, who had been hitherto oblivious to the king's plans. They were trained for anything his majesty asked of them, unquestioning in both loyalty and commitment to the Eternian cause. They would travel to the ends of the known world for their king; for there was no greater honour than to sacrifice their life in his direct service. Alectorious thought it fitting to address all of his men together prior to departure. He gathered the Elite Guard, who looked around at each other in naïve bewilderment, with not a hint of what the king was about to impart. It would be pendulum moment not only in their lives, but the history of the known world. As the king readied to speak, he tightly gripped the hilt of his sword.

"And so it finally begins, my fellow Eternians: we march on together, united in this noble quest in search of the great dragon to a place unseen in countless eons. The path ahead may not be easy nor will it be clear; but, with the courage of the purest parts of our hearts and conviction of every piece of our souls, we, like so many brave Eternian warriors before us shall overcome any obstacle that destiny dares throw upon our path. Look around to the one who stands next to you and remember the people of our nation - see the hope in their eyes and willingness to sacrifice *all* for the greater good of the known world. Feel the spirit of change in the air and *know* that the gods will walk with us - step by step, breath by breath, moment by moment through all that the path before us lays. Know this will be the greatest moment, our finest sun and most unforgettable adventure in our long and proud history! Ride with me now and together, we shall create legends that will be remembered a thousand eons henceforth! Onward we venture, Eternians!"

The king's powerful sentiment hit a raw nerve in the group, and was duly echoed.

"Onwards!" the Elite Guardsmen cried as one, raising their shining swords to the air.

"To the ends of the known world!" they zestfully added, knowing it *would* be so.

There was a sense of purpose in the Eternians' eyes as they made their way to their horses, contemplating the king's words, with not a soul amongst them wishing to take a step back. Before long, they had secured their belongings and were ready to embark on their grandiose adventure into uncharted lands. Soon the Eternians were travelling on the winding forest path towards the magnificent snowy peaks of the great Buvarious Mountains, unaware what fate or fortune might soon behold.

ANCIENT DELPHOESIA

Before venturing further on the path to the great Buvarious Mountains, the king and his men passed through the remains of Ancient Delphoesia: a mystical sanctuary not far from the Oracle's enigmatic stream-side abode. According to "The Great Book of Heroes", Delphoesia was once believed to be the centre of the known world and by some even, the very origin of creation itself. There was not much remaining of this once-sprawling sanctuary other than numerous scattered ruins and a small circular temple, but the spirits of the ancients could still acutely be felt, whispering their words of divinity to those adept enough to hear.

Over the eons, many would travel here from afar in search of spiritual guidance, wisdom or insight, much in the same way they now did the Eternian temples. From seekers to kings, soldiers and mystics, they would come to connect to the spirits of the gods and their ancestors in search of the wisest path to follow. It was popularly theorised by scholars that ancient adventurers would pass through Delphoesia before heading on to the Buvarious Mountains, in the belief this deeply spiritual place would bless their onward journey. It was for precisely *this* reason the king and his loyal knights were here.

As they drew their mighty steeds to a halt, the Eternians were in awe of this majestically spellbinding sight, capturing their imagination unlike anywhere else in the known world. Alectorious was most especially taken; overwhelmed by the sense of history he could feel permeating the countless weathered but impressionable stone ruins. There were remains of several temples and houses, a forum, theatre and most notably, perfectly intact cobblestone streets criss-crossing the entire sprawling complex. The king wondered how it might have been when Delphoesia was once a thriving place of worship as he visualised the many travellers, soldiers and seekers alike moving to and fro along the narrow streets and wide open arenas. He was moved beyond all conceivable words of description as he absorbed his tranquil surroundings.

"Can you not feel it, Thelosious?" Alectorious asked in a low voice, turning discreetly to his noble companion standing but two paces distant. Thelosious was in equal measure spellbound, wondering of the countless stories that lay hidden within this majestic abode. If only these weathered walls could utter but a whisper of Delphoesia's captivating tales, the cerebral one imagined in a fleeting instant of wonder.

"With all of my heart and soul, Alectorious," he resolutely concurred. Thelosious held, along with the king, a keen interest in the history of the ancient ones, having from his very youngest eons, especially middlehood, been fascinated by the Eternian heroes and their countless tales of daring and adventure. It was remarkable to think this was once a bustling place of dwelling and worship, revered throughout the ancient world and beyond. These feelings of wonderment were not shared by all present, however: Gavastros was quite unable to make any sense of why his companions were so mesmerised by what he saw as nothing but an indiscriminate pile of rubble…

"What *is this* unholy place, my king?" he asked, gazing around the surrounding remains in utter bewilderment. Alectorious had expected such a reaction from Gavastros but was sympathetic to his vivacious companion. The prodigy was still young, and one sun would come to truly appreciate the history of his illustrious nation. The king looked meaningfully into his eyes, enlightening him as to the origins of this captivating place.

"This is Ancient Delphoesia, Gavastros. Since and *even before* the Age of Heroes, it is said our ancestors travelled here for guidance when the path ahead unclear or when in search of a stronger connection to The Great Spirit. It was a place of divine inspiration, guidance and worship, revered and glorified throughout the then known world, as it still is by many learned, enlightened souls in our present age," Alectorious explained with great zest.

Gavastros seemed quite unmoved by his king's answer, unable to feel any particular sense of wonder at what he believed was exactly… what he saw…

"It seems as but a pile of old stones!" he uncouthly baulked. Thelosious was unsurprised by the predictability of his companion's reaction, but understanding as was the king. Thelosious remained unusually composed, resisting his often scathing outbursts.

"These are the remains of a deeply sacred place - of great wisdom, insight and healing. If you could only see beyond what your eyes tell you, Gavastros, you would discover a bounty of untold precious treasure," Thelosious wisely professed, revealing his more natural, philosophical side. Alectorious raised his chin as if in salute to his companion.

"Most astutely put, Thelosious; I could not have said it better myself," he agreed, hoping Gavastros would soon move on from his ephemeral ways. The king looked around and took a breath of fresh air, absorbing the mysterious surroundings deep into his body and soul. Alectorious felt if the divine had blessed this revered place, it would be for eternity.

The king and his knights spent some contemplative moments wandering the remains of temples, houses and shrines, trying to picture how it might have been for one who had travelled here all those eons ago to pay homage to the divine. Even Gavastros began to sense what it would have been like in these long past suns; such was the power this enigmatic abode held within its sacred boundaries. The prodigy sat upon the remains of an old stone wall, looking around as he imagined travellers, soldiers and worshippers alike walking gleefully along the cobblestone streets. He began to inadvertently connect to the spirits of those long-past peoples, feeling a special fondness for this beguiling place that he simply could not describe; it was as if he had been here many eons ago, in a past life now long-forgotten. The young Eternian of twenty-three eons could almost feel the ancients passing him by, whispering words of curiosity to each other about this lone seated stranger.

"Gavastros!" ….. "Gavastros!!" the king dramatically alerted. The prodigy shook his head as if having been deeply entranced. "It is our moment, my companion; we must move on," he encouraged, as Gavastros brought himself back to the present. There was an unusual look of despondency on the prodigy's face as he reluctantly stood, having quickly grown fond of this ancient abode. Gavastros looked to Alectorious with a deep sadness in his eyes.

"I felt a connection here, my king - a peace that I simply just... cannot explain…" he began, unable to articulate his profound sense of awe. Alectorious was in no doubt of what it had been, smiling with a look of tremendous satisfaction.

"You felt the spirits of the ancients, Gavastros: *your* ancestors," the Eternian leader replied, proud his companion had finally managed to see beyond his limited five senses. Gavastros, in this realisation felt completely overwhelmed, as a tear of emotion rolled down his right cheek. "It is alright, Gavastros; you will see them again, upon your return," the king resolutely promised, realising his companion was sincere in his feelings.

The prodigy wiped away his tears and reluctantly made his way back to the horses, saddened to say goodbye so soon to this truly captivating abode. As the Eternians began to trot away on their noble steeds, Gavastros took one last look back, vowing never to forget this moment for the rest of his eons on this mysterious known world.

PATH TO THE BUVARIOUS

The king and his knights departed Ancient Delphoesia with a tremendous sense of upliftment, with all now very much ready for the journey to the great Buvarious Mountains. Indeed, there was no knowing what the following suns might bring: only that their collective destiny lay somewhere up there in those majestic snow-capped peaks. These feelings of excitement only grew as the Eternians made their way along the winding wooded path, unbeknownst of the magnificent adventures awaiting them in those far off summits.

Alectorious took several reflective breaths to absorb the beauty of the mystical forests surrounding; a world he so rarely had the chance to appreciate, such was the nature of his position as Eternian leader. He allowed himself to relax from all the stress and worry that accompanied his life as King of Eternity, which allowed little opportunity to pursue his *true* heart's calling. Alectorious looked around at the giant, thick brown-barked trees on either side of the narrow path stretching as far the eye could see, feeling a genuine sense of homeliness within this natural abode; so distant that it was from all the pomp, ceremony and prestige that beset the Eternian court. As much as he *did* love his nation, he often wondered what manner of life it would be to live deep within the tranquillity of the forests, far away from the many annoyances and complications of life in the city. It would be much as the Catharians, he imagined, completely immersed in the beauty of nature and oneness of all creation. There were no castles, court nor walls - only the endless expanse of enchanting forests, gently flowing streams and majestic snow-covered mountains to captivate his spirit and sooth his weary soul from all the hardships of life in the ever-dynamic world of Causians: the name commonly used to describe the people of the known world.

"What more could one possibly ask for?" Alectorious thought in a brief moment of reflection. It would surely be the most idyllic life the king could possibly dream: deep in the vast creation - and very heart of The Great Spirit itself. The king often wished he could simply escape from all his worldly troubles into this endless expanse of lush alpine forest and dramatic mountaintops where none could ever find him: immersed and protected in the *true* sanctuary of the gods. Alectorious imagined more of such an idyllic life, living each and every sun freely exactly as he wished, exploring this limitless natural abode - the trees, streams, waterfalls, animals and majestic peaks - all those wondrous bountiful creations. He intuitively looked up to the mountains and the suns shining from high above: light from the great twin beacons was beginning to break through the tree branches as crisp autumn leaves fell silently on the forest floor, creating an enchanting carpet of many colours and hues on which the knights could tread.

The king promptly returned his attention to the path, reflecting more on what the Oracle had said during their meeting in her stream side cottage. Alectorious wondered if he had been right in following his heart's path and if indeed, the gods *would* protect and guide him, all the way to the great Buvarious. He also pondered as to where the known world was destined and if it was as The Prophecy had written, to rise up to a higher place. It would surely be a world where all were free to follow their heart's *true* desire, without the oppression, conflict and pain that now so scarred these ancient lands. Alectorious hoped it would be soon, for he could not much longer bear to live in this ever so fractured land, where the many suffered so needlessly for the benefit of those so few. He then began to wonder if the empire would *ever* be defeated: their power and influence was so great it seemed some suns like an almost impossible task. *Even if* this happened - and freedom and peace was *finally* restored, for how long would it endure? Perhaps another, more insidious individual than Nerosis would rise from the ashes of the empire and attempt to seize control of the seven city states - or it could even be a threat from lands beyond, never before set foot in by Eternian kind?

The king thought more of the Higher Worlds spoken of in the scrolls, wondering if Eternians would *ever* be as one with the gods in the stellar heavens. Even if it were to be so, he wondered how and when it might come to pass. Perhaps Reiactus, if they ever found him, could answer this, and many other such perplexing things. As more questions without answers formed in his mind, the king's thoughts were fittingly interrupted by the convivial Gavastros, who had hitherto been in an unusually pensive mood. He pulled up alongside on his mighty brown-white steed, with curiosity difficult to restrain as he cast a wayward glance to his king.

"Alectorious, my old companion; if I may be so bold, there is something I wish to ask of you." The dreamy king shook his head, swiftly returning his thoughts to reality. It was an appropriate interruption; almost as if the gods were telling him not to over-burden his mind. In any case, conversation with the prodigy was likely to be direct as much as it would be entertaining; something the king would no doubt appreciate, as well as enjoy.

"Please Gavastros, go ahead, it would be a pleasure, as always it is," he concurred. The prodigy looked to the roof of the evergreen forest, then to the snow-capped mountains in the distance, mulling over his words. After a brief reflection, he finally spoke.

"I have been wondering much this fine sun of the Great Reiactus and if he *is* up there... you know... high in the Buvarious... and if we shall ever find him. What think you of this, my king - do you *truly* believe that we will?" Shifting his gaze from the mystical peaks back to his companion, Gavastros inquisitively continued. "I mean, I have *always* believed in the dragon as you have, but to actually *see* him in reality, well, it would be quite something else entirely," he added, before eagerly awaiting his king's response. Alectorious carefully pondered before offering his wise insights.

"Gavastros, you know I have *always* believed in The Great Spirit *and* that our nation has been watched over and protected by the gods for eons immemorial. This powerful force has spoken through the scrolls, guiding us to embark on this glorious quest into the mountains: *is* Reiactus somewhere out there, awaiting our arrival? Our Myths, legends and folklore most certainly suggest he once graced these lands and indeed, it was *many* eons ago the scrolls were written: ancient words with little tangible proof of their authenticity. Logic might suggest it impossible that he still lives and breathes; however, the discovery of the scrolls have changed much in my, and many others thinking. I personally and truly believe that if we trust in *and* follow our inner guidance, we shall be led to where we are destined and achieve beyond what anyone could have *ever imagined*." Gavastros respected his king's words of reflection, yet still held a sentiment of doubt as he shook his head.

"The scrolls were a significant discovery, my king, but should we listen *only* to them? We cannot even be sure by whom they were written - and by the gods, for what reason! There is no real proof at all!" he controversially reasoned, but the king was rather unphased.

"You have a fine point, Gavastros. Indeed, ultimately, we cannot prove their authenticity. However, if each of us is to look within, we will discover a truth and wisdom much greater than any scrolls or ancient texts have *ever* possessed. I have always believed one should listen to and follow that most powerful voice, Gavastros. Although I may not have always done so myself, I do believe that through it, The Great Spirit has spoken, leading myself and my fellow knights to the path we now so boldly tread. Do I believe that we *will* find Reiactus? It is indeed, only when we can see and touch something with our own bare hands that the excitement and passion of that reality can be *truly* ignited. If and when it does transpire - and we do meet Reiactus - *then I will believe*. As much as I wish it, Gavastros, I cannot see the future - I can but read the signs the gods throw upon our path - and I firmly believe it is our duty to have the courage, fortitude and determination to follow them," he further proclaimed, with his convictions stronger than ever. Gavastros mulled over his king´s words, trying to decipher them into a more palpable form.

"So you mean, Alectorious; that you will not believe in something until you see it with your very own eyes?" he deductively asked, in his typically blunt manner.

"Something of that nature," the king jovially answered, bemused by the prodigy's simplistic interpretation of his words. Gavastros continued with gusto.

"A part of me believes so strongly that I just want Reiactus to be real no matter what, yet, until I can see it with my own two eyes and touch, with my very own hands, it is nothing more than a fantastical dream – something unattainable," the brave one lamented, wishing he could be whisked away to a mystical faraway land where all his dreams could come true in but an instant. The king was sympathetic to his sentiment, having as the prodigy, all his eons dreamed of meeting the great dragon. Alectorious had no doubt their path would take them to all those places they had hoped for, and so many more.

"Know Gavastros, that every moment from now, we are living that dream." The prodigy was very much taken by his noble king's words, silent as he returned his focus to the path. The two companions fell into quiet contemplation of all that had been spoken as they continued into the enchanting forests, onwards to their bright destiny.

EYE OF THE STORM

The Eternians continued on their quest to the mystical Buvarious Mountains, led from the front now by Jalectrious, the most senior knight after the king. Venturing ever higher upon the increasingly winding path, the group were surrounded on both sides now by thick green pine forest as far as the eye could see. They maintained a strict silence; the only audible sounds were of the wind passing through trees and constant singing of birds from the branches, high above. It was eerily tranquil; the Eternians began to feel a distinct sense of unease as they looked around for possible signs of danger. Their suspicions were soon vindicated as countless feathered creatures took off in unison from their perches, flying into the distance in apparent distress. Moments later, countless animals including deer, squirrels and antelopes dramatically followed, escaping into the depths of the forests.

"The birds - they flew away!" exclaimed a startled Alectorious, looking instinctively around in a circle. His men did likewise, frantically trying to make sense of what was happening. Something was definitely not right, thought Alectorious, wondering if the perils spoken of these paths were true, after all. As if on cue, Jalectrious swung his head round to his companions trotting close behind, issuing a stern order.

"Eternians: halt now!" he demanded, in more than a strong whisper. He raised his clenched blue-armoured fist to the air as his other hand reached for the hilt of his sword. Positioned at the front of the group, Jalectrious was well-placed to spot any oncoming threats. He carefully scanned the forests as the Eternians pulled hard on their collective horses' reins, grounding to a standstill in the middle of the forest path. Anxiously looking around, they wondered what manner of thing could have silenced an *entire forest.* Deep down, they knew, but would not admit it to themselves. As several moments past, the tension increased to unbearable levels. The king was particularly anxious as his heart missed several beats.

"What is it, my companion?" he nervously asked, drawing up beside his able deputy. "If it is as I fear, may Promaestious protect us all," Jalectrious chillingly replied. Concentrating on the path ahead, he tried his best to decipher the faint noises in the distance. "I thought I heard horses up ahead, sire... it was faint but..." he continued. The king quickly concurred as their worst fears were suddenly realised.

"Wait, I heard it too - and can see who it is!" Alectorious added in startled disbelief.

"Gomercians soldiers - arm yourselves!" shrieked Jalectrious, as he duly finished the king's sentence. Gavastros panicked, having been caught completely off guard.

"By Guerris!" he cried. The prodigy grabbed the hilt of his sword as a wave of both fear and adrenalin swept through each of the Eternians' bodies. They mentally readied themselves for inevitable confrontation, thinking of the possibility, as there was in any battle, that they would not make it out alive. Eternians believed their souls lived forever and that the physical body was but a temporary vehicle for their terrestrial experiences - however, *this particular life* was the only one they had - and they would protect it with all of their might.

"Eternians - be ready!" Jalectrious ordered, raising his sword with commanding zeal. As one, the knights and Elite Guard drew their shining blades, positioning their shields for protection from the rapidly approaching threat. Alectorious gripped his sword tightly as his heart pounded faster and a trickle of sweat poured down his face, realising confrontation was imminent. At least the king could draw solace from the fact he was in the company of an elite group of warriors. Although their number was small, one Eternian was worth at least three enemy soldiers.

"'Tis the Gomercians sure, my king - they have seen us - and prepare to attack!" screamed Gavastros at the top of his lungs. Pumped up and ready for action, the prodigy tensed his powerful biceps and pectoral muscles as he tightly gripped his sword.

"Eternians - form a line - protect the king!" Jalectrious barked. The Elite Guard instantly responded, forming a protective barrier in front of their noble leader. From over the hill in the distance, a group of Gomercian cavalry was rapidly approaching the Eternian position with unnerving confidence. Flanked on either side by heavily-armed foot soldiers, it was an intimidating sight for even the most hardened of warriors: that shining black and gold armour only added to their terrifying aura.

"How many can you see, Jalectrious?" Alectorious nervously demanded. The king was clearly flustered, judging by the quivering tone of his voice.

"I count some fifteen horsemen and *at least* that many infantry!" Jalectrious replied.

"Wait, more in the forest - on the left and right flanks!" Gavastros added. The king panicked as the enemy number rapidly swelled and sweat began to trickle down his cheeks.

"NO! NO!" he whispered, trying in vain to stay calm. Although having been involved at Dragon's Pass, Alectorious had never been one for the heat of battle. Unable to restrain his fright, the king sensed this might be his final sun upon this fragile known world.

"By Aphroedisia, how can we possibly survive *this*?" he panicked, looking in trepidation to the approaching hordes. "We are outnumbered and outflanked by more than three to one!" he added chillingly, as Jalectrious did his best to restore calm.

"Fear not their numbers, my king; for the finest warriors in all Eternity fight with us!" he replied, hoping to provide some measure of reassurance. Jalectrious knew it would take far more than sheer ability to win this battle: without reinforcements, it would take a near miracle to emerge victorious against so many. Flanking the king and his knights, the Elite Guard remained cool and composed, eager to engage the enemy and serve their king: they would stand and fight to the end for their nation as the ultimate warriors they were.

In moments, the superior commanding officer, Jalectrious, barked his final orders. Unintelligible to the outsider, the Elite Guard knew *exactly* what to do.

"Form up tri-five left right on one!! Four front on two me!!!" he commanded. His subordinates instantly responded: forming a triangle of protection around the king, the Eternians were now a lethal fighting unit only the bravest in all the lands would dare challenge. With the three knights heading the front, they were ready for anything the Gomercians could dare throw in their path. Jalectrious turned once more to Alectorious, confident that all would be well.

"My king, we do all that we can to protect you! If duty so requires, every one of us to a man shall fall before you!" he promised. The king stared deep into his companion's eyes and shook his head.

"It will not be so, for I *will* confront my fears this sun; if you are to fall, I shall with you!" he bravely insisted. Jalectrious raised his sword in salute as the Eternians readied themselves. Adrenalin rapidly began to pump through the king's throbbing blue veins, knowing he would soon be in the thick of the action. The stage was set: the Gomercians in their black and gold armour stood from a distance, watching like a wild animal staring upon its imminent prey. The Eternians stood some fifty spears distant, ready to defend all they held dear. After what seemed an age, the enemy commanding officer finally raised his sword, issuing the final call to arms.

"Gomercians: for the glory of the empire, ATTACK!!!" he cried, ordering his legion promptly into battle.

"AHHHGGH!!!" cried the Gomercian infantry in frenzied unison. They rushed at the Eternian position from multiple angles, from both the path ahead and hiding places in the forests. Realising they would soon be surrounded, Jalectrious had to act fast.

"Eternians, we take out their cavalry first! Alectorious, on the rear guard: we go full forward, split two on my mark!" he ordered, as the men prepared to charge.

"FORWARD!!!" he yelled, raising his sword to the heavens. His fellow Eternians did likewise: as one, they dramatically charged the approaching enemy in perfect formation. As they gained speed, Jalectrious waited for the right moment to execute their well-rehearsed battlefield manoeuvre.

"MARK!!!" he yelled. The galloping Eternians split evenly into two groups, riding round the Gomercian horsemen's flanks. Causing great confusion, the Eternians threw the enemy into complete disarray. As they passed on the right and left side of the Gomercian cavalry, Jalectrious delivered the decisive order.

"ATTACK!!!" he screamed, at the very top of his lungs. As one, the Eternians lifted their shining blades and engaged the shell-shocked Gomercians with unbridled ferocity, instantly falling many of their number. The imperial soldiers were simply unable to match the skill, speed and sheer dexterity of the highly-trained knights and Elite Guardsmen. The Eternians retreated up the forest path as the remaining Gomercian cavalry chased, seeking revenge for their fallen comrade's lives. The king and his men quickly turned to face their adversaries, attacking again, hopelessly outclassing their more inexperienced rivals. The Gomercian foot soldiers were quickly closing in: shocked as they were furious at the rapid demise of their cavalry. The Eternians regrouped to brace for another attack, again forming a protective perimeter around the king. The Gomercian infantry charged the mounted Eternians with unrestrained zeal, some without even the remotest sense of fear.

"AHH!" they screamed, swinging swords like men possessed. "You shall pay for this, Eternians!!!" cried one fanatical Gomercian, as the Eternians responded with equal fervour.

"Gomercia will fall!" said one Elite Guardsman with unbridled fury.

"Give this to Nerosis!" yelled another, as the two groups fought heavily. "Ching!" "Clang!" "Bang!" came the various noises as swords, shields and armour alike clashed with a thunderous clamour. Many cried out in pain as warriors from both ranks fell - the king hoped it would not soon be he - may the gods protect their souls, he thought for the briefest of moments. Alectorious was faring much better than expected, managing to compose himself well despite all the madness surrounding.

"Pull out - reform the line!!!" Jalectrious screamed, with his men quick to comply. The Eternians would attempt to run down the remaining soldiers with their massive Clydosian horses: animals originating from lands said to exist beyond The Great Plains. Indeed, they could try and outrun the remaining infantry into the mountains but it would most certainly alert more Gomercians to their presence: the Eternians *had* to face them now. The king and his men managed to break free from the enemy, again galloping up the path to regroup. Reforming the line, they readied for one final attack. The king instinctively turned to his loyal deputy, noticing a nasty gash on his shoulder.

"Jalectrious, you are wounded!" he exclaimed, pointing to the gaping cut.

"I am fine, Sire - it is but a scratch, I assure you. How do *you* fare, my king?" Alectorious put on a brave face for his fellow Eternian and soldier.

"But a few scratches my companion, nothing more: let us finish this!" he ordered with great fervour. Jalectrious looked to the men in the knowing he might not see these courageous souls again, delivering his final orders with a passion never before seen.

"Eternians, you have fought bravely this sun: now *this* will be our final stand. We charge at full attack - may the gods be with you all!" he shouted at the very top of his lungs. The Elite Guard flinched for not an instant, proudly holding their heads high. At the age of some thirty-one eons, Jalectrious had proven a very capable leader, having been chosen for knighthood for his ice-cool nerves and tactical nous on the field. Forming a single impenetrable line, they turned to face the quickly advancing Gomercian foot soldiers.

"For Eternity!!!" screamed Jalectrious, raising his shining sword aloft. The remaining twelve Eternians charged the enemy hordes with all their might, as if the god of war himself had possessed their very souls. Almost half the Gomercians were crippled or badly wounded on impact, such was the ferocity of the Eternian charge. Before the knights and Elite Guard could turn for another attack, they were quickly enveloped by swarms of enemy foot soldiers screaming the most terrifying of cries. The king and his men fought on heroically, managing to thwart the initial imperial onslaught. Despite their most valiant efforts, the Eternians were again, quickly surrounded by endless waves of Gomercian soldiers emanating from the surrounding woodland. As if in the eye of a proverbial storm, the king realised they would need a near-miracle to make it out of this alive.

From the corner of his eye, Alectorious spotted another group of soldiers hidden in the forests, seemingly waiting to enter the fray. His immediate thought was they were Gomercian reinforcements, but at closer inspection, realised it was nothing of the sort. Dressed in light-brown earthy coats and limited silver armour, it was in stark contrast to the black and gold of the Gomercians and for that matter, Eternian light blue. The king looked up in fascination to these mysterious warriors, wondering by whose bidding they were here. As the mystery forestmen waited for what appeared to be their leader to order them into battle, the king wondered if they were perhaps mercenaries in disguise… or… could it be? Surely it was not possible… not in a thousand suns. If it *was* who he suspected, they would *most certainly not* be helping the Gomercians - but he could not understand why they would come to Eternity's aid, either. In that moment, the king's spirits immediately lifted, realising the gods had answered his prayers. The leader of the forest men dramatically stepped forward, drawing his sword from his sheath before raising it to the heavens. He turned to his band of warriors, issuing the order to charge.

"For The Great Spirit!!! Show no weakness, fear nor mercy!!!" he screamed. An instant shudder reverberated through the king as he watched in awe. The forest leader turned to the duelling armies and charged - in mere moments breaking into a full sprint.

At unparalleled speed, the mystery man hurled himself towards the action, with his loyal followers not a handful of spears behind. With an apparent disregard for their own lives, the forestmen threw themselves fearlessly into the fray, taking Eternians and Gomercians alike completely by surprise. So engrossed in battle were they, the Gomercians thought at first the forestmen were on *their* side. Instead, they were given the shock of their lives - in moments taking heavy casualties to the enigmatic new arrivals.

"Who *are* these mysterious warriors?" thought Alectorious, watching in amazement as the forestmen engaged the hapless enemy. Within a blink of an eye, the forest leader had taken out three Gomercian soldiers before four, then five - and even more. His men fought with almost equal ferocity, moving with such blinding speed it seemed somehow unreal – almost like mythical Eternian heroes...

"ALECTORIOUS!!! WATCH OUT!!!!" Gavastros dramatically cried, as the king turned in panic to face his companion. Having been distracted by the arrival of the forestmen, Alectorious had momentarily forgotten he was in the heat of a battle. His fellow Eternians however, had been strangely unmoved by these mysterious men fighting by their side. The king instinctively looked in the other direction from the prodigy, seeing a lone Gomercian who had taken a horse from a fallen comrade, launching an all-out drive towards him. In battle mere moments are life - and it was all Alectorious had now - for this smallest lapse in concentration might have just cost him all. The Gomercian rammed his horse directly into the side of the king's steed, with Alectorious not realising until it was too late. Sephalos was dramatically unbalanced by the impact of the enemy charge, throwing Alectorious from his saddle to a hefty thump on the ground. The mysterious forest warrior saw the Eternian king fall from the corner of his watchful eye, moving rapidly to help as though a servant of many suns - but in truth, just moments. Seeing their opportunity, several other Gomercians moved rapidly toward the fallen king, raising their swords to deliver a fatal blow. With the

Eternians not quick enough to act, the mysterious forestman knew only *he* could save the stricken king's life. As if it his own life hanging in the balance, the forest leader took an extra sword from a fallen Gomercian soldier and threw himself fearlessly at the enemy with all of his might. With a single swipe of each shining blade, the forestman instantly felled his shell-shocked adversaries with but moments remaining: the king's life had been saved. Realising they had been completely outclassed, the remaining Gomercians soldiers fled from the scene of battle. The sight of such skilful swordsmanship had left them with little choice, knowing that by fighting on, they would have made a certain journey to the afterlife.

As the Eternians and forestmen scrambled to assist their respective wounded, the forest leader turned his attention to the escaping Gomercians, knowing a captive would be an invaluable asset. Picking out an escaping soldier, he instinctively raised his sword and hurled it though the air at great velocity. It struck the poor soldier right in the back, piercing solid armour and stopping him right in his tracks.

"AHHH!!!" he cried in tremendous pain, before falling to the ground in agony. The forest leader rushed to the fallen enemy, showing him no mercy at all. He knelt down, grabbing him tightly by the throat and demanded some very straight answers.

"What are you doing here, Gomercian? This is *not your land*!" he angrily commanded. The mystery man spoke in a typically gruff forest accent, squeezing the last remnants of life from his apparent enemy, who was struggling to respond from the tightness of the forestman's grip. Meanwhile, the king was eager to know all that he could.

"Please - loosen your grip - I think he is trying to tell us something!" Alectorious persuaded. Casting a contemptuous glance back, the forestman grudgingly complied as the captured Gomercian coughed and spluttered. Finally regaining his breath, the enemy soldier spoke in a trembling, but surprisingly compliant voice.

"Please, for the sake of my family - I shall tell you all that I know, if only you allow my life to end in peace!" the shell-shocked soldier responded. Gomercian foot soldiers were usually thought to be fiercely loyal to their leader and extremely uncooperative as captives. The forestman was naturally taken aback - and with a somewhat puzzled expression simultaneously obliged, completely letting go of the weakening soldier. By now, the Eternian knights and several other forestmen had gathered round, curious as were their newly-found companions to know all they could from the "enemy". Realising his captive was now willing to cooperate, the forestman repeated once more, but in a quieter, kinder tone. Speaking in almost a whisper, the forest leader again tried to communicate with the struggling warrior.

"Why are you here, soldier?" he evocatively asked. The man began to cough in his attempt to explain but was severely dehydrated by his wounds. "Water - get me some water!" the forest leader demanded. Doing all he could to help comfort the fallen Gomercian, he realised this poor, unfortunate soul was not fighting by his own will, but by virtue of circumstances well beyond his own control.

"Gavastros - give him some of that water!" the king impulsively ordered. Still very much in shock, Alectorious was unable to believe what was transpiring before his eyes: Eternian and forestman standing side by side as equals for a common cause. Realising he was trying to repent for his once ways, the forest leader felt it only appropriate to offer any comforts he possibly could in the last moments of this man's life. It was an act of chivalry perhaps - a show of respect between fellow warriors. The Ancient Code of Virtue, reflected the king, remembering that much-revelled age in which he had never actually lived yet knew so well. It was the path of a true knight and warrior - something long forgotten by all but a few honourable souls. Alectorious looked on helplessly, feeling a deep sense of sadness as he watched this unfortunate man draw his final breaths. Still unintroduced, the Eternians handed the forestman some cool mountain water. The forest leader carefully handed it to the fallen soldier, whose breaths were becoming shorter by the instant. The man sipped the icy spring liquid, enjoying it like the very nectar of the gods themselves. Taking several deep, reflective breaths, he gathered his thoughts and feelings before imparting them in words.

"I thank you for your kindness in my final moments upon this known world," he struggled, as the gathered Eternian and forest warriors listened intently. The man continued. "I joined this army not of my own choosing but of forces against my will. They said if I did not fight, those whom I love dear would not live to see another sun. Truly, I had no other choice - for it was my life - or theirs. What is one to do?" he reasonably asked, feeling understandably helpless. The forestman was sympathetic, offering words of support.

"You did nothing wrong, soldier - you sacrificed yourself for a cause much greater than yourself. You are a virtuous soul," he said, pausing for a moment. "Are there many other of your kind?" asked the forest warrior, with the Gomercian nodding in the affirmative.

"It is the way with many of Nerosis' imperial soldiers: blackmailed and tricked into fighting a war, for a nation and ideal that is not their own," he replied, as the king took his chance to speak. He leaned forward, whispering quietly to the man.

"Tell me soldier…" he began, with the others turning to face the Eternian leader. "Would those such as you fight for us if they were *not* bound by the empire?" he asked, with a sense of great anticipation.

"I have… no doubt of this..." the fallen soldier replied, only to be met by a collective gasp. The king realised if Eternity was able to capture *just one* of the occupied city states, they could harness the strength of countless others willing to fight against the empire. As he thought further of the implications, the others were utterly transfixed. The struggling Gomercian was clearly uncomfortable with all the commotion; Alectorious and Jalectrious realised this, instinctively disbanding the crowding soldiers. In matters of such sensitivity, it was best that as few as possible heard what would doubtlessly be priceless information.

"Back to the wounded, men - they need all the help you can afford them," Jalectrious ordered. The Elite Guard acted promptly in compliance as the crowd dispersed, with only the forestman and his apparent two right-hand men stood around the fallen soldier, along with Alectorious and his three knights, Jalectrious, Gavastros and Thelosious.

"I understand your choice - you acted for the ones you love and were loyal to them above *all else* - remember this, if nothing else I say," offered the mysterious forestman, as he motioned to the compassionate Eternian king. Alectorious knelt on the path, offering the fallen soldier some more refreshing, chilled water, while Thelosious removed the man's helmet and placed his head upon a bundle of clothing.

"Oh thank you; that feels *much* better. You know, they told us many awful things about you Eternians - they had us believe we would be shown no mercy and that you cared for yourselves and no others. How wrong were they… have I been… I thank you, truly," he sincerely offered. The king was naturally humbled by the man's words.

"We do only as we would be done by… my companion," he affectionately replied. The man smiled appreciatively as he began to feel a bit more comfortable.

"How did you find yourselves in these forests?" Jalectrious inquisitively asked, realising the man might not have much longer to live.

"We came to fight the forestmen but were never told the reasons for this. Perhaps more importantly, we came to find possible weak links in Eternity's defences. We were searching for caves or other potential hideouts to encamp, in preparation for an eventual invasion. Our commander as did we, never expected to meet you in battle so soon…"

admitted the man in vain, his spirit now weakening with every breath. Alectorious' eyes widened in disbelief: he immediately realised the implications of this terrifying revelation.

"Invasion you say?" was all he could muster, as Thelosious and Gavastros looked at one another with an equal sense of dismay.

"Oh yes… Nerosis is in the advanced stages of his invasion plans for Eternity… he…" the man continued, his voice rapidly weakening. As the man's soul prepared to enter the spirit world, the king frantically pushed for answers.

"What is his plan - when will this invasion take place?" he desperately asked, making his tone as soft as possible in the knowing the soldier would soon be gone. Wishing to help all he could, the fallen soldier summoned his last reserves of strength.

"The defeat at Dragon's Pass taught Nerosis a crucial lesson - he will not make the same mistake again. When he attacks, it will be in much greater numbers - and he will not stop until *all* the known world is consumed. Eternity is the ultimate prize: one that I and many others pray he does not capture," he explained, with the king anxious to know more.

"But when does he plan to invade? It is of paramount importance we know, to save many others who have suffered as you from imperial tyranny!" The soldier struggled to respond, with so little life left in him. Alas, it was to be the last thing he would ever say. "S…Soo…oon..." the poor soul whispered as he took his final breath. A collective silence was followed by a sense of complete disbelief. The forestman gently put his hand over the fallen soldier's face before closing his eyelids forevermore.

As the man's spirit drifted peacefully into Athepothesia, the gathered Eternians and forestmen stood in complete silence, with a deep sense of sadness in their hearts. Alectorious was particularly affected, having never witnessed one pass over in such a way. He did not display any emotion though, knowing as king, he must always project strength. The lead Forestman turned and walked away as the Eternians remained to pay their respects to this unfortunate soul; sad that such an innocent life need so senselessly be taken. Alectorious realised on reflection the man had been a victim of circumstance rather than by actions of his own choosing. As the king looked instinctively up into the treetops, he sensed the man's spirit smiling back down upon them, and that he was finally at peace. Deep down, he knew it *was* so.

Soon Alectorious returned his thoughts to matters of the moment and the impending Gomercian invasion, realising there was still very much to ponder in the fight for freedom from all that was not right and true.

MEETING OF DESTINY

Alectorious and his knights stood together speechless, shocked by the dramatic series of events to have just transpired before their very eyes. But moments ago they had been on the brink of re-uniting with the ancient heroes in Athepothesia; instead they now stood as victors, side by side with the mysterious forest dwellers. Indeed, the forestmen having come to the aid of Eternians was something no-one could have envisaged in their wildest of dreams.

As the group of soldiers came to terms with this unfamiliar predicament, the king's mind was consumed with a thousand different thoughts. Alectorious wondered if what the fallen soldier had spoken of *was* true, and that the Gomercians would soon invade, before pondering how he as Eternian leader should best respond. The king wondered if he should turn back and prepare for such an eventuality or continue with his quest into the mountains in the hope of realising his long-cherished dream of finding the great dragon. While deep in reflection, Alectorious had momentarily forgotten about the forestmen's leader, who was, along with his companions, preparing to set off into the distance. As if something had guided him, the king instinctively looked up. Uncharacteristically raising his voice, he attempted to capture the elusive forest dweller's attention.

"Wait... man of the forests! To where do you go?" the king cried to the beguiling stranger, with whom he had yet to directly communicate. The forestman turned his head round slowly, reluctant to engage in any further conversation. He knew he would need to confront the Eternian leader one sun - but wished it not be this. The forestman grabbed the reigns of a fallen Gomercian's steed and stared the king directly in the eye. For one eternal moment neither spoke a word, as if they were trying to read each other's thoughts.

"I go home," was the forestman's simple reply, placing one foot in the stirrups before mounting the large dark-haired animal. He drew the mighty steed round to face the king and his men as the Eternians and forestmen alike watched with great curiosity. Alectorious instinctively took a step forward to thank this intriguing soul for his selfless acts of valour. Slightly raising his palms to the air, he continued.

"Mysterious man of the forests; I owe you a debt I could not even begin to repay," The grateful king imparted. Moving closer, he was naturally curious as to why this enigmatic personality had risked everything to defend the Eternians. If the forestmen *were* Catharians as Alectorious had suspected, it would defy all logical explanation. For certain, they were no allies of the Gomercians; but what motive they had for fighting on Eternity's side, the king could not possibly fathom. He dearly wished for answers to this, and so very much more.

"*Owe*, great king? You owe me *nothing* at all…" the forestman began, in a somewhat patronising tone. The knights were clearly unimpressed but the king was ever more intrigued. The forestman continued as he looked around the remnants of battle: bodies, armour and swords alike strewn across the once-peaceful forest path.

"On the contrary, you gave me the chance to vanquish these sacred lands of the heathenous empire: I did what was but my duty to The Great Spirit *and* the forests. Know that the Gomercians are *my* enemy more than they will *ever* be yours," responded the mystery man in a blunt, emotionless manner. It was on reflection, not a particularly unexpected reply; the forestmen were of the belief they had everything they needed out here in the vast expanse of the natural world. The king remained calm, hoping to elicit what he wished to know.

"Well, put it another way if you will: what boon could one bestow upon a soul of such courage, I then ask? It is not often one becomes a saviour," he praised. The forestmen was unable to disguise a light chuckle, momentarily casting his eyes to the treetops.

"A Saviour... I? Well, that's the first I have heard *that*! Please, king, save your illusory words of flattery for those who know only vice and shallow vanity. I bade farewell many eons ago to the world of matter: I am *now* a man of the forests," he responded, as if trying very hard to prove a point. The king was unwilling to concede as he stepped ever closer.

"There must be *something* I could impart you as a token of my, and my humble knight's gratitude," he insisted. All eyes shifted expectantly back to the forestman, who looked around his spectacular natural surroundings and took a large breath. He suddenly raised his hands to the air before addressing the king and his men.

"I have all I need here in the forests, deep in the heart of the lands of The Great Spirit - trees, animals, rivers, streams... purity - things that neither gold, riches nor fair maiden could *ever* buy," he brazenly responded. As the Eternians observed their enchanting surroundings, it was difficult to argue with this. The king was becoming increasingly frustrated but was steadfastly unwilling to give in. Despite the forestman's rather difficult nature, there had been nothing stopping him from simply riding away; yet here he remained. The mystery man seemed reluctant to reveal too much but this was perhaps understandable considering the many perils in the wilds of the forests. The king was intrigued by the reasons for the stranger's selfless actions, wondering why he would risk so much for no apparent reason at all. The forestmen had been under no visible threat from the Gomercian forces but they had so willingly thrown their bodies into the fray. The king's curiosity as to the motives of these fascinating souls was insatiable and would not cease until the truth revealed.

"Yet, you would risk your life for a complete stranger?" the king queried, as he began to circle his forest-dwelling counterpart in the middle of the path - as if an animal closing in on its prey. The stranger was unflustered, acting as though completely in his element.

"I must say, your modesty is greatly commendable," the forestman quipped, before continuing. "I know as well who *you* are - and think the reward more than paid for the risk, Alectorious, *King and Knight of Eternity*," he unexpectedly added. Thelosious and Gavastros looked to each other, rather unamused by the forestman's quite blunt attitude. Despite his obvious renown across the lands, Alectorious was oddly taken aback by being addressed by his first name. There was a peculiar familiarity about this mysterious forestman - as if they had met before in eons long past - or in another life, even. Unperturbed, the king continued.

"Well, since you clearly know who *I am*, might I have the due pleasure of *your* name? If of course, it is not too great a burden for you to bear…" he insisted, disinclined to submit to the forestman's stubborn nature.

"My name, indeed; but does a king need know the name of a wanderer - one who calls the forests his home - the trees and animals his companions?" replied the man, motioning to the magnificent forests surrounding. Attempting to evade the king's questions, the forestman trotted upon his steed in a near perfect circle, as if the hunted evading its hunter. The king continued unabated, unwilling to accept anything but the answers he sought.

"I need to know the name of a warrior: one who against tremendous adversity displayed bravery and swordsmanship that I have never before witnessed in my lifespan. It is in recognition of a stranger who, in the face of great danger would risk his life for another. *That*, my dear companion; is why I ask of you now," Alectorious solemnly demanded. The forestman continued his evasiveness, relishing the chance to speak to a king in such a way.

"Does the king believe it his right to know this humble warrior's name?" he asked. The other Eternians meanwhile, most especially Gavastros, were becoming visibly upset by the forestman's uncooperative nature. Alectorious was simply unwilling to allow another to get the better of him and continued to play the forestman's little game. The king realised that if it were not for this man standing before him, he would no longer be here now, living and breathing. Alectorious persisted with an increased sense of curiosity.

"It is indeed my wish to know, but it is naturally every man's right to choose his own path." Realising he was currently out-with Eternity, the king accepted he would be seen in the forests as an equal by any he encountered. The perennially impatient Gavastros saw things in a much different light though, unable to accept such words be spoken to his noble leader. He confrontationally moved toward the forestman and spoke his mind.

"Sire - let us not waste our sun on this vagabond! He helped us sure, but shows you - and Eternity - *our* nation, no respect at all!" he asserted, pointing disdainfully at the mounted forestman. The young knight had, from the beginning, taken a dislike to the stranger, mistrusting his secretive, evasive nature. However, perhaps it was as much the threat he posed to Gavastros' rising star. The prodigy had clearly touched a raw nerve: the forestman jumped dramatically from his horse and moved aggressively at Gavastros.

"Respect? *You* talk of respect, *Knight* of Eternity? I'll have you know my men and I just saved *you and your king* from a certain end. Why don't you show *that* some respect before you accuse *me* of unvirtuous actions?" he retorted, pointing evocatively at Gavastros' chest. The prodigy did not hesitate in retaliating.

"How dare you insult me in this way - I shall show you what it is to be a *real* warrior, forestman!" Gavastros countered, reaching for his shining blade as the forestman did likewise. As tensions dramatically mounted, the king was quick to intervene. Taken back by the sudden escalation of events, Alectorious moved forward with open palms raised.

"Gavastros - enough of that!" he boomed, infuriated by his knight's selfish belligerence. The prodigy grudgingly released the grip of his sword as he stared contemptuously into the eyes of the forestman. Finally he conceded, turning away in a huff.

"I have had enough of this *vagabond* - I shall be gone!" Gavastros announced in utter disgust, before storming off angrily to his steed. Alectorious and Thelosious remained, eager to know all they could of this mysterious soul.

"If you will tell us not your name, forestman - may I ask - are you those known as the Catharians?" Thelosious boldly questioned, hoping to elicit *something* of meaningful value.

"I most certainly dress as they - but in truth, are we not *all* sons of this world and ultimately, The Great Spirit? Catharians live and fall, feel and think exactly as Eternians - something *even I* took many suns to accept," the forestman cryptically retorted. The king sensed something uniquely different about him, but could not put his finger on what it was.

"You are quite unlike what I had expected of a Catharian - I have heard of your people's great dislike for Eternity - so why I then ask, were you so compelled to help us?" the king thoughtfully probed. The forestman began to open up a little as he relaxed his shoulders, his tone now less defensive than it had been before. He spoke bluntly.

"The Gomercians have come to wipe out every last Catharian that walks these sacred lands - *if* Catharia is to fall - mark my words, Eternity will soon follow. A clear message must be sent out that these forests will *never* be theirs. The empire is as much Catharia's enemy as it is yours. That is all for now, *King of Eternity*. I must return to the forests, for there is much to be done this sun," the gruff forestman answered, hastily preparing to depart.

"Be gone if you must, mysterious forest wanderer; if you would only tell us your name!" the king pressed, knowing it would make it a lot easier to track him down later on.

"Sandros," the brash Catharian replied, before jumping back on his steed. He pulled hard on his horses' reins before speeding off into the forests with companions in tow. Some of the Elite Guards readied to give pursuit but were quickly restrained by their wise leader.

"Let him go!" the king ordered, raising his hand steadfastly in the air. Alectorious sensed he would meet the forestman again when the moment right; for now, he had a dragon to find. The king's curiosity was greater than ever as he wondered about the stranger's origins. "Sandros…a most unusual name for a Catharian," he reflected. Alectorious could have sworn he had heard it before but was unable to place his finger on exactly where. Thelosious was more familiar as he drew on his vast knowledge of such scholarly things.

"It means "defender of men" in old Catharian," he pronounced, recalling his extensive studies from middlehood. The king's eyes widened with intrigue as his noble companion continued. "I read it once, many eons ago in The Ancient Book of Heroes; apparently it is a name given in these parts to those descended from great warriors," he added with intrigue, as Alectorious further pondered the significance of their serendipitous meeting.

"An appropriate name, it is indeed. Well, if the gods will it, we shall meet our forest companion again," he said, but Thelosious was not so sure of this.

"There can be no knowing when or where that might be, my king: these forests stretch further than the eyes can see," he observed, as he looked into the dense surrounding woodland. The king was dismissive, knowing they would be drawn to him if it was meant to be.

"That may be so, Thelosious, but as a wise man once said: that which is ordained by The Great Spirit to be will not pass one by. I have the distinct feeling it *will* happen, much sooner than we realise," he prophesied, sensing the forestman would have a significant role to play in the fight against the empire. Standing not a few spears away, Thelosious was full of questions, wondering as the king did, if there *was* a deeper meaning in all of this.

"I sense we shall, my king; but his unforthcoming nature could prove to be a *particularly* significant obstacle," he observed, but Alectorious was quite unperturbed.

"We must give him a chance, Thelosious. These Catharians are a most guarded lot - it has always been their way. We share the same enemy, remember; it will only be a matter of suns before the forest people recognise this and inevitably we have no choice but to work together." Thelosious was unable to argue with his leader's observations. For the pragmatic Jalectrious, there were far more pressing concerns at hand. Stepping forward, he made his views plainly heard.

"My great king, in as much as I share your interest in this Sandros character and what he might offer our cause, I am deeply concerned about this talk of Gomercian invasion. The safety of our nation is of paramount importance and as such, I frankly question the wisdom of continuing into the mountains. Perhaps it *would* be better to return to Eternity. You heard the fallen soldier, Alectorious: it might only be a matter of suns! We stopped them at Dragon's Pass, sure, but they were always going to return - and in far greater numbers than ever before. I truly fear the full force of the Gomercian army will soon march upon the gates of our nation," he reasoned, before pointing in direction of the eternal city. Even Thelosious was showing signs of worry as the group of knights pondered, such was the imminent nature of the threat. The king was sympathetic to his companion's fears but was confident the path they now tread would serve Eternity's highest good. He peered off into the forests as if in search of inspiration before responding in a reassuring tone.

"My loyal knights: as king of Eternity, I have a tremendous responsibility to my nation, people *and* this known world of ours. As such, I must ensure *all* avenues in this quest to defeat the empire are pursued, no matter how unreasonable they may at first seem. Know that Eternity is in the hands of our most trusted fellow knights, and some of the greatest strategists ever to have graced these lands. I can assure you, she has nothing to fear in our absence," the king resolutely promised, raising his palms for emphasis. It eased the thoughts of Thelosious and Gavastros but Jalectrious remained wholly unconvinced.

"I fear that when the people become aware of your absence they might begin to lose hope - even faith in the kingship. In such suns of crises, the populace can be ever so fickle - you know this only too well, Alectorious," he boldly remarked, but the king was unmoved.

"When the people hear their king and his knights are on the most noble of quests, all of that will change, my dear companion. Eternians hold their history, mythology and legends in the highest regard, for it inspires a sense of belief beyond compare. When they know it is Reiactus we seek, their deepest passions will be ignited."

"It would be unwise to turn back now, Jalectrious; not when we are so close to our dream. We *must* finish what we have begun, for the gods have summoned us!" Thelosious enthused, as the king did not hesitate to add his thoughts.

"Trust in The Great Spirit, Jalectrious; for it is watching over and protecting us, as always it has. At Dragon's Pass our prayers were answered, just as they were this sun as we stared down the jaws of defeat. And so they shall be again," he promised, as he looked out longingly to the sweeping alpine forests.

"Very well, Alectorious - as you wish," Jalectrious finally conceded, before shifting focus back to the forestmen. "What of this… Sandros and the Catharians, my lord, do we pursue them?" he asked. The king nodded promptly, with there being no question.

"We pursue them indeed - but with caution. They can be a timid, even insular people; however, I sense there is much they can offer us, and we them. This Sandros character could prove a powerful ally against Gomercia: he fights like none I have encountered," Alectorious answered, recalling in vivid detail the enigmatic forestman's sublime combat skills, imagining the difference he could make. Thelosious was becoming impatient, keen as were the others to return to the path on their noble quest in search of the dragon.

"Do we make now for Catharia, my king?" he inquisitively asked, looking out to where those mystical lands of the forest dweller were thought to be. The king was pensive for a moment but realised there was only one path left to follow.

"We do not. First, we continue our journey to the great Buvarious. If and when we find what we seek, we shall pursue the Catharians - agreed?" he asked, looking to his loyal band of knights. The response was unanimous. "AGREED!" they bellowed in unison.

The knights had been greatly impressed by how Alectorious had grown in confidence, decisiveness and resolve since the beginning of the journey. The punishing nature of their thus-far path had been very much the catalyst, but none could have imagined such a dramatic change. Alectorious himself had been astounded by how his outlook had transformed, having never imagined he would embark on such an ambitious venture.

The king, Jalectrious and Thelosious returned to their steeds, with much ground to cover before the setting of the suns. Gavastros and the Elite Guard were already mounted and ready for departure, with the prodigy especially keen to continue the adventure into uncharted lands. The king cast an instinctive glance to Jalectrious, whose shoulder had been badly damaged during the skirmish, effectively disabling use of his preferred arm.

"Jalectrious, I fear for your wound - you do yourself no favour by continuing - I think it best you return home," the king wisely advised. His second-in-command found it difficult to argue, having tried in vain to keep his nasty abrasion a secret.

"Indeed my king, it grows weaker by the moment - I shall only slow your progress," he admitted despondently, touching his shoulder in agony. The king nodded in agreement.

"Then so it shall be: two Elite Guardsmen will accompany you to Eternity. The remaining Gomercians will have dispersed by now so your passage should be unhindered."

"Very well, my king - should I order a relief force?" Jalectrious asked, realising many more Gomercians might be lurking in the forests, ready to strike.

"We will be too far into the mountains. However, if we have not returned seven suns from now, order a detachment of Elite Guard to follow this path until we are found."

"Very well, sire," Jalectrious nodded, agreeing it the wisest option. "I shall send word. And what of the council?" he queried, knowing they and the citizens would be deeply concerned as to his majesty's wellbeing.

"Tell them of all that has transpired, and that our return is imminent. Inform the people their king and his knights have embarked on the most noble of quests into the Buvarious Mountains in search of the great dragon, Reiactus," the king commanded, knowing without question at all they would rally behind him.

"Very well, my king, it shall be done," Jalectrious acknowledged. The king mounted his trusty steed, Sephalos, before turning to face the towering snow-capped peaks in the distance as Thelosious, Gavastros and Jalectrious did likewise to their respective paths. As Jalectrious departed, he bade a final farewell to his fellow knights.

"May the gods be with you, my companions!" he shouted. Yanking the reigns of his steed, Jalectrious launched himself dramatically along the forest path. The accompanying Elite Guardsmen followed, ensuring their superior officer was well protected.

"With you also, Jalectrious!" Alectorious bellowed, waving. "I only hope it is so," he then whispered, as he watched his companion gallop into the distance. Overhearing, Thelosious offered some words of comfort as he patted the king affectionately on the shoulder.

"They shall be watching over and protecting us *all,* my king - of that I am sure," he heartedly encouraged. Alectorious smiled as he, Thelosious, Gavastros and the remaining seven guardsmen continued towards the mystical Buvarious Mountains.

As the Eternians trotted along the path, the king began, for reasons quite unbeknownst think about his mother, who had passed in mysterious circumstances many eons ago. Although he had no memory of her, he thought often of the suns they might have spent together playing in the colourful meadows just northwest of Eternity as many other children and domesticated animals did. Suns of such innocence, bliss and perfection would they have been. Together they would play, swishing through the tall flowers as if the garden of the gods themselves, as the twin suns shone brightly in the crisp blue sky, and the snow-capped peaks towered like angels in the background. The king was a baby when she passed over, but Alectorious knew her as a woman of deep compassion, close to nature and the heart of The Great Spirit. In light of recent events, he wondered what she would make of the world now and indeed, Eternity in its current predicament and furthermore, how she might resolve the startling predicament they now found themselves in. He was certain she would choose the path of peace and love, as most women the king believed would. Indeed, such menacing creatures that man could be. It made him wonder what a world it would be if it were ruled by the feminine kind; one of peace, fairness and equality he imagined, shackling the seemingly insatiable desire for these childish games known as war that men craved to indulge in at no end. What truly was the reason for this? In his view, the pursuit of battle only ever resulted in pain, suffering and torment for all. She would have made a fine queen in his stead, he resolutely believed; but alas, in his imagination only these thoughts would remain. Perhaps many eons from now, men and women would live as *true equals* - and the balance between these feminine and masculine aspects above all other things was the key to peace and stability in the world. He felt that unfortunately, he would not live long enough to see that sun. The king began to wonder if his mother was now watching over him and if one sun, they would be reunited when he finally passed into the realms of afterlife and he hoped, the fields of Athepoesia. Deep down, he knew it *would be so*.

While thinking of such things, the king wondered about Sephia and how she might be faring in what felt now like a world away in distant the City of Eternity. He wondered what she might be doing at this moment; perhaps a peaceful walk in the temple gardens or around the city markets; or perhaps she was, similar to the king's childhood, taking a stroll through the meadows picking all manner of colourful wildflowers. Or maybe she was secretly practising her acting skills and pursuing that dream she had so sadly abandoned. Alectorious truly hoped she had a change of heart on this and indeed, all those who had ever given up on their dreams. He missed Sephia dearly but knew he had a duty to fulfil for his nation, and indeed, people of all the known world. With those peaceful thoughts in mind, the king returned his attention to the path, with a feeling that if something was *truly destined to be*, The Great Spirit would allow it to be so.

FOLLOWING ONE'S HEART

The Eternians continued along the path still very much enthused, pondering as they went, the many thrilling possibilities awaiting them in far-off mystical lands. Before long, the towering snowy peaks of the Buvarious Mountains became acutely visible from above the treeline of the pristine alpine forest as the sense of anticipation reached greater heights than ever; for before long, they would be high in that heavenly abode, living a life they could have only ever dreamed of but moons ago.

Despite the Eternians' desire for adventure, the tumultuous events of earlier in the sun were playing heavily on their collective conscious, with mixed feelings about the recent skirmish in the forests. For Gavastros, it had been a heroic victory against the odds, befitting the Age of Heroes themselves. Having survived two battles with his Gomercian foes, the prodigious swordsman had grown ever more in confidence as a knight. He certainly felt quite the accomplished warrior and was now ready for any test the gods could muster. Thelosious was simply relieved to have survived such an attack, knowing that without the forestmen's divine intervention, they might now be wandering the fields of Athepothesia. The king meanwhile was excited by what lay ahead but did in part question the rationale of what had already been a perilous and costly journey. Some of the finest Elite Guardsman had lost their lives: irreplaceable warriors to whom he owed an incredible debt. Feeling the need to share his thoughts, Alectorious pulled up alongside his companion of many eons.

"I feel very much for those who fell this sun, Thelosious," he admitted, pausing briefly to reflect. "I wonder if their sacrifice will not have been in vain." Thelosious looked thoughtfully to the treetops, realising the sensitive nature of the topic.

"It would be natural for one to question in light of all that has transpired; but remember, Alectorious, this is the path you chose and it was with *all of your heart.* Your men believe in you, my king, and gladly sacrifice themselves for our cause. You made the *right* decision, despite any lingering doubts you may hold," Thelosious encouraged, sympathetic to his companion's dejected plight. Alectorious displayed a hint of a smile, relieved there were others who shared his point of view.

"Thank you, Thelosious, it means the known world to me; truly it does. Deep down, I *do* believe it was the wisest decision to embark on this noble quest, but I wonder if we shall ever find what we seek, and if the great dragon awaits upon mountains high; only the gods could possibly know," he candidly admitted, as Thelosious was thoughtful.

"Know that I have *always* believed in The Great Prophecy, as you, my king, and that we were meant to travel this path laid out before us. Perhaps it *was* for reasons unbeknownst we were guided to the mountains, and that Reiactus and the forestmen are only a small part of the whole story. Whatever is to be, I am sure the sacrifice will have been worthwhile in the end," he asserted, lifting his eyes to meet his companion's.

"If only we knew for certain, Thelosious; such things have always baffled me so. I imagine only the passing suns will reveal the answer." Thelosious was much in agreement.

"Indeed: we can only follow our path and hope the gods guide us to a better place."

"Quite, Thelosious, quite," the king agreed, as Thelosious expanded on his thoughts.

"The most important thing is that in deciding this path, you followed the calling of your heart: it is something that few kings *have ever* had the courage to do," he inspired. Alectorious' eyes brightened as he felt a sense of upliftment.

"I do so with the most humble of intentions, Thelosious. While I admit that following such a path is not easy, it is far from impossible. I often wonder why others are not compelled to do the same," he pondered, despite the many sacrifices made on their thus-far gallant quest. Thelosious was thoughtful, wondering much the same as his companion.

"Only the gods could know the answer to this: perhaps those souls have a deep-seated fear of failure, ridicule or even success and the enormous expectations it might bring."

"A feeling I can well relate to, Thelosious; I only wish I can live up to the hopes and expectations of our people," the king admitted, realising the consequences of not doing so.

"Have not fear or doubt, my king, I believe you *will* fulfill your destiny, for it is with the noblest virtue you are blessed; cherish and honour that *always*," he offered. The king nodded in appreciation as they continued along the forest path.

"You know, Thelosious, it seems in *this* world, when one follows the path of their heart they suffer dearly as a consequence; it is something that I shall never understand about this great mystery that is life," he keenly observed, as Thelosious appeared reflective.

"Perhaps those who follow their heart will suffer, for *some* suns; but I believe it will be those souls who will *ultimately* be victorious," he said with utmost conviction.

"A profound thought, Thelosious, and one I shall not ever forget," the king commended, having not expected such an empathetic response. Alectorious continued. "For certain; I would rather live following my heart's path than ignore the calling of the gods, only to discover even the smallest chance to make a difference had passed me by - and live the rest of my eons wondering what might have been," he professed. Thelosious was greatly taken by his king's insights, realising how much the journey had impacted his companion.

"Those are words of great kings, Alectorious - and it is as *that* I believe you will *always be* remembered." The king looked to his loyal knight without a word being said, smiling in a way as if to say thank you. With that, the two Eternians went silent as they continued along the tranquil forest path.

It was late noon and the group of noble adventurers had advanced ever further on their quest to the Buvarious Mountains. The light of the twin suns was breaking sharply through the crisp autumn leaves into the eyes of the mounted warriors as if to warn that night would soon fall. There was still a great distance to travel before the Eternians reached their destination and they would require a safe place for the night to recover from their exertions.

The plan was to depart in the morrow as soon as the suns rose, with the aim of reaching the foot of the mountains by the moment they set again. These were unfamiliar paths to the king and his knights, and there was no knowing what perils they might encounter. The forests, by contrast, were relatively peaceful: most known species of animals and birds posed little threat to the Eternians' safety and that of their horses. In any case, the king was confident the forest god Caledoesious would keep a watchful eye while they slumbered.

"Alectorious, the suns will set before long; we had best find a place to rest for the night," Thelosious advised, motioning to the setting stars in the spectacular purple-blue skies. The king looked up, acknowledging the moment for respite had finally come.

"Very well Thelosious - at your order," he agreed, motioning for his companion to take charge. Alectorious gazed up to the suns shining through the trees, marveling at the striking range of hues they cast upon the forest floor. It was quite a sight, beguiling both the king and his men.

"Eternians, ready for camp!" Thelosious duly ordered, raising his hand commandingly to the air. The Elite Guard drew a collective sigh of relief, for the sun's events had already proven most testing for their otherwise rugged spirits. They all looked very much forward to a peaceful sleep in nature in the fresh mountain air, under the innumerable stars soon to be shining in the skies, high above. They frantically searched for a suitable spot to camp, knowing it would not be long before night fell. The king had to ensure it was well protected from any passersby, but near enough the path to resume their journey quickly in the morn. Their prayers were soon answered as Thelosious discovered a prime spot, waving to his companions from the forest.

"My king, over here - on the other side of those rocks!" he exclaimed, pointing to a collection of large boulders on the east side of the path. Located on top of a small hill, he was adamant the gods had guided him. The king was in total agreement with his companion.

"Well done, Thelosious: we will be well-shielded there." Looking at stones with intrigue, a dramatic sense of déjà vu washed over the king. This place felt so familiar, yet he had never in his life set foot here before - perhaps it was memory from another life. Gavastros was equally enthused as he galloped ahead to investigate. Jumping from his hefty steed, he ran up the natural path to the top of the hill before disappearing behind the collection of mysterious oval-shaped rocks. He quickly reappeared, shouting back in the affirmative.

"It is perfect, my king! There is a clearing behind with enough space for everyone, including the horses. We can make a campfire too - and the rocks will prevent anyone from hearing us!" he promised, knowing it was ideal. Alectorious had his reservations but there was little other choice: night would soon be upon them and they desperately needed to rest.

"Eternians - prepare for camp!" the king authoritatively commanded. Each of the travellers dismounted his steed before negotiating the narrow path with steeds in tow, concentrating fully on the task at hand. As they reached the top, the men secured their horses to the trees before unloading their equipment to the soft forest floor, covered as it was by innumerable leaves from the recent autumn fall. Unpacking their belongings, the Eternians set up camp for the night in their cosy surroundings. For the king, this was a dream come true; for never had he slept in the depths of the forests, as one with the natural world. His companions were simply looking forward to a well-earned rest from the sun's tumultuous events, knowing their adventures had only just begun.

UNDER THE STARS

Before long night had fallen and a myriad of constellations were sweeping gently across the mysterious night sky, sparkling like precious diamonds in a bounty of great treasure. The Eternian adventurers had gathered around a cosy little campfire, warming themselves from the cool mountain air now permeating the encircling forests. Alectorious sat nearby his companions resting against an ancient tree-trunk, which had most probably fallen from a thunderstorm many moons ago. He looked up peacefully into the towering trees as birds intermittently chirped and branches swayed in the gentle breeze, in complete wonderment of this magnificent creation. Alectorious felt an inexplicable, mystical presence that he had never before: a deep sense of connection with the forests and natural world. Indeed, it was the first instance he had dormed under the stars in the depths of the wilderness, and it was sure to be an experience he would for long cherish.

Alectorious looked beyond to the innumerable lights drifting across the night sky, marveling as they shone through the swaying branches of the trees. He began to wonder what these shining beacons *truly were* and what manner of force could have created such phenomena. It was as if it the gods themselves watching over this courageous band of souls, protecting their each and every step into uncharted lands. Alectorious was thoughtful as he gazed silently into this endless sea of shining light, contemplating all that had transpired and would soon be on this most grandiose of quests. He wondered where this adventure was ultimately destined to lead, and if it would be all he had ever hoped and dreamed.

Alectorious reflected on the Catharian forestman named Sandros who had shown such bravery in the face of adversity: the king had never in all his suns witnessed a soul so passionately come to the defence of a people and indeed, nation not his own. It was also strange that one with seemingly nothing to gain would risk so much. Perhaps it *was* as

Sandros intimated due to the Gomercian threat to Catharia that he had helped the Eternians, but Alectorious sensed there was a lot more to it than this - there *must* have been another reason Sandros had come to their aid - and the king was wholly determined to find out what it was. There was certainly a distinct familiarity about the forestman: what that was he could not say, but was sure the answer to this and many other questions would soon come to light.

Alectorious sat directly in front of the enchanting campfire, relaxing with his loyal companions Thelosious and Gavastros, contemplating as often he did the many ancient Eternian legends and mythologies. He began to gravitate towards thoughts of Reiactus and The Great Prophecy, wondering if it would as the scrolls had foretold *finally* come to fruition. Alectorious made himself comfortable for the night on the soft forest floor as he quietly reflected, shifting his eyes from the stars to the mysterious flames as they flickered tellingly in their own shadows. The king then looked to his nearby companion, who also seemed to be in rather a pensive mood. Thelosious had always been partial to a bit of philosophical discussion, being one of the few souls Alectorious could communicate with on such existential matters.

"I wonder, Thelosious; what are your thoughts on Reiactus' legend?" he casually queried, shifting to rest his head against the soft bark of a tree towering into the night sky. It was something they had spoken of on many occasions before but the king simply could not resist, such was his fascination with the subject. Alectorious looked up and out through the branches reaching high above their heads before fixing his gaze hypnotically on the stars. It was a fine evening, and one that he would not forget for countless eons. As Gavastros in the background slowly drifted into the ethers, Thelosious suitably spoke his mind.

"Many a sun have I contemplated the history of our great nation, my king; its legends and mythology. As you, I have often wondered what it all means and the deeper message the gods and The Great Spirit wish to impart," he pondered, equally curious as to the *true* meaning of such things. The king sat up, focusing his thoughts.

"Then, what do you believe they are saying to us, Thelosious; our revered myths and legends?" he curiously asked. Thelosious placed one hand upon his chin, pausing in contemplation. In the other hand he caressed a small pebble he had found on the forest floor.

"Well, more than anything else, I believe they exist to give us hope and inspiration in suns of great uncertainty. Myths and legends tell of mystical forces that exist within this world and beyond, guiding Eternity and her people to a better place: one that knows not the suffering, hardship and pain we now so burden," he contemplatively replied. The king was engrossed as his eyes sparkled in the light of the countless stars above.

"And The Prophecy that speaks of Reiactus' return - do you *truly* believe in it?" he probed, knowing it a topic which both were most passionate about.

"In spite of what many souls and even logic might say to the contrary, I in fact do. There is no question in *my* mind that Reiactus did once grace these lands. However, it would be unimaginable that he still lives, even if he *did* survive the first Eternian war. As we already know, it is impossible for any physical being to live much beyond eighty eons - one hundred at a stretch - and Reiactus passed some seven hundred eons ago! Yet, there is something inexplicable that makes me believe he *may yet still* live, somewhere up there in those enigmatic peaks," Thelosious emotively answered, motioning through the thick forests in direction of the mountains. The king remained silent as he sensed his companion had yet more to say. Thelosious continued, folding his arms as he gazed into the enchanting stars.

"It has led me to conclude one of two things, Alectorious: that his kind have the ability to live for an exceptionally long period *or* that he simply disappeared to another place, for all these eons since the Age of Heroes." It was indeed a most controversial thought, but he and the king had long known each other to think outside the realms of normality.

"Do you mean to suggest Reiactus travelled *beyond* the known world?" the Eternian leader asked, wondering of all the exciting possibilities. Thelosious was thoughtful as he peered into the innumerable constellations in the starry skies, as if searching for an answer.

"Beyond, yes, but not in the sense you might think. You know, many of our scholars believe when Reiactus passed, he ascended to the stellar heavens. For countless suns I contemplated this idea before finally concluding that the heavens are in fact like another world - a place quite similar to our own but of a much lighter density, where beings such as Reiactus live - even travel to and from at will. If *this* were to prove true, it might help explain his long absence." Thelosious and the king intuitively looked above, wondering which shining beacons might be the blue dragons'. Alectorious had long been fascinated by the concept of other worlds and that there might be several, very similar to their own, somewhere out there in *that* endless ocean of light. As he wrapped himself tightly in his warm blanket, Alectorious could not imagine anything more exciting than to travel there. He silently contemplated how that might possibly be done.

"A truly fascinating insight, Thelosious: perhaps it *was* a world of dragons Reiactus had travelled to after the first Eternian war - one where many other of his kind still exist. It could well be from where has just returned, and now awaits us in the great Buvarious. The possibilities are quite simply limitless," the king reasoned, utterly immersed in this captivating discussion. Thelosious was equally engrossed, contemplating the possibilities as he continued to gaze into the starry night skies.

"If it *is* that he travels between these two worlds, it would pose many questions, Alectorious. For example, where is this world to which he ventures and *how* does he travel there?" Both Thelosious and the king found it difficult to address this most perplexing of questions as it was well beyond their current understanding of the known universe.

The nature of existence was something that greatly fascinated both; the king had always had a deep desire to expand his level of conscious understanding of all things.

"That is *exactly* what I wish to know, Thelosious, but I imagine these things can only be answered by the gods themselves, or Reiactus, if we are *ever* to find him," he sighed. Alectorious picked up a branch and threw it into the forest in frustration, resigning himself to the fact he might never know the answers to all that he wished. There was so much yet to be explained about the universe that he wondered if these things would *ever* be known. Alectorious leaned back against the rough bark of the tree, peering longingly into the countless luminescent beings of light above.

Gavastros had been lying quietly on the forest floor pretending to be asleep, but had in fact been secretly listening to every word of his companions' conversation. The prodigy was baffled by what he believed to be nothing more than utter gibberish. As always, he chose the perfect moment to join the discussion: whether it by chance or design was another matter entirely. Sitting up from his resting place, Gavastros turned to face his startled companions with a familiarly smug expression.

"Here you two old philosophers are on this fine starry evening, talking of dragon worlds, other realities and all that cannot see with one's own two eyes. I shall tell you, my dear companions, if *I* could travel to another world, it would be where Eternity ruled supreme and *I* had a kingdom *all* to myself. Oh - and I should not forget to mention, many a fair maiden to satisfy my most *noble* of needs," he cheekily proclaimed, before folding his arms with a mischievous grin. The king and Thelosious were both rather unimpressed by their companion's tactless intrusion and were all too often frustrated by his shallow, overly convivial outlook on life. Thelosious was particularly vexed, as he believed the younger knight had always been unwilling to look beyond his limited perception of reality. He thought

Gavastros might have had a change of heart since the visit to Delphoesia but realised it would take considerably longer for the prodigy's experiences in the ancient abode to truly sink in.

"Gavastros, do you ever think of anything *other than* satisfying your carnal desires; have you *ever* thought of what might lie beyond the known world and that, there might be so much more than what we already know? Or did it also perhaps even occur that you might just be a tiny, insignificant pebble in the infinite pond of The Great Spirit's creation?" Thelosious scolded. His ephemeral companion was rather dismissive, superciliously waving his hand in response. Gavastros had little interest in such things, tilting his head back and rolling his eyes as if being lectured like a child.

"My dear old companion," he sarcastically jibed, putting his arm round Thelosious briefly before standing, theatrically waving his hand. "I see the known world *exactly* as it is presented before me - each and every challenge, obstacle and opportunity the gods bestow upon my path. I live each sun to overcome their tests, satisfy that which I desire *and* to perform my duty as a Knight of Eternity to my noble king and nation. *If* and when that other world you speak of *does* collide with mine, I shall deal with it, exactly as I see fit. Until such a sun, I shall live life as I see it - with my own two eyes and one foot in front of the other." As Gavastros finished, he placed his hands on his hips and looked proudly into the treetops. The king was listening silently in the background, rather bemused by his companions' striking verbal bout. Secretly urging them to continue, he was fascinated by this tense clash of quite contrasting personalities.

"If that is your wish, Gavastros, do as you please and continue living that way; but know that one sun, you will experience something that will open your eyes to a *much greater* reality, and you will remember what I said this night," Thelosious retorted, now increasingly frustrated. He stood to face Gavastros eye to eye as tension increased.

"I shall do just that, Thelosious! And know that one sun *I* will be remembered as the greatest swordsman that *ever* lived!" he claimed, with more than just a hint of hubris.

"Well that just about sums you up, Gavastros - it really does," Thelosious retorted, shaking his head in disgust. Gavastros was quite unrepentant, replying in kind.

"Well if it helps us to victory over the empire, what harm is there in that?"

"And if it does not?" Thelosious hissed. The king at that point decided it best to intervene, sensing things were beginning to escalate out of control. He dramatically stood, moving between the two clashing knights.

"Gavastros, Thelosious, listen to me this instant!" he demanded crossly. The king raised his hands as Thelosious and Gavastros intensely eyed each other off. "Long have we been firm companions - all three of us - let our differences in opinion *never* fall in the way of the bonds that we share. Gavastros - no one doubts your commitment to your nation, loyalty to companions *or* bravery on the field - you are a great knight and warrior of Eternity. I understand it is difficult for you, as it is *many* Eternians to see beyond what is in front of their eyes - Thelosious and I are no exception to this. If you could just *some suns* take a moment to think outside the boundaries of your life and consider what might be out there, it could *not only* open your eyes to a whole new set of possibilities, it might also help us in our struggle against the empire," the king encouraged, trying his best to reason with his stubborn companion. Gavastros was left momentarily speechless, having not expected such profundity.

"By the gods, Alectorious - I never knew you had such wise words within you!" the prodigy replied, unsure how to react. Gavastros hesitated for a moment, scratching his head.

"Well, if thinking outside my reality will help defeat the Gomercians *and* make life better for my fellow Eternians, I might well have to consider such things more often!" As a large grin appeared on his face, Alectorious was suspicious Gavastros had somewhat ulterior motives for this newfound wisdom. Although relatively harmless, the king wished not to think of what they might be. Even for his relatively young age, Gavastros was seen by many as immature. However, by virtue of his immense courage and commitment to his nation, the king had been *convinced* Gavastros was fully deserving of his place amongst the revered "Knights of Eternity". At this stage in life, the prodigy seemed more preoccupied with fair maidens and fighting than he was other worlds and realities, but he was still young and should be allowed to be so; for he would undoubtedly grow into a great knight and leader of men. It was known Jalectrious had been in many ways similar to Gavastros in his younger eons and had matured into a fine example of chivalry and Eternian knighthood.

Thelosious had already conceded the futility of this particular conflict in light of the long path ahead. The cerebral one gathered his things for a good night's rest under the stars, ready to drift away peacefully into Astrala - or land of dreams as it was also known.

"I could not have said it better, my king. Many adventures await us in the morrow; I think it best we now retire," he tactfully suggested. Alectorious resolutely concurred.

"I must agree, Thelosious. Ensure we have two Elite Guards on every watch: there is no knowing *what* lies in these forests." the fretted, concerned the enemy was still close by.

"As you wish Sire," Thelosious answered, before motioning to the relevant guardsmen. As Gavastros stomped out the remains of the campfire, Thelosious and the king readied for their night's dorm. Alectorious was soon resting upon the forest floor taking one long last look out through the towering trees into the spectacle of light above. The king gazed longingly into the stars, pondering if the gods would be watching over them this night, and of the exciting adventures the morrow might bring. Alectorious rested his head gently on his improvised pillow and closed his weary eyes, drifting quietly into the mysterious realms of Astrala. The Eternians were soon fast asleep under the evergreen trees and watchful eyes of the gods, sailing into the limitless world of dreams.

DREAMING OF DRAGONS

The king lay peacefully upon the soft forest floor under the many constellations shining brightly in the enigmatic skies above. An unworldly presence now infused this sacred wooded land, which was a place quite unlike anywhere else in the known world. The forests had come alive in the mysteriousness of the night; the ancient trees were alive with a mystical energy force as they swayed gently in the wind and their branches reached out as if to protect the sleeping adventurers, far on the sacred ground below. Throughout the peaceful woodland, many birds and animals intermittently made their presence known; owls in the branches whispered their words of wisdom into the cool night air while their smaller feathered counterparts enjoyed the curious star-lit skies, chirping away as if it a bright, late noon sun. On the tranquil forest floor, numerous small animals scurried to and fro while squirrels could be heard high above, grappling and scratching the thick-barked trees. Jumping from branch to branch, it was as if these tiny creatures were on their own little adventurous quest of the night, searching for something that was quite unknown.

Alectorious began to drift into a deep sleep as the mystical land of dreams supplanted that which he had believed to be reality, and the two worlds merged into one. The king began to dream a dream unlike any he had had before, as he was suddenly transported to a mysterious land of indescribable beauty and wonder - it was unparalleled to anything he had ever seen - a place so similar, yet different to the world he now knew. It was lighter, brighter and with a peaceful tranquility that words could not even begin to describe: an age many eons from now and a great distance from *this* world.

Alectorious suddenly found himself riding on the back of a great blue dragon, gliding over dramatic valleys, rivers and mountains of this mystical abode, marveling at its remarkable natural formations. The dragon had a bright scaly coat not unlike Reiactus' might have been, although the creature's identity was quite uncertain. Together, king and dragon flew over a range of magnificent snowcapped peaks and mystical forests, then through dramatic tree-lined valleys with gently flowing rivers and streams, passing all manner of animals, people and natural phenomena. Dramatic mountaintop castles could be seen throughout the land, which was brightened by a spectacular sky of indescribable colours and hues. After what seemed a great distance, the dragon dramatically flew up and rested upon the highest peak in the lands, where they could view this mysterious world in all its glorious magnificence. The king climbed from the dragon onto the mountaintop's rugged surface, looking in amazement to all that he saw, wondering if this could be the reality Eternians had been prophesised to rise up to. It was of such indescribable beauty that he wished never to leave, feeling that here he could spend the rest of his suns. As the king absorbed the tranquility of this enchanting abode, the dragon placed his mighty claw on the Eternian's shoulder as if to capture his attention. In that moment, Alectorious was dramatically spirited back into the waking world.

"My great king - it is the moment to rise, for we have a long sun ahead!" whispered a distinctly familiar voice. Alectorious awoke with a jolt, lamenting the premature end to his slumber. It was none other than Thelosious, gently shaking the king's shoulder.

"By Promaestious, you could not have chosen a worse moment - I saw it, Thelosious - in my dreams!" exclaimed a bleary-eyed Alectorious, shaking his head to properly awaken.

"Saw what, my king?" Thelosious asked with intrigue, wondering what his companion was jabbering on about. The king stood, feeling utterly invigorated.

"The world to where we are destined - oh, you should have seen it, Thelosious - truly beyond all words of description, it was!" Alectorious wistfully replied. His companion naturally wished to know more but realised there was yet much ground to cover this sun.

"I doubt you not, my king, and most certainly wish to hear all; but we must continue on to the mountains," he wisely insisted, knowing the path would be long and arduous.

"Very well," the king conceded, still greatly vexed his dream had come to a premature end. It was so typical, he thought; just as it had become interesting. Perhaps there was a reason for this, as there often was for these things, but he could not see it now. Dreams of such vividness were a rare occurrence for the king, and he certainly wished he could experience them more often, or at will, even. Alectorious wondered if *that* were at all possible and if so, the unimaginable places he might venture as he drifted through the endless realms of Astrala.

As the king hastily packed his belongings in readiness for departure, he reflected on his dream and its unbelievable clarity: in many ways it had been *more* real than the waking world. He also wondered how this had been possible, leading him to question what was *more real* - the waking or dream world. Perhaps the *dream* world was reality and the real world was but a dream - it was a most perplexing idea that could encourage eons of insightful enquiry amongst philosophers and scholars throughout the known world, he reflected. Alectorious thought that Reiacus, if they *ever* found him, might shed some light on this, and many other questions he had for countless eons sought answers. With that, the king turned his mind back reluctantly to the moment, more focused than ever on the path ahead.

THE JOURNEY ONWARDS

The king and his knights soon resumed the path to the great Buvarious Mountains, drawing ever nearer with every gallop upon their noble equines. A growing air of anticipation could be felt amongst the intrepid adventurers as they edged towards their cherished destination, which was now so close they could almost taste it in their very mouths. Alectorious was quite content with his decision to embark on this most gallant of quests, utterly convinced he had made the right decision in following the calling of his heart and that of The Great Spirit. He glanced evocatively to his men, seeing that bright glow of adventurous Eternian spirit that had for so many suns laid dormant: it was alive and well once again now, and would doubtlessly help deliver their nation to a glorious destiny.

Alectorious thought more of his dream from the previous night and the spellbinding place he believed they were destined, pondering if it had indeed been the Higher Worlds the ancient scrolls had spoken of. The king dearly yearned for this enchanting paradise but knew that before it could ever be realised, The Gomercian Empire had to be vanquished and peace restored to the known world, forevermore. Indeed, it was difficult to believe Eternians might soon be free of all those terrible things that had for long plagued these sacred lands.

In all the excitement of their journey, Alectorious had almost forgotten about his eloquent home: The City of Eternity. It seemed in some ways like a distant memory: like a faraway land in another life. Realising he had never been so far from his lofty castle abode, the king wondered what the citizens' reaction to his dramatic departure might have been. He knew that many would never understand the reasons and he would be branded as irresponsible and rash, following the dreams of deluded ancient romantics. There were many, however, that *would* see the deeper, more profound reason behind his quest, and most certainly be supportive of the king's outwardly at least, reckless actions. Plasos was certainly one with the ability to see beyond the limited five senses: despite initial objections, his mentor would surely have been more sympathetic had it not been in suns of such crisis. The king was nonetheless convinced he was following the divine guidance of The Great Spirit and that there *was* a higher purpose to his bold expedition. They had already found in the forestman Sandros one with the potential to affect tremendous change, and the king was certain there were others like him willing to join the Eternian cause. Indeed, following one's heart would often lead to acting in a way contrary to reason and logic - it may even bring about some degree of misfortune - but Alectorious knew that *ultimately*, souls who followed that inner calling were destined to take their place amongst the gods in The Higher Worlds. Realising his mind was beginning to drift away, the king shook his head profusely, bringing himself back into the moment. Alectorious looked around in bewilderment to the endless teeming forests, wondering where in the known world he now found himself.

"I say Rhoedas, where is that map?" the king asked, turning promptly to his navigator and expert tracker. A foremost expert on the mountainous regions of the northern known world, there was not a better man in whom Alectorious could place his trust. Thelosious looked to the king as both realised they would need to stop.

"Eternians, we break now!" he ordered. The unit of Elite Guardsmen came to a steady halt as the king, Thelosious and Gavastros huddled close together. Rhoedas approached as a somewhat nervous anticipation grew amongst the three companions: they had progressed well but there was yet far to travel. Rhoedas reached to the side of his horse, pulling out the ancient parchment from the worn brown satchel attached to his saddle. Unraveling it carefully, the precious edges were creased and colours faded from countless suns exposure to the elements. It was in rather decent condition despite its countless eons of use. The map was surprisingly detailed as the king keenly observed mountains, forests and rivers - even small settlements and long-lost, ancient ruins. Alectorious gazed dreamily at the Buvarious

Mountains which were marked in the north-eastern edges, wondering if they would ever see its great heights and if Reiactus awaited them in its majestic snow-capped peaks. Resting the weathered map carefully upon his horse, Rhoedas scanned the valleys, forests and mountains strewn across the ancient parchment, trying his best to locate their current position.

"It is difficult to pinpoint *precisely* where we are, my lord; this map was made many eons ago and is not *exactly* to scale," he sheepishly admitted, prompting a round of nervous reactions from his gathered superiors.

"Can you at least give us an approximation, Rhoedas?" enquired the king, anxiously biting his lip. He glanced briefly to Thelosious, who was in equal measure concerned.

"Using my best judgment, I would say we are somewhere along this path, *here*… between these two winding streams," Rhoedas intelligently deduced. Pointing to the long meandering, seemingly endless forested mountain path, Alectorious felt quite satisfied with the distance thus-far travelled. "…and are approaching this river… over *here*…" continued the navigator, pointing to a large body of water bisecting the mountain trail not far ahead.

"So, how far would that make us from the Buvarious?" the king questioned, excited, as the knights simultaneously turned to face Rhoedas.

"I would say, approximately one full sun's ride to the base of the mountains; the Prejosian caves, not half a sun more. As for ascending the peaks themselves; well, that could be any man's guess..." the tracker responded, as Thelosious' face lit up in anticipation.

"It will not be far, my companions; glory will soon be ours!" he vigorously proclaimed, already tasting the crisp mountain air in his lungs.

"To the roof of the known world!" Gavastros dreamily added, looking in the direction of the alluring icy peaks. The king was more cautious though, knowing the map had been forged many eons ago and was not an accurate representation of the surrounding lands.

"That river you mentioned, Rhoedas - are you sure it can be crossed? There appears to be a bridge but this is a very old map - it may no longer be safe - or could have disappeared completely!" he remarked with understandable concern, realising it might be their only way into the Buvarious. Rhoedas however was quite re-assuring.

"The bridges up here were built to last, my king; I am confident it *will* be crossable. Remember, the snows fall high now upon these mountain ranges; much of the river at higher altitudes will be frozen so it will not be as wide as usual. In the worst case scenario, we can rebuild the bridge; we have the manpower *and* the expertise," Rhoedas assured, as the king nodded in agreement. The Elite guard and hoplites were not only skilled warriors but well-versed in many arts; they were trained to be resourceful and react appropriately to any challenging situations that may arise, wherever in the known world they might be.

"Very well, Rhoedas - and the horses?" the king asked. "Even if the bridge *is* intact, I fear it may not take their weight," he added. Rhoedas appreciated his leader's concerns.

"We had best be cautious. We shall most certainly have to dismount upon crossing, but it *should* hold. The mountains, when we reach them, could prove rather more troublesome with such large animals..." the tracker conceded. Alectorious narrowed his eyes suspiciously.

"Troublesome - could you somewhat elaborate?" he asked with considerable unease. Thelosious and Gavastros were meanwhile peering at the ancient map, realising there were many more obstacles than at first realised. Rhoedas answered somewhat apprehensively.

"I am not sure how to explain this Sire, other than that we shall only be able to go so far with the horses - there simply is *no way* we could take them up into the Buvarious - the mountain paths are far too dangerous, with sheer drops from the edge. The elements are also *extremely* unpredictable: rain, wind and snow could fall upon us at any instant," he explained, raising the ire of the king, who was incredulous.

"We cannot just abandon the horses to the mercy of the mountains!" he scathingly recoiled. Thelosious and Gavastros were equally flabbergasted, expressing as such.

"Surely there must be *somewhere* we can safely leave our steeds whilst we scale the Buvarious!" Thelosious insisted, with Gavastros also quick to voice his concerns.

"My king, we cannot leave our horses behind - they will surely perish in the elements!" he agreed in trepidation. The prodigy looked to Rhoedas equally disbelieving, unable to fathom it had even been suggested. Horses were held in the highest esteem by Eternians - even considered equals by some. Rhoedas frantically scanned the map for a suitable location, hoping to appease his visibly upset superiors.

"Well, there is a valley here, my king - it is not *entirely* clear but appears to be surrounded by thick alpine forests, and there is a river running right through it! The horses would be well sheltered - there will be plenty of shrubs to feed on - and water to drink from the river. Under the circumstances, it would be our best option," the tracker admitted, as Thelosious quickly warmed to his idea.

"I am inclined to agree, Alectorious," he remarked, with a telling nod.

"We can build temporary shelters, of that I am sure, and leave a unit of Elite Guardsmen behind to protect the horses while we ascend the Buvarious. The Gomercians would not venture that far - the animals will surely be safe in the valley," Rhoedas added, knowing how much the king cherished his fine steed, Sephalos. Alectorious peeled his eyes from the map, casting them skyward in frustration. All was not proceeding as he had envisaged but on reflection, realised there were always going to be obstacles such as this. Despite these setbacks, the Eternians were still well on the way to realising their dream; and the king was not about to turn back now after all they had been through.

"Very well, it will be done: we make for the valley and set up camp in the forest. In the morrow, we ascend the great Buvarious," the king concluded. Alectorious seized the old map from his navigator, scanning the countless towering peaks and deep valleys. "At this point *here* we leave the horses. Gavastros, Thelosious and Rhoedas; you will accompany myself and three Elite Guardsmen into the mountains. The rest will remain behind with the animals," he ordered, pointing on the map to where the mountains dramatically shot up from the river valley.

"How about the return, my king?" asked the prodigy. If we are to journey the same way, the Gomercians might await us - and in much greater numbers!"

"A fine point, Gavastros," conceded the king, turning again to his tracker.

"Rhoedas; is there any way back to Eternity apart from the path we took?" he asked, searching the ancient map for possible routes. Thelosious also looked, noticing the faint outline of a path running almost parallel to that which they now walked.

"How about this one, my king - it is rather faded but clearly marked," he suggested.

"Indeed; why did we not use it in the first place, Rhoedas?" asked the king in bewilderment, with it having seemed a far more reasonable proposition.

"Well my lord, I could not have been sure if those paths still existed - if they do, no-one to our knowledge has ever travelled them - at least any Eternian. Furthermore, there could be numerous bandit tribes roaming those parts. It is also the lands of the forest dweller, thus deemed unsafe for travel." The king was greatly frustrated with his tracker, in light of their recent experiences with the Catharian forestmen.

"Yet, it is the men of the forests who just helped save our lives, Rhoedas!" he uncharacteristically fumed. Rhoedas hung his head, apologetic for his lack of judgment.

"I could have never foreseen what would befall us, my lord." Thelosious was quick to defend the innocent tracker, knowing they were circumstances well beyond his control.

"What is done, is done, Alectorious; neither Rhoedas, I, nor any other of us could have envisaged what was to transpire. For all we know, it might have been even more perilous, had we taken the other path. The most important thing is that we are alive and safe, on the path to the Buvarious: our destiny." Alectorious bowed head, politely conceding to his follower.

"I do apologise, Rhoedas, truly I do; you could have never foreseen it," he admitted, as the tracker nodded in acceptance. "Well, we shall return to Eternity upon *that* path. When our quest complete and the gods will it, we will meet once again, our forest companions," the king added, hoping that would include the elusive Sandros. Thelosious could feel his regal companion's frustrations, doing what he could to console him as they readied for departure.

"They say, my king; that one should never walk upon paths once trodden. Perhaps for some reason, it was meant to be - and that we *will* encounter the forestmen, when the moment right," he encouraged. The king looked to Thelosious with a mischievously warm smile.

"I am counting on it." With that, the king handed the map to Rhoedas for safe keeping before signalling for Thelosious to assume command. Although officially the Eternian leader, it was a duty that did not always come naturally to the king. Alectorious preferred to delegate responsibility whenever possible; not only to lighten the burden on his *own* shoulders, but to ensure all his knights were capable of leading whenever the need arose. Thelosious was content with the responsibility, issuing orders as if the king himself.

"Eternians: single file and not a word spoken!" he commanded. The remaining group of Elite Guardsmen mounted their horses, which all neighed furiously as they started back along the path. "We may not have seen the last of the Gomercians, my companions, and must be ready for any eventuality!" the cerebral knight cautioned, knowing the enemy might lurk around any corner. The Eternians continued on the mystical tree-lined path to the great Buvarious Mountains with a feeling that all would be well - and the gods would be with them every step of the way.

As the Eternians rode closer to the mountains, Alectorious was awe-inspired by the astonishing natural beauty that blessed his eyes this sun. It *truly was* the land of the gods described by his mentor, Plasos; with enchanted forests, crystal-clear streams and countless species of exotic animals to be seen at every turn. Indeed, it was something he could have only imagined in his most vivid of dreams. The higher the Eternians rose, the more dramatic the scenery became - the endless snow-capped mountain peaks piercing the heavens, with countless spectacular waterfalls streaming from their rocky pinnacles into peacefully flowing rivers and streams, far below. It was all the beauty one could imagine but a suns ride from Eternity, which seemed like another world now - a far-off land in another life, indeed.

Soon, the path began to whiten with a scattering of mountain snows, as the king began to feel an overpowering sense of freshness throughout his body and soul. It was a stunningly beautiful sight to behold, and one he would never forget for the remainder of his eons.

THE BRIDGE OF LEGENDS

Alectorious delved into increasingly peaceful thoughts as the Eternians travelled further along the tranquil forested path, making ever greater strides towards their cherished dream. They were now so close; with this very fact reflected in the collective inner knowing of an imminent discovery of spectacular proportions. It encouraged the Eternians to press on, for before they knew it, the bold adventurers would come face to face with the towering Buvarious Mountains, in all their magnificent glory.

As Alectorious rode upon his fine steed, Sephalos, the cool, crisp mountain air and peaceful forests had a magical effect upon the young king; his conscious awareness of all things had risen to a level not yet experienced in his life thus far, allowing him to perceive things he could have never before. He felt his spirit mysteriously connecting to a much higher and profound level of understanding, transcending the reality to which he had hitherto become so accustomed. All barriers and divisions seemed to disappear as he felt an inseparable connectedness with all living things; it was as if that connection had *always* been there, but simply forgotten over the eons, living as he had been in the known world of Causians. The passage of the suns also seemed different - one seeming as though it were two and their journey like many moons, indeed. *Everything* was different: it was something he simply could not find the words to describe. The king no longer had any sense of fear as he sensed the constant presence of otherworldly beings watching over, protecting and guiding himself and his companions on this epic mountain adventure.

Alectorious wondered if his men also felt these things but decided for the moment at least to keep the matter to himself. The king saw his place in the world so very differently now: he could perceive the interconnectedness of all things in the vastness of The Great Spirit's creation and the deeper purpose each and every soul was here to serve for the ultimate betterment of all. He had come to realise that, while the empire's actions directly contravened the fundamental laws of the universe, it was ironically, the Gomercians who had galvanised the king and his men to look within and walk the path they now did. It had compelled them to uncover that inner strength needed to rise up against the most incredible of odds, testing their resilience and every last fibre of their mortal being.

Despite his status as king of a powerful nation-state, Alectorious in many ways felt so minute and insignificant; certainly in comparison to the vastness of all creation. He was in awe of all that had been forged by the hand of The Great Spirit; something he was certainly far more aware of deep in the forests. It was most especially the case when Alectorious gazed out into the night sky and saw a myriad of stars and constellations shining back upon him; as if the eyes of the gods themselves were watching over and protecting, waiting for him to return home. The king would often look up in wonderment to those shining beacons of light, spellbound by their endless possibilities. He believed, as did many other thinkers, that each of those stellar bodies were suns as their own, supporting worlds where countless other, perhaps similar civilisations existed. Eternians all knew of course their world revolved around the twin suns once each eon but they were unsure exactly as to what their world was and how many others of its kind existed. Extensive research had led scholars to conclude it was in fact an enormous sphere: smaller but similar in nature to the twin suns. If *that* were the case, the area Eternity and the other six city states took up was a very small part of the *whole* world.

Imagine all the civilizations that were yet to be discovered, Alectorious dreamily thought: the possibilities were simply staggering. He dearly wished to travel beyond to those places of great myth and legend, to know once and for all what lay out there. There was a deep superstition of the lands uncharted amongst Eternians, for it was believed that countless dangers lay in wait: from gigantic monsters to the extremes of nature's wrath, ready to block any attempt to venture out-with the known world. This, coupled with the rather inconvenient matter of war with the Gomercian Empire meant the king had been unable to fulfil his lifelong ambition of travelling beyond his native land.

Alectorious cast his thoughts back to the stars and the idea they might in fact be other suns, each supporting their *own* spherical world: it truly was mind boggling to think. With their current level of technology and understanding, it was very difficult to substantiate these outlandish ideas, but it would be utterly ridiculous for one to think *there would not be* other intelligent civilisations somewhere out there in the universe. The Great Spirit would surely not have gone to the trouble of creating all those countless stars for the sole purpose of one minute civilisation to look upon them in wonder each night, as the king often did. Perhaps in many thousands of eons henceforth, travel to one of these stellar island bodies would somehow be possible. How exactly he was quite unsure, but was certain it *would* be so. It was certainly a tremendously exciting thought. Alectorious was saddened he would never have the opportunity to fulfil this far-flung dream but was adamant that, many eons from now, Eternians *would* travel to that endless sea of stars, high in the night sky above.

In contrast to these rather inexplicable feelings of insignificance, Alectorious had been feeling a heightened sense of empowerment. The king had achieved things he could have only dreamed of just moons previously by reaching into his deepest reserves of strength and courage to follow his heart's *true calling*. By defying a council of many wise souls, he had followed this inner guidance to these uncharted lands and chased his dream of finding the great blue dragon. There was no promise of success, but Alectorious was determined to see his epic quest through to the very end. The king was finally, after his twenty-eight eons, walking the path he had always dreamed, convinced it would best serve his nation and indeed, greater known world. He was quietly confident he *would* achieve all he had set out to: find the great Reiactus, form an alliance with the Catharians *and* defeat his arch nemesis, Nerosis and the Gomercian Empire, once and for all.

Alectorious was ever more excited by the possibilities ahead, in particular what the known world might be like *without* the tyrannical empire. He dreamed of a place where all were free to live as they pleased - to move between city, nation and town - to speak one's mind and the *truth* without fear of persecution or imprisonment. It would be a place where *all* were able to pursue their heart's truest desire without worry of judgement or condemnation - a world where one could venture deep into the forests and mountains and connect freely with the spirits of all existence. What a splendid place that would be - exactly as in the Higher Worlds, the king dreamily thought - was that *truly* to where Eternians were destined? It was so exciting to think they could be so close to a place where all could live in peace, without want or need of anything at all. Alectorious soon brought his mind back to the moment, wondering if they might encounter more souls that would join the Eternian struggle against the empire. Much had been written of the mysterious peoples living beyond the known world - the edge of which they were now rapidly approaching. Alectorious would soon discover if all that had been written was true, and that his prayers for divine assistance would be answered…

"ALECTORIOUS - WATCH OUT!!!" screamed Gavastros at the top of his lungs, abruptly interrupting the king's thoughts. Daydreaming had seized Alectorious' concentration from the moment with almost fatal consequences, as the path had dramatically narrowed as it turned into the steep hills. It was a most welcome interruption, for the speed of the king's horse would surely have spirited him over the edge. Alectorious reacted quickly, pulling hard on the reins of his steed before coming to a dramatic halt. The others did likewise as the king drew several breaths of relief before turning to fittingly thank his companion.

"That is I believe, one more I owe you, Gavastros," he said, gasping. The prodigy saw the humour in this, squinting his dark brown eyes.

"I shall overlook *that* occasion my king - but the next…" he jovially replied, as both managed a playful chuckle. The Elite Guardsmen were altogether more concerned as Quintos approached the slightly shaken king.

"Are you alright, Sire?" he asked, but Alectorious was quick to allay any fears.

"Yes, thank you, Quintos, perfectly; I allowed my mind to wander for but a moment - shall we continue?" he asked, pointing to the bend in the path ahead. Without a word said, the knights and Elite Guard nodded as the king again took the lead. They cautiously approached the perilously tight turn, with curiosity mounting as to what they might discover on the other side. The expert tracker, Rhoedos issued a gentle warning in concern for his leader's safety.

"Tread carefully, my king; we know not what lies beyond; it could very well be…" he began, but was unable to finish his sentence. The king was incredulous as he turned round the bend, reacting as if struck by a thousand bolts of lightning from the heavens above.

"By the Gods!" he exclaimed in beguilement. Before them, an ancient stone bridge reached out from one end of a divide in the path to the other. Eliciting memories of countless myths and legends, it was exactly as the ancient map had depicted and much as Alectorious had imagined. Behind the bridge, a spectacular waterfall hissed and sprayed as endless streams of crystalline water poured down from a preceding mountain river, with the residue forming shifting clouds of vapour in a scene reminiscent of a mythical tale in the books of Eternian heroes. Beckoning his followers, the king rode ahead. "Come, my companions, I think we can cross it!" he exclaimed, with eyes focused on the stone construction as the others followed. The Eternians negotiated the perilous turn with great caution, careful not to ride too close to the edge, from where there was a near vertical drop to immeasurable depths.

Once safely past, they pulled up to the side of the path still some way from the bridge. From what the king could gather, the structure was of very ancient origins; possibly from a tribe of peoples long lost to these parts. Arching across a deep, seemingly bottomless gorge, the rough stones of the bridge had weathered storms of many eons, and footsteps of a thousand souls upon their indelible surface. The giant waterfall tumbling but a few spears behind the walkway churned out wall-upon-wall of the purest liquid one could imagine into the rivers and streams, far below. It would have most certainly originated from high in the Buvarious Mountains: *truly* the nectar of the gods. Alectorious was spellbound as he gazed in awe, wondering what manner of abode he now found himself in.

"I could have never in all my suns imagined such magnificence," he tellingly remarked as his companions moved closer with an equal sense of awe.

"Nor I, my king," agreed Thelosious, with the cerebral knight likewise astonished by these remarkable wonders of creation. The king was captivated by the contrasting image of falling waters and the bridge, unmoved as it was in many eons. It was quite a sight: the creations of man and The Great Spirit before their very eyes, standing together as one. As the observant Alectorious looked closer, he noticed peculiar wooden railings stretching from one end of the bridge to the other. It seemed this ancient construction might have been used in suns not long past; but by whom was the question upon his inquisitive lips.

"Come now, let us move closer!" the king encouraged, so enchanted was he. The Eternians proceeded to an area just to the foot of the bridge, which was somewhat wider than the path itself - not more than two spears. The king and his knights dismounted their steeds and walked closer for inspection as the Elite guardsmen waited nearby. Alectorious,

Gavastros and Thelosious approached the edge of the bridge, careful not to lose their footing on its slippery wet surface. They peered at the perfectly intact stony structure, then to the tumbling cascade of transparent essence streaming ever so evocatively behind. All were in wonderment, silent as they absorbed the beauty of their surroundings. It was a most unusual sensation; as if the water spirits themselves were flowing throughout their bodies, cleansing the very depths of their souls.

"It is certainly rather larger than I had envisaged," Thelosious admitted, as he admired the unique design of the stone arch. "The map had indicated but a small footbridge over a winding river; quite a pleasant surprise, I must admit!" he gleefully added, with eyes cast to the bridge, then to the walls of water thundering behind, completely mesmerised.

"It is that, indeed," the king agreed, feeling the strength of the gushing waters reverberate throughout his body. It was something quite indescribable - as if he were looking into the very heart of creation itself. Alectorious took several deep breaths as he gazed enchanted into the waterfall, absorbing this great natural power. Gavastros was equally moved as he shook his head in disbelief.

"I am quite lost for words, my king - a beauty unlike any I have ever witnessed," he tellingly remarked. Thelosious by contrast sensed a distinct familiarity about the place.

"It feels as though I have been here before…" he said, before suddenly realising. "By the gods - this might well be it!" he excited, before shifting his eyes left then right.

"Be what, Thelosious?" the king asked, mystified, unable to pull his gaze from the perfectly clear blue falling waters.

"I think I read of it once in "The Book of Eternian Heroes and Myths" - an ancient text written several hundred eons ago by a wise old sage named Socrasious. It spoke of a place fitting *exactly* this description, referring to it as "The Bridge of Legends": a gateway into uncharted lands and the first of many steps into The Unknown. It is said only those of purest intentions may cross, and those unworthy shall be cast into the bottomless abyss," Thelosious acutely explained. The king was perplexed, for it was the first he had heard of it.

"Most interesting, indeed; the danger is obvious but there must have been more to it than what he had written. Perhaps Socrasious was trying to deter people from venturing further into the mountains and discovering their many secrets."

"Yes; something *someone* wished to hide…" Thelosious acknowledged. The king pondered the mysterious bridge; the creators of which were now long forgotten to history.

"I am sure we will discover soon enough," he concluded, excited by what might lie beyond the short expanse of stone. Gavastros had been closely inspecting the curious arch, unaware of his companion's conversation from the noise of cascading waters.

"My lord; the railings on the bridge are not more than a score of eons old!" he exclaimed abruptly. The king moved in for a closer look, greatly intrigued.

"Yes, I had noticed before; most unusual," he replied, running his hand across the slightly weathered wood. Thelosious followed Alectorious as he considered the permutations.

"There must be tribes inhabiting the area; perhaps even hostile," he worried, likewise sliding his hands across the unusually smooth wooden railings. The king felt a sense of apprehension as he looked to the forests on the other side, wondering what might lay in wait. Thelosious was also uneasy but knew it was the only way forward.

"Be that as it may, my king, we have no choice but to cross if we are to make it to the Buvarious Mountains." Alectorious was unable to argue as he focused on the other side of the plunging watery crevice.

"There is no question of that, my companion - and cross we shall," he said, as Gavastros displayed his typically confident exuberance.

"And we *will* be ready for any who dare block our path!"

"That we shall, my companion," the king assured, still concerned about the safety of crossing. "I do question the strength of this stone - will it hold the horses? It has weathered many eons of nature's wrath," he fretted, but Thelosious was quick to allay any fears

"It should be, if we take them slowly in single file. Judging by its sturdy construction, the bridge was most certainly built with animals in mind." the cerebral one concluded.

"I shall be first to cross!" Gavastros insisted, but Alectorious was quick to stop him; if only because it presented the perfect chance to prove *his own* mettle.

"No - let it be I," he bravely proclaimed. Thelosious quickly rebuked his king's rash reaction, knowing any manner of threats might await them on the other side.

"Alectorious, please - allow one of the guardsmen to cross in your stead - your life cannot be risked! As a loyal knight of the Eternian realm, it is my duty to ensure no harm befalls you," he insisted, but the king protested, having tired of being told what to do.

"I shall do no such thing, Thelosious - it would not be prudent!" he said, wholly determined to prove his valour. "I am king of Eternity *and* your leader. As such, it is my regal duty to take these first steps into uncharted lands. I have a legacy to uphold, and from this symbolic moment on, I shall lead my nation to a much brighter world." Thelosious conceded with a humble nod, unable to argue with his brave companion's words. The king often felt he lived in the shadow of his knights, protected from danger at every waking moment. Alectorious had been hitherto unable to *truly* stamp his authority on the kingship: now he would prove once and for all he was a true knight and *the* leader of Eternity.

"Alectorious!" cried Thelosious, as the king readied to cross the ancient stone bridge. "Be careful, my king." Alectorious simply smiled back. Thelosious had seen great change in his companion: he was *finally* reclaiming the power within he had for so many suns denied. It was not only that which was rightfully bestowed upon Alectorious as king, but his *own* life's path. Alectorious no longer allowed the expectations of others to affect his decisions and refused to wait for the hand of fate to rescue him, grasping every opportunity to effect positive change. There was no question or doubt that recent experiences had changed Alectorious in many ways: he had *twice* been victorious on the field of battle and now led his loyal followers into uncharted lands where few had ever dared venture. The king himself could sense a profound shift - a spiritual awakening occurring from deep within - his spirit growing with every passing sun. Soon, all the world would change for the better - of this he was certain. Meanwhile, Alectorious had his attention firmly focused on the task at hand as he issued the necessary orders before crossing.

"*When* I make it over, follow in single file," he commanded, before turning slowly to face the narrow stone bridge. Thelosious concurred with a nod before passing the order onto the Elite Guard. Holding his noble Sephalos tightly by the reigns, Alectorious the 2nd of Eternity slowly but surely made his way across the mysterious bridge into uncharted lands. Some seven to ten spears in length, it was an ancient relic built in an era and by a peoples long forgotten to the chronicles of history. Alectorious thought of where they had disappeared to and how many since had crossed, wondering if any fortunate souls had made it as far as the great Buvarious; perhaps they had, but decided never to return.

Step by step the king proceeded on as the magnificent waterfall thundered into the deep gorge to a raging river far below: a drop surely no man could survive. Reaching halfway, he paused, relieved to have encountered no danger thus far. The king moved forward with one hand on the hilt of his sword, ever wary of threats. Such bridges were said to be inhabited by the most terrifying troll-like creatures that would devour you in the blink of an eye. All these fears and superstitions quickly dissipated as before he knew it, he reached the other side safely with horse in tow. Alectorious stopped and took a sigh of relief, thankful no misfortune had befallen him. His sense of peace was short-lived as suddenly a giant, heavily-armed man emerged from the nearby forest, blocking the king's advance. With a long dark beard and some one and a half spears in height, the mountain man was an intimidating sight to behold. Startled, the knights and Elite Guard quickly armed themselves, with Gavastros instinctively readying to charge across.

"Alectorious!!!" he screamed, but the king was quick to stop him.

"Wait, Gavastros - the bridge cannot take you all!" he cautioned, raising his hand.

"He is right; we had better do as he says," Thelosious duly advised, sensing that all would be well. The cerebral knight was now second in command after Jalectrious' departure and proving a worthy deputy. "Nonetheless, we keep our swords at the ready. If something happens, *then* we risk crossing," Thelosious added. Alectorious meanwhile kept his cool, sensing the man meant no harm.

"It is alright, his weapon is not drawn - I shall handle it!" he steadfastly assured, having carefully analysed the large brute. The king trusted his intuition: if the man had had hostile intent, his weapon would already be drawn and ready for combat.

"Who goes there? Why dost thou come to these here lands?" demanded the strangely-clad man in an equally odd, unrecognisable accent. His towering frame lunged over the king, with arms neatly folded and feet spaced wide apart. While in awe of this hefty character, Alectorious sensed he was relatively harmless, responding in an amicable fashion.

"Why my good fellow, I am King Alectorious the 2nd of Eternity; I merely seek passage with my brave knights into these lands uncharted, to our destination of the great Buvarious Mountains. If you would only be so kind as to allow, we shall trouble you no more," he graciously expressed, bowing his head as a sign of respect. The man seemed rather unphased by his regal guest, probing Alectorious further.

"And what might be the reason for thy journey, king?" curiously demanded the large figure, whose arms and legs were comparable to tree trunks. The Eternian king hesitated, momentarily questioning if he should impart their *true* purpose. He finally decided it best, sensing that despite the man's rather rough exterior, he was a benign and virtuous soul.

"We wish travel to the Buvarious Mountains in search of the great dragon, Reiactus - I have word he has returned to these lands," the king explained, quite unsure of the reaction. The man was surprised by his answer, having heard no talk of such an occurrence.

"Well really, king; is that a fact?" he rhetorically questioned. "Very interesting indeed," he added, rubbing the rough stubble on his chin as he quietened his tone. The large man's curiosity had been clearly awakened as he probed. "And why *exactly* wouldst thou seek the great dragon?" he asked, in a tone suggesting he *might* know something of Reiactus' whereabouts. The king remained calm, answering his questions honestly and directly.

"I seek his wise council and guidance on the best course of action for my nation - and The Great Spirit willing, his help." The big man somewhat relaxed, placing his right foot upon a large boulder before resting his forearm upon his hefty thigh.

"And what would it be that so threatens thy nation, knight?" he enquired in an inquisitive but quieter and rather concerned tone, as Alectorious began to sense the man was more companion now than foe. Gavastros and Thelosious were meanwhile looking on curiously from the other side, unable to decipher the nature of the conversation as the king answered the brooding giant's question.

"The known world has been engulfed by a tyrannical empire that has swept throughout the lands without mercy or remorse, plundering countless treasures and riches at will. My nation of Eternity is all that stands between them and total conquest of the known world. It may not end there, even - they might venture here also, to *your* sacred lands," he added, hoping this would be enough to convince the man to allow them safe passage.

"Well, quite unaware of this, was I. Indeed, it is a noble and virtuous path thou walk, knight and as such, I shall suffer thee to pass - but first, thou must pay thy fare," he demanded, much to the astonishment of the Eternian. He was momentarily lost for words, having never in all his suns been treated in such a fashion. Alectorious was furthermore surprised by the man's unawareness of the empire and the *very* real threat they posed.

"I am The King of Eternity - and shall do no such thing! You do not own these lands, nor do you have the right to tax them!" Alectorious insisted, shocked that he was by these ludicrous demands. The hulking man abruptly retorted, further infuriating his majesty.

"Thou are a king and should be respected as such, but thou are not king of *these* lands - and shall pay passage akin to any other! Thou are no longer in Eternity; these are "Dragon's lands" or "No-man's land" as some of us prefer to call it!"

"This is tantamount to extortion, if I may be so bold!" he stubbornly argued, unable to fathom what he was hearing. The man was quite unrelenting in his lofty demands.

"Thou tax thy citizens as we do those who wish to cross this bridge: thou *must* pay!" he insisted, displaying a surprisingly witty turn of intelligence. The king still refused to give in, looking to his companions on the other side of the tumbling, hissing waterfall.

"I shall have you know the finest soldiers in the entire known world await on the other side of that bridge: I shall *not* be threatened in such a way!" he protested, uncharacteristically losing his cool. The hulking man merely smiled mischievously, obviously relishing the chance to lay down terms to The King of Eternity - and no less.

"And I, king, hast not more than thirty of my *finest* warriors waiting not far fro here, each and every one of they, very much bigger and stronger than thy knights. The choice of course is thine - but I *do* believe the odds are stacked rather against thee!" replied the large brute with a chuckle, knowing the king would inevitably submit to his demands. Alectorious could simply not believe he was being talked to in this way as he struggled for a response. "Who are you people and for whom do you work?" he demanded, as if trying to change the subject. The man was rather bemused, taking his foot from the large rock to resume his previous stance.

"Why, thou do not recognise us? Surprised be I of thus! We are none other than... hmm... I shall wait til thee pay before I consider knowing thee of that. This much I shall impart thee - we work, worthy king Alectorious, for none other than ourselves - Oh, and that fellow up there thou might otherwise know as… The Great Spirit!" he replied, pointing up to the bright blue skies. He hoped the king's curiosity would encourage him to yield, firmly believing it was wrong to favour one by virtue only of his title, riches or birth. The king knew he would eventually have to give in to the man's incessant demands, knowing that even the Elite Guard would struggle against such massive beings. It was nonetheless a most curious thing, as Alectorious had never heard about any souls inhabiting these parts. Such was the extent to which Eternity had lost contact with the outside world; there were surely many more surprises in store.

It was possible these giants had at some point migrated from The Great Unknown: the lands said to exist beyond the Buvarious Mountains. Or maybe they had always been here living in isolation, far from the injustices of the known world. It was certainly very curious that the giant still used vocabulary from Middle Eternian. Whatever the case, they might one sun prove to be powerful allies and should be accorded all due respect. The king finally came to the realisation the man wished for nothing more than a small payment and perhaps to be treated as an equal, as all people in truth were. It was a humbling experience for Alectorious but a lesson duly learned. He allowed his nerves to cool and took a few breaths before finally and perhaps a little grudgingly, offering his willingness to negotiate. There was no way he could hope to overpower this individual and his companions lying in wait.

"Very well; just how much is it that you ask?" Alectorious enquired, as the side of the giant's mouth curled up in a wry smile. The big man rubbed his mighty hands together, knowing he had won his little game with the Eternian king. On the other side of the bridge, the knights and Elite Guard were becoming increasingly agitated: they were unable to hear anything at all over the thundering waterfall. The man was blunt as he stated his demands.

"Eight pieces of gold and thou shall pass," he said, as Alectorious froze in shock. He possessed nowhere near that sum, having not expected need of gold in such a remote place.

"*Eight* pieces! Why, I have not two pieces to give!" the flabbergasted king protested. The man looked disappointed, stroking his chin, knowing the king spoke the truth.

"Then surely thou or thy men hast something else of value?" insisted the giant, surveying the king and his knights for valuables. "Oh my, that dagger thou hold is particularly nice," he remarked, glancing to the elegantly crafted weapon attached to the king's belt. Alectorious greatly valued his sidearm but realised it was only a material object and quite easily replaced. He really had little choice, finally conceding to the man's demands.

"Very well," the king sighed. "The dagger it is," he added with great aversion. Ever so reluctantly, the king removed the beautifully decorated weapon and handed it over to the beaming brute. Although a treasured possession, it was not *even* close to the value a potential alliance might have. The man took the dagger appreciatively from Alectorious' hands and held it to the bright rays of the suns. Smiling, he knew he had struck a *fine* bargain indeed.

"King of Eternity and thy noble knights - thee may pass!" he gleefully announced. The giant stepped politely to one side, waving the king and his men on. Alectorious turned to his knights and Elite Guard, beckoning them over the bridge.

"It is alright - you can cross now!" he shouted, trying to be heard over the incessant roar of cascading waters. Gavastros and Thelosious looked at one another rather baffled, unable to comprehend what was going on.

"Whatever was all that about?" questioned a bemused Gavastros, scratching his head.

"I have no idea, but we shall find out soon enough - come, my companion - let us make haste!" Thelosious encouraged, making for the edge of the bridge. He signalled for the Elite Guard to follow, warning them to keep their eyes peeled. The giant man walked away from the bridge to the edge of the woods, where several other of his kind awaited. Similar in size and heavily armed, the king was greatly relieved he had negotiated. As Alectorious mounted his steed, he shouted to the retreating stranger before it was too late.

"Wait - you have yet to tell me from what tribe you hail!" he asked, still unintroduced despite their lengthy conversation.

"Why, free and worthy king, we been none other than Prejosians: some men of lesser intelligence wish us be known simply as cave men," he quipped, unafraid of a bit of self-deprecation. Alectorious was incredulous as his eyes dramatically widened.

"Prejosians?" he gasped, cocking his head forward before removing his helmet.

"Well aye, as we hast *always* been," the man replied, bemused by the king's reaction.

"You mean you live in *the* caves of Prejosia?" Alectorious further inquired. Believing it was to where Reiactus had been taken, he was unable to contain his excitement.

"Well, we do inhabit caves in the region known as Prejosia, far up in the mountains, as well as these here local forests. There are countless interpretations of the word "Prejosia" mind, so I am unsure if it be the caves to which *thou* refer. There been many of such kind, so it could, or could not be..." admitted the Prejosian, doubtfully shrugging his broad shoulders.

"Hmm..." responded the king; somewhat confused. "Well, if you *are* Prejosians as you say, then surely you must know *something* about Reiactus and if he has returned as was prophesised..." The knights and Elite Guard were all gathered round listening intently.

"In honest truth, worthy king, we Prejosians do not trouble ourselves much with myths and legends as do thee Eternians. We been a simple folk - we enjoy our lives in the caves, forests and mountains, close to the elements and The Great Spirit. We very much value each other's company; whether it be around a campfire or walk in the vastness of nature. We wish not bother ourselves with the affairs of those who seek power and control over others," explained the giant but gentle Prejosian. Alectorious felt a profound sense of admiration for this virtuous soul, expressing his feelings as such.

"I greatly respect the life path you have chosen to walk - even envy it in many ways. However, I cannot change the path upon which I now find myself, and must do all that I can to bring about the end of imperial rule of the known world. If Reiactus is here and you know of his whereabouts, I would be greatly indebted if you were to impart this knowledge," the king pleaded, bowing slightly. The man wished to help but, frustrated, was unable to do so.

"Truth be told, it is long since any Prejosian to my knowledge hast encountered the worthy Reiactus. Tell thee I would if I knew, but it is... that I do not. All I can say to thee is thus - the path upon which thou now tread, king - follow it until thou can go no further, and thou will be taken to where thou must be. This is all I can impart to thee for now," the Prejosian offered, motioning to the path winding up into the mountains. The king offered his gratitude, knowing without question he had found a firm new companion.

"I appreciate your efforts to assist and honesty with which you speak - I sense you Prejosians to be a wise, virtuous people - I duly salute you for this." The man replied in kind.

"What thou see in me is but a reflection of thyself, worthy king of Eternity," assured the Prejosian with a meaningful smile. In that very moment, a gust of wind swept up dramatically from the foot of the gorge as if in recognition of these two wise souls. The king was very much concerned for the safety of his new mountain companions.

"Tell me Prejosian; what would you do if the Gomercians were to come thus far?" he asked. The giant was confidently dismissive of any such threat.

"That, they will never do, king. The Great Spirit protects these sacred lands upon which thou now walk, and the empire thou do not realise *well* knows this," he assured.

"I hope you are not mistaken, for the sake of us all. I shall bid you farewell, Prejosian, and will not ever forget," promised the king, preparing to move further up the path.

"My name is Prosious," replied the giant, with a hitherto unseen emotion in his eyes.

"Thank you, Prosious, and may The Great Spirit *always* be with your peoples," the king humbly offered. Alectorious had a new-found respect for these mysterious cave beings, whose only desire it seemed was to live in peace and harmony with their nature surroundings. In this world, not even a simple desire as this could seemingly be fulfilled.

"And The Great Spirit with *thee,* worthy Alectorious, King of Eternity," the noble Prejosian replied. With a respectful bow, he disappeared into the dense forest with his companions, perhaps never to be seen again.

The King, Thelosious, Gavastros and Elite Guard assembled, having taken their first steps into wild, uncharted lands. It was a place not trodden by Eternians in many eons and would require every bit of strength if they wished to reach those esteemed mountain peaks. Alectorious felt a dramatic shift in the air now they had finally crossed over and a pure, powerful presence permeating all that surrounded. He thought more of the Prejosians, wondering if they would encounter these simple yet benign souls again. In spite of his doubts, deep down, he knew it *would* be so. With that in mind, the king and his fellow Eternians mounted their steeds, heading ever further along the sacred path of their destiny.

INTO LANDS UNCHARTED

The Eternians continued their quest to the mystical Buvarious with zealous aplomb, knowing their elusive dream was finally within grasp. Despite all the uncertainties, they were enlivened by the innumerable possibilities for adventure and discovery that lay ahead. The king and his men had ventured further than any Eternian in living memory into lands untouched for many suns - and with each and every step, another page in their illustrious history books was being written. There was a pure, innocent energy now permeating their surroundings, through the thick forests and mountains high, deep into the fibre of every man's body and soul. The Eternians rode their steeds proudly into these majestic lands to where few had ever ventured and yet fewer ever returned: a place that had been held in great mystery and intrigue for countless eons. The allure of the Buvarious was simply too strong for any ambitious adventurer to resist, and Alectorious could only imagine the mysteries waiting in their mythical heights. The twin suns were now edging ever closer to the imposing icy mountain peaks that shimmered like bejeweled crowns in the dreamy blue skies. It would not be much longer, the king thought with captivated anticipation.

The path up to the mountains was beginning to narrow and before long, it became wide enough only for a single man and his horse to pass. On one side there was an almost vertical drop and on the other, a mixture of steep rock faces, small trees and various shrubs.

"Eternians, dismount!" the king ordered. "From here, we ride in single file: Rhoedas, take the lead," he commanded, turning to his expert tracker standing but paces away. Rhoedas understood this environment better than any in the group, with his countless suns spent in the northwestern mountains an indispensable asset to their chances of success. Also known as "Higher Lands", the mountains were a place demanding utmost respect from whoever was brave enough to venture here. Following Rhoedas, the Eternians proceeded in single file with steeds in tow, as close as was possible to the side of the path. They carefully negotiated the trail as it snaked round the side of the steep hill, with all very aware that one foot wrong could prove fatal. As they looked ahead to the narrow twisting path, a wave of trepidation swept throughout the group. Rhoedas kept his cool, turning to address his fellow Eternians.

"We must exercise the greatest of caution, my companions; for one false step could well be our undoing," he starkly warned. The men slowed their walk to an almost standstill in response, fearful they or their steeds might lapse in concentration for a moment too long. They truly had nothing to fear though, for Eternian horses were immensely intelligent creatures: highly trained and very aware of their surroundings, they had to cope with not only the rigours of long distance riding but the brutal intensity of battle. Trained from birth in the lands of Clydosia, the animals knew their duty as well as the knights did to king and country. Tightly gripping his reins, Rhoedas continued. "One step at a moment, my fellow Eternians, and we shall reach the end before long. Trust in your steeds - and they will in you," he assured, trying to ease the increasing tension he sensed amongst his companions. The king was supportive, expressing his total trust.

"Listen to Rhoedas, men - he knows well of what he speaks!" Alectorious encouraged, equally sensitive to the unease felt by all. The Eternians moved nervously along the precarious meandering path, with many secretly questioning the wisdom of taking such enormous risks. They managed to negotiate several twists and turns, staying as close as was possible to the side of the cliffs, careful not to look to the dramatic drop but a spear to the right. The horses it seemed were far more relaxed than the knights and Elite Guard, moving along as if it just another trot in the forests. Gavastros was particularly frightened, as an inexplicable sense of dread reverberated throughout his body and soul: he had so fearlessly flung himself into the perils of battle, yet found the idea of his life placed in the unpredictable hands of the nature gods utterly terrifying. At any given moment the path could collapse and his life swept away, forever into the abyss. What an inglorious way for it all to end, Gavastros thought in a fleeting moment of trepidation. His heart began to pound faster and hands tremble with fright; his now only wish was to stand on safe ground again. The mighty Gavastros: he had once thought himself invincible, now humbled by the natural world.

After several more harrowing twists and turns, the path began to widen, much to the relief of the Eternian travelers, whose nerves were incessantly beginning to shred. Gavastros was particularly relieved, collapsing to the ground as he reached the end. He took several deep breaths; thanking the gods above he was still alive. The king looked over, perplexed to see the prodigy in such a state. He approached his loyal knight with due concern.

"Gavastros; whatever troubles you, my companion?" he asked, as he knelt down on the rough stony path. As the prodigy answered, his voice began to tremble.

"Never in all my suns have I felt such fear; we were so close to the edge, my king: one wrong step and it all could have ended," he gasped. Alectorious tried to be reassuring.

"But it did *not* end, my companion; and we continue on through lands uncharted. To be certain, the gods watch over us; come, there is yet much to discover." Thelosious was equally encouraging, stepping forward to offer his thoughts.

"The worst is over, Gavastros; know that a great destiny awaits," he enthused, as his companion nodded reluctantly. The prodigal young knight returned to his feet still somewhat shaken, pausing and taking several deep breaths to regain his composure.

Before long, the Eternians were on their steeds once again, continuing their journey to the mystical Buvarious Mountains. As the path began to widen, it led the adventurers away from the cliff's edge closer to the forests before swerving right onto a wide rocky plateau. From there, a break in the tree line offered an awe-inspiring view of the entire known world.

The Eternians were collectively breathless as they approached, gazing out in amazement to the magnificent splendour before their eyes.

"Rhoedas, Halt, I say - we shall rest here!" the king ordered, raising his voice above the noise of trotting horses and strong winds sweeping up from The Great Plains.

"Very well, my king!" Rhoedas excited, as he signalled to the others. The king dismounted first, leading his trusted steed to a nearby pine tree before tying him firmly to one of its thick branches.

"You will be safe here, Sephalos; it will not be for long, I promise," he said, stroking the mane of his noble equine, which replied with a nod and animated stamping of hooves. Alectorious made his way swiftly to the rocky platform, hoping to catch a glimpse of his cherished city, far off in the distance. The others moved to quickly secure their horses, exuberantly following to likewise witness the stunning panoramic vista. The Eternians gathered not far from the edge of the cliff and gazed longingly out, silenced by the vast magnificence before them: they had never in all their eons born witness to such an incredible sight. Most of the known world was visible: from the sweeping plains and teeming forests to the seven city-states strewn throughout the lands. Their beloved Eternity was barely visible, with former allies Brasovia, Calgoria and Saphoeria seen equally afar. So small and insignificant thought the king, as he scanned the endless horizon.

"There she is, my companions - our beloved Eternity, in all her magnificent glory," he evoked. Alectorious focused on the spectacular blue and white castle towers gleaming in the light of the twin suns: truly beacons of hope for all the known world.

"It is difficult to believe we have made it thus-far, my king," Thelosious remarked, wondering if they would *ever* return. Alectorious was very much in agreement.

"It seems so small from here: almost like a painting in the knight's chamber," he gleefully admitted, observing the beauty of all that his eyes could see. Gavastros was equally taken, scanning for other recognisable landmarks across the sweeping plains as a gentle breeze blew across the Eternians' faces, as if in recognition of their presence.

"Over there to the west, my king, the colossus atop that small mountain: Brasovia, if I am not mistaken," he remarked, pointing to a fortified structure on a large volcanic rock.

"That it is, Gavastros; the most inconquerable city in the known world, some would have had you believe," Alectorious concurred. There was a feeling of longing in his voice, knowing capture of this illusive fortress-nation was key to freeing the people of these troubled lands. Thelosious noticed several other recognisable landmarks, marveling at how small they seemed: like pebbles scattered across a giant pond, indeed.

"There, further to the east, our old allies Saphoeria - to the west, Calgoria - and our great adversary, Gomercia, barely visible in the distance. Never have I seen our world like this: simply awe-inspiring," the cerebral one remarked. Scanning the stunning scenery, it was as if it had been created by the most talented artist in all the lands.

"Wait! Is that not Dragon's Pass? I thought it was *much bigger* than that!" exclaimed Gavastros, pointing dramatically in a south-easterly direction. "Hardly can I believe we fought *and* won a battle there," he somberly added, remembering the place he had almost met his end: here he now stood, looking down in defiance at what might have been his fate. To the east and west, right to the very south, teeming forests stretched out to the edges of rolling mountain ranges, which were *not quite* as high but almost as impressive as the great Buvarious, with their cragged, snowcapped icy peaks. Countless rivers reached out in all directions - the enchanting Glasovia flowed from the magnificent Buvarious Mountains, wrapping round the city of Eternity and out to their auld allies, Saphoeria. The Great Plains of Marathosia, which covered much of the known world, stretched far off into the distance, with the clear blue skies providing the perfect backdrop to this otherwise imperfect world.

"I wonder my king, will these lands will *ever* see peace?" Thelosious pointedly reflected, dreaming of a better world as he gazed out into the mesmerising vista.

"Only with our actions can we ever hope to answer that, Thelosious. The gods and Great Spirit know we mean well upon this world, and surely wish for the harmony of which you speak. We must continue to have faith and trust they will support us in our moments of greatest need, as they have already on this most noble of quests." The cerebral one was unable to argue as he nodded, continuing to contemplate.

Alectorious stood back, allowing his men to rest and absorb the majesty of all before them, in appreciation of the many hardships they had suffered and countless tests that were sure to come. The Eternians continued to look out to the vastness beyond as the wind blew gently across their eyes and the glimmer of the majestic suns cast a brilliant array of colours and hues across The Great Plains to the never-ending forests and mountains ranges stretching out in all directions. It was a sight unparalleled by anything they had ever witnessed, leaving an impression that would last for the rest of their eons. The king realised they had not much longer, encouraging his men to return to the mountain path.

"My fellow Eternians, in as much as I wish to admire this great beauty, we must continue: the suns are setting fast and we know not how far it is to the valley," he decreed, rallying for one final push. The Eternians withdrew aversely from the rocky plateau, returning to their horses and path to the mountains. Alectorious sensed something very special would soon be upon them: what that might be, he could but only wait and wonder...

VALLEY OF THE GODS

The path continued to wind up steadily through the forests towards the mystical Buvarious Mountains, widening the higher the band of noble travellers ventured. Their journey had been long and the Eternians would soon need to replenish their tiring bodies and souls, as well as find suitable shelter for the long night ahead. The king hoped it would be soon, for the mountain air would soon become bitterly cold and their lives placed in perilous danger *if* they were to be caught out in the open. It was fortunate Eternians were, in addition to fighting, trained to adapt to any environment imaginable, using all that nature provided to protect themselves from the merciless elements of nature gods: in these parts, namely freezing winds and heavy snowfalls that came with the much higher altitudes. Indeed, both the king and his steed were very much on their last reserves of strength. Several of the others were also suffering greatly from the tribulations of their thus-far arduous journey, with scars of battle still fresh upon their sprightly limbs. To some of the group, it seemed only a miracle could deliver them successfully to the Buvarious and home to Eternity. Alectorious however was confident his great dream *would* be realised.

The king's prayers were soon answered as the winding forest path soon opened out onto a wide grassy plateau, revealing a dramatic valley of the most breathtaking natural beauty. Every Eternian to a man was stunned into bewildered silence as they gazed at the divine magnificence before them - it was like some kind of hidden paradise - a place imaginable only in one's most fantastical of dreams. A wave of relief swept through the band of intrepid travellers knowing that *finally* they had reached safety.

The valley was covered in a lush, thick green grass, with a variety of multicoloured flowers growing throughout its fertile pastures. A number of exotic animal species including deer and squirrels roamed freely, oblivious to the arrival of these mysterious visitors - and a peaceful, crystal-clear river flowed gently down from slightly to the north-west. It was a truly idyllic setting, very much reminiscent of a place in the Eternian books of mythology. The path continued north from their position along the river before disappearing into the trees. The valley was populated on its edges by thick evergreen forest, with dramatic mountain peaks rising to the bright blue skies above, glistening like bejeweled crowns in the late-noon suns. Alectorious was utterly spellbound, struggling to articulate his feelings of amazement.

"By Aphroedisia; where in the known world have we found ourselves?" Drawing his horse to a halt, the king was in awe of his enchanting natural surroundings as he gazed along the gently flowing river, past the forests and up to the imposing snowy mountains towering what seemed like a heartbeat away. Marvelling at the imposing peaks, they emanated an aura quite unlike anything he had ever encountered; as though these alluring summits were a living, breathing being, beckoning, enticing the king and his men further into this ancient realm of wonder, mystery and intrigue. Alectorious had no question that he now looked upon the great Buvarious Mountains, in all their majestic glory. From Eternity they were spectacular, but from such close proximity there were not words to describe their captivating beauty. The Buvarious were every bit the enchanting sight described by Plasos - if only his old mentor could have been here to witness their divine magnificence.

"I think we might have reached Athepothesia, my king," gasped an equally beguiled Gavastros, referring to the place Eternians travelled upon their passing from this world; a heavenly abode of the most indescribable beauty and bliss where one could experience anything they desired. There, one would rest and contemplate their life before continuing on their soul's journey in the worlds of matter - or perhaps even beyond.

"You might not be mistaken at all, Gavastros," Alectorious resolutely agreed, lost for any other words of description as he shook his head in bewilderment.

"I could have only imagined such divine beauty," added Thelosious, with the Elite Guard equally enticed by the natural riches abounding the valley. As well as an impressive tapestry of flora, the Eternians observed several types of animal including deer, squirrels, wild cats, various species of coloured birds and even several wild horses, all existing together in perfect harmony. It was almost like a dream; much as a place in ancient mythological texts or great works of art. The king wondered if it were all truly real, thinking it might be some kind of illusion fashioned by the mountain god, Arturious. He also pondered why he had never been inspired to venture here before - perhaps he had merely been waiting for the right moment - one which had finally arrived. It all felt so familiar… as if he had been here before… perhaps in another life. Whatever these feelings of familiarity, Alectorious was so close he could feel it in his very bones - the excitement of achieving what he had for so long dreamed. He felt a deep sense of satisfaction, knowing that by following the calling of his heart he had been brought to this very moment and place. Looking to his companions, he encouraged them onward.

"Shall we continue?" Alectorious asked with meaningful intent, trotting ahead on his fine steed. The others needed no second invitation, enthusiastic as was their king to discover more of this majestic paradise. The Eternians continued along the tranquil riverside path, observing their spectacular alpine surroundings at they went. Alectorious spotted the ruins of a castle roughly halfway up to the east upon a small hill and further to the north, what appeared to be an ancient temple. This was most certainly the valley Plasos had travelled to in his younger eons as the king recalled conversations with his mentor. The castle was exactly as described, where Plasos had sheltered from the thunder, lightning and rain, all those eons ago.

"Amazing, truly something; never in all my suns could I have fathomed it," the king gasped, looking around in continued wonderment. The knights and Elite Guard seemed equally taken by this hypnotizing utopia as Thelosious fittingly remarked.

"My king, I do believe I once read about this place in "The Eternian Book of Heroes". I recognise the castle and temple further up. It must be what the heroes called "The Valley of the Gods"," he explained, pointing to the intriguing ancient structures.

"It would fit that description perfectly," the king agreed, gazing up the valley as Thelosious continued to divulge more of what he knew.

"It was written that before one travels into the great Buvarious they will encounter a valley of such captivating beauty they will wish never to leave. Many believe it an attempt, or test even by the gods to tempt people away before they venture further and discover the mountain's hidden secrets." The king nodded in recognition of this.

"I can see why; I could live here for the rest of my suns!" he remarked, with eyes gleaming like proverbial stars in the night sky. Now very much at ease with his new surroundings, Alectorious continued. "Truly amazing - befitting the gods themselves. What fascinates me more than anything is the castle ruin to the east and the temple further up. I wonder who could have possibly built them, all the way up here in the mountains and more significantly, for what purpose?" he pondered, pointing up to the brace of intriguing ruins.

"Only the gods could ever know," Thelosious concluded, shaking his head in bewilderment. Gavastros had been detached from the conversation busy scanning for danger, noticing a lone figure further up the valley crouched on his knees.

"Alectorious, someone by the river - he appears to be beckoning us!" the prodigy exclaimed. The king reacted with surprise as he looked up along the narrow river's edge.

"I had not noticed - it is as though he appeared from nowhere!" he flabbergasted. Thelosious concurred, seeing an opportunity to find out more about this mysterious abode.

"Nor I - he must have just emerged from the forests - in any case, he might be able to enlighten us about the castle and temple." The king could only concur with the cerebral one as the Eternians readied to trek up the river to meet the man.

"He appears to be unarmed but we approach with caution - he may not be alone."

"What of the horses, my king?" Gavastros asked.

"Let them go for now - they need water and rest," he wisely ordered, knowing their loyal steeds would not venture far from the plush green meadows. The horses were set free in accordance with the king's wishes, running out into the fields as content as could be.

Alectorious, his knights and the Elite Guard walked up the narrow path in direction of the man, who was busy refreshing himself in the crystal-clear waters of the river. Nearing his position, the king ordered the Elite Guard to remain as he, Gavastros and Thelosious moved in closer. Reaching the river's edge, the stranger seemed quite unperturbed by the Eternians' presence - almost as if he had been expecting their arrival. The curious character continued to splash his face with the icy-cool waters, turning as the king and his knights approached. The man's reaction took the travelers rather by surprise.

"Welcome, Eternians, if that is indeed who you are," he said, in an amiable but somewhat guarded tone. He stood to face the startled king, brushing the soil from his tired old knees. The man then coolly placed his hands on his hips as if to invite answer. The king was momentarily speechless before he was finally able to muster a response.

"That we are; I am King Alectorious the 2nd of Eternity and these here are my loyal knights and companions, Thelosious and Gavastros. It is a pleasure to make your acquaintance," the king offered, bowing graciously. Thelosious and Gavastros relaxed, sensing the man posed no serious threat - for now at least.

"As it is I," the stranger replied, turning to gaze at the magnificent peaks of the great Buvarious, then to the northern ranges continuing on from there, as if in search of fitting words of expression. The sound of silence fell suddenly upon the gathered men as the king tried to break the awkwardness. He looked around, reflecting on his beguiling surroundings.

"So this really is it - the Valley of the Gods. I had heard much of its beauty, but never in my wildest dreams imagined such a place - *truly* heavenly." Alectorious fittingly remarked, before removing his shining blue and gold helmet. The man could only concur.

"That it is, king. When I first came here oh… many suns ago now, I just couldn't bring myself to leave no matter how hard I tried to resist the desire to stay," he replied, proudly admiring the magical place he now appeared to call home. The Eternians were greatly curious as to what he was doing all the way up in this isolated river valley.

"May I boldly ask - how long *have* you been up here?" the king queried, intrigued, wishing not to pry too much as the man cast his mind back.

"Oh my, it's been many a sun… many, many indeed. One *does* tend to lose a sense of the passing eons, being way up here. It's like nowhere else in the world, if it could even be considered part of it at all… You think but a few eons have passed you by, then before you know it, your skin has wrinkled and hair turned grey!" he added with a light chuckle, brushing back a silvery mane behind his broad, once powerful shoulders.

"I know that feeling very well," agreed Alectorious, as the man looked thoughtful.

"When was that now…. hmm… I suppose it must have been since around the fall of Saphoeria, oh… whenever that was," he hastily concluded. Although reasonably pleasant and intelligent, the man appeared to have somewhat lost touch with reality. The fall of Saphoeria - that really was *many* eons ago, thought the king - what *has* he been doing up here all these eons? Alectorious had many questions for this mysterious character but decided not to be too forthright, knowing he would discover the answers in due course.

"Pardon my saying so, but is it possible you might hail from the forest lands of Catharia?" the king probed, having noticed a strikingly similar speech pattern to the forestmen he had encountered earlier in his adventure.

"Very perceptive of you, king - it is in fact those great lands that, long ago, I *did* hail from," he candidly admitted, sitting inconspicuously upon a nearby shapely boulder. "Please, relax with me for a while," he added, beckoning the king and his knights to be likewise seated. Alectorious, Thelosious and Gavastros sat comfortably on the soft grass close to the boulder as they listened to the sounds of the river trickling and flowing ever so serenely nearby. The mystery man continued unabated.

"Very few of us, Catharians that is, dared ever to venture this far into the mountains; why this is, I cannot say for all. Perhaps it was for fear of getting lost and never finding our way back; not *only* in a physical sense, but a spiritual one also." a look of perplexity appeared upon the king and Thelosious' faces. Realising this, the man continued to explain.

"You see, Catharians really are a deeply spiritual folk - close to nature and The Great Spirit - the purest connection to which they believe exists only in the forests, rivers, mountains and animals. They simply cannot bear to be away from their homeland for too long, believing they'll lose that ever-so sacred link with the all-that-is. I was one of the few willing to take that bold step out into the uncharted lands to see what lay beyond," he evocatively explained, while displaying a subtle hint of pride.

"I understand that feeling well - from here, Eternity seems like a world away - almost like another life now," the king admitted, as the mystery man smiled in understanding. Alectorious probed further. "Tell me, have you ever felt that loss of connection of which you speak?" The Catharian clasped his hands together in deep contemplation.

"In some ways, yes, I have; but for all I've ever lost, I made anew in this great valley. There are powerful forces up here that have opened my heart and mind to a *whole world* of possibilities. So powerful are they, it is said that hidden gateways to other worlds exist in these mountains. So I must say that for I, where one path has ended, another has presented itself. Some might say I sacrificed these connections but I feel it was *ultimately* for a much higher purpose and am content with my decision. No matter how much you love somewhere, king; it's never wise to close yourself off from other possibilities. There really is a world of unknown lands to explore out there. Well, I call this valley "home" - for now at least," he finished with a meaningful smile. Alectorious deeply appreciated the man's wise insight, going on to expound his own perplexing predicament.

"It sounds very much like ourselves - many had warned us against coming here and of the dangers we might face, but I believe in the end, we chose the right path," he admitted, looking around at the striking beauty of the valley once again. The king noticed a group of curious deer, pausing to admire the magnificent animals.

"A worthy sacrifice is it not?" noted the man, looking to the approaching creatures.

"Without question," agreed the king, taking a deep breath to absorb all that surrounded as Gavastros slumped dramatically to the grass in exhaustion from all the sun's excitement. The deer suddenly ran away, believing it had been an act of hostility.

"If I may, do you know of any others herein the valley?" Thelosious asked, curious as to the extent of settlement in the area. There was not a soul in sight apart from them - a feeling of remoteness unlike anything the cerebral one had ever experienced.

"Well, there are *some* around but you'll have trouble finding them. People up here just want to forget about the world and its problems - they don't want to be reminded of all that they left behind and what they might face if they are ever to return. Sadly, I doubt very much if they would reveal themselves to you - most of them are merely kindred spirits the world no longer cared for, feeling the only place for them is way up here, safe from the insensitivities and harsh judgments of the world," the Catharian sighed. The king's curiosity only grew.

"On the contrary, you have welcomed us warmly; why are you so different?" he asked. The old Catharian displayed an inexplicable hint of unease. He was unusually cordial for one who apparently distanced himself from any form of civilization; there was certainly a lot more to him than at first seemed, thought the king, who was ever more eager to know all he could of this intriguing character. The Catharian reflected, nodding in understanding.

"A fair and reasonable question, king - perhaps *I am* unlike the others; I want to let go of past wounds, like all men do, but at the same moment, I wish to stay in touch with the world I left behind and all the things I loved in it. I want to move on yet hold on, in the hope that one sun I *can* help in some way to make a change in this world, for the betterment of *all*. You know, many of us Catharians tried to make a difference - we *truly* did - to make the world free of oppression and tyranny; one where all were free to live as they pleased… a better place for those we would leave behind, long after we pass into the realms of spirit."

The man took a deep sigh, glancing to his own shimmering reflection in the glassy blue waters of the river, recalling his many eons past as they rippled before his eyes, lamenting his inability to fulfill the wondrous dreams he had had for himself, the world and its people. The king looked equally saddened as he likewise gazed into the streaming blue waters, sensing the hardships the Catharian had suffered, wondering why The Great Spirit allowed such misfortune to befall well-meaning souls.

"It seems you have endeavored greatly to help this world: a most noble thing indeed," offered the king, sensing the feelings of disappointment within the man.

"Oh yes, I tried, so very hard did I: one labours for so many suns, only for his dreams to be ruthlessly crushed by an empire that cares for nothing other than the hollow pursuit of wealth and power over innocent, helpless souls," he irately expressed.

"We know of this, Catharian, very well - many Eternians have fallen to defend our nation from this power of which you speak - we have suffered as much as you in the fight for freedom and all that is good," Alectorious sympathetically replied. The man seemed appreciative of the king's sentiment, replying in equal kind.

"Our suffering is so very needless; all I ever wished for was to live a peaceful life free of such tyranny and oppression. I am sure, Alectorious, that you desire no less for your nation and people," he admitted, while staring meaningfully into the king's deep blue-green eyes.

"I do - but some suns, I ask why the few must spoil it for the many - and if one's actions of virtue will ultimately mean anything to anyone at all. However, these I believe are the tests the gods and The Great Spirit lay before us - and we should endeavor with all our might to overcome them. I have always believed one should never give up hope for this world or their life - ever," Alectorious passionately countered, trying his best to reason with the Catharian. He had a genuine feeling the man could still offer much to the world, despite being of an age relatively advanced to that of the king. The Catharian continued, expressing a realisation he had come to over his eons spent in the tranquil valley.

"Well, I think that's one of the reasons I came here: a feeling that all hope had been lost for the world. Yet, there seemed to be another part, deep inside of me that's waiting for the right moment to once more answer the calling of The Great Spirit - *if* it so requires my humble service. It's almost like some kind of Athepothesia up here - a transition or healing place between lives - or in my case, a life within a life," he philosophically reflected. As the Catharian finished, Alectorious and Thelosious contemplated the insightful words of this virtuous soul. Meanwhile, Gavastros had taken off to explore the valley, with topics of such depth having yet to capture his erratic interest. The king deeply sympathised with the man, sensing he had genuinely endeavoured to make a difference but for reasons hitherto unclear, had been unable to fulfill his dreams. Alectorious offered his thoughts of concern.

"Your actions of goodwill were not in vain, my companion; nor I do believe, will *ever* be forgotten by the gods now watching over us. Perhaps the right moment and place *does* wait to call upon your most noble service once again."

"And that moment could fast be approaching; perhaps much sooner than you could have ever expected," Thelosious added, in a far more serious tone. The Catharians' expression dramatically changed, sensing his calling might indeed have arrived.

"He speaks the truth," Alectorious concurred, looking around at the snowcapped mountains shimmering in the background. "Before long, all the inhabited lands will be at war: The Gomercian Empire has swept across the known world and is soon to launch an invasion of Eternity. He will not stop there: Nerosis will eventually attack Catharia and perhaps even this valley," he chillingly warned. While fascinated by this turn of events, the Catharian reacted with a confident smirk of defiance as he sat up and spoke his mind.

"The Great Spirit will *never* allow those tyrants to come this far. The valley is protected by forces beyond anything you, I or any living thing could *ever* comprehend."
It was very much what the Prejosian had said, remembered the king: that anything of an impure nature would be unable to travel beyond The Bridge of Legends. Perhaps it *was* true after all. It did not however make Eternity any safer from Gomercian attack, and evacuating the entire population up here was simply *not* an option. The Catharian dramatically changed his expression at the thought of his homeland being threatened.

"I do genuinely fear for Catharia though, very much so. If the Gomercians are to invade Eternity, they might first attempt to subjugate Catharia; if indeed they have not already. If and when they do, I shall happily offer my services to help in any way I can. I had honestly expected the Gomercians would leave Eternity alone, as they *should* know it is virtually impossible to lay siege to," he admitted, with a stark look of bewilderment.

"I am sure you could still do a great deal to help thwart the Gomercian advance. Remember that as Catharia, Eternity now fights for her very survival and ultimately, I do boldly believe, that of the *entire* known world," the king insisted, sensing the Catharian could offer much to help the struggle against the empire. His past was still very much unclear but

Alectorious, as Thelosious, was certain the man had extensive military experience, judging by the cuts and lacerations on his arms and face, as well as the manner in which he spoke of soldierly matters. The king decided he best not ask too much for now, certain the answers would present themselves soon. It was important to show respect to one's elders in Eternian culture - to pry too much into their lives was considered quite inappropriate.

"Then perhaps *now* is that sun," acknowledged the Catharian. The king nodded meaningfully, knowing there was nothing left to be said on the matter. Silence fell upon the small group of souls as Alectorious cast a meaningful glance to the forests, not far from where they sat by the river's edge. He noticed a family of squirrels running up and down the rough bark of a tree collecting necessary provisions before scampering back up a thick brown trunk. Upon seeing the king, the small furry animals leapt high into the branches, believing he was a monster hunting its prey. Alectorious was inexplicably reminded of Sandros and the Catharians he had met not a few suns previously on the forest path. Surely this man would know something of him, if the Catharians were indeed the closely knit bunch they were believed to be.

"I must impart that on our adventures we encountered others of your kind: they helped us fight off a Gomercian ambush, saving my men and I from a certain end. Among them was a brave warrior who fought like none I have seen: his name was Sandros. Do you know him?" the king inquisitively asked. The mysterious Catharian seemed to hesitate ever so slightly before calmly answering. It was as if he had expected this very question.

"I know *of* him, but have never met in person… A real loner I hear - doesn't let *anyone* in… waging a lone, one-man war against the Gomercian Empire. You could probably do with a lot more like him fighting for Eternity…" he not too subtly suggested, and with a somewhat curiously nervous chuckle. It was an interesting point: the king remembered Sandros had been with several other Catharians during the skirmish.

"Do you know where we might find him?" Alectorious probed, excited to find someone who knew *something* of Sandros whereabouts.

"Somewhere in the lands of Catharia, I would imagine. Know however, he is a *true* forest dweller; lives, breaths and sleeps on the forest floor; rarely as I understand it, ever visits any of the villages. There are a few others of his kind roaming around, Catharian purists: those who believe that only by an inseparable bond with the forests can one achieve a true, meaningful and lasting connection to The Great Spirit. There is *some* truth in this belief but there are not many who follow such a strict doctrine. I personally feel that same connection is possible in this mystical valley." The man looked to the range of snow-capped peaks glistening above, feeling a warm glow of satisfaction with the path he had chosen.

"A fascinating insight; I had never known such people existed," the king replied, realising the extent to which Eternity had lost touch with its closest of neighbours.

"There are many interpretations of what the Catharian way truly is, as I'm sure there are for Eternian," the man remarked, casting his wise old eyes back to the king.

"Indeed there are. Well, when our purpose in the Buvarious has been fulfilled, we are sure to seek him out," Alectorious promised, ever more fascinated by this mysterious Sandros character. The Catharian became silent again, curious to know more of the Eternians and their reasons for travelling so far into the mountains.

"May I ask what brings you Eternians to these lands? It's a long way to come just to see a pretty river valley. In recent eons, your people have not been known for their adventures, with of course the greatest respect. Mind you, the Gomercians have admittedly not helped much in this…" he free admitted, and with a noticeably disgruntled sigh.

"That, we have not been," the king concurred with a smile. "But all people change,"

"That they do," agreed the Catharian with a sensible grin. The king decided to be forthright, speaking as the old man sat back and folded his arms, listening intently.

"We embarked on this quest in search of the great dragon, Reiactus, and have reason to believe he has returned to this world and his once ancient home, high in the Buvarious Mountains," the king explained, motioning to the lofty peaks above. The man struggled at first for words, as if unsure of what to say.

"Ah… The great dragon Reiactus… Rei… actus. Well… I haven't heard his name in countless suns indeed. It's been eons since he last graced these lands but that magnificent name has *never* been forgotten," he suggestively offered. The king was surprised by this response, which suggested a far greater awareness of the dragon in Catharia than had been at first realised. He sat up, utterly flabbergasted.

"You know of his legend?" Alectorious exclaimed, unable to hide his excitement.

"Oh, it's no legend, king; not at all. He was - and still is, very much real - flesh and bone, just like you and I," the Catharian assured. He smiled broadly as his mood dramatically changed. Alectorious was beside himself with delight.

"So he *has* returned, after all!" he elated, impatient to know more.

"Returned; well, that's not *quite* the right way of putting it, king, for he never truly went anywhere at all…" he explained, leaving Alectorious rather bewildered.

"I don't understand," he admitted, confused. The Catharian was sympathetic.

"Reiactus is a being like none that has gone before; it is something I cannot now explain but one sun, you will know the whole truth," he promised. Alectorious conceded, realising it would be imparted when the moment right.

"But do you know where Reiactus might be now?" he asked, hoping it be not far.

"It is believed by many he lived - or lives somewhere up there, high in the Buvarious as you said, although no-one's sure *exactly* where," the man answered, looking up to the magnificent snowcapped peaks illuminating the clear blue skies. The Catharian turned back to the king with a tone of caution in his voice.

"It's a dangerous place to go, king - if unprepared, you could suffer a terrible fate. Nature's wrath is most unforgiving in those mountains - freezing winds and blinding snowfalls could end your challenge in the very blink of an eye - or the earth thunder could shake you from its very edges. If you *do* decide to go, there is no guarantee of your return. Not even *your* gods can protect you up there, Alectorious," he starkly warned, expressing genuine concern for the regal Eternian. The king was unwavering, determined more than ever to see his heroic quest through to the end.

"We have come thus far, and shall not shirk this challenge," he promised, showing his clear intent. The Catharian was not at all surprised as he smiled to the valiant king.

"I thought you'd say that. Pure Eternian it is - brave, fearless and bold - never give up until the battle is won, your fears conquered and enemies vanquished forever. A great Eternian king once said that," recalled the man, in a salute of respect to his regal visitors. Thelosious knew immediately of whom the man spoke.

"Ah yes indeed, King Alectorious the 1st," he acknowledged, surprised a Catharian would have known such a thing. There was certainly a lot more to the man than had at first been apparent. The Catharian smiled faintly before turning north, his eyes glazing as if looking out to a long-lost companion. He knew it would be dangerous in those perilous mountains but could do nothing to stop the adventurous young Eternians.

"Follow the river until the path goes skywards - and from there, the hand of The Great Spirit will guide you. If it is meant to be, you *will* meet your dragon," the mysterious Catharian promised, delicately casting his hand in direction of the magnificent snowy mountains, piercing the skies as though the swords of great warriors.

"I *truly* believe we shall," the king replied, adamant he *would* fulfill his promise and find the legendary Reiactus. Looking to the skies above, the Catharian realised it was far too dangerous for the Eternians to begin their ascent this late in the noon.

"It would be madness to attempt now - the suns will set before long and the temperature will fall dramatically. You may rest in the valley this night; early in the morn you can begin your ascent into the Buvarious," he intelligently advised, knowing all too well the unforgiving nature of this harsh mountain environment.

"I think that would be wise, Catharian," acknowledged Thelosious, as he, along with the king and their new companion stood from their places by the peacefully flowing river.

"But we have nowhere to stay - and there are not less than ten Eternian souls to house this night," worried the king, looking to his Elite Guardsmen across the tranquil river valley.

"Oh yes, you do - right there," the Catharian responded, pointing to the ancient castle ruins. The castle was well sheltered by a thick forested area from where the mountains reached dramatically into the skies above. The king had forgotten all about the mysterious structure, so fascinated had he been by the Catharians' alluring tales.

"I had thought it was but a ruin," he remarked, looking to the turreted building not half way up the valley. Appearances could most certainly be deceiving, Alectorious thought.

"Well, not as you might have imagined. There are still several rooms perfectly intact and the living area is more than large enough for everyone. We can make a fire for warmth and prepare a meal for the evening there," the Catharian explained. Alectorious smiled broadly, gladly accepting this kind offer, very much looking forward to the evening ahead.

"Splendid; it shall be one to remember, of that I am sure," he smiled, with a boyish excitement. A night in a castle by the mountains in a distant river valley - something only read of in folktales thought the king, feeling as though he was living out a middlehood dream.

"Well, it seems Gavastros has already rather warmed to the idea," Thelosious observed with a chuckle; pointing to the prodigy in the distance, who was busy clambering the protective walls of the castle.

"Oh Gavastros - he never lets us down," whispered the king, shaking his head. The Catharian seemed unconcerned, inviting the Eternians to continue to the other side.

"Shall we?" he asked. Motioning with his hand, he began walking in direction of the ancient castle ruins Gavastros was climbing. Alectorious and Thelosious followed, likewise making their way through the colourful grassy fields. A number of animals ran by in curiosity of the mysterious bipedal creatures, having never seen so many, and dressed in such unusual colours. The king acknowledged their presence before looking up to the twin suns creeping into the edge of the mountains in the northwest, casting an array of captivating hues across the peaceful valley - a sight he would never forget. Turning back, the king looked to the horses running playfully in the grass, concerned they would never make it out alive.

"I worry of our horses - they will be in need of shelter also." The Catharian was quick to reassure the king, pointing up ahead.

"Worry not of them. There are a few stables at the rear of the castle: they'll be safe and warm there. You won't be able to take them much beyond this valley though; the mountain paths are far too treacherous for such large animals," the man warned, with the king immediately lamenting this rather inconvenient oversight.

"That *does pose* a considerable problem," he understated, as the three men glided through the soft grass of the valley. The Catharian was re-assuring, waving his hand.

"Not at all; you could leave them here for another moon and they wouldn't even notice your absence - there is plenty of fresh water and grass for them to feed on until your return." Looking to their lush surroundings, the king felt a little more at ease.

"Very well; but I fear we shall not be able to go back to Eternity by the same path," he stated, concerned the Gomercians would be awaiting them.

"There will be no need, king; before you venture into the Buvarious, there is a path leading past the northwest range towards Catharia. It's mainly along a wide forested path and much safer than the one you came here by. You won't find any Gomercians there, I promise,"

"But what of the Catharians?" the king asked, understandably concerned.

"I'm sure they wouldn't object to your passing through their lands; there is no malice felt towards Eternians, despite what you have been led to believe," the Catharian reassured.

"If only we had known that before - we suffered much upon the path we chose," the king admitted. The Catharian was philosophical, drawing on his eons of life experience.

"I believe the paths we choose in life are for a purpose much deeper than we at first realise, Alectorious: reasons of learning, understanding and growth," posed the man of some fifty-seven eons. He continued, revealing more of his insightful nature.

"Some men are blinded by their heart's desire to follow its true path - but there is no shame in that," he thoughtfully added, as he saw the great ambition within the Eternian king.

"I truly do struggle to understand these reasons. I feel like I am stranded all alone on this path, halfway between the worlds of men and the gods at the mercy of fate as to which way I shall fall," Alectorious admitted, lamenting his struggle to *truly* grasp his destiny and indeed, nation's. The Catharian was sympathetic to his plight, offering his thoughts.

"I can never know how it is for you, but I'm sure it is not easy being a king. The one thing I have *always* believed, above all else, is that you have to live like a one man army to survive in this world, Alectorious - it's the only way to overcome adversity." The king was taken by these simple yet profound words, vowing never to forget.

"I know that only *too* well," he forthrightly admitted, nodding profusely.

"Live like a one-man army - fight like a hero," Alectorious unexpectedly added.

"Ha-ha! So the Age of Heroes returns!" the Catharian playfully laughed.

"For I, it never ended," the king admitted, revealing his great passion for classical Eternian history. As they marched toward the castle, a light breeze blew across the fields and countless flowers swayed to and fro as if alive with the spirit of the Aphroedisia herself.

"Wait!" said the Catharian, dramatically stopping in middle of the valley some halfway between the river and castle. The king looked him in the eye, curious.

"Look around for a moment - the animals of the valley." The king and Thelosious did exactly this, looking at the many curious species roaming throughout as they lived their carefree existence in the lush, grassy meadows, unconcerned what might befall them the next sun, moon nor eon: a way of life the king could only dream of.

"A seemingly perfect existence, one would think," he acknowledged.

"It is that, indeed - they live a life of peace, innocence and bliss - we on the other hand, one of hardship, tests, and struggle. Why that is, one truly wonders…"

"A life in the valley is easy for one to envy; it truly questions the necessity of all the struggles we face, sun after sun," the king observed. The Catharian was philosophical.

"Yes, Alectorious; but it is in these very struggles we are compelled to rise up and overcome all obstacles; to *truly* know, understand and appreciate what it is be alive, and to cherish, in each and every moment, those feelings of bliss we so seldom feel in this world; that which those innocent creatures experience so effortlessly, each and every sun of their lives." Alectorious finally began to grasp his cryptic meaning.

"I have spent my *entire life* trying to recapture that elusive bliss of which you speak; that only the purest of innocent souls seem ever to find," the king replied, wishing for a world free of the suffering he had known now for too many eons.

"It is the most noble of devotions, King of Eternity," the Catharian admired. With that, he, Alectorious and Thelosious continued through the brightly coloured meadows towards the mysterious castle ruin not far in the distance.

THE ANCIENT CASTLE

Alectorious, Thelosious and the enigmatic Catharian approached the castle perched quaintly atop a small rocky hill on the far-east side of the tranquil river valley. From there, a low, weathered stone wall stretched all the way up to the mysterious temple in the north where a larger settlement had apparently once existed. The cosy-looking castle was surrounded by a patch of thick forest and behind that, a series of mountains rose dramatically into the skies. Unlike the king's opulent residence in Eternity, the castle consisted of but a high tower conjoined by a number of smaller buildings, which presumably served as living quarters for the once-inhabitants of this enchanting natural paradise. The small fortification was surrounded on all sides by walls not more than two hoplites high, with almost perfectly circular turrets at each corner. As the Eternians approached, Alectorious and Thelosious marvelled at the long-forgotten ancient stone structure, curious as to how it had come to be all the way up here in the chilling climes of the mountains.

"It is as a dream, indeed - I could have only imagined such a place," the king tellingly remarked as he looked to the castle, feeling as though he were caught in the midst of a fantastical tale. Thelosious was equally impressed by this unknowable finding.

"It looks strikingly familiar but I cannot quite put my finger on it," he replied in frustration, remembering an ancient myth he had once read. As the two knights keenly observed the imposing structure, a familiar voice bellowed from the ramparts.

"It is perfect my king - befitting the heroes themselves!" cried the prodigy.
The king was furious with his subordinate's unruly behavior, beckoning him wildly.

"Gavastros - come down this instant and rally the guardsmen - we have an evening meal to prepare for!" he scolded, raising his voice as it echoed across the valley.

"As you wish, my king," Gavastros somberly replied, before climbing down to fulfill his duties. The Elite Guard were meanwhile scattered throughout the meadows, relaxing as they could not elsewhere on the plush green grass. It was an opportune moment to recuperate from all the hardships of their thus-far tumultuous adventure as the soft, vibrant energies of this natural utopia provided the perfect elixir to their many wounds of battle. It was a moment they wished would last forever, for there was no knowing what perils lay in wait.

The king's attention was meanwhile firmly fixed on the castle, with much interest growing as to its mysterious origins. He queried the Catharian who was standing nearby.

"I have been wondering; do you know who once lived here?"

"Well, it's a relic of a long past age; that is sure, king. I learnt much of its history from an old hermit who inhabited these parts when I first arrived in the valley. He told me all that he knew; a treasured companion, he was indeed," the Catharian replied, with a distinct look of sadness in his eyes. The king quickly picked up on this, probing sensitively.

"Whatever became of this… companion?" he asked. The Catharian peered off into the snowy peaks, taking a deep sigh before lowering his head. The king waited patiently, sensing he perhaps should not have asked. The old man raised his head and finally answered.

"He was a great lover of those mountains…" the Catharian began, signalling up to the imposing peaks of the Buvarious. "…Obsessed with stories of gateways to other worlds and mysterious dragons, much as you are now, determined to find out if all that was spoken of the Buvarious were true. I tried to talk him out of it - there's no way his frail old body could have taken him up there - but he listened not. And on a lone windy sun in a late autumn much like now, he set off unannounced into the Buvarious Mountains. I tried to give pursuit but it was all in vain," the Catharian expressed with visible remorse, as he shook his head angrily.

"Whatever happened to him?" the king asked, utterly flabbergasted, eyes widening.

"Well, that's the very thing; I have no idea at all. I rode as fast as I could to the crossroads, then on foot up the mountain path as far as I could go - but there was not a trace of him. I met several other souls along the way; in those suns, it was a far more popular route than now, but they had not seen him. He could not have gone further than I had chased - certainly in his state. It is a great mystery what happened to my old companion, Androsious. Perhaps he made it, high into the Buvarious and discovered its secret gateways - or maybe that old fox had me deceived all along and travelled north into The Great Unknown. Either way, he could not have made it all alone," the Catharian explained, suggesting a tremendous feeling of loss. In this realisation, the king took some moments before offering his thoughts.

"I am so sorry, you must have been close," he sympathetically conveyed.

"He was like a grandfather to me - like the one I never had - if only I could have said goodbye," the Catharian lamented, shaking his head with a profound sense of regret.

"Perhaps you will see him again," reasoned the king, knowing it *would* be so.

"Yes - when I reach Athepothesia - and I'll find out where he's been these last twenty eons!" the Catharian chuckled, trying to shift himself into a more positive state of mind.

"Indeed!" smiled the king, doing his best to express such a disposition. All were silent as they looked around, still very much in awe of their surroundings. The Catharian continued.

"Androsious told me much of the valley's once population; a people similar in many ways culturally to Eternians. The castle was the residence of a powerful lord who, upon discovering this hidden paradise, was so captivated that he wished never to leave. He had been a hard tyrant for most of his suns but the valley pacified him, greatly changing his outlook on life. Seeing the error in his ways, the lord settled here permanently and built this castle, inviting his former vassals, servants and any others who wished to live a more peaceful existence. Many built their own houses and eventually formed a village, of which only the walls now remain. They also created small dwellings deep in the forests - some of whose remains still exist. The land was surprisingly arable too, providing for every need, wish and desire of the once residents. The passing of the seasons have sadly, swept away almost all remnants of these lost peoples; their memories passed on only by the ancient spirits still inhabiting the valley," the Catharian concluded with a regretful sigh. The king was instantly captivated by this enchanting tale, curious to know all that he could.

"What ever happened to them?" he asked, fascinated, with eyes fixated on the castle.

"When the great rebellion against the lords began in the lower lands, many returned to Eternity or other cities in the plains such as Saphoeria to fight for their respective native nations. The castle and village were eventually abandoned, with so few souls left to maintain them. It's strange; there should be a lot more remains yet almost everything but the castle itself has mysteriously disappeared," the Catharian explained. The king was surprised by these startling revelations, with little real knowledge of the area himself.

"It is most unfortunate and I must say, surprising that none others ever desired to settle here," he pointedly remarked, imagining life in such a magnificent natural abode.

"Well, that's not *exactly* accurate. During the Age of Heroes, the seven great warriors and their followers are believed to have stayed here for a number of moons or perhaps even eons before venturing further into the now "Known World". Their legacy: that temple you see up there," the Catharian revealed, pointing to the ancient structure to the northeast.

"By the gods, the heroes themselves on this very ground," the awestruck king replied, imagining them standing in this very spot, all those eons ago. The Catharian agreed.

"Quite a thought, is it not? Well for me, the castle is home, for the while being at least. I've restored what I can - rebuilt the roof and some of the old rooms. It's simple but does me reasonably well. A bit chilly in the winter months, mind, but there's a nice little fireplace to keep me warm. You will be my most honoured guests," the Catharian wholeheartedly offered, looking forward to some much-needed company.

"It will be *our* honour, truly," the king appreciated, greatly relieved to have found a place for the night. Moments later, Gavastros approached from the valley with the Elite Guard. There was a clear look of trepidation on his face - an unnatural expression for him.

"My king, I have assembled the men and horses. Several of the steeds are badly injured: I fear they may not make it out of here alive." Gavastros was known as was the king for his love of horses and could not bear the thought of losing a single one.

"Allow me to have a look," the Catharian calmly offered, as he, along with the Eternians approached the troubled equines that were struggling to stand upright. The old man knelt down and inspected the swollen leg of one of the animals.

"It's just a bit of fatigue - a few suns rest in the valley and they'll be fine," he assured with a smile, gently patting the horses' throbbing leg. There was a collective sigh of relief from the Eternians but it raised some immediate questions.

"But my king, I thought we were to leave in the morrow?" Gavastros asked.
Thelosious interceded on the king's behalf, despite knowing the prodigy would not approve.

"We are, Gavastros, but without horses - it is far too dangerous for them in the mountains - we shall have to come back for them upon our return," the cerebral one explained, as the prodigy took the news slightly better than expected.

"I do hope so, my companion, for I could not live with myself if we returned to Eternity without them," he firmly replied, deeply concerned for the animals' wellbeing. Thelosious was calm, knowing the gods above would protect their animal companions.

"Allow the land and The Great Spirit to look after them - as is their natural way - you must trust." Gavastros nodded as the Catharian spoke, shifting focus back to the moment.

"Well, the suns will set before long - you'd better get the horses into the stables for the night - it'll be much warmer for them in there," he insisted. Alectorious looked at once to the prodigy, who took the hint well. Gavastros nodded in acknowledgement.

"I shall make sure of it, my king," he promised, as if having read his leader's very thoughts. Moving quickly into action, the prodigy turned to his subordinates.

"Elite Guard - horses to the stables - on the double!!!" he barked. The guards duly obeyed, taking the tiring steeds by the reins to the sheltered area in the rear of the small fortress.

"Meet us inside the main tower later; we have a rather large meal to prepare," Thelosious added, as Gavastros acknowledged with a simple salute. The king was still very much concerned for the group's safety, fearing the possibility of an imperial night attack.

"I worry the Gomercians will track us up to this valley," he expressed, concerned about retribution for the previous sun's events.

"Worry not of them; they'll never in a thousand suns find you here, Alectorious. Remember, only those of purest intentions may enter this valley; all that you have read is true," the Catharian assured, as a wry smile appeared on his battle-hardened face.

"But surely they could simply walk same the path as we?" Alectorious doubted.

"So you may think - know however that The Great Spirit is an all-powerful force and must *never* be underestimated. It makes the eye see things that are not there and blind them from what really is. The more you respect its divine power, the more it will open up to you…" the old man cryptically explained. The king was rather perplexed by this notion.

"I would *never* question the power of The Great Spirit; but I do begin to ask myself why I had never ventured here before," he replied, looking appreciatively to his beautiful surroundings, feeling fortunate to have been blessed with such a bountiful discovery.

The Catharian was philosophical as he drew on his vast spiritual knowledge.

"It is often said that the path only opens when the seeker is ready to receive the wisdom of the ages - perhaps you and your nation were waiting for that moment, Alectorious - a moment I believe might now be upon you..." he wisely professed.

"I believe it could well be," the king agreed, his eyes squinting. The Catharian realised there was nothing more to be said, turning his attention to more practical concerns.

"Well, I'd better collect some supplies for the evening. Feel free to wander around; it's your home now too," the old man promised, before disappearing into the forest in search of wild berries and wood for the fire. It would be a while before the suns set, so the king thought it fitting to explore. He looked intuitively to the entrance of the castle, noticing a faint outline of some ancient inscription marked upon its indelible surface.

"Thelosious, do you see that?" Moving closer to the stone, he tried to make out what was written. ""Werphoesia", it says. I wonder if that was the name of the village." Alectorious curiously wondered. Thelosious was of little doubt as to its meaning.

"More likely the castle - in those ancient eons, each fortress was given a name as an expression of affection for the place. They were very parochial suns, indeed," he explained, with the king ever more intrigued by what lay within.

"Werphoesia," he whispered, wondering what it might have been like living here all those eons ago. Alectorious looked to Thelosious, who encouraged him forward.

"After you, my king," he said, motioning with his palm wide open.

"It would be my honour," Alectorious replied, before taking his first steps inside the castle. The two companions walked through the small archway into the courtyard of the ruin, quite unsure what to expect. They looked at the mysterious stone walls, feeling a sensation of being magically transported into that long forgotten age when heroes and creatures of terrifying proportions roamed these ancient lands. Alectorious looked around the courtyard, noticing a large white tree dominating the centre, imagining the many stories it could tell of the souls that had passed through over the eons.

At each corner of the courtyard, there was a turret holding the four walls together, with each rising to some three to five hoplites in height: a relatively small castle, obviously built for practical purposes. At the rear of the courtyard was the main tower, which in turn was flanked by some smaller buildings: presumably housing for the long-past residents.

Alectorious thought more of the peoples that had once inhabited these walls, wondering how they had seen the world and if they had viewed it the same way Eternians now did. The king longed to know more of these forgotten suns: if the world had changed much since then and if man had learned his lessons over the passing eons. The ever-expanding empire suggested otherwise, but there have *always* been those who have sought control over others. Of course, these heinous actions were ultimately those of a small number of souls, with the populace being innocent pawns in their pursuit of power, wealth and control.

"I can almost feel the presence of those long-passed souls," Alectorious tellingly remarked, looking around the mysterious courtyard with a sense of grandiose mystique.

"A feeling unlike never before," agreed Thelosious, as the king took a step forward.

"Shall we?" he asked, motioning to the main tower ahead.

"Most certainly," Thelosious replied. The two companions walked straight across the courtyard, past the mysterious tree and through the doorway into the main castle tower. It led directly into a large, high-ceilinged room, which at one end was slightly elevated and at the other, a large fireplace could be seen. Thelosious gasped in awe as he looked around.

"This must be the main hall: the inhabitants of the castle would have feasted here each night long after the setting of the suns. I can only imagine the countless stories of adventure exchanged," he evocatively remarked, picturing a vibrant chamber full of banqueting lords, elegant ladies and noble knights.

"I can only imagine," agreed the king with a smile, looking to one end. "They would have warmed themselves at the fireplace on those long winter nights, speaking their minds of a great many things," he added excitedly. Thelosious was much in agreement, expanding.

"I imagine the lord of the castle would have sat atop the elevated part, over there, unlike we have in Eternity," he noted, pointing to the other end of the chamber.

"I wonder who he *really* was…" the king pondered, glancing over in curiosity.

"A man just as you and I, my king; with the same thoughts, feelings and fears that we *all* have," Thelosious professed. The king was impressed by his companion's words.

"Succinctly put, Thelosious, indeed," he agreed, unable to add to this simple profundity. "Shall we continue?" Alectorious asked, barely giving his companion a chance to answer. The king began up the narrow spiralling stone staircase in the corner of the chamber leading up to the next level; it revealed three more rooms, with each significantly smaller than the main dining hall. As he looked around, he wondered how it might once have been. "I imagine these were for the family of the lord: they are very small but cozy I imagine in the long, cold winters," Alectorious said, as he and Thelosious inspected each dwelling carefully.

"Yes; this one must be the Catharians'," reasoned Thelosious, finding a chamber with a small bed, chest and strewn with various personal belongings.

"And we had best respect that," the king suggested, motioning to the spiral staircase. Thelosious nodded as they ventured further up, one room before the top of the tower.

"Ah, the lord's chamber, no doubt," the king said, immediately recognising the purpose of the large room. It was completely undecorated apart from some ancient inscriptions still barely visible upon the stone walls. The king looked with fascination, moving closer for inspection. "Can you make out any of it?" he enthusiastically asked. Well-versed in Ancient Eternian, Thelosious edged closer to examine the mysterious writings.

"Barely, my king; it is a dialect I am quite unfamiliar with but shall do my best," the cerebral knight promised, placing his finger below the first line as he concentrated deeply.

"In these valleys of great beauty, I did discover again my heart and my soul; who I *truly was* and all that I am. I wish that one sun, I shall have left this world a brighter place than I once found it, and hope that in a thousand eons henceforth, souls more virtuous and benign than I once more rule these lands, and never again allow the ways of the dark to hold sway over the innocents of this world.

For any man who is to read these words that I write,

remember the gods watch over thee always; and shall lead thee unto thy destiny,

if thou are but willing to listen to the whispers of thy heart, and the poems, deep within thy soul...

Farewell noble traveler from afar, to whom I humbly impart my words, and may thee safely be guided unto that which thou do so humbly seek."

"It is a very old dialect, Sire; I am afraid that is the best I can do," Thelosious humbly conceded, as he took a step back in quiet reflection. The king was utterly captivated.

"Profound, truly; words of a noble soul, indeed," he said, wondering who might have written it. "Such a kindred spirit; yet unable to see his own goodness," the king added, seeing it as unfortunate that one of such virtue saw only his misgivings.

"I believe they are words of the castle lord; the once-tyrant of whom the Catharian had spoken. So captivated by the beauty of the valley, he was forever transformed. Yet so haunted by his once ways, he was unable to forgive himself for misdeeds to his fellow man," Thelosious extrapolated. The king was philosophical as he caressed the grooves in the stone.

"Would you, Thelosious or indeed, would I? If I had caused the suffering of a great many souls, I dare think it would be something *very* difficult to ever forgive myself for." Thelosious was somewhat in disagreement as he paced around the stone chamber.

"I humbly do think, my king, that one sun, you would inevitably have no choice but to do *exactly that* - forgive - and forget. Surely, it would be the only way for one to move on to a more positive path; not only for oneself, but ultimately, the known world," he intelligently reasoned. Alectorious returned to his feet, reflecting on Thelosious' insights.

"Maybe so, but the past is something we can neither deny nor ever *truly* forget..." Sensing further discussion would only cause argument, Thelosious' answer was simple.

"It is not," he said, casting his eyes to the stairs. The king read his companion well.

"Well, to the top it is," he said, smiling, eagerly moving to the winding stone steps. Alectorious and Thelosious departed the lord's chamber, making their way up the final set of winding grey stone steps to the top of the castle tower. As he reached the open air, the king walked out to the impressive parapets and leaned precariously over the edge. Marvelling at the natural beauty before him, Alectorious felt truly blessed to be alive.

"Even more captivating from up here," he gasped, gazing out from his bird's eye view in the tower to the stunning valley below. The brilliant array of coloured flowers swayed gently in the breeze that swept dramatically up from The Great Plains, as countless animals grazed peacefully in the fields with not a care in the known world. Across the valley to the east, the river flowed down elegantly from those dignified snowy peaks as if the essence of life itself. Scanning his magnificent surroundings, Thelosious was moved beyond words.

"I see why so many wished never to leave," he managed, utterly captivated by all that he saw. The king had only one reply as he cast an evocative glance of mystique.

"That is why, my companion, they named it The "Valley of the Gods"."

THE TWIN SUNS

Alectorious gazed out from the castle tower to a small mountain rising to the east of the river valley, noticing a narrow winding path leading all the way up to its highest point. Starting not a short walk beyond the castle walls, it was a chance simply too good to miss. He intuitively turned to the Great Buvarious, watching as the twin suns set upon her majestic snowcapped peaks, casting an untold array of colours and hues across the Eternian Ranges in the North West, far into the valley below. The suns emitted an energy force with intensity unlike anything Alectorious had ever felt - he imagined what a sight it would be to witness them setting from the mountaintop - it would be like looking into the eyes of the divine itself.

"I believe the gods are calling you, Alectorious," Thelosious said, as if reading his companion's very thoughts. To watch the suns set was a favourite pursuit of the king, as it was with many an Eternian; for they believed in those final moments in the late-noon skies, the worlds of men and the gods would ever so briefly cross. At that concise moment, a connection with beings from the Higher Worlds would ever so fleetingly be possible, and their divine teaching and wisdom open to all of those adept enough to hear.

"You know me only too well, my old companion," Alectorious replied with a bemused chuckle. Knowing it something he must do, the king wasted not a moment more.

"I shall not be long," he added with a smile, starting toward the winding staircase.

"You had best leave your armour behind; it will only burden you," Thelosious cleverly advised. The king nodded in total agreement.

"Very much so," he replied, as he moved steadily forward.

"May the gods be with you, Alectorious!" his companion enthusiastically added. The king acknowledged once more before disappearing down the spiral stone staircase. As he reached the main hall, several Elite Guardsmen were on hand to assist in disassembling his blue-gold plated armour. They hurriedly took it apart piece by piece before placing it on one of the seats imbedded into the wall of the main hall.

"Thank you, men; tell the others I shall not be long," the king instructed.

"As you wish Sire." they replied. Alectorious leapt up and made his way into the courtyard and through the main castle gate before passing Gavastros, who had been busy collecting berries and other luscious consumables for the evening meal.

"To where do you go, my king?" he asked, looking up in bewilderment.

"The mountain, my companion; for the suns will soon set!" he exclaimed. Gavastros immediately understood his king's intentions, expressing only words of encouragement.

"But of course; may the gods impart you much wisdom!" he exclaimed, before the king made his way round the side of the ancient castle toward to the winding mountain path; he could hardly wait to reach the summit and witness the twin suns, in all their magnificent glory. Alectorious very much enjoyed watching the setting titans from his tower chamber back in Eternity; but from here it would be simply incredible. The climb up would not only be the perfect opportunity to release all those inner tensions but to deeply contemplate his current predicament. If the king were fortunate enough, he might even receive some guidance as the known and Higher Worlds ever so briefly touched. In more practical terms, it would provide a clear view of the surrounding area and hopefully, reveal a safe passageway into the jutting peaks of the great Buvarious.

Alectorious soon reached the foot of the small mountain, stopping briefly to summon his strength for the steep ascent. Looking up the meandering path, he knew he had not long before the twin beacons silently edged behind the snowy peaks; and it would most certainly require all his efforts to reach the top. Alectorious started at a brisk pace, quite unsure of his journey's duration. The path shot up steeply, first through a small patch of forest, rapidly sapping the king's energy as he tried to maintain an even pace. It twisted and turned like a wild winding river, flattening the higher up he traversed. Alectorious soon made it through the trees back out into the open. The setting suns shone into his eyes with a blinding brightness at every corner he turned as the path blew up dust with each step. The river and castle became smaller with each returning glance and his breaths ever deeper in exhaustion. The king pushed harder, turning once again as the summit came dramatically into view. He summoned one last burst of strength, using all his energy for the final push to the top. Within moments Alectorious was there, collapsing as the path reached its proverbial crescendo.

"Made it!" he whispered in exhausted relief, desperately trying to catch his breath. Alectorious finally but slowly rose to observe his surroundings, marvelling at the breathtaking snowy peaks stretching into the distance, and the majestic river that was flowing peacefully, far, far below. The king felt truly privileged to witness to such magnificent splendour. Alectorious realised that, while similar opportunities might again present themselves, it would not *quite* be the same. He found something exhilarating in this, experiencing a moment that would not be repeated for the rest of eternity. It was quite a profound notion, the king thought, as he looked longingly across the peaceful mountain ranges in wonderment of all that surrounded.

Alectorious felt a strong sense of déjà vu as he watched the setting suns cast a brilliant array of indescribable hues across the mountains, valley and entire known world. He realised how strikingly similar this majestic place was to one of his recent dreams, wondering if it was a moment that had always meant to be. The king looked across the range of snow-covered mountains leading up to the great Buvarious, pondering what force of nature could have created such a colossus and how long it had watched over the world. He imagined it would have been countless eons before *Eternians* had graced these lands. He then looked into the valley in equal amazement, where the multitude of colourful flora and fauna were like a rich tapestry of creation itself, with the crystal-clear river winding gracefully down from high in the great Buvarious, further illuminating this alluring sight of perfection.

Alectorious glanced with a tremendous sense of yearning to Eternity in the south-west, which was now but a spec in the distance; he wondered of all he had left behind - his nation, people and companions, before fleetingly, if he would ever see them again. He then looked over to Saphoeria and Dragon's Pass in the southeast, then to Brasovia and The Great Plains of Marathosia stretching far off into the distant southern horizon.

The king sat on a nearby boulder to relieve the strain in his legs and watch the final moments of the twin suns: the eyes of the gods themselves as they set peacefully across the clear blue skies. Before long the twin stars began to set, casting a spellbinding blanket of colourful hues over the snowy mountains. It was an indescribably beautiful sight, thought the king, as he took several deep breaths to relax. Alectorious stared further, more meaningfully into the setting beacons, knowing it was the perfect moment for contemplation of all that had transpired on his grandiose adventure. He squinted his eyes from the sun's brightness and the wind blowing gently across his face, reflecting on all that had passed and was soon to be. From Dragon's Pass to the council and Oracle, the mysterious forestmen and finally this magnificent river valley - things he could have only dreamed of moons ago - yet it had all transpired. He took great inspiration in this, believing *anything* was now possible. It had already been quite an adventure, befitting tales of the ancient heroes and all those who dared to ever dream of a life beyond that which had been taught to them. Indeed, he felt it only the beginning of an even *greater* journey into lands uncharted as he looked forward with much anticipation to the suns and moons ahead, and all the magnificent discoveries soon to be had.

Alectorious was so close to his dream of reaching the Buvarious he could almost touch it with his bare hands. Before long, he would know once and for all if Reiactus lived *and* if The Great Prophecy held true. He dearly hoped that the dragon, if they found him, would assist in the fight against the empire - or perhaps as the Oracle had said, others would come to Eternity's aid. Maybe it *would* in fact be another who united the people of the known world in this common cause for freedom. The king realised the Eternian standing army had not the numerical might to *directly* challenge the Gomercian forces, so some outside assistance would most certainly be required to overcome their arch-nemesis. It was now a case of finding those willing to assist, wherever in the known world they might be.

The king suddenly remembered his dream from several suns ago of a magnificent mountain range - a place exactly like he now found himself. While memories were faint, Alectorious knew it had been a sign he was *exactly* where he was meant to be. He gazed deeper into the majestic setting suns as if searching for answers to all those unanswered questions. He then spoke, as if it to a companion of many eons.

"Noble gods and Great Spirit; show me the way of virtue, righteousness and truth; protect and watch over my nation of Eternity, for I have only ever wished to serve the people of this world, in any way that I can," he pleaded, hoping his despairing call would somehow be heard. Alectorious fell silent as the suns continued to creep down, hoping, however unreasonably there might be a response... but there was none. The king sighed in disappointment; he felt helpless, all alone on this remote mountaintop. It was not moments later a soothing voice dramatically began to speak, almost as if from somewhere within.

"Release your doubts and fears, Alectorious; for you have *always* been protected and watched over. Remember to always follow the pathway of your heart, and you shall find the truth of all that you ever sought." The king then took a deep breath before opening his eyes in shock, expecting to see someone standing there. In that moment, a deep-blue Aieglos flew directly in front of him, screeching as it turned into the twin suns' beaming rays, then back around the mountain in a wide, sweeping arc. The magnificent bird then dove suddenly into the valley from whence it had come before disappearing, as if it had never been. The king immediately knew it was a divine sign; for Aieglos had long been the forbearers of good fortune and symbolic of great victory. Alectorious knew without question the gods had spoken and that he had chosen the right path.

As the king relaxed, he reflected more on the journey ahead. He realised the dragon might never be found but was confident the mountains would open up an entire world of possibilities. The king watched as the great shining beacons finally disappeared behind the rugged snowcapped peaks, feeling truly blessed to have witnessed this magnificent display of natural grandeur. As the thin mountain air began to cool, Alectorious reluctantly picked himself up and returned to the path, promising to never forget the divine words of wisdom imparted upon this mystical mountaintop.

A NEW ACQUAINTANCE

Alectorious returned to the castle exhausted, ready for a hearty meal and well-earned rest. Night had fallen quickly and a steady stream of smoke was emanating from the roof of the ancient castle stronghold. He stopped instinctively before entering, glancing longingly up to the stars awakening slowly in the night skies, winking as if in recognition of his noble presence. A deep a sense of fulfillment washed over the king as he observed these proud shining beacons, feeling much had been accomplished on his thus-far tumultuous adventure: it was more than he could have possibly imagined but there was so much yet to come. In that moment he thought again of Sephia, wondering if she was faring well in distant Eternity.

Alectorious was ready to feast and settle in for the night, knowing he would require every bit of energy for the gruelling ascent into the Buvarious; for it would be a most testing examination of willpower and desire to overcome adversity. He made his way inside the main gate, through the courtyard and into the dining room of the main hall. A large fire now burned brightly at the far end where Gavastros, Thelosious, the Catharian and Elite guardsmen were all huddled round busy preparing the evening meal.

"Blessed be the gods above, my king - you have safely returned!" the prodigy exclaimed, somewhat overstating the point as he announced the meal for the evening. "We have prepared a delightful banquet, Alectorious; Cloesian stew served with the finest of Ibroesian brews," he proudly stated, hastily adding some finishing touches to the rather scrumptious-looking meal. The prodigy enjoyed boasting of his culinary prowess, which was equaled only by his deft swordsmanship and immense physical strength. It was not the regal meal Alectorious was perhaps used to, but it would more than suffice in replenishing his weary body for the arduous climb in the morrow. The king removed his coat and shoes, chuckling heartily in response.

"It sounds truly splendid, Gavastros," he gleefully answered. Alectorious joined his companions Gavastros, Thelosious and the Catharian, sitting on a rug near the fire and wrapping himself in a thick blanket. The cold night air could acutely be felt whistling through the arrow loops of the castle walls and around the large rectangular chamber as the king warmed himself as best he could, holding his hands to the crackling flames while Gavastros helped serve the evening meal. Each man received a sizeable proportion of Cloesian stew: a mixture of local vegetables, nuts, herbs and spices, covered in a sweet tasting sauce the Catharian had created with native berries and juices. All were gathered round waiting for the king to offer prayer, as was the Eternian tradition.

"May the gods above bless this banquet and guide us all to our highest calling," he announced in thanks. With that, everyone began to consume their well-earned dish, devouring every morsel with joyous aplomb. The Elite Guardsmen were quickest to finish, before scattering around the chamber to rest from the sun's exertions, knowing they in particular would need all their energy in the morrow. The king, Thelosious and Gavastros had much to discuss this fine evening as they made themselves comfortable upon the thick rugs strategically placed around the fireplace. Alectorious was first to break the silence, between the whistling winds and hissing logs on the fire, so eager was he to find out more of the mysterious lands he now serendipitously found himself within.

"I really must apologise; in all the excitement of making your acquaintance, I forgot to ask the pleasure of your name," he remarked to the Catharian, who was dismissive.

"Oh, it's really I who should apologise, king; for as host, I should have done so long ago. In all the excitement, I completely forgot," he admitted, equally embarrassed. The Catharian was hesitant at first, as if holding something back. "You know, it's been many eons since I entertained guests…" he vaguely remarked, before allowing for a short pause. He then dramatically changed tact. "My name is Skolastros; it's with humble pleasure that I welcome you to my home, worthy Knights of Eternity," he cheerily offered, motioning around the dimly-lit stony chamber. The king was honoured, replying in kind to his unassuming host.

"It is a great pleasure to meet you, Skolastros, and is with equal humility I accept this cordial invitation," he replied, looking in gratitude to the cosy surroundings of the castle, with its expertly constructed stone walls and small fireplace; it would certainly keep the intrepid adventurers warm this starry night. It was almost too perfect: as if having been created for this very purpose. It was odd that at exactly the right moment, The Great Spirit provided all that one required, the king briefly reflected.

"I thank you also, Skolastros," Thelosious added, bowing his head.

"And I," concurred Gavastros, raising his hand in a respectful salute. The men sat back and relaxed, feeling more at ease now they had been formally introduced. Alectorious looked about the chamber with curiosity, wishing to know of this mysterious ruin's past.

"Skolastros, could you tell us more of this castle and its origins?" Thelosious and Gavastros were equally curious. The Catharian paused and took a deep breath, as if a wise man with much knowledge to impart, elaborating on what he had spoken of earlier.

"Well, according to legend, it was owned by a wealthy lord who had originally come to these parts seeking to discover the secrets of the Buvarious Mountains, believing he could find a way to acquire yet more land and power for his own greedy ends. On his way through the valley, this hitherto power-hungry man underwent a dramatic transformation: he suddenly came to realise the error in his ways and that his insatiable desire for wealth, power and control over others served no good end at all. No-one knows why this occurred - some think it is due to the valley's inextricable link with the divine - others, its captivating beauty. Whatever the reason, these harsh once-ways were washed away forever as the lord fell in love with the valley, desiring never to leave. He abandoned his lands in the plains and sold them for a handsome sum, using the gold to build this here castle. Upon hearing of the valley's beauty, the lord's vassals and many others pledged their loyalty, following him to build a new life, free of the conflict and hardships of the Lower Lands. They built several small villages, living off the forest and working the land as best they could," Skolastros succinctly explained, as the Eternians burst with countless questions. Gavastros was particularly taken by this inspiring story.

"Why ever did they leave, Skolastros?" he inquisitively asked, before leaning forward. Alectorious and Thelosious were also very much in wonder. The Catharian delved deep into his knowledge of the area's history, casting his mind back to those long-past ages.

"Well, after The Great Rebellion against the lords, the lord of *this* particular castle lost support of the kings of the known world. Most of the people who had moved here returned to the ever growing city-states of Eternity, Saphoeria and many others, fearing they would otherwise, no longer be safe. The lord and those closest to him are said to have remained, seeing out their final suns in the peace and tranquility of this magnificent valley. After they had passed, the castle and surrounding village simply fell into decay, with no-one left to maintain them over the passing eons." Gavastros appeared somewhat lost, with his awareness of such things leaving a lot to be desired.

"My knowledge of history is somewhat hazy, Skolastros - the great rebellion? I think my memory needs refreshing," he acknowledged, taking a sip of his warm Ibroesian brew. Thelosious was clearly unimpressed, always quick to berate his companion's misgivings.

"By the gods above, Gavastros - you of all people should know these things! The history of the known world affects Eternity to this very sun, yet you know not the reasons we fight for our nation!" he scolded. The king was more forgiving as his history was also a little patchy. He leaned forward and spoke in a rather serious tone.

"Well, now would be a perfect opportunity to learn," he offered, knowing this would be a very long night indeed...

AGE OF LORDS

Skolastros merely smiled in reaction to Gavastros' question, as if it reminded him of his own younger, carefree suns, which were so many eons ago it seemed like another life. At the behest of the Eternian Knights, he would impart a tale of when powerful lords ruled the lands and people lived every sun as if it their last - such eons of uncertainty were they.

"Oh yes, this grandiose castle; from an age now *long forgotten* to the people of the known world," the Catharian nostalgically began, as he began to recall all he knew of this disremembered age. Relaxing, he allowed his mind to drift back to *that* distant era.

"It is so very much unlike the castle of Eternity: much smaller and less fortified," noted Gavastros, intrigued by what life might have been like here, all those eons ago.

"That it is, my companion, and so very much more," agreed the king, as Skolastros took another deep breath before continuing with his captivating tale.

"Indeed, my companions; it was an unimaginably trying age when rich and powerful lords ruled over all. They amassed huge fortunes of gold and silver through the acquisition of land, trade and war, sparing no expense in protecting their vast quantities of wealth. They built many castles throughout what you *now* call the known world, employing a large number of builders, craftsmen and even small armies. These lords would pay homage to the king, who would in turn recognise their legal right to rule, calling on their vassals' service in periods of war. In truth, it was an age of great hardship and suffering for the many, with tremendous inequalities existing throughout the common populous. So for all its opulence, it benefitted only the wealthy, powerful and their extended aristocratic families," he intricately explained, as the Eternians felt themselves magically transported back to these long-past eons. Alectorious took a moment to interject, giving Skolastros a short break.

"It was known as the "Age of Lords". There was a constant struggle between the king and lords, with none trusting each other's true intentions; such was the unrestrained pursuit of individual wealth and power. There were many uncertainties, with the constant infighting between the lords themselves meaning one could never know *what* to expect," he succinctly explained, remembering discussions with Plasos on this most fascinating historical period.

"Yes, thank you, Alectorious; you know your history very well indeed," commended Skolastros, with a respectful nod. Gavastros was very much eager to know more.

"Whatever happened to these lords, and how did this era come to an end?" he curiously asked. Moving closer to the fireplace, the prodigy stretched out, making himself comfortable on his warm fleecy rug.

"May I, sire?" asked Thelosious, looking meaningfully to the king.

"Please, go ahead; your knowledge of this era is *much* clearer than mine," he conceded, as all then turned to Thelosious. The cerebral one rubbed his hands together, showing his enthusiasm for this long forgotten age.

"After many eons of rule, people became deeply resentful of the tremendous power the lords wielded, as much as they did their lavish and greedy ways, when most ordinary people were struggling merely to survive. The vassals and many others directly under the lord's power organised into a vast underground movement before surfacing to directly challenge their authority, demanding fairer treatment and equality. A reasonable enough request, one would have thought - but the lords, in all their hubris, ignored these desperate pleas, believing it their divine right to rule over all. The people eventually lost patience, resulting in wide-spread rebellion throughout the lands. Many of the lords' castles were ransacked of their valuables, sending the lands deep into turmoil. Soon, virtually the entire known world had turned against the lords, isolating and eventually overthrowing them. The king by contrast had always been held in high esteem by the people, but had been unable to stop the proliferation of the lords' power due to their immense wealth." It had all become clearer to the inquisitive prodigy, who nodded with much interest.

"Oh Yes, "The Great Rebellion"," added the king, as Thelosious continued with unabated enthusiasm, not allowing for further interruption.

"The seven kings of the known world saw the opportunity to realise their dream of restoring the once-ways of the ancients - powerful centrally-controlled city-states, free of the greed and corruption of the lords, whose only desire had been for wealth, power and control - the wellbeing of their subjects having always been a secondary consideration. The King of Eternity led the way, offering everyone citizenship and equal rights in exchange for their direct loyalty and homage. The king would therefore circumvent the lords; have direct control over the entire populace and most importantly of all, gold and military resources. The kings of the other city states including Saphoeria, Brasovia and Gomercia soon followed suit, laying the foundation for the seven city states we now know. It is to be noted that, to this very sun, countless ruins of the lords' castles lie strewn throughout the known world."
The prodigy's eyes began to widen in amazement, unable to believe what he was hearing.

"So after the fall of the lords, the king could have done *exactly* as he pleased; for there was no council to tell him what to do!" he voiced in surprise, having never studied this age of history in any great depth. Thelosious was quick to explain this discrepancy in detail.

"Well, yes; therein lay the problem…" he impatiently replied. "…The lords argued exactly this, suggesting that they be placed together in an advisory council to the king, speaking on the people's behalf. Although now greatly weakened, the lords still had at least collectively, a considerable amount of wealth - and therefore power. The king of Eternity, wishing to appease them, created "The Council of Lords". The people were naturally, greatly displeased by this. They argued it was merely a return to the past ways, calling for a more democratically elected council. The king eventually gave in to enormous public pressure, permanently disbanding the lords' council. The Eternian High Council was thus established, finally delivering a *true* voice of the people, for the people *and by* the people," Thelosious proudly replied. Gavastros was still rather baffled, probing further.

"But the king - now of course our noble Alectorious, still in theory had and *still does* have absolute power - does he not? To this very sun, no-one can *directly* challenge the king's authority!" Gavastros thoughtfully pointed out. In the background, Alectorious was quietly enjoying the discussion as he kept warm in his thick blanket, curious where it all might lead.

"In theory that *is* correct, but the council as you know already, Gavastros wields tremendous influence over the king and his knights," Thelosious defensively retorted. "Remember, it was *they* who successfully appealed to the king to disband the Council of Lords. It was also they who, by unanimous voice, ultimately convinced our previous king to withdraw plans for the invasion of Saphoeria: a decision that saved many lives, indeed." Gavastros had a stark look of concern, realising the deeper meaning in all this.

"But what if the people were to tire of the kingship and one sun demand a democratically elected ruler?" he most controversially posed, perhaps if only to wind up his cerebral companion. Alectorious and Skolastros listened keenly in anticipation of Thelosious' answer. The king was surprisingly unconcerned by such a possibility, feeling the burden of the kingship was all too often far too much to bear. He had secretly wondered what life might be like without this great responsibility, living freely as he pleased. Skolastros remained silent and chose only to listen, feeling it best to leave the Eternians to their own affairs.

"Gavastros, how could you suggest such a thing - in the presence of the king himself, no less!" Thelosious incredulously scolded, but Alectorious was unphased.

"It is alright, Thelosious - Gavastros asks a valid question - please, continue!" he demanded, keen to hear his deep-thinking knight's response.

"Very well," replied Thelosious, continuing without hesitation. "It was of *some* concern, Gavastros, but you have to consider that for the people of this age to have any voice at all was unheard of just eons previously. Furthermore, the people then, as they do to this very sun, had the utmost respect for their king and his knights. It would have been *unthinkable* to challenge his majesty's rule," he added, confident the divine right of kings would *never* be broken. Gavastros was far less convinced, expressing his due concerns.

"I support our king every bit as much as you, Thelosious; but do *genuinely* fear for the future. None could have predicted the fall of the lords nor indeed rise of the Gomercians - yet that they did - and here we now are," he reasoned, expressing a hitherto unexplored philosophical side. Whether these were his *true* thoughts, or he merely sought yet another bout with his perennial sparring partner was another matter entirely. Thelosious responded defensively as the conversation became ever-more intriguing.

"None can predict the course of history, Gavastros: even the gods themselves! However, in as much as the council has tremendous influence, the king still *is* commander-in-chief of the armed forces, whose each and every member have sworn their undying loyalty to him. Perhaps *even more* significantly, the treasury falls directly under the king's control: all major expenses require his explicit consent. Even if there *were* calls for a democratically elected leader, that person would have neither the loyalty of the army *nor* the knights, without whom, Eternity would be utterly defenceless." Gavastros still held serious reservations.

"I doubt nothing you impart; only to say that when there is a will by one, there is always to be found a way," the prodigy reasoned, reciting a quote passed on by his mentor, Scalegrious in hoplite training before entry into knighthood. The king and Skolastros were still listening quietly in the background, following Thelosious' every word with intrigue.

"That maybe so, Gavastros; but remember that in addition to the full support of the army, the kingship is held in the very highest esteem by the minestros-hood, who firmly believe he rules by divine right of the gods themselves; against whose will, the people would *never* rebel. These two great pillars of Eternian society will *never in a thousand eons* be threatened," the cerebral knight upheld. Gavastros was forthright, venting his honest feelings.

"Well frankly, Thelosious, I just do not trust the council at all," he admitted. "For all *we* know, they could be sitting around this very moment, scheming and plotting our very downfall. With the king and ourselves away from Eternity so long, it would be the perfect moment for them to strike, would it not?" he suspiciously added. Thelosious was incredulous the prodigy would even *suggest* such a thing.

"By the gods, what treasonous talk is this? They would dare no such thing, Gavastros! With Eternity in an effective state of war, anything to destabilise the leadership would compromise our very *existence* as a nation: each and every one of the council well know this! Furthermore, any weakness would soon be exploited by our enemies. The king has always deeply respected the council and they in turn his divine right to rule. The kingship is inextricably ingrained in our culture, Gavastros; something no *true* Eternian would *ever dare* to jeopardise," he defensively replied, promptly sitting upright and folding his arms. The perennially suspicious Gavastros was still quite unconvinced.

"Well, whatever is to be of our great nation, I shall do all that I can to ensure we *never* fall to the heathenous rule of the empire," he proudly assured. "And I shall enjoy my position as knight of the Eternian realm for every sun that it be so," he added, as the king and Skolastros looked to rejoin the conversation. Alectorious leaned forward with intent. "And know that whatever befalls the kingship, we shall *always* be faithful companions," he promised with a broad smile. All were very much in agreement as Thelosious made a toast.

"To companionship!" he proclaimed, fittingly raising his cup of heady brew. The others did in kind, gulping a portion in recognition of their many eons spent together.

REIACTUS' LEGEND

Silence fell upon the knights as they sat around the sparkling fireplace, pondering what fate might behold them in the morrow. It was sure to be a sun more testing than any other on their daring adventure into lands uncharted - and would require every last piece of resolve, determination and courage to succeed in the perilous climb into the Buvarious Mountains.

The king's now only wish was to fulfill his lifelong dream: to discover once and for all if the great Reiactus still lived. Nothing else mattered. It would go beyond all that he had ever imagined possible and it now felt so close. The others' thoughts were dominated by other matters, with Gavastros wondering if he would ever see his beloved Eternity again; he so dearly missed the adulation of the citizens and hoplite warriors, many of whom looked up to the prodigy as a modern-sun hero, with his deft combat skills, guile and unparalleled strength. It was a feeling unsurpassed by anything he could possibly fathom. There was also the comfort of his knightly quarters: a veritable world away from this ancient valley ruin. Thelosious by contrast was more concerned by what might befall Eternity in their absence, in light of the apparent Gomercian plans for invasion. With no means of directly communicating with their companions back home, it was naturally of utmost concern. Skolastros was simply content to avoid questions about his own elusive past, yet was equally curious as to the Eternians' purpose in the great Buvarious. There was much he had yet to reveal about himself but felt it best to wait; at least for now. The Catharian turned to break the silence, hoping to divert attention away from any awkward questions and maintain his state of secrecy. With the air cooling and night growing on, he knew it would be the moment to ask the one thing he truly wished to know…

"You say you seek the great Reiactus, Alectorious; have you reason to believe he awaits your arrival?" Skolastros suggestively asked, with a subtle hint he knew *considerably* more than at first intimated. The king responded calmly, sensing no harm in the question.

"In Eternity, there is a prophecy that speaks of the great dragon's return..." he began, before going silent in reflection. All that could be heard were the crackling flames and howling winds in the background as all listened in anticipation. "...It is written that he would come to aid Eternity once more in her darkest moment as in the Age of Heroes over seven hundred eons ago. His return has long been dismissed by scholars as hearsay and the ramblings of delusional romantics..." the king furthered. He again paused as all were captivated. "...Until that is, we discovered a set of ancient scrolls corroborating this very thing. They were found in a cave nearby an abandoned castle, in many ways similar to this one." Skolastros' eyes widened with intrigue as he quickly drew conclusion.

"It must have been a lord's castle: they more than anyone else had a vested interest in hiding the *true* history of the known world. Any message of hope for the ordinary person would have been quickly suppressed and hidden away. What did these scrolls say?" the Catharian inquisitively asked, sitting upright in pronounced fascination.

"All has yet to be translated, but one of the passages said "When the earth shakes like thunder, a great dragon will soar, and a vast empire shall fall". The earth has shaken Skolastros, yet we still wait..." Skolastros sat back, peering thoughtfully into the flickering campfire and then to the ceiling, enquiring further about the king's journey.

"Yet, you have come so far to seek the great one's audience," he keenly observed, with Alectorious going somewhat on the defensive. It was indeed a major decision to make, leaving everything behind on such an audacious quest with no guarantee of success.

"It might seem like the actions of a madman, Skolastros, but to venture into these mountains was a calling stronger than anything I have ever felt; as if the gods themselves were willing me on to those enchanting peaks, guiding me to my destiny. Already indeed, we have made many fascinating discoveries. Perhaps it *was* Reiactus that summoned us; as a test of resilience, resolve and commitment to our cause," he reasoned, as his companions intimated their agreement. Skolastros was less than convinced though, knowing far more than he was willing to disclose of the enigmatic dragon.

"I'm not so sure, Alectorious. Reiactus is very reluctant to reveal himself - especially to those of The Great Plains - I think he would much rather leave the affairs of men to rest." he expounded. The three knights sat up as one, surprised by his unforeseen admission. Skolastros immediately regretted what he said as the king duly probed.

"Wait - how could you possibly know that, Skolastros? Reiactus has been absent from this world for countless eons - longer than any man could possibly live!" Skolastros hastily tried to backtrack in realising his mistake but managed to keep his cool.

"As we came to understand in Catharia, Reiactus' purpose was never to be a saviour. Rather, he is a being of great knowledge and wisdom, with much to impart to the world; it is his responsibility to guide those of good heart *back* on the path to the Higher Worlds." The Eternians were left speechless by this startling revelation; Gavastros was particularly miffed.

"So, *he did not* save Eternity during the Age of Heroes?" he asked in startled disbelief, having never heard this aspect of the dragon's life. Skolastros was quick to placate the prodigy's fears as he sat up with meaningful intent, folding his arms over his knees.

"On the contrary, Gavastros, without Reactus' help in the first Eternian war, your city would *most certainly not* stand as it does now. You must understand; there is so much more to this magnificent being than the eyes could possibly tell." The king, being very much in agreement, further clarified his position.

"I can well appreciate your sentiment, Skolastros; I have *always* known Reiactus to be a wise and noble being. Please, misinterpret not my intentions: I seek only his wise guidance and the gods willing, help in our struggle - *never* to be our saviour. I must further divulge that your words seem to confirm my intuition that he has indeed returned - or perhaps even, never left us at all," he deducted. The Catharian realised he could hide the truth no longer.

"It would serve you well to listen to this insight, for his presence has never been absent from these mountains…" he confirmed, as the three knights gasped.

"What are you saying, exactly?" the king asked, astonished. The others were equally taken as Skolastros divulged more of his clandestine knowledge.

"Throughout the ages, there has not been a moon gone by that he has been unsighted in these parts: the mythical Lands of the Dragon. Know that Reiactus is an immortal being: a thousand suns are but a blink of the eye to his kind." The Eternians were in unison quite disbelieving as the king animatedly probed.

"Have you yet encountered him?" Thelosious and Gavastros wondered much the same as they huddled closer. The Catharian went on as his voice rose evocatively.

"I believe I have once, many moons ago. It was but a flash; a mere moment in the span of my eons, but those unmistakable blue scales upon that mighty flying creature were most certainly that of the great dragon," Skolastros assured, as he vividly recalled his brief sighting a score of eons ago. The king was astonished, bursting with more questions.

"If what you say *is* true, why would he have hidden in the mountains all these eons?"

"Perhaps he was never hiding at all but rather, waiting for the right moment, and person to appear," Skolastros explained, drawing on his vast reserves of inner wisdom.

"Perhaps so, and is the very reason we were drawn here in his search," the king imagined. The Catharian was without reason to argue, nodding in agreement.

"It could very well be, Alectorious. In these mountains there do exist powerful forces well beyond our comprehension, enabling beings such as Reiactus to live *much* longer than they might have otherwise done. How this is so, I cannot say; only that it is. In any case, I am sure if it is meant to be, you *will* find the great dragon." The king responded with a boyish excitement as he recalled numerous ancient Eternian tales, myths and legends.

"It will be exactly like the Age of Heroes: man and dragon, united again as one," he dreamed, longing for a better world than the one he now knew. "His words would inspire us to great things and his strength help defeat the empire, once and for all," he added, evoking ancestral memories of the dragon's actions in the First Eternian war.

"I pray that it be so," Skolastros unequivocally agreed. The knights' imaginations were ignited as the prodigy imagined how they might be remembered.

"They will speak our names for a thousand eons: The Great King Alectorious the 2nd and his noble knights, Gavastros and Thelosious!" he zestfully claimed.

""The Heroic Eternian Quest into the Buvarious: in Search of Reiactus" - that is how our story would be entitled, I am sure," Thelosious pensively agreed, imagining how their adventures would be retold by writers and scholars many eons from now.

"So the Age of Heroes *does* return," declared Skolastros, sensing the many parallels with those legendary suns of mystique, intrigue and boundless courage.

AGE OF HEROES

The three knights sat around the fireplace focusing on Skolastros, surprised he had spoken so highly of *that* legendary age so treasured by the Eternian people. It was revered like no other before or since, heralding the very birth of their nation's history and remembered most of all for The Seven Heroes. These men's acts of gallantry inspired countless generations to rise up and beyond what any had thought possible, defying all those who dared threaten Eternity's existence as a shining beacon of hope for *all* the known world. It was the age that defined what it meant to be Eternian, the reason they fought with such passion for their country and all that it stood for. From the virtuous King Alectorious the 1st and mythical Achtreias to the celebrated victory in the First Eternian War, it was an age etched deeply in the consciousness of every man, woman and child throughout their ancient kingdom. No matter what befell them, Eternians would never in a thousand eons forget the tremendous sacrifices of their cherished ancestors to whose valourous actions they were forever indebted.

"Skolastros, you seem to know much of the Age of Heroes - I had thought it an era quite unknown to Catharians - I am fascinated to hear more of what you have learned," the king insisted, having hitherto assumed the forest people to be uninterested in such matters. Skolastros was desperate to prove to the contrary; he clasped his rough hands together, readying to captivate the king and his knights with enthralling tales of this enigmatic bye-gone era. Clearing his rusty throat, he continued with unbridled zest.

"There could not have been an age when braver souls walked these lands; men who sacrificed *everything* in the name of their civilization and all they believed in. It is a tale that has inspired me throughout my life and helped through countless hardships; for Indeed, I would not be sitting here now if it weren't for these brave souls. As you understand it, the heroes *were* Eternians, but they were also men; valiant warriors who would never in a thousand suns gave sway to adversity or gave up hope of achieving all they had ever dreamed. It was an era that defined the course of history for not only Eternity - but the entire world - including, perhaps even *especially* Catharia. For the birth of Eternity was ultimately, the birth of what *you* refer to as "the known world"." The knights were quite taken by these poetic words, urging him to continue as they huddled closer.

"Please go on, Skolastros, we wish to know all - truly," the king encouraged, intuitively sensing the Catharian knew far more than even *he* of this most revered age.

"Oh yes, Skolastros, you must!" Thelosious enthused, rubbing his hands together with glee. As expected, Gavastros expressed a genuine show of interest.

"My favourite era of them all; you have my undivided attention," he fervently assured. Skolastros nodded in acknowledgement, falling silent as he summoned his impressive knowledge of this long-forgotten age. He had to be cautious, for what he was about to impart might come as a surprise - even to the Eternians. Skolastros was well aware of the vast amount of knowledge lost, forgotten and even deliberately hidden throughout the ages to suit whatever powers might have been. He would reveal only what he must for now, and would divulge the full extent of his knowledge when he sensed The Great Spirit willed it.

As the Eternians sat in eager anticipation, the heavens in the night skies above began to open up; rain was soon falling heavily on the ancient stone castle as if to usher in the opening of this grandiose tale of adventure, drama and boundless intrigue.

"I think the heroes have spoken," the king evocatively remarked, as bolts of thunder lashed off in the distant mountain peaks and streams of water cascaded upon the roof of the castle. The stage was now perfectly set for this captivating but very real story of daring and courage. All smiled with the king, knowing it would be an epic retelling.

"They honour our presence," Gavastros agreed, looking above in the genuine belief that higher forces now watched over them. The cerebral one was in full agreement.

"It is a sign, to be certain," Thelosious affirmed, convinced it was their ancestors in Athepothesia, while Skolastros was unconcerned by the brewing calamity above.

"Are you ready?" he asked, as the knights all nodded in unison. The rains were now falling like a thousand thrusting spears and the thunder and lightning like the incessant screams of a great dragon. They had truly nothing to fear in the sanctuary of the castle though, protected as they were by its robust stony walls. Skolastros looked around at the knights before taking a deep breath, embarking on what would be an exhilarating retelling of these valourous forgotten eons.

"It was written in now lost ancient texts that well beyond the Buvarious Mountains and deep within the heart of the great unknown exists another world: one of such captivating beauty there are not words in our language to describe. These long-forgotten mystical lands are said to be heavenly beyond *all* belief: dramatic valleys of breathtaking beauty carved by the hands of the gods themselves; the purist forests and pastures of a thousand unseen mesmerising colours; cities of such glorious majesty that would capture your heart for a thousand suns if only your soul were pure enough to enter. As ancient legends have it, many eons ago, there was a band of seven brave young warriors originating from within these mysterious lands, wishing to reach out to where none had ever gone before.

There had been much written of a land far beyond populated by wild, savage peoples: a place where no other of their kind would dare venture in a thousand eons. This brave band of souls saw an opportunity to prove their valour, adamant they could pass any examination the gods could conceive. And so they boldly set off into the mountains on a heroic quest with their loyal followers, seeking the immortality of glory. They sought not only excitement and adventure but to explore these wild uncharted lands, hoping ultimately to create a glorious city; a mirror image of the one they would leave behind. So powerful were their convictions, the heroes believed it their duty to spread the greatness of their civilization to these alien lands and enlighten those unfortunate souls who still slumbered in the shadows of barbarism.

After many suns of hardship, struggle and toil, the seven explorers finally brought their audacious dream to realisation, finding themselves in the now "known world". For untold suns, the heroes had ventured through the treacherously high mountain passes of the great Buvarious, enduring the bitterly unforgiving conditions of freezing cold, howling winds, incessant snowstorms and thunderous skies. In their long and perilous journey, the heroes faced many obstacles from both within and outside themselves that would test every fibre of their mortal being. As well as icy winds and steep winding passes, they fought all manner of hideous beasts that would dare oppose their challenge into lands uncharted. Mythical creatures of tremendous size and the strength of many warriors stood in the heroes' path, threatening to devour them in the blink of an eye. There were winged, fire-breathing monsters of the most frightening appearance - half-man and half-dragon - that, with a single breath would burn you alive. There were giant four-legged monsters with heads of several animals living deep in the caves that would spring out and attack at any conceivable instant.

Not a man in their paradisiacal homeland of the unknown could understand why they had gone; risking everything in such hostile environments, only to find themselves in equally wild, inhospitable lands. So determined were the heroes to realise their grandiose dream; however, not even the wrath of the gods themselves could halt their relentless drive. The heroes and their loyal followers defiantly overcame all that was thrown before them, enduring every extreme of nature and overcoming every obstacle that dared thwart their advance. Never for a moment did they consider turning back, knowing the immortality of greatness itself beckoned for each and every soul that was to survive these most punishing tests of resolve, willpower and sheer self-belief. They knew their names would echo for a thousand eons in legend, poem and song *if* they were to rise up and achieve what most had believed to be impossible.

After many suns of struggle, the heroes finally made it through the perilous mountain passes, with their will to succeed unbreakable and their determination, unbreakable. They had the inextricable belief they could overcome any obstacle and achieve beyond what any had thought possible. Their leader, Alectorious the 1st, had the unrelenting conviction they followed the will of the gods themselves; guided, protected and watched over by the many divine beings of the Higher Worlds. The heroes continued their path down the mountains, eventually reaching this magnificent river valley. So captivated by its beauty, they duly named it "The Valley of the Gods". Many of the heroes' followers were instantly taken by the natural world beyond the great Buvarious, which reminded them very much of their homeland in the depths of the unknown. The hardier of them chose to remain in the mountains where their forbearers still live: the Prejosians, as you now know them. There was yet another group who, further on, discovered forests of indescribable beauty and beguiling mystique, unlike anything they could have imagined. These souls decided to remain in this enchanting paradise where they felt most at home, close to nature and The Great Spirit. They named their lands after a word meaning "purity" in an ancient dialect, one sun coming to be known as "Catharians". The seven heroes and majority of others decided to venture further, beyond the forests to the edge of what is now The Great Plains, resolutely determined to recreate the glory of their civilization. They discovered a perfect site for their new city: a small hill long thought by the native population to be cursed by an ancient spell. The heroes were convinced their gods had merely been protecting what had been ordained for them countless eons ago. Upon this hill, their glorious fortress was established, with Alectorious the 1st naming it as promised "Eternity": the city that would never fall. They are the direct descendants of the now Eternians - your ancient ancestors.

So you see, my companions, in ultimate truth, we are all connected in one way or another. The heroes are our forefathers, our creators: they wanted to spread their noble ideals to new lands and create a world where *all* could prosper, as in their glorious homeland. They came not for riches or glory but to spread what they truly believed to be the greatness of their civilisation, with their inconquerable spirit having never given into the adversity of their noble quest. It was the Age of Heroes and the birth of Eternity, captivated by men of such strength and courage there was nothing in the world that could douse their spirits nor will to overcome any thinkable adversity. Many have since attempted the intrepid journey back to these mysterious lands, retracing the steps of the seven heroes beyond the great Buvarious, but none have ever returned. Some say they were vanquished in the perilous journey through the unforgiving mountain peaks; others that they had reached it, and what they had found was so captivating that they decided never to leave. Yet others suggest they were simply unwilling to risk the return journey, so perilous an ordeal had their travels been. Perhaps we shall *never* know what lies beyond the Buvarious or that there is really nothing there at all: simply the wild imagination of scribes, scholars and mystics. I for one *firmly* believe it exists and that one sun, we *will* return to discover the answers to all that has troubled the minds of thinkers and philosophers alike, for thousands of suns."

As Skolastros finished, he allowed the Eternians to absorb this startling series of revelations. So captivated by his enchanting tale, the knights were speechless. The king in particular was struggling to articulate a meaningful response.

"I am utterly lost for words," he admitted, looking to the ceiling pensively as the rains continued to mercilessly fall upon the roof of the castle. "I had always been taught Catharians and Prejosians were here *long* before the arrival of the heroes. Why ever was this truth withheld, I do wonder?" he asked in bewilderment, with the prodigy also struggling to come to terms with it all. Thelosious was rather unsurprised, calmly offering his explanation.

"Well, there are many reasons, my king. National pride for one - the early Eternians might have wanted to feel different - somehow unique. So it was quite natural they would seek to differentiate themselves," he intelligently offered, as Skolastros completely agreed.

"Exactly!" he said, pointing his finger meaningfully at the cerebral one. The king could not deny his companion's words of reason and logic.

"It makes *perfect* sense. They wished to feel separate from everyone else - perhaps even enhance the idea that they - *we* were The Great Spirit's chosen people," Alectorious starkly admitted. The others nodded, very much in approval of his sentiment.

"Were the heroes not without opposition?" the king asked, somewhat changing the angle of the conversation. The Catharian moved to answer, clearly and succinctly as he could.

"Well of course; many of the native population didn't take well to these foreign settlers arrogantly claiming territory as they saw fit. However, the local tribes wouldn't dare come near the Eternians at first due to their, albeit, unfounded superstitions. They nonetheless feared these new arrivals would unsettle the balance of power and bring many unwanted influences. In this, their fears would prove true. The Eternians brought not only their culture and beliefs but weapons, fighting techniques and armoury never before seen. They were also highly organised, with a system of rule unheard of and a language that would come to dominate the known world to this very sun. It was quite unlike the native ones but relatively easy to learn, ultimately bringing this once fractured world ever closer together. The early Eternians sought to appease the local tribes' by companioning them and introducing them to "Eternian" ways: customs, culture, farming methods, construction, weapons, warfare and all manner of other things to help their new neighbours. Many of the northern peoples had a dramatic change of heart and took enthusiastically to these ideas, and warmly embraced the arrivals. Keen to establish a more centrally-controlled government, the northern tribal leaders believed the civilized ways of the Eternians to be a boon - a breath of fresh air away from the warlike tribalism that had hitherto dominated the lands. Before long, the northern regions had adopted many of the Eternian ways including their language, culture and belief systems. They would soon become firm allies, dividing themselves into two major city-states alongside Eternity: Brasovia and Saphoeria. A third city, Calgoria, was also soon established. It was loosely associated but chose to take a more neutral stance in periods of conflict.

The powerful tribal confederation of the south, which had until that point dominated the political landscape, was not particularly impressed with these foreign upstarts stealing their proverbial thunder. Their furiously jealous leader swore to vanquish the heathenous foreigners from what he saw as *his* rightful territory. The tribal confederation finally declared war on Eternity and her allies, determined to swing the pendulum of power back in their favour. Mustering every able-bodied man they possibly could, the confederation assembled an enormous force: the largest ever seen in the history of the known lands. They marched north, swearing to send the upstart newcomers beyond the mountains from whence they had come. And so thus began "The First Eternian War"," explained Skolastros, as vivid images of these dramatic historical events formed in the mind's eye of the Eternians.

"I can almost see it now: so very clear," said Gavastros, quite taken by Skolastros' skillful, as well as captivating story-telling. The king was also deeply moved.

"The might of the confederation armies must have been terrifying," he imagined, visualising the hordes of enemy soldiers as they descended upon Eternian city walls. Skolastros nodded, continuing as the king and his merry men listened, utterly mesmerised.

"Despite the overwhelming numbers faced, the Eternians and their allies managed against all expectations to thwart the relentless attacks of the tribal confederation. The Seven Heroes fought gallantly from the vanguard, encouraging their men to fight on, never wilting in the unshakable belief that *they* were destined for a glorious victory. The allies took heavy casualties but fought on undeterred, surpassing their numerically superior enemy in every facet of field combat. The heroes inspired Eternity and her allies to dramatic victory that sun, with a little help of course from a certain dragon…" Skolastros subtly divulged. As the king listened spellbound, Thelosious recounted an ancient text he had studied in middlehood eons.

"From out of the shadows of the great Buvarious appeared a grandiose creature; a dragon so large it blocked out the very rays of the twin suns themselves. With such blinding speed did it approach the field of battle, that neither companion nor foe could one tell. It swooped down into enemy lines, terrifying with its deafening screams, scattering the heathen like pebbles across the plains to the lands from whence they came…"

"That is all can I remember; we recited that passage on more occasions that I could possibly remember," the cerebral one acknowledged, as the king's eyes lit up.

"From the "The Eternian Book of Heroes" - if I am not mistaken - may I continue?" he asked. Alectorious was a keen student of his nation's long and turbulent history

"Please my king; it would be an honour," Thelosious encouraged, sitting back as his companion enthusiastically continued. Gavastros was meanwhile engrossed, imagining himself in the thick of the action during *that* glorious battle. Skolastros was also relishing the moment, with the thunder and rain only adding to the dramatic effect. The king went on…

"…Forever was this gallant soul immortalized by these heroic acts of valour by those to whom loyalty he swore, in this one eternal moment that was but a blink of the eye. For a thousand eons and more, he would be remembered as the greatest hero of them all…."

"And to this very sun, he is remembered as though it were but moons ago," Thelosious added, visualising the magnificent blue-scaled giant soar across the skies. The king was still full of questions, probing the wise Catharian for more detail.

"What I do not understand, Skolastros, is why Reiactus sided with Eternity?" he asked, having never heard a plausible explanation for this most perplexing of questions.

"There was a reason for this that is long forgotten to Eternians..." Skolastros responded. The king was beside himself in anticipation, beckoning for an answer.

"Well, whatever was it?" he asked, quite unable to contain his excitement.

"It all goes back to the heroes' journey through to the known world. It is said that while traversing through a perilously high mountain pass, the heroes discovered a pile of rocks that had come crashing down in an avalanche during a recent storm. Upon investigation, they discovered a small, scaly creature trapped underneath and seriously harmed. The ancients had initially thought to end the being's life, believing it to be yet another monster that would mercilessly devour them. Their leader, Alectorious the 1st instead took pity on the young creature, seeing it was of kind heart and without hostile intent like the many his men had already vanquished. He duly ordered his soldiers to clear the rocks and set it free. It was to the protest of many but Alectorious the 1st would have none of it. After much toil, they finally managed his bidding, uncovering what appeared to be an infant dragon. At this point, a magical thing was said to have happened: the young creature spoke, but curiously, could only be understood by the king. The dragon promised he would never forget the king's gracious actions and that if he or his people were *ever* in danger, he would come to their aid. Alectorious the 1st thanked the dragon, saying he had wished nothing but gratitude in return. The Eternian heroes continued on their quest, expecting never again to see the mysterious creature: how wrong were they.

The tale became folklore amongst the adventurers and eventually spread to the natives of The Great Plains, who believed the dragon to be the offspring of the gods themselves. It only served to heighten the status of the early Eternians, who many were convinced had been sent by the divine. It was not until eons later in the heat of *that* decisive battle the dragon returned to fulfill his promise, halting the tribal confederation's relentless advance on allied lines and catapulting him into mythical, almost godlike status. The dragon met with

Alectorious following the battle, thanking him again for his act of kindness from all those eons ago, hoping he had gone some way to repaying the recently-crowned leader. The king was naturally euphoric, promising him anything he wished. The dragon asked only that Eternity act as a keeper of peace and never to walk the destructive path of war and conquest. Alectorious swore in that very moment that every Eternian king thenceforth would be bound by this noble promise and their nation would respect the sovereignty of *all* free peoples. The king told the dragon he would always be welcome and remembered as a symbol of hope to this aspiring nation. The dragon was last seen disappearing into the mystical Buvarious Mountains from whence he had come; never, in recorded history at least, to be seen again. The blue colossus soon became legend; a symbol of Eternity, and inspired many acts of virtue. Alectorious the 1st felt this noble creature required a name befitting such magnificence, duly calling him after one of the brightest stars in the night sky: the legend of Reiactus was born." As Skolastros finished, the Eternians were awestruck by this captivating story of valiant heroes, forgotten lands and mythical creatures expertly retold.

"I could hear this tale a thousand fold and it would *still* inspire me beyond words," Alectorious admitted, feeling he could now achieve all he had ever dreamed.

"It makes me feel privileged to have been born in this, our great nation," Thelosious proudly expressed, as Gavastros displayed an equal sense of pride.

"If only we could travel back to this ancient era, I would have been honoured to stand side by side with our brave heroes in battle," he humbly offered, with this particular age being his personal favourite. Thelosious' response was rather contrasting to the prodigy.

"I must admit, the names of the heroes do escape me; those apart from king Alectorious the 1st of course," he rather sheepishly admitted, perhaps in a subtle attempt to get the better of Gavastros. The prodigy reacted angrily, unable to hold himself back.

"Of all the hypocrites, Thelosious!!!" he scalded. "You attack *me* for my ignorance of the lords, while you forget the names of our greatest heroes - how by the gods could you?" he snapped, prompting a somewhat nonchalant response. The king merely rolled his eyes as the never-ending saga of his two companions bickering continued.

"Please Gavastros, do enlighten us all," Thelosious haughtily invited. The prodigy was not at all hesitant, thrilled to reveal all he knew of this most celebrated ancient age.

"It would be my most honourable pleasure," he proudly replied, truly relishing the chance to impart his knowledge of The Seven Eternian Heroes. The group of adventurers moved closer to warm themselves around the cosy fireplace as the next chapter in Eternity's long and turbulent history duly began to unfold…

ACHTREIAS: GREAT HERO OF ETERNITY

It was late, but the Eternians would gladly hear stories of the ancients well into the cold mountain night. The convivial Gavastros was particularly enthused as he prepared to speak of his very favourite; the legendary warrior and hero of men: Achtreias. The king and Thelosious meanwhile relaxed in their warm blankets as Skolastros picked up a pile of firewood from the corner of the room before placing it gently onto the dying embers of the fire. It was becoming ever colder as the chilly biting air seeped in through the cracks of the ageing castle walls and along its stony grey floor. Indeed, the gathered men would require every last bit of warmth to see them through the night. Skolastros hastily returned to take his place amongst the intrepid Eternians, motioning to Gavastros to begin. The prodigy suitably took his cue, doing his utmost to accurately recount the lives of his courageous ancestors.

"The great heroes of Eternity were warriors of skill, bravery and valour unequalled to this very sun: men whose names are so treasured in folklaw, their very mention alone could inspire an entire army to rise up against the most overwhelming of odds. Their legend was and still is so revered by Eternian soldiers that it an honour to be even mentioned in the same breath; for they were such god-like souls that one could only ever *dream* of equalling. In total there were seven heroes, including and led by the legendary Alectorious the 1st, who in his own right is remembered as one of the greatest kings in Eternian history. The next of the heroes was Krakos; he of a proverbial lion's heart and strength of the finest steeds, with the ability to defeat ten men all on his own. There was Graos; remembered for his deep intuition, humble graciousness as much as his deft swordsmanship on the field of battle. Then there was Presoerious; a man of powerful charisma equaled only by his unrelenting determination to overcome all the obstacles the gods could possibly set upon his path. The third, Reispious, was one of powerful vision and foresight, sparing the heroes many a danger on their perilous adventure through icy mountain passes. There was Saephilious, whose stealth, speed and deceptive strength formed an equally indispensable part of this brave band of seven warriors.

But there was one soul who stood out above all others as a shining light of strength, courage and fortitude to the Eternian nation: his prowess as a warrior was equaled in every part by his authoritative charisma and ability to inspire men to victory with but a swing of his sword. His name was Achtreias: he with the heart of a dragon and god combined, they said; as strong as ten men and as fast as the howling winds themselves. Throughout his legendary life, Achtreias achieved many unimaginable feats of endurance, skill and of sheer courage, never in history to be equalled and for a thousand eons will not be. They say he travelled once, deep into the lands of the unknown with but armour, shield and sword, single-handedly defeating all manner of insidiously terrifying creatures on his path through the perilous mountain passes and bitter freezing winds. Some even claimed he scaled the sheer face of the Buvarious with his bare hands, and upon reaching the summit, he conversed with the great Reiactus himself. Such was his prowess on the field, Achtreias had an unmatched ability to inspire those around him with his heroic swordsmanship, boundless courage and unequalled strength. His reputation was such that many of the enemy would refuse to fight if they knew he was amongst the Eternian divisions.

Legend has it that after the triumph in the ancient battle of Largoerisia, Achtreias took it upon himself to run all the way to Eternity to inform the people, such was his delight in victory. It was not a few suns later he inexplicably passed to Athepothesia, much to the shock of the entire nation. Some say it was from sheer exhaustion, others that it was his chosen moment and yet others that there were more mysterious reasons. Little do Eternians realise that not only was Achtreias a powerful warrior, he possessed a mind equalled only by the greatest thinkers in the lands, with a tremendous fascination in all manner of subjects; most especially the history of his nation and people. As well as a fondness of the arts and history, he had a deep interest in philosophy and theology, having received countless teachings on the nature of the world by the many great minds of the era, such as the revered Astrious and Soctraious. Achtreias was also a keen patron of the arts, participating in some of the age's most famous plays; he even tried his hand at painting, would you believe! Achtreias, as many of his teachers, believed these lands to be an unjust place full of trickery, deceit and greed - everything a *true* Eternian detested. He *firmly* believed it was his noble duty to do all in his power to defend the innocent and uphold the values of freedom his people so dearly cherished. Achtreias wished to be remembered as more than just a great warrior, but as a learned individual with a genuine concern for the plight of his nation and people. Achtreias believed it was his place to defend all those who could not fight for themselves, protect the meek and ensure the strong follow *always* the ways of virtue, truth and compassion.

He was much loved throughout the lands for his countless acts of bravery, as well as his kindness. Countless warriors looked to him as a hero; wishing but knowing they would never equal his gallantry, valour and skillful swordsmanship. Achtreias was without a doubt, the greatest of all Eternian heroes, my companions: his devotion to king and country unquestionable, his bravery unmatchable and his legend, quite unbelievable." Gavastros paused, proud to have been able to recount the life of his favourite historical figure in such vivid detail. It was a story he had read a hundredfold and more in the books of heroes, inspiring him to be the valourous knight he now was. The others were simply spellbound by this captivating tale, with the king quick to offer his satisfied commendation.

"Thank you, Gavastros; that was truly profound. I am sure that one sun they shall remember you with equal admiration," he kindly offered, knowing how much this enchanting story meant to his companion since middlehood suns.

"Thank *you* my king, it would be an honour to be *even mentioned* in the same breath," he humbly replied, secretly dreaming it *would* be so. Thelosious also spoke graciously, subtly conceding his previously condescending remarks.

"I *am* impressed Gavastros, indeed - your knowledge of heroes surpasses even my own!" he admitted, as the prodigy took it on the chin.

"But there is never a great warrior without a rival, Thelosious," Gavastros suggestively said, before readying to finish his enthralling story. All listened with much enthusiasm as the rains lashed evocatively on the roof of the ancient castle...

"Yes, there was one... a rival to Achtreias from the distant lands of the tribal confederation where is now the Gomercian Empire. Deeply resentful of the Eternian Hero, this unnamed soul claimed to be the vastly superior warrior, swearing he would prove it by felling his prodigious opponent in battle. In truth, he was merely jealous of Achtreias' tremendous feats of strength, bravery and swordsmanship, as much as the adulation he enjoyed from his fellow countrymen. The Gomercian was a cruel, unkind being who derived morbid satisfaction from the power over and suffering of others - *nowhere near* the strength, intelligence and class of the legendary Achtreias - and deep down, he well knew it. The Gomercian believed himself to be the greatest warrior the known world had ever seen; but his delusional hubris was to be his very undoing. On the eve of a great battle, several eons after The First Eternian War, this unnamed Gomercian decided to challenge Achtreias to a duel to the end on the vast Plains of Marathosia. The clash was witnessed by the entire armies of Eternians and Gomericans, with both believing *their* hero *and* respective nations to be unbeatable. Many experts believed the battle would last an age, such was the skill of each warrior; Achtreias the quicker and the more agile, while the Gomercian bigger and stronger, but significantly slower.

The battle began surely enough at a ferocious pace, with neither warrior able to make headway over the other as they delivered enormous blow after mortal blow. They repelled each other with equal skill and dexterity, captivating to a standstill every last soul who bore witness to this enthralling duel. After what seemed an age, the larger Gomercian began to tire from the endless volley of powerful blows both delivered and received. Finally, the Eternian saw his opportunity: as his enemy dropped his guard for the briefest of moments, Achtreias, well aware of The Gomercian's renowned cruelty, mercilessly finished him off, severing his head clean from his body, stunning the onlookers into bewildered silence. Such was Gomercian shock at the sight of their fallen hero; they lost all appetite for battle, retreating in utter humiliation. They vowed that for the rest of existence they would not rest until this inglorious defeat avenged. This dishonor has haunted the dreams of Gomercians ever since that fateful sun. Even their imperial conquests have done little to erase this bitter memory, and will likely only be forgotten when their empire *finally* complete.

Achtreias' legend has been celebrated throughout the ages, with many an Eternian aspiring to emulate his noble, heroic deeds. None have thus far managed to reach the stellar heights Achtreias did in his celebrated lifespan, for he was a soul without comparison or compare; one through which the dragon spirit flowed so freely that his strength was equalled by only the gods themselves. Many have said we shall never see his like again; but I believe he *will* return, when our nation once more calls." As Gavastros stopped, a wave of inspiration surged dramatically through each of the gathered men. Alectorious felt invincible, sensing the spirit of their greatest hero was with them this mystical night.

"Truly moving, Gavastros - Eternity shall never forget his legend, I promise you," he steadfastly assured. The king was impressed by his companion's intricate knowledge, realising how one's passion could strive them to excel beyond all expectation. The prodigy smiled proudly as the Catharian offered his own plaudits.

"There are some things *even I didn't know*: very impressive, Gavastros," Skolastros admitted with intrigue, before placing more wood on the fire to ensure it would last the night. Thelosious meanwhile rubbed his chin, looking his usually pensive self.

"As much as we admire the seven heroes and their feats of valour, I dare say they lived in an age very much dominated by the sword and shield," he observed. It was a point well worth mentioning, thought the king, but would almost certainly upset the prodigy. He was not to be mistaken as Gavastros took it rather the wrong way.

"You do not *truly* respect the heroes, do you, Thelosious?" he angrily retorted, swift to defend these valourous souls that had been such an inspiration throughout his life.

"On the contrary, Gavastros, our heroes' feats of courage have defined who we truly are as Eternians and all that we live for. Indeed, they are to be revered for this; but there is more to our history than fighting, war and conflict," countered the cerebral knight. The king could only agree with this, further risking the ire of Gavastros.

"That there is, Thelosious, and it was many eons until we as Eternians came to this costly realisation. It was long after the Age of Heroes and well beyond the Age of Lords that a new age arose; one where deep philosophical enquiry overtook the insatiable desire for glory on the field." As the knights paused and rubbed their hands over the sparkling fire to warm up, they readied to hear another enthralling episode in their long and vibrant history.

AGE OF REASON

There was an age that had transformed the known world more than any other, opening the hearts and minds of the people to ideas, concepts and beliefs they could have never before imagined or conceived. It was an era unlike any hitherto, where the pursuit of the mind and spirit supplanted all that of ephemeral, worldly matter. The Age of Reason has arrived.

After so many eons living in a world dominated by conflict, struggle and the pursuit of power, people could finally turn their attention to more creative, fulfilling pursuits such as the arts, intellect and that which was philosophical or spiritual in nature. Finally, they could think freely without fear of ridicule, persecution or prejudice. While it was an age embraced by the many thinkers of the era, it was not as popular with those of the warrior class. Many of them believed this age of introspection had only served to weaken Eternity, allowing the empire to sweep across the lands while people were lost in their thoughts. Gavastros was one who believed this but was careful not to voice his opinion, knowing Alectorious was a great admirer of this much revered period. As he spoke, the prodigy tactfully chose his words.

"My king, the Age of Reason is one I have never quite understood; how exactly did it come to be and what, if anything, has ever come of it?" he cleverly asked, significantly understating his *true* feelings on the matter. The king was now tiring, with the morrow's arduous task of scaling the great Buvarious Mountains permeating his thoughts.

"The night grows old, Gavastros; I fear we must rest for the night," he wearily admitted, realising the challenges that lay ahead. Thelosious was of a rather different opinion.

"Oh come now, Alectorious; it will not take long!" he zealously encouraged, punching his fist in the air. "It is my favourite age; I would so relish the chance to hear it again," he fervently added. Eventually, the king yielded as he rubbed his weary eyes.

"Very well; but it will be the last of the evening," he insisted. Warming his hands close to the fire, Alectorious began to recount the next enthralling chapter of Eternity's long and turbulent history. Gavastros, Thelosious and Skolastros were intently waiting despite their much-needed journey into the dreamy realms of Astrala.

"As the Age of Heroes gave way to the pursuit of wealth and power in the Age of Lords, great suffering and hardship was experienced by the many and untold riches for the few. It inevitably manifested a longing for a better way of life; something more than just the constant struggle for survival and pursuit of individual glory. The Age of Lords thus came to its inevitably spectacular end. With the closing of this most oppressive age, a desire was born deep within the hearts and minds of the Eternian people for a more profound understanding of their nation's mysterious past and the vast worlds of creation. People had tired of war, conflict and the constant glorification of such, wishing to discover answers to things by means *other* than the sword and spear. They began to ask questions of this great mystery that was life, pondering the reasons their world had been brought into being and their *true purpose* in this land so scarred by war, conflict and the glorification of any one soul. More than anything else, they wished to discover a deeper meaning to their *own* lives beyond the constant struggle for survival. This enlightened age inspired a whole generation of free-thinking souls, with many philosophers, writers, astronomers and spiritualists coming strongly to prominence, wholly determined to answer those untold questions that had hitherto puzzled the minds of the populace. The mysteries of life, the gods, The Great Spirit and universe were passionately discussed, debated and endlessly inquired, as well as countless other matters of the mind, spirit and soul.

For untold suns, philosophers and spiritualists pondered why Eternians had been brought into this world and what purpose they were here to serve. There were many ideas concerning this; one of the most popular was that we had originated in the Higher Worlds, where we had once lived amongst the gods themselves. Some theorised we had been sent to this world as a test of our strength, courage and fortitude; to rise up from the labyrinth of darkness that is this known world, and thereby prove our worthiness of re-entering the *Higher Worlds* of spirit. Many realised this to be an enormous undertaking, concluding it would take many lifespans to achieve through countless incarnations in physical matter. Throughout this adventure that was life, they believed all would be protected by the gods, who would gently guide them onwards and upwards to their highest truth.

The early thinkers during the Age of Reason sought to examine the first Eternians and why they had been inspired to come from deep in the unknown to this barbaric, uncivilized land. Many believed they had been guided to serve as a beacon of hope and inspiration for the native souls and help lead them to return to the light of The Great Spirit.

There were also the famed Eternian astronomers such as Lumious and Anterious, who would each night look up in wonder to the stars in the sky, contemplating what might exist out there in that vast ocean of stellar light. They noted that the stars, as our own twin suns were never stationary, moving from one end of the lands to the other like mythical sailing ships on open waters. While at first controversial, astronomers concluded our twin suns were in fact stars themselves - and our world a giant spherical ball which revolved around them. The implications were extraordinary: the great stargazers realised an endless number of worlds just as our own might exist out there in the vastness of the universe. While it created much furore and excitement, we were unable to travel to or communicate with these far off stellar worlds and sadly, never pursued this realisation to any great length.

The philosophers also questioned the gods themselves and their purpose, wondering where they might exist in the limitlessness of The Great Spirit's creation. Some believed it was in a distant far away land and others that they lived high in the mountain peaks. A popular theory suggested the gods were spiritually advanced beings from the Higher Worlds, travelling to the lands of the *known world* in moments of tremendous need, assisting in any way that was possible in the people's journey back to the source of The Great Spirit.

Throughout the Age of Reason, writers scribed countless an enthralling tale; recounting amongst other things, the audacious journey of the heroes through the Buvarious Mountains. It inspired many courageous souls to emulate their legend, setting off in search of the mysterious lands from which their ancestors had originated all those eons ago. None are believed to have returned, further deepening the mystique, intrigue and mystery of what came to be known as "The Great Unknown". And so to this very sun does the Age of Reason continue, awaiting its much prophesised end." As the king's speech came to a close, he paused to rest, looking to the ceiling of the ancient castle in reflection. There was a pensive feeling in the room as Thelosious was next to offer his insights.

"An age quite in contrast to that of the 'Heroes and 'Lords, but a fitting conclusion to so much unnecessary, fruitless conflict," he fittingly acknowledged. The Catharian had rather mixed feelings on the topic before also speaking his mind.

"Yet, it didn't stem the tide of the empire, Alectorious: it seems the way of war and conflict dominates more than ever before," he starkly recognised, having witnessed so much of it in his long eons. Gavastros was quick to show his support for Skolastros' point of view.

"He speaks the truth, my liege; it seems all this thinking has led us nowhere," he boldly proclaimed. The king found himself very much on the defensive as he scrambled to conclude his story. Alectorious continued as the winds howled powerfully above and water from the tumbling rains trickled down the side of the ancient stone walls to form countless puddles around the mysterious valley castle. The Eternians listened as they revelled in the safety of their surroundings while cosying up to the bright flickering fire. The king carried on, clutching his hands together in deep concentration.

"Indeed, as historians looked at the three Ages of Eternity, they realised how much they had been dominated by war, conflict and the pursuit of wealth and power. They recognised that the known world had been in a constant battle between the forces of light and dark, where each and every individual's willpower, resolve and ability to rise up against adversity was persistently tested. They concluded that one sun there would be a grandiose battle where the forces of the light and The Great Spirit triumph over those of darkness and despair, forever vanquishing the heathen from these lands. When this occurs, Eternity and her followers would be catapulted back to where they *truly* belong in the Higher Worlds: a place of pure bliss where no harm would befall any soul. There, one would continue on their journey within and outside of themselves to an even greater understanding of all existence. After an untold expanse of eons, every soul would finally reunite as one with The Great Spirit: the source of all creation." As Alectorious finished, his knights were utterly spellbound, imagining the boundless possibilities *if* what the king had spoken of *was* true. Thelosious was particularly enthused, with the firm belief their present reality was but a drop in the proverbial ocean of life. The cerebral knight held nothing back in his expressiveness.

"Truly exquisite, my king; it makes one realise what might be out there in the vastness of all creation. I furthermore wonder if we shall *ever* know all there is to of this world and the universe; perhaps we will not, until we ourselves reunite with The Great Spirit in the Higher Realms above," Thelosious articulated, as the king looked thoughtful.

"Perhaps it *is* that we shall never know all there is to of this world, but we *can* strive with every fragment of our heart and soul to make it a better place for all."

SKOLASTROS' PAST

The night was growing old and the prodigy had drifted far off into the mystical realms of Astrala with the Elite Guard, who had long been slumbering on the stony floor of the ancient castle chamber. Thelosious, Alectorious and Skolastros were still enjoying the warmth of the fire and absorbing conversation, which was a welcome remove from the rigours of their thus-far tumultuous journey. The remaining three could acutely feel the bite of the ice-cool air sneaking in through the castle walls, with only the fireplace and warm blankets keeping them from freezing to the bone. Skolastros had grown increasingly quiet during the evening, for reasons that were quite unbeknownst to the two awakened Eternians. As much as he had wished, the king had hitherto refrained from asking anything even vaguely personal; but his curiosity was now overwhelming and Alectorious could simply not help a passing remark. The Catharian would simply tell half-truths or craftily evade the question if he wished not to answer, the king reasoned. Alectorious readied himself for the proverbial plunge, bracing for all manner of responses.

"Skolastros, you have been in this valley a great many suns; may I ask what compelled you to venture all the way up here in the first place?" he tactfully asked, unsure of the reaction. Skolastros froze as an awkward silence fell upon the castle chamber, with only the crackling flames and howling winds to be heard. Alectorious instantly regretted having asked, sensing he had stepped over an invisible boundary. Thelosious felt an equal sense of unease as Skolastros stared into the fire as if desperately looking for a way out. After what seemed an age, the Catharian managed to drag his gaze away to face the nervous king.

"Forgive my silence, Alectorious. In truth, ever since you arrived I have tried to evade such questions. I admit it was wrong to do so and shall now face up to my past," he unexpectedly replied, as the king desperately tried to backtrack.

"I do apologise; I wished not to upset you in any way. We need not speak of it any further," Alectorious said, waving his hand, but Skolastros was adamant; almost embarrassed.

"No, Alectorious - I *will* tell you," he insisted. The king and Thelosious felt much more at ease now, with their attention firmly fixed on Skolastros. He continued, much to the Eternians' curiosity as they relaxed, intermittently warming their hands on the fire.

"Indeed, I *do* hail from the lands known as Catharia - that much is true - but it is a place I have spent few of my living eons. As a young man I was an ambitious warrior, wishing for a greater challenge than my homeland could ever possibly afford me. In my view, most Catharians simply wanted to hide in the safety of the forests, away from all the problems of the world. In the unwilting belief that *I could* make a difference, I set out in search of an army that would have me; a noble force of virtue, valour and gallantry, exactly as in that legendary Age of Heroes: The Kingdom of Eternity was the obvious choice. And so I travelled to that luminous city, hoping I might join the ranks of the famed hoplites and The Great Spirit willing, one sun work my way up to the Elite Guard. A number of Eternian commanders were not particularly enthused by the idea of a lowly Catharian within their haughty ranks, believing me to be unworthy of such a prodigious honour. Others were indifferent, with one officer named Hectrious greatly sympathizing with my plight. He suggested I head to Saphoeria where Catharians had been warmly welcomed for many generations. So I heeded his advice and rode out across The Great Plains to the mysterious eastern city, where, as was spoken, they embraced me as one of their own - like a brother, indeed. I found a home in a battalion of peoples from many origins across the known world, including several Catharians and Eternians. I took quickly to this soldierly life, impressing my superior officers with my swordsmanship and ability to inspire those around me. I rapidly moved up through the ranks to battalion commander and before long, tactical field command, where I was jointly responsible for the entire Saphoerian army. I became the pride of

Saphoeria and Catharia, revered and celebrated by many for what could be achieved with but hard work and commitment. It was the pinnacle of my life and something I could have only ever dreamed of as a young soul back in Catharia," Skolastros explained, casting his mind nostalgically back to those long-past eons. He could almost feel again the adulation of his fellow soldiers; the companionship he had so dearly cherished and the touch of the hilt of his golden sword, so vivid were his memories. The king and Thelosious were naturally quite taken back; having never imagined one of such humble beginnings could ascend to such a position. Looking deep into his wise old eyes, Alectorious could see the battle-hardened warrior Skolastros was born - and had always destined by the gods to be.

"This is a most honourable achievement, Skolastros; and I duly salute you for this. It is for certain, a great privilege to be in your presence," the king respectfully offered, intuitively sensing the many hardships suffered throughout the Catharians' life.

"That it *was* indeed..." smiled Skolastros, his expression suddenly dimming as he continued. "... But it wasn't long after my appointment to joint field command that the Gomercian army marched on the very gates of Saphoeria, bent on adding it to their burgeoning empire. We all knew it would be a decisive moment - a battle that could determine Saphoeria's fate for a thousand eons. Knowing they were a highly immobile and centralised force, we boldly laid down the challenge to fight on the open plains of Marathosia: the Gomercians of course, gladly accepted. We thought we could outflank them with our faster, more agile forces and send the imperial army into complete disarray; but how wrong were we. The enemy legions held fast and strong, thwarting our every attempt to draw out their flanks and expose their centre. Instead it was *our* army sent into confusion, forced back behind the Saphoerian city walls to defend as best we possibly could. The overwhelming number of Gomercians eventually broke down our defences with their siege weapons and by the end of the sun, the ancient city was *all theirs.* I was subsequently expelled and told never to return, forever burdening the loss of Saphoeria on my shoulders.

From that moment on, I swore to never again to be responsible for another soul and not in a million suns ever to forgive myself. I simply couldn't bear the shame of returning to Catharia as the great hope that had become their humiliation. In my dreams I saw the faces of all those who looked up to me and the country I had failed: it was simply all too much to bear. Wishing to escape the indignity of being responsible for Saphoeria's end, I set off into the mountains with the intention of never returning. On one fine sun of my travels, I stumbled upon this enchanting valley. I immediately knew I had found my place in the world - where I *truly* belonged - my home." The Eternian king was unsure as how to react, unable to fathom the sheer sense of loss Skolastros now felt. Thelosious was far more knowledgeable of this era than the king, offering his sympathies to the embattled Catharian.

"I have read of this conflict, Skolastros," admitted the Eternian knight, in an understanding tone. "There was *nothing* you could have done; not even the greatest generals would have been able to stop those kind of numbers," he added, remembering in detail from his extensive military studies. Alectorious also recalled reading about it in one of his favourite books during middlehood not long before he had been crowned as king.

"I remember this - The Battle of Saphoeria - I read of it once in "Great Battles of the Known World"!" he admitted, evoking memories of this well-known text on military history. Alectorious recalled those countless nights he would stay up late, reciting many a tale of courage on the field. The king continued, supporting his companion's thoughts. "Thelosious is right, Skolastros - those numbers were unbelievable! Even if you *had* stayed behind Saphoeria's walls, the city would have fallen all the same. It has never been as fortified as Eternity or Brasovia. You did *not* deserve what you received," he steadfastly maintained. Still unconvinced, Skolastros looked straight into the Eternian leader's eyes.

"How could you *possibly* know that? You were *not there* Alectorious. We could have won that battle, *I swear*. There was a chance - we were so close," the Catharian insisted. Clenching his fist in frustration, the veteran soldier found it so very hard to let go.

"It matters not anymore, Skolastros - it is all in the past, and there is nothing you can do to change it - you simply have to move on. Even the gods *themselves* cannot alter what has been. It is of no service to anyone for such talent to go to waste in this distant valley; you could do much to help those struggling in the world," the king insisted, sensing a burning desire within the Catharian to again make a difference.

"But I have nowhere else to go, Alectorious," Skolastros sighed, looking around the ancient walls of his castle home, certain that here he would spend the rest of his eons.

"You would be most welcome in Eternity; I feel there is much you could impart to help in our struggle," Alectorious suggested, genuine in every word he spoke. Skolastros' looked to the roof of the castle in reflection as he contemplated the king's words. His expression suddenly brightened, sensing he *could* make amends for those long lost eons.

"I would wish only to impart my knowledge - not take up a command, you do understand," the veteran subtly replied, wishing desperately to avoid a repeat of the past. The king was fittingly delighted, providing all the reassurances he possibly could.

"Whatever is your wish; any contribution would be *invaluable*," he promised elatedly, hoping the Catharian *would* join them. He was still doubtful, hesitating for a moment.

"I shall have to sleep on it," Skolastros responded, rubbing his tired, wrinkled eyes.

"Take all the suns required," encouraged the equally exhausted king, more than ready for a good night's rest. "Well, I think it best we retire for the night; for there is a great journey ahead of us in the morrow." Skolastros and Thelosious nodded in agreement. Wrapping themselves in their thick, warm blankets, the three men lay down close to the fire on the ancient stony castle floor. Their spirits soon drifted peacefully into the realms of Astrala - the land of dreams - in rest and readiness for the morrow's adventures, unbeknownst of what fate or fortune might soon behold…

VALLEY TEMPLE

Alectorious awoke dramatically from his slumber to a bright sunny morn, enlivened more than ever by the path ahead. The king had dreamt of the most beautiful paradise in all the worlds imaginable, with deep valleys, towering mountain peaks and an enormous body of water stretching as far as the eye could perceive. It was a place quite unlike any other, with a brilliance and tranquility equalled only by the abode of gods themselves. Alectorious remembered the tales he had heard the previous night of mysterious lands beyond the great Buvarious Mountains, wondering if it had been to there he had ventured in his dreams. If it were so, it would be a land, and a place well worth fighting for.

"Forgive me, my liege; the sun grows on and there is a long journey ahead," whispered his cerebral companion, knowing they would need every last bit of sunlight to reach their esteemed destination. Alectorious nodded in complete understanding, putting aside for now, his lofty thoughts. The king sat up and rubbed his eyes to gather his senses.

"I shall be ready soon, Thelosious." Standing up straight, he stretched every limb in his nimble body before Gavastros approached with a small bowl of enticing-looking food.

"This will help awaken you, my king, and give strength for the journey ahead; eat, for it is a good meal," the prodigy encouraged, handing his eons-long companion some freshly made soup. The king sat on the stone cold floor of the castle to enjoy his glorious sustenance, washing it down with a swig of tasty natural juice that Skolastros had prepared with some orange-coloured fruits from the local forests. Upon finishing, Alectorious put on his armour with the help of several Elite Guardsmen. The armour was made from a strong, lightweight alloy unique to Eternity. Instrumental in bettering the Gomercians on many occasions; the shiny blue metal composite was created from a formula shrouded in utmost secrecy.

"Where are the others?" the king asked, looking around the empty castle hall.

"They await you outside, my lord," replied Quintos, the assisting Elite Guardsman, as he motioned to the narrow stone entrance. Allowing the king to rest as long as was possible, the others had already made the necessary preparations for their onward journey.

"Sire; your sword," offered the Elite Guardsman, Segaerious. Handing over the elegantly decorated weapon, Alectorious took a firm hold of its handle.

"Thank you, Segaerious," the king replied, as he hastily attached the fine blade to his weapons belt. "You both go ahead," he insisted, motioning to Quintos and Segaerious, who duly went outside to join the others. The king desired to be alone in his final moments in the valley castle, wishing to reflect on all the wondrous memories he had made here. He would never forget staying awake, long into the mountain night with his noble companions, talking of great heroes and victories as thunder and rain tumbled down outside, or feeling that deep bond of companionship with his fellow knights as they shared the history and myths of their glorious nation. Alectorious took a long, deep breath, looking around the ancient chamber as if to absorb those incredible memories deep into his body and soul.

After some peaceful reflection, the king finally stood up. He walked to the entrance of the chamber before making his way briskly through the courtyard to the main gate where his knights and Elite Guard were patiently waiting along with the Catharian, Skolastros.

"My fellow Eternians, my humble apologies; I am not usually one to slumber so long. Our status, if you please?" he politely asked. Thelosious stepped forward from the group of waiting soldiers, answering his companion in detail.

"My king - Segaerious, Chamelious and Mykos have volunteered to stay in the valley with the horses - Aeirious, Quintos, Rhoedas and Lacoenious will journey with us into the great Buvarious," he announced, naming the Elite Guardsmen that would stay and go.

"Will it not mean we will have to return to the valley?" asked the king, frustrated, remembering the plan to travel through Catharia on the return to Eternity.

"Worry not, Alectorious; it won't take long to double back," Skolastros assured, knowing these lands as well as he did. The king nodded in quiet relief as he turned to face the veteran Saphoerian commander, who was saddened to say goodbye so soon.

"Well, it has been my most humble pleasure, Skolastros. I do hope we meet again before long *and* that you carefully consider my offer. The known world needs people like you, now more than ever before," he warmly encouraged. The king firmly grasped the hand of the Catharian, who expressed his equal disappointment in having to bid farewell.

"It was an honour to be your host and a memory I shall *always* cherish, Alectorious. I bid farewell for now, but I'm sure we'll meet again, very soon," he amiably replied, in a subtle implication he would accept the king's offer. Alectorious knew without a word being said, it *would* be so. With that, Thelosious ordered the Elite Guardsmen into formation.

"Eternians - prepare to depart!" he bellowed, as his subordinates suitably obliged. Skolastros spoke once more, imparting some rather invaluable information.

"Remember, before long you'll reach the crossroads: to the east will lead you where you wish to go, into the Buvarious Mountains where Reiactus is said to be," the Catharian advised. As he motioned to the peaks in the distance, the king felt a tingling sensation run straight down his spine - of excitement or trepidation - he was not sure which.

"And to the north and west?" he asked, looking up beyond the enchanting forests to the north, sensing that his destiny lay there.

"Follow the path west and you shall reach the lands of Catharia - and thereafter, Eternity," he promised, nodding his head in that general direction; but the king was still very curious about the mysterious lands that lay beyond.

"And north?" he asked with intrigue. Skolastros shook his head in uncertainty.

"It is believed to be the path into The Great Unknown, but none have ever returned to tell the tale." Alectorious smiled, sensing this was soon to change.

"When all of this is over, I promise…" he began, looking out beyond the distant snowy mountain peaks with meaningful intent. Skolastros interceded, adamant it *would* be so.

"I *know* that you will, Alectorious," he replied with confidence. The king simply nodded as he started up the valley towards the forests in the distance. After only few steps the Catharian spoke again, stopping the king right in his tracks.

"Wait! Forget not of the temple, Alectorious - I sense something of great importance will be imparted to you there," he insisted, pointing to the ancient structure further up.

"By the gods, of course - the temple! In all the excitement I forgot to ask - do you know anything of it?" the king wondered, signalling for his men to halt. He turned around and edged a little bit back along the path to the Catharian, unable to believe they had not spoken of it until now. Skolastros happily explained as Alectorious listened intently.

"It was built by the Eternian Heroes upon their passing through this valley in honour of the mountain god, Arturious, and sky god, Siriosious. Later settlers regularly worshiped there, praying for good fortune in all kind; be it harvest, trade, rain or even snow in the long winters," answered the Catharian. The king was somewhat mystified by this.

"Rain I understand, but snow?" he asked, squinting his eyes, a little bit confused. Skolastros explained a little more as the king listened pensively.

"The snow and rain were considered sacred to the ancients, as indeed they still are for many. The rains were like tears of the gods purifying the landscape of all its impurities; the snow on the other hand was believed to be a blanket of protection from wayward spirits through the long, cold dark winters. I imagine it to be somewhat similar to your Eternian temples - quite amazing really - after untold eons, still very much intact. Visit while you still have the chance, Alectorious, for it may *never* be so again," Skolastros encouraged. It was indeed, a unique opportunity the king simply could not afford to miss.

"That I will, Skolastros - thank you - and farewell," he replied, as the old Catharian bowed graciously. Alectorious bid his final goodbye before returning to his fellow Eternians.

"Thelosious - we must visit the temple before leaving the valley," he insisted, knowing it paramount to show their respects to the gods, The Great Spirit *and* their ancestors.

"I very much agree, sire; we shall await you near the entrance when we arrive," Thelosious promised, realising it wise to pray for good fortune. As the Eternians made their way up the long narrow path through the valley, a feeling of tremendous sadness came over them. The adventurers admired their striking surroundings, knowing they might never set foot here again. Many eons from now they would speak of this enchanting abode and its many curiosities: the plush meadows, crystal clear river and sweeping mountains. Like somewhere out of a fairytale, these were memories that would remain for the rest of their suns.

As the Eternians neared the valley temple, Alectorious broke off from the main group before moving closer to the intriguing structure. He immediately noted its remarkable condition, despite having been constructed many eons ago in *that* heroic age. To his knowledge, there were few other examples of its kind anywhere in the known world. Alectorious felt greatly privileged to be able to visit this masterful creation of the ancients and would relish every last moment. There were numerous trees and shrubs growing around the perimeter, in many ways similar to the Eternian Temples. The elegant building was surrounded by large circular columns on each side, which were all decorated with intricate engravings and pictures from a long forgotten age, still visible despite many eons in the harsh climes of the mountains. Warriors, birds and wild animals adorned its ancient surface, in homage to the powerful beings that had once graced these mysterious lands. The roof was equally familiar in design to the Eternian Temples - slanted slightly on both sides and pointing to the bright blue skies above. The king approached the ancient structure with an overwhelming sense of déjà vu, as if having been here just a few suns ago. It was an incomparable sense of familiarity: perhaps from memories of another life. In that very moment, a gust of wind blew up from the valley floor, sweeping scores of fallen leaves in the king's direction. It was like a wave of invisible energy welcoming him into this sacred realm of wonder, mystery and boundless intrigue.

Alectorious stopped but paces from the bottom of the temple steps in awe of the mystical presence he sensed emanating. He absorbed the peaceful enchanting energies deep into his body and soul, imagining The Ancient Heroes standing on this very spot. He continued with eager anticipation, sensing that same otherworldly presence experienced in the Temples of Eternity. Alectorious took each step slowly up to the thick marble decorated columns, stopping once more before walking inside and taking a deep breath. As the king edged inside, he felt a wave of mystical energy surrounding and soothing; calming, relaxing and releasing every bit of tension from throughout his body and soul. It was a feeling of almost total bliss; as if he had entered the realms of the Higher Worlds. The presence of the gods was immensely strong here, thought the king, surprised they still graced this ancient temple after so many eons of disuse. Perhaps it was that they had just returned - or had maybe been here all along. Alectorious gazed around the highly-decorated walls and ceiling, observing numerous perfectly-preserved paintings of enchanting mountain landscapes and mysterious animals, amazed so much detail was still visible after so very long. The king moved closer to the middle of the temple where the presence of the gods was strongest, hoping to connect with this divine enigmatic presence. He knelt down, taking several deep breaths to relax his body and to receive their divine wisdom. The king breathed deeper and silenced his thoughts, concentrating as much as was possible.

"Oh gods and Great Spirit, speak unto to me now; what words of wisdom dost thou have for thy most humble servant," he asked, in an almost quiet whisper. Alectorious waited patiently for some moments, receiving at first, no answer. He was surprised, for in Eternity the response had usually been relatively swift. Then again, it had not been on his previous visit to the temples. Sensing it a test, he persevered, continuing his repetition of deep reflective breaths. Before long a quiet, whispering voice spoke softly in his ear.

"Patience, my dear companion…" it unexpectedly heartened. Alectorious was rather taken aback. The Eternian king continued to wait, breathing deeply in concentration. Before long, an image began to form within his mind's eye as he fell deep into a trance.

Alectorious suddenly found himself soaring high over the mountains upon a great blue dragon towards a destination unknown. The king looked out to the high mountain peaks stretching out to seeming infinity and the vast plains, far below: it was a vision so real he could have sworn he was *actually* there. Alectorious glanced over his shoulder to the left and saw a large golden dragon with bright blue-green piercing eyes, ridden by who he believed to be the legendary King of Heroes, Alectorious the 1st. He turned back to his right as a Dragon of earth-colour appeared, ridden by a man dressed in Catharian attire. His identity was unclear but was strikingly similar to the forestman, Sandros. The three dragons swooped down in unison over the forests and the City of Eternity before turning dramatically east toward the much-revered Dragon's Pass. The dragons flew over the legendary pass before changing direction once more, heading southwest to the mountaintop fortress of Brasovia. As they approached the imposing citadel, bowmen from high in its parapets began to shower the flying creatures with wave upon wave of arrows, but they merely bounced off the powerful beings as if protected by an invisible energy shield. The three soaring titans circled thrice-fold before diving at the Brasovian fortress, unleashing a stream of bright-blue coloured flames from their nostrils, freezing the enemy solid with a single blast. Not moments later, the soldiers shattered into thousands of fragments before disappearing as if they never were.

The three dragons dived into the castle of Brasovia at blinding speed as everything blurred into a dreamy haze. In that moment Alectorious woke, breathing heavily as he opened his eyes. He was stunned by the sheer vividness of his vision - it truly was mystical - the likes of which he had never seen before. Perhaps it was by virtue of the higher energies of the valley such powerful apparitions were possible; he might never truly know. In any event, the king knew it was a message of tremendous importance. The Great Spirit had spoken and there was little question what he was being encouraged to do. After all, Alectorious thought, the Eternians *were* destined to take that great mountaintop fortress. The king decided it best to keep it quiet for now and await the most appropriate moment to impart to his companions.

With that, Alectorious rose to his feet and made his way out of the temple into the bright blue skies and mystical energies of the captivating river valley. He looked around to the natural wonder surrounding, which was now more vibrant and colourful than ever. The king's visit to The Heroes' Temple had been a profoundly transforming experience, affecting him in many ways yet to be seen. It was a literal breath of fresh air, putting him in good stead for the remainder of his intrepid journey. The king turned to his knights and Elite Guard waiting not twenty spears distant, ready for the arduous climb into the mountains. Thelosious in particular sensed a change in his companion's spirits.

"I hope your meeting with the gods was fruitful, my king," he subtly suggested.

"It most certainly was; but a story for another sun," Alectorious replied, taking hold of his weapons. Thelosious understood well, knowing the king would as always choose his moment. Alectorious turned to his men with unusual zest, feeling more inspired than ever.

"Are you ready to fulfill your destiny, fellow Eternians?" he asked, elated, prompting an equally positive response from his loyal followers.

"We have been ready all our lives, my liege!" an ardent Quintos replied. Gavastros was equally enthusiastic, itching for action as usual.

"For Eternity!" he passionately cried, as the king delivered the orders to depart.

"Onto the Great Buvarious!" he exclaimed with great fervour. The king and his men trekked diagonally across the valley from the temple to resume the forested path, which would eventually lead them to the foot of the towering Buvarious Mountains; further than any Eternian since written records began. It would be an adventure unsurpassed in their long and turbulent history, and one that all were truly proud to be a part. With a heavy heart, the travellers bade their final farewell to the enchanting river valley before turning towards their destiny, believing that whatever was to pass, they had changed Eternity and her people's fate, forevermore. The warriors departed The Valley of the Gods in one part deeply saddened, but in the other knowing it was a memory that would *always* remain, deep within their noble spirits.

TOWARD THE GREAT MOUNTAINS

The seven remaining Eternians; Alectorious, Thelosious, Gavastros, Aeirious, Quintos, Rhoedas and Lacoenious made their way briskly north along the valley path towards the thick alpine forests, which would eventually lead up to the foot of the mystical Buvarious Mountains. A series of towering peaks reaching into the skies from just beyond the river valley, the Buvarious were truly a sight to behold: higher than any other in the known world, their cragged snowcapped tops only added to the dramatic effect. There were many tales as to what could be found in the heights of these imposing behemoths; from powerful dragons, giants and monsters, to enormous crystal caverns or even gateways to other worlds. Their allure was clear, but only until the Eternians reached those lofty peaks would they know if the legends spoken were true and the great dragon Reiacus indeed lay in wait.

As the group finally departed the valley and entered the forests, there was a definitely heightened sense of purpose amongst the three intrepid knights, who were all now confident they *would* realise the dream they had for so many eons yearned. The king was relieved to feel those all-too familiar soothing energies of the forests once again, which brought a deep sense of calm to his tender body and soul. It was something Alectorious had grown so accustomed to on this fine adventure, making him wonder if he could *ever* return to life as leader of a powerful nation-state. It was nonetheless exhilarating to be on this most valiant of quests: one that so few kings had ever the audacity to embark upon. It was *especially* encouraging that he was on the final stretch of realising his life-long dream of reaching the Buvarious Mountains - and if most incredibly fortunate, meeting the legendary dragon, Reiactus.

The rest of the Eternians felt a collective sense of relief to be back on the path, so close to those mystical peaks they could almost touch them with their own bare hands.

As much as the Valley of the Gods had been an enlightening, awe-inspiring experience, one did as the legends alluded, feel a strange sensation of being trapped there; for it was a place so enticing there was a feeling of wishing never to leave. Yet, what lay ahead was so daunting, there was an element of desire not to continue. Alectorious had thought much of this, concluding that while an alluringly beautiful place, the actualised level of growth for any soul living in this sheltered valley would be relatively limited. He realised there was nothing to really compel one's spirit to rise up and fulfill their *true* potential here. For those like Skolastros, it might serve to ease difficulties faced at a particular moment in life, but for one to live *all their suns* in the valley, well, that would be another matter entirely.

The king thought more of Skolastros and their initial meeting - the fact he had been sitting at the riverside in that *exact* moment had seemed rather odd - co-incidental even. It was almost as if the Catharian had been awaiting the Eternians' arrival, for reasons Alectorious was yet to completely fathom. In any case, there was certainly much more to Skolastros than had been revealed and the king was determined to find out all that he could.

Alectorious cast a meaningful glance to his knights and Elite Guard, who all were seemingly content to be back on the path. Eternians were generally a very proactive people: waiting around for things to happen had never been their way. Thelosious was very much his usual self, quietly trekking along while his mind lost in the heavens contemplating all manner of things, while Gavastros seemed even by his standards, unusually zealous. The prodigy was apparently unconcerned about leaving his beloved steed behind in the valley and was now leading the group from the front with confident ease. Indeed, it was heartening for the king to have seen his companion grow in so many different ways...

Gavastros balanced his sword and sheath over his broad, powerful shoulders, relaxing in the knowing there was little chance of encountering his arch nemesis, the Gomercians, in such a remote region. As much as he relished the heat of combat, there was *even* for he, moments for quiet introspection. The prodigy had been thinking more of what Alectorious had spoken a few suns previously at the forest campfire, realising there *was* a lot more to him than a valourous knight of the Eternian realm. Gavastros acknowledged that he really should begin to ask more questions of himself and his life's purpose; for one sun, he would pass into Athepothesia and look back upon all he had done, wondering what it had all been for. Life as an Eternian knight was without question a privileged one - to be recognised, adored and revered by one's fellow countrymen - a position most could only dream of. But there was something even *he* admitted was inexplicably missing that even this glamorous life of heroic battles and daring adventures could not provide. He wondered what could possibly fill that gaping void within, wondering if it was something everyone felt in this worldly realm of matter. Maybe it *was* only by entering the Higher Worlds that *true* fulfillment could be realised - and was this, therefore, the ultimate goal Eternians were destined to achieve?

Gavastros further contemplated life in the Higher Worlds and how one might spend one's suns in this heavenly abode: it was hard to imagine Eternity was destined for such a dazzling place considering her long history steeped in turmoil and conflict. He wondered what manner of place the Higher Worlds were and how the gods amused themselves in their lofty paradise; if they ate, drank and were merry, or adventured into wild uncharted lands as he and his fellow Eternians now did. The prodigy chillingly realised that without Gomercians and wars, there would be no knights - and almost certainly not any fighting. Whatever would become of him, he thought in a moment of sheer trepidation, shuddering at the thought of having to lay down arms and be a knight no more. He wondered if he truly wished to go to the Higher Worlds at all if it were not possible to test one's physical prowess, swordsmanship and valour there. Gavastros thought further as to what he would do in a world without fighting or conflict, nor adversary or foe. Struggle was all he had ever known in life, as had been the quest to obtain the highly-esteemed title of "Knight of the Eternian Realm". It was an honour for which so many had fought yet so few ever achieved; for including the king himself, only seven righteous souls could become a knight at any given moment. It only highlighted the privileged nature of this position the prodigy had managed to achieve. From his eons as a young esquire to hoplite, the rigorous demands of the Elite Guard and finally entry into knighthood, it had been a struggle each and every sun of the way. Against the countless others wishing to better him, the indomitable Gavastros had been victorious. Indeed, it was difficult to imagine another way of living. If only he could catch but a glimpse of the Higher Worlds' magnificence, he might even grow to like it. Perhaps after all, there *would* be tournaments or other such contests to test one's valour, resilience and bravery.

What Gavastros might become with neither sword nor shield, he could but only wonder with great foreboding. However, even in *this* world he was able to test his physical prowess in many other ways - embarking on an adventure beyond the Buvarious Mountains into the lands of the unknown was one such example - in search of challenges, adventure and excitement or fair maidens, even! It would be greater than this intrepid quest, if it even possible to travel that far at all. Gavastros had heard many a tale of the perilous dangers that lay in the unknown lands, firmly believing he was man enough to face whatever tests the gods could possibly throw at him - and venture where no other Eternian ever had. He felt deep within that whatever was to be, many yet unseen possibilities would in due course present themselves. For now at least, it was best to concentrate on the path ahead *if* he and his companions were to return safely home. Gavastros intuitively looked up from his vantage point at the front of the group, noticing the path dramatically begin to widen.

"My king - a clearing!" he exclaimed, pointing animatedly with his shining sword.

"I see it, Gavastros!" Alectorious replied, squinting his eyes to focus on the opening in the trees ahead. Thelosious had no question what he saw before him.

"It must surely be the crossroads, sire!" he concluded in equal excitement. The knights made their way briskly forth, unbeknownst what lay ahead.

SERENDIPIDOUS ENCOUNTER

The Eternians gathered at the mysterious clearing in the forests where the path as Skolastros had explained split into three directions; onwards north through the mountain ranges; to the west, towards Catharia and Eternity; and to the east, it ascended dramatically into the highest point of The Great Buvarious Mountains. The king and his men looked up in awe to the unimaginable colossus of rock, snow and ice staring down upon them, with some naturally beginning to wonder if it were indeed wise to continue. The unpredictable nature of the high mountain passes was well documented by learned Eternian cartographers and scholars; and the smallest mistake would have the most catastrophic consequences. Alectorious knew the perils all too well but was completely unphased by the daunting challenge ahead.

As Gavastros scanned the cragged mountains covered in a thick white blanket of snow and ice, he felt a sense of fear he had never before in all his eons. The Elite Guardsmen were equally unaccustomed to taking such risks, with several wondering how long they would survive in those unforgiving peaks reaching high into the skies above. Meanwhile, Thelosious' mind was wandering elsewhere; he intuitively looked to the right of the path junction where he noticed a peculiar flat-faced boulder. As his companions stared up, mesmerised by the imposing snowy summits, the cerebral one moved in closer for inspection, noticing an unusual script carved deep within its aged, smooth surface.

"My king, look; there is something written on the stone!" Thelosious announced, frantically beckoning the others, so instantly captivated by the mysterious writings was he. His companions gathered round in haste, with some more impressed than others.

"It is just a lot of old scribbles!" bemused Gavastros, unable to see any real meaning.

"It is far more than that," countered Alectorious, realising its *true* significance.

"It is a pictorial alphabet, my king, and very ancient: one of the first written languages of the known world," Thelosious excitedly claimed. Alectorious was deeply intrigued.

"Can you understand any of it?" he asked, kneeling alongside, greatly impatient.

"It has been eons since I have studied this particular script but I can more or less decipher it. Give me a few moments," he promised, concentrating on the mysterious writings. Clearing his throat as he ran his finger along the smooth surface of the stone, he began.

"Noble travellers to whom these words I do impart; choose wisely the path thee now follow, for in a thousand suns henceforth, thou shall remember this moment and the destiny thou chose. One may discover untold mysterious wonders in the great Buvarious; but beware the wrath of these enigmatic mountains, for their beauty is truly the most deceptive of all.

Beyond the known world to the north is a land of beauty and mystique that one could only imagine in their wildest of dreams; I urge thee on to these uncharted lands, only if thou are prepared never to return.

If the dangers of the unknown tremble thy limbs, to the west thou shall find the lands from whence thou came.

Choose wisely brave and noble travellers; for thou do write the very course of history with each step dost thou take."

Thelosious took a few moments to catch his breath as his companions mulled over the curious writings. The king was genuinely moved, shaking his head in disbelief.

"Profound - the words so alive - almost like a living story," he observed. Moving in for closer examination of the complex pictorial alphabet, Alectorious caressed the fine grooves of the characters with his delicate fingers. In that moment, he felt the most unusual presence - as if someone was secretly watching him…

"Expectations… curious things are they not?" whispered a nearby, unknown voice. Startled, the king turned round to see a slightly-built young man standing not a few paces distant. He was dressed in blue and golden robes much like those worn in the Eternian temples, except more finely adapted to this cold mountain environment. He seemed slightly younger than Gavastros, with the king imagining some twenty-two eons or so. Having not heard his approach, the other Eternians turned around in equal dismay, quite unsure how to react. The young man was carrying a long wooden walking staff but was otherwise unarmed and seemingly harmless. The mysterious soul was seemingly, completely unperturbed by the heavily-armed guards that had moved around the king as he smiled at the group of warriors.

"Stand down men, he is not dangerous," the king ordered, sensing the man posed no serious threat. The guardsmen duly complied, lowering their swords. The king waited as if in invitation to the stranger, who began to pace around the forest clearing speaking his mind.

"Indeed, we expect much of this life and the world, yet, so rarely and for so few souls do these hopes, dreams and expectations ever seem to be realised. I have asked as I have pondered for a countless many suns: is this something in itself that should be expected and, is it but the way of the known world? Or perhaps it is that the hardships we suffer are designed to galvanize us to achieving what we never thought possible," he articulately posed. The Eternians were mostly speechless but the king was very much intrigued by what the man had to say. He responded with calm, only too happy to engage in some impromptu philosophical discussion, as much as he wished to know more about this curious soul.

"Well, I have come to believe, he who appears from nowhere, that the challenges of life in the known world compel us to rise up and beyond anything we could have ever expected of ourselves," Alectorious countered, as though to a companion of many suns. The young man nodded in appreciation of these thoughtful words while the others stood back, listening intently. The stranger had stopped his incessant pacing around in the soft grass, looking directly at the king with arms slightly folded. Alectorious continued as the others wondered where this perplexing conversation was leading.

"We must walk the paths we have chosen in our hearts to follow; for with no doubt it is to where we are destined," the king added. The man contemplated the king's words before resuming his pacing around the edge of the forest clearing.

"And has life thus-far, for you and your noble knights, king, I assume of the great city of Eternity, compelled you to such?" replied the man, apparently rather well-travelled.

"Well, it is for *that very* reason we stand upon this soil, on the verge of these here Great Buvarious Mountains," Alectorious responded, with calm and increasing intrigue.

"Then I applaud, as do I convey my most humble words of respect and admiration unto you, and your courageous warriors," the traveller offered, before bowing graciously. The king nodded in kind as Thelosious probed further, his curiousity now overwhelming.

"Tell me, have you heard much of our homeland?" he asked, stepping forward.

"Oh yes, most honoured knight, I know Eternity very well: the city of many hopes, dreams and courage: standing as a proverbial one-man army in defiance of imperial tyranny, never wilting, faulting or *ever* giving in the identity of who they are and where they come from. They are a proud nation, indeed - a *truly* great nation. And I shall say it an honour to humbly stand before her noble king and his knights: it is something I shall always cherish," he whole-heartedly offered. Alectorious was flattered, expressing due words of appreciation.

"We stand before you in equal humility, great mystic - if that is indeed your path in this world," he replied, sensing the man was one who followed the inner ways.

"I follow many paths as do we all, but that is one of them, yes," he elusively replied, clearly trying to avoid the question. The king realised his unease before changing tact.

"How, may I ask, did you find yourself in such a remote area - do you hail from these lands?" he asked, wondering by what means one with so few possessions survived out here in this harsh, unforgiving alpine wilderness.

"From deep in the mountains is my true home, although I have traversed much of the known world searching… seeking… reaching out to those who wish to receive..." the curious mystic replied, as Alectorious probed yet further as to his meaning.

"Receive… what exactly?" he questioned, squinting his eyes with interest.

"Well, knowledge of course - a deep understanding of The Great Spirit that I have garnered from my endless inner search and many wise masters throughout my travels - one of whom I believe you now seek," the man answered. The king's eyes excitedly lit up, subconsciously knowing *exactly* of whom the beguiling mystic alluded.

"Wait - you speak of Reactus?" Alectorious gasped, with his mouth wide open. The young mystic answered in no uncertain terms, quite to the delight of the gathered.

"That it is, I do; his noble spirit shines like a thousand suns throughout these mountains out to the souls of all spiritual seekers - those with the courage and fortitude enough to follow their *true heart's calling*. I do believe he has summoned you here for reason of great importance, King Alectorious. It was no coincidence, nor folly in your thoughts at all to venture to the Buvarious. I believe you *will* meet Reiactus, but there shall be one more test," the mystic tellingly replied, as he peered out ominously to the imposing peaks shimmering in the brightness of the morning suns. The king could hardly contain his excitement: his lifelong dream now so close to realisation. Alectorious moved closer.

"How could you know this?" he whispered in bewilderment, as the mystic was calm.

"Perhaps it is but a feeling; for a great king would never risk so much if it were not for a great end," he explained intuitively. Alectorious could not argue with this logic.

"There is much truth in what you say," he admitted. Thelosious was still doubtful of the man's claims as he looked up, daunted by the behemoth of ice and snow above.

"These mountains are enormous! *Even if* Reiactus *is* there, it would take many suns to find him that we simply do not have!" he remarked, wondering how it could possibly be done. The mystic shook his head as he peered up at the imposing peaks.

"It need not be that way; for if you continue on the path to the east into the mountains, you will eventually reach the ice caves of Prejosia. From there, if The Great Spirit means it to be, you *will* be drawn to that which you seek…" the young man elusively replied. He gazed longingly with walking stick in both hands as a giant cloud of snow dramatically blew over the icy mountain peaks. The king was heartened as he was beguiled by the path ahead.

"Do you mean to say that whatever one seeks, he shall find up in the Buvarious? It sounds almost like magic," he imagined. The mystic shook his head, correcting the king.

"No, not magic, for there is no such thing; but powers beyond your comprehension," he explained with eyes gleaming. The king simply nodded, knowing there was only one way of knowing. Realising what had to be done, Alectorious brought their discussion to a close.

"Well, the sun is short and there is yet far to travel. I thank you for your words of insight, mystic; they shall *not* be forgotten," the Eternian leader offered, priming for the climb into the hazardous peaks. The mysterious stranger was equally gracious in reply.

"I bid you farewell, worthy King Alectorious. I hope as I do pray that, along with your brave knights, you vanquish the heathenous empire from these once-benevolent lands. I must say that it is deeply saddening that so many suffer at the hands of so few and that great kings are unable to fulfill their bright destinies. Easy it is for one to attack that which is vulnerable and so very wrongly misinterpreted as weak - and an *even greater* misfortune it is that so many give into the temptation of power, attacking those innocent souls who are unable to defend themselves. Know that you *can and will* defeat the forces that are not of the light, King Alectorious. My heart, thoughts and my prayers will be with you, always," the mystic offered, heartfelt. The king was deeply inspired and felt the need to express his gratitude.

"It has been many a sun since my ears have been blessed with such words of wisdom and fortitude. I think it thus appropriate to bid you welcome in my city at any moment of your choosing," the Eternian leader kindly insisted. Alectorious reached into his pouch, handing the mystic a shining gold coin bearing the seal of Eternity. "If you ever *do* make it, show this to the guards and they will guide you to me: it is the mark of the Eternian king," he promised, hoping it *would* be so. Thelosious was meanwhile concerned for the young man.

"These lands may not be safe for much longer, mystic - it might be wise to seek refuge with us in Eternity - the empire will not be as sympathetic to your beliefs as we," The mystic appreciated Thelosious' sentiment but was elusive as he readied to depart.

"It would be an honour; I feel we shall meet again, my dear companions."

The king pushed no further, offering his final farewell to the curious stranger.

"So long, mountain mystic, and may The Great Spirit *always* protect you."

The enigmatic young traveler bowed before quietly walking away toward the snowy mountain peaks. Alectorious looked confused as he turned to his fellow Eternians.

"Are you alright, my king?" queried Thelosious, with Gavastros equally concerned. The king shook his head profusely as if trying to snap out of a trance.

"I had the strangest feeling of déjà vu when I spoke to that mystic; it was quite inexplicable, almost as if I was looking into a mirror," he admitted.

"Well there was a *slight* resemblance; perhaps you met him once before or maybe you followed that path once in another life…" Thelosious suggested, as the king momentarily froze. Alectorious instinctively looked around but the man was nowhere to be seen.

"He has disappeared - impossible - no-one could ever move that fast!" he exclaimed. Thelosious was not at all surprised, knowing the mysterious nature of the mountains.

"Nothing here is as it seems," he remarked with a smile. Feeling as though he had been dreaming, Alectorious searched within for answers. Eventually, he resigned himself to the fact that some things were simply just not meant to be known - for now at least.

"It certainly is not. Well, I sense we shall meet him again, when the moment right,"

"I also," agreed Thelosious, as they shifted their focus back to the path. The king looked to the Elite Guard, who had been busy preparing for the impending ascent.

"Eternians! Are you ready?" he asked with great fervor. The guardsmen responded in unison and with much gusto, ready to sacrifice their lives if duty so required.

"Sire, Elite Guard, ready!" they roared in unison, swiftly assembling before the king and his valiant knights. The intrepid group of Eternians then moved into single-file for the ascent up the eastern path to their destiny in the towering icy peaks, high above.

INTO THE BUVARIOUS

The king and his men readied to embark the narrow winding path that led all the way up the side of the steep rocky mountain face to the summit of the Great Buvarious Mountains. They all knew this would be the most challenging part of their thus-far stirring adventure, with icy winds, high altitude and potential for avalanche a constant threat to their mortal lives; but it would doubtlessly prove rewarding *if* the Eternians were to succeed in their ambitions of finding the great Reiactus. Alectorious and Thelosious felt a sense of exhilaration not experienced since those long-past middlehood suns, having never ventured this close to the heavens. As they imagined the wonders lying in wait, Gavastros was secretly questioning the rationale of what they were about to do: for the potential danger as much as his recently-discovered dislike of great heights. The king sensed his unease, casting a concerned glance.

"Are you ready, Gavastros?" he asked, with no expectation of answer. The prodigy looked to the snow and ice-covered rock faces, shuddering at the mere sight of those daunting peaks reaching high above. He attempted a brave face, wishing not to show sign of weakness.

"For Eternity - *always,* my king," Gavastros boldly asserted. His body language, which normally had such a cool, confident aura about it, was wholly unconvincing. The tracker Rhoedas fittingly interrupted, having been vigilantly assessing the path ahead.

"My king, if we make haste, it should take us until early noon to reach the summit. We shall most certainly make it back before the night falls," he promised, having carefully analyzed the contours and topography of the precarious mountain face. The king was satisfied with what he had heard; confident his men were fully up to the task.

"Very well, Rhoedas - it shall be done. Gavastros, if you would have the honour," Alectorious asked, inviting the prodigy to lead the way. He accepted, knowing it the perfect chance to prove he *was* man enough to face the rigours of these colossal mountains.

"Eternians - to the great Buvarious!" the prodigy cried, casting his arm dramatically forward. The group of adventurers followed in single file up the winding rocky trail, with mixed feelings of excitement, anticipation and sheer trepidation running through their brittle bones. One by one they followed the harrowing mountain path, hugging the steep faces of hard rock as they progressed. The travellers took every step with the greatest of care, knowing that one wrong move could end it all and plunge them into the endless abyss. After several meandering twists and turns, the Eternians soon found themselves at a considerable height - as much as two thousand hoplites, the king imagined, and were afforded a spectacular view of the tree-lined valleys, far below. At the king's behest, they stopped to absorb the stunning scenery as the ice-cold winds bit hard on their battle-hardened faces. The Eternians gazed out as one, utterly beguiled by the mesmerising vista.

"Breathtaking, is it not, my king?" Thelosious asked, almost lost for words. The king absorbed the magnificent sight before his eyes, struggling to express his feelings of awe.

"I could have never imagined I would live to see something like this, Thelosious," he admitted. Alectorious scanned the valleys of evergreen trees before looking across to the range of snowcapped mountain peaks shimmering in the distance to the west, gasping. It was like the abode of the gods themselves, such was the brilliance of this natural wonder.

"You have come so far, Alectorious, and you should be truly proud of that," his loyal companion commended. The king acknowledged this but was not entirely in agreement.

"Not yet far enough," he rather sternly replied, glancing meditatively to the icy summits, hoping beyond hope his great dream would soon be realised.

"We shall be there before you know it, Alectorious," encouraged Thelosious with a playful pat on the back, as if having intuitively sensed the king's thoughts.

"I only hope the gods allow it be so, Thelosious," Alectorious replied, mesmerised by the impressive snowy pinnacles. The Eternians absorbed the beauty of their surroundings for a while longer before continuing up the gigantic mountain.

"We must move on; for the gods will not wait for us," realised the king. With that, the Eternians departed their unique vantage point. As they ventured higher, the path was covered in an increasingly thick blanket of snow, as ice was formed all along the imposing mountain face. The need for care was greater than ever as Rhoedas sounded warning.

"Be cautious my king, for the surface is most slippery!" he cried, realising one wrong step could prove fatal. It was a tremendous risk for such inexperienced climbers to be so high in the mountains, he thought, praying the gods above would protect them. The king suddenly looked up ahead then behind, seeing the prodigy had completely disappeared from view.

"Where's Gavastros?" he asked, as the others looked on in equal concern. Their worries were short-lived as the convivial knight appeared from around the corner some ten spears distant, having been quietly walking ahead. So lost in his thoughts, the king hadn't even noticed. There was an odd expression of mixed relief and worry on Gavastros' face: all naturally wondered what it could possibly be.

"My king, we cannot go on - the path has disappeared!" the prodigy exclaimed, almost breathless from the thin, high-altitude air. As he pointed further down snowy path, the king and Thelosious immediately feared the worst. "Impossible!" frustrated Rhoedas, having already examined the map in detail. "Unless of course...." he added in trepidation. There was only one way to find out: the Eternians started round the mazy bend of freezing snow and ice, eventually arriving at a large gap in the path.

"Avalanche!" the king gasped, concluding it was the only explanation. Looking to the pile of rubble far below, he wondered how they might ever be able to cross the gaping hole stretching between the two ends of the path. At almost three spears in width, the king feared it might thwart any further advance up the mountain path.

"We cannot go on," he whispered in great disappointment, slamming his palm on the hard icy rock face as he felt his lofty dream rapidly begin to fade. Thelosious was equally dismayed as he stared incredulously at the perilous gap in the rock.

"Surely it is far too dangerous," he imagined, with the Elite Guard nodding in seeming agreement. Only Rhoedas believed to the contrary, confident they *could* cross.

"Really, not at all - give me some rope!" he chirpily demanded, turning to his fellow guardsman, Quintos, who duly passed a coil of thick cord from his broad shoulder to Rhoedas. Meanwhile, Gavastros looked anxiously down into the abyss, gasping in fright.

"This is madness, Rhoedas - we shall never make it!" he baulked, but the tracker was confident. "Watch and learn, my companion," he insisted, unravelling the coil of thick rope in readiness to climb. The others looked on disbelievingly as they began to tremble from fear and the biting cold infusing their bodies, feeling very much as Gavastros now did.

"What *exactly* is it that you propose, Rhoedas?" asked the king in bewilderment, gulping nervously. The tracker calmly explained, calling on his deep well of knowledge.

"The path might have fallen away but there are a large number of indentations across the face of the mountain - if we can wedge the rope in on the other side of the path we will be able to use them as footholds to make our way over - I shall go first!" he fearlessly professed, but Alectorious wished not to unnecessarily risk the lives of his men. He looked to Thelosious, who was at equal unease with Rhoedas' proposition.

"Your call, my king," he responded, knowing it a decision for the king; and he alone. Alectorious thought intensely but eventually conceded, knowing there was no other way.

"Alright Rhoedas, tie yourself into the rope; we shall hold you fast," the king ordered. Rhoedas did so: he tied the rope through a solid metal climbing loop on his belt and readied to cross the icy divide. Quintos had already chiselled another loop into the rock and tied the other end to it as the Eternians all held firmly onto the rope to safe-guard Rhoedas.

"When you are ready, Rhoedas!" Quintos exclaimed, motioning to his brave companion. The tracker began to make his way onto the sheer face, skillfully placing his feet in the small indentations across the rocky wall. He used the other cracks and protrusions for his fingers and hands, dragging his nimble body across the perilously steep cliff. The king, Thelosious and especially Gavastros looked on in trepidation, knowing it would be *they* who soon crossed. Rhoedas made his way over and without incident, much to the relief of the king and his men. As Rhoedas set foot on the other side, he quickly wedged metal loop into the rock with a small hammer. He rapidly threaded the rope through and tied it tight before pulling down hard with all his weight, as the men at the other side of the gap did likewise.

"Ready!" Rhoedas shouted to the others, few of whom shared his enthusiasm.

"Attach your belt to the rope and try not to let go of the rock: I know not how much weight we can hold!" he warned, as Quintos bravely stepped up.

"Wait, I shall go next!" Gavastros insisted, brashly pushing the Elite Guardsman aside. He took a small metal loop and attached it to his belt before fixing it to the main rope spanning the gap in the mountain path. It was a tried and tested technique for Eternian climbers but for those inexperienced in mountainous regions, understandably daunting.

"Take it slow and sure, Gavastros; it will be over in but a moment," encouraged the fretful king. As the icy winds began to relentlessly howl and waves of snow swept across the icy rock face, Alectorious sensed his companion was far more fearful than he appeared. Gavastros moved further toward the edge, first placing his hands on the thick rope. He grabbed it as tightly as possible and placed his foot firmly in the first foothold on the cliff face before shuffling hastily across. Gavastros was at first unshaken, methodically moving his feet and hands as if an expert climber of many suns - but it was not for long...

"AHHH!!!" he screamed. A part of the rock had suddenly given way as the prodigy's knee smashed hard on the side of cliff face. As a thousand icy particles began to rain down, panic infused the group of Eternian warriors. Gavastros' body dangled uncontrollably as he tried to grab hold of something, knowing it could soon be the end of it all. The king screamed in terror as his companion's life hung precariously in the balance.

"GAVASTROS!" he bellowed, as Rhoedas tried his best to restore cool.

"Stay calm!" the tracker shouted, as the Eternians called on their collective strength to support their endangered companion. "There is a crack to your left, Gavastros; try to place your foot in it!" he advised, as the prodigy scrambled desperately to pull himself up.

"I cannot - it is too far!" he cried, with the tension now almost tangible.

"Quickly, Gavastros!" whispered the king, as the others looked on in trepidation. The prodigy finally managed to wedge his foot into the rock, dramatically pulling himself upright. He froze still on the mountain face as everyone breathed a collective sigh of relief. The king called out to his companion as his words echoed across the cliff face.

"Gavastros, are you alright, man?" After several tense moments, the prodigy spoke.

"My knee is a bit sore, but I am otherwise okay; I shall be across in but an instant," he assured, taking several deep breaths to calm his shredded nerves. The prodigy continued, arriving at the other side before he knew it. Looking back, he thanked the gods for their mercy. The king was next and carefully attached his belt to the rope. Having identified a somewhat safer route, Alectorious made it over confidently and without incident. Thelosious followed close behind and to his relief, also managed to avoid the dangers suffered by his overzealous companion. Finally, the remaining Elite Guardsmen made their way to the other side of the rocky abyss, with all greatly relieved to have averted an early passage to Athepothesia. Yet again, the gods had watched over these brave and noble warriors.

SNOWSTORM

The Eternian explorers trundled further up the winding mountain path, more determined than ever to see their divine mission through to the end. Alectorious felt the pure mountain air as it soothed his tiring body and soul, clearing his weathered spirit of all those unwanted energies and opening his mind to a plethora of intriguing possibilities. He felt a great sense of calm as he looked to the path ahead, which was so clear now there was only one direction to follow. There was something dreamlike about these mystical mountains, which were so far removed from civilization and the known world that it was difficult to fathom he was living the same life but a handful of suns ago.

The king had heard whispers from certain knowledgeable Eternians of mysterious occurrences in these mountain passes and wondered if they held any truth. Perhaps most fascinating of all was the story of a secret gateway within the Buvarious' lofty peaks, if through which one were to pass, would be instantaneously transported to another world. Alectorious was utterly captivated by the thought, pondering if it was by this means Reiactus had returned to *his* world; and if souls who had ventured in his search ever discovered it. Perhaps those who had, had been whisked off to a far-away land, finding themselves in a place from which they wished never to return. The king hoped he would soon find the answer to this and many other secrets of these revered mountains, intuitively sensing that in due course all would be revealed. Returning his mind to the present, it seemed unbelievable they walked upon the mighty Buvarious - it had been a dream just a handful of suns ago - *now* they were finally living it, the king happily realised.

Before long, heavy snows began to fall all around, encompassing the intrepid adventurers and covering the narrow path with a blanket of pure-white powdery essence. The Eternians' advance slowed as the snow rapidly tumbled down, quickly thickening on the once rocky ground. The man in front was barely visible as the winds relentlessly howled, with footprints the only way of recognising the trail ahead. After another twelve spears' march, a blinding white had totally encapsulated the bold adventurers, who were now knee-deep in snow and barely able to move. The ever vigilant Rhoedas delivered appropriate warning.

"My king, we cannot continue in this blizzard, it is far too dangerous - we *must* find shelter!" he advised, as countless tiny icy-white particles drifted and swirled all around. Rhoedas was a climber of many suns' experience in the high mountain passes northwest of Eternity: his advice was never to be taken lightly. The king was in total agreement, yet unable to see any escape from the blizzard of chilling powder.

"Very well, Rhoedas, but to where?" he fretted, squinting to see through the waves of snow thrashing upon their, and the rocky mountain face. Shivering as the icy temperatures continued to plummet, Alectorious worried they would freeze before finding suitable shelter. As if on cue, the exploratory Gavastros appeared from through the misty cloud of snow.

"My Lord!!!" he bellowed, trying to be heard through the howling winds. The king looked up in anticipation, sensing his prayers might just have been answered. Having been walking a considerable distance ahead, Gavastros had been well-positioned to identify safe places of refuge. Alectorious struggled to hear over the deafening noise of the icy winds, anxious the prodigy would be the bearer good tidings.

"Not twenty spears ahead - a cave!" he jubilantly announced, frantically pointing up the snowy path. The king gasped in relief, knowing deep within they had been saved.

"Can we find shelter there?" he nervously asked. Gavastros nodded affirmatively.

"I am sure of it, Sire!" he promised. Snow continued to fall heavily as visibility worsened by the moment. Quick thinking was required as the king turned to the tracker.

"It is our only hope, my king," Rhoedos concurred. Alectorious nodded.

"Eternians, we follow Gavastros!" he ordered. The group continued along the narrow icy path, staying close as was possible to the smooth frosty walls. Every step required the greatest of care, as from the edge of the path was a fall to unfathomable depths. The Eternians soon reached the curious grotto embedded deep within the side of the icy mountain face; the entrance was small and barely visible through the thick snows of the blizzard but just about large enough for each of the knights and Elite Guard to squeeze through. The seven wasted not a moment as, one by one they crouched down and crawled swiftly inside. As the Eternians spilled into the cave, there was a huge collective sigh of relief. Gavastros was first to express his delight and was immediately taken by his new surroundings.

"Very cosy; I might even dorm here this night!" he thankfully remarked. Feeling very much at home, the prodigy huddled up against the hard rock wall of the mysterious cavern, with the howling winds now like a distant echo through the narrow entrance. It was certainly a lot larger than the king had expected: roughly three-and-a-half spears wide and just over a hoplite high, with rough grey stony walls and a grainy surface. It was more than enough space for all to rest until the snowstorm blew over.

"Truly a sending from the gods; amazing how they always answer when one is most in need," the king remarked, marvelling at the coincidental nature of their finding.

"I pray it not for long, for there is yet much to climb," Rhoedas pragmatically recognised, as the others made themselves comfortable against the rough edges of the cave. Thelosious was meanwhile busy inspecting his new surroundings, catching sight of several curious pictorial designs scattered across the primeval walls with a torch hastily made by the Elite Guardsmen. He moved closer, examining in greater detail as he beckoned the king.

"Alectorious, look; hieroglyphs!" the cerebral one remarked, fascinated, noticing the series of unusually-shaped pictograms. The king moved to join him, equally captivated.

"By the gods, you are right!" he excited, carefully examining the uniquely formed illustrations strewn across the cragged grey cave wall.

"Animals, mountains and dragons, even!" Alectorious observed with intrigue, marvelling at the intricately-crafted drawings of clearly prehistoric origin.

"And men dressed in the strangest of clothing: whoever could have drawn such wondrous things?" he questioned in admiration. There had once been many such cultures scattered around The Great Plains, but these mysterious writings bore little resemblance to anything they had ever written. Thelosious was equally bewildered as to their origin.

"I have absolutely no idea, my king - a writing system I have never seen - almost certainly from *long* before the Age of Heroes. I could only guess as to their meaning, but certainly of a people long lost to history," he admitted, curious as to who these souls might have been. "One can only wonder," the inquisitive Thelosious added, as the king remembered some ancient texts he had seen in the vast archives of the Eternian Libraries.

"Perhaps they were of a people that travelled between this world and another; I once read of a secret gateway within this very mountain to other worlds, exactly as Skolastros had alluded," Alectorious divulged, as he imagined some mysterious far-off lands.

"It is possible, my king - perhaps Reiactus can speak more of this - when we find him, of course," Thelosious encouraged, quietly confident it *would* be so.

"Ah yes… Reiactus… *if* we find him… indeed," sighed the king, crouching despondently against the rough, cavernous wall. He relaxed and made himself as comfortable as was possible in the mysterious abode, quietly pondering the nature of its origins.

"It is too perfect; almost as if this cave was made by the gods for this very moment," Alectorious whispered, following on from what he had previously spoken.

"Perhaps it was, my king; this mountain has magical powers of illusion," Thelosious acknowledged. Gavastros however, found it a possibility quite unable to fathom.

"Do you mean to say the mountain in fact *created* the cave, Thelosious!?" he replied disbelievingly. The king was by contrast supportive of his thoughtful companion.

"They say that *anything* is possible in the great Buvarious, Gavastros," he said in a tone of quiet mystique. The prodigy was without reply, silently nodding. Suddenly, the primeval cave became eerily silent as all quietly contemplated this intriguing possibility.

As the snowstorm raged on, the Eternians warmed themselves as best they could from the incessant cold, rubbing their hands together and stamping their feet on the rocky ground. It had been made considerably easier to bear by the Elite Guardsmen, who had previously managed to build a small fire by implementing their daggers and twigs gathered earlier from the forests. Although the cave was markedly warmer than the bitterly freezing conditions outside, it was still well below the far milder temperatures they were used to in Eternity. Gavastros warmed his hands over the flames before moving to peer out into the blinding white from his safe vantage point and comfort of the cosy little cave.

"My king, the snowfall is heavy: I pray it not hinder our progress much longer," he vexed, as the snows seemed only to thicken by the instant. Rhoedas gazed out in kind but was quickly dismissive of the prodigy's concerns.

"It will soon pass; the weather is most changeable in these parts. I have experienced much of this in the northwest mountains." he reassured, making himself comfortable against the cave wall, folding his arms to retain as much warmth as possible. Gavastros soon re-joined his circle of companions, doing his utmost to lift their spirits.

"Well, we are here for now; and had best make the most of it!" he jovially exclaimed, laying back and resting his head upon his rucksack, expecting some good old-fashioned conversation. The others seemed otherwise content to rest and recover from their thus-far arduous climb, with their eyes already half closed and ready for a good night's rest. Silence soon fell upon the cave, with the howling blizzard winds and slow crackling of the flames all that could be heard. It seemed somehow unreal to be sat in a remote cavern high in the mountains, thought the king; a world away from their beloved city, with its elegant tree-lined boulevards, stunningly beautiful gardens and magnificent castle, wondering if he would ever see it again. The others sat in collective thought of the path ahead, questioning if they would *ever succeed* in finding the great dragon and return to tell the tale, or if they would disappear somewhere in these foreboding icy mountains, never to be seen or heard from again. There was no telling what might befall the Eternians in this most unpredictable place: for indeed, the changing of the winds alone had the power enough to alter one's destiny. Gavastros was particularly worried, expressing his concerns.

"My king, what if we are not to make it back - what shall become of our nation?" he asked in trepidation, considering the permutations as Thelosious tried to offer calm.

"It is but a snowstorm, Gavastros; it will pass soon enough!" he said, feeling his companion was being overly melodramatic. The prodigy shook his head.

"It is not only *that* I worry of, Thelosious, but the path home. There could be untold Gomercians blocking our way," the prodigy expounded - and with good reason.

"We shall be taking the western path through Catharia: the Gomercians are unlikely to be found there," the king assured, but Thelosious was wholly unconvinced.

"They could be *anywhere,* my king - there really can be no knowing," he chillingly remarked, suddenly recalling the ambush of but a few suns ago in vivid detail.

"Indeed, but it is a far safer path than the one we initially took. In any case, we *have to* go to Catharia," the king insisted, instantly reminding the prodigy of his new rival.

"Oh yes, to find that little upstart of a forestman," he bitterly spat, expressing his clear dislike of the mysterious Catharian. The king was unimpressed, speaking sternly.

"We need all the help we can find in the fight against the empire, Gavastros; if we are to be victorious, you must learn to put your personal feelings aside." As much as

Gavastros hated to admit, it was difficult to argue with his king's reasoning. The empire had grown much larger than anyone could have imagined and there was no telling how far it might eventually reach or how audacious become. Another period of silence ensued before the Elite Guardsman, Aeirious, spoke in an attempt to uplift the mood in the secret cave.

"If I may so boldly ask, Gavastros, what will you do when the Gomericans are *finally* defeated?" he impertinently posed, knowing it would illicit some interesting responses. He was not to be disappointed as the others became unusually animated.

"The world will no longer have need of your sword," guardsman Lacoenious brazenly added, as the others chuckled in unison. Gavastros took it in good humor at first, laughing along with his entertaining companions before finally mustering a response.

"There is always *someone* who wishes to fight, Lacoenious! History remembers that where one power falls, another *always* rises to take its place. Perhaps there will be invaders from yet undiscovered lands beyond the known world, or maybe even those from within we are yet unaware of," he replied, but the Elite soldiers were unwilling to yield. Lacoenious took his cue, cleverly rephrasing the question to meet his own ends.

"Suppose for but a moment there were no longer *any* threats to Eternity," he cleverly posed, with the others listening with much anticipation. Gavastros was shocked by the mere suggestion, so much had his life been dominated by the sword and shield.

"Well… I… could not say," he at first mumbled, predictably struggling to answer. "Perhaps I would devote my life to fighting in tournaments, presuming of course *they* still existed," he doubtfully added, brightening as he thought of an even more creative possibility. "Or perhaps I would travel deep into the unknown and visit the lands of our ancient ancestors, fighting all manner of hideous beasts along the way."

"And encounters with fair maidens perhaps also?" Lacoenious playfully suggested, as all chuckled in good humor. Gavastros did not take it well though, upset at being made to look the fool. He did well to hide his feelings, cleverly deflecting the question.

"My king, what shall you do at this conflict's end?" the prodigy asked. Alectorious struggled for a response at first, looking up pensively to the dim cave ceiling.

"A fine question, my companion - for in all my eons I have known as you only struggle and conflict - a world of peace is so very difficult to imagine now," he admitted, with a deep sigh of regret. Thelosious pushed as everyone listened with intrigue.

"Please try, my king!" he encouraged, as Alectorious began to scratch his head.

"Well, I imagine as Gavastros, I would explore those distant lands I could not before. Perhaps it would firstly be to Catharia then beyond these great mountains, deep into the heart of the unknown. Then I would search for the mythical City of Heroes in the land of our ancient ancestors," he dreamily replied, excited by the countless possibilities. The prodigy was baffled, finding it difficult to fathom the king's fixation with the forest dwellers.

"Catharia - but why, Alectorious!?" he incredulously asked. Thelosious was quick to come to the king's defence, knowing the prodigy should respect his wishes.

"Gavastros, be silent; it is not your place to comment!" the cerebral one scolded. "I think it would be a magnificent adventure, my king," he enthusiastically agreed. Warming his hands on the crackling fire, Thelosious imagined as the others what these far-off lands might be like. The king focused his attention on his more thoughtful of companions.

"And you, Thelosious; what would you wish at this struggle's end?" he pointedly asked. Thelosious was silent for some moments, considering this unimaginable possibility.

"Truth be told, my king, I would be inclined to follow you into the unknown; I have long wished to see the land of the ancients and discover the truth of our origins.

Otherwise, I might contently spend my suns contemplating upon a mountaintop or catching up on my favourite book: "Tales of Ancient Eternian Heroes"," he replied with a broad smile.

"That would be splendid; I hope that sun shall soon be upon us, my companion," the king professed, with the others nodding in agreement. Sensing a change in the air, Rhoedas cast an instinctive glance outside, hoping the falling snows had subsided. The tracker rushed out to assess the conditions before promptly returning inside the cave.

"The blizzard has passed, sire - the path should be safe to continue!" he gleefully announced. The king, Thelosious and Gavastros reacted with a look of curious disappointment, having very much enjoyed the cosiness of this clandestine mountain abode. It had been quite a memorable experience, but duty now called for greater things.

"Well, my fellow Eternians; in as much as I have delighted in this comfort, the gods summon us to move on," the king emphatically ordered. The others reluctantly complied, gathering their belongings before venturing out into the open air and now clear-blue skies. The mountains and forests were covered in a thick blanket of pure white essence, shimmering and sparkling in the twin suns' reflection, blinding in their sheer brilliance; all the lands were shielded like a tablecloth of the gods, indeed. The Eternians looked around in awe at this proverbial winter wonderland, having never witnessed such divine magnificence in all their eons. They took several moments to absorb the surrounding beauty into their bodies and souls before continuing on the intrepid path, high into the peaks of The Great Buvarious Mountains.

THE FINAL STRETCH

The king continued with his loyal followers along the narrow snow-covered path, more determined than ever to realise his long-cherished dream. He encouraged his companions fervently on, with their advance having been slowed considerably by the snowstorm.

"Let us make haste, my fellow Eternians; there is yet far to journey!" he said, while trudging slowly through the thick white snows. There was no knowing what else might hamper their progress into these perilously unpredictable mountains, with the journey having already defied all expectations. The reality of these lofty peaks was in stark contrast to their peaceful appearance from a distance and it was impossible to determine the innumerable challenges they might soon bring. The Great Buvarious was sure to leave an indelible impression on the king and his men; and it would be an experience that would live with them for the rest of their eons.

Alectorious cast his eyes forward along the precariously narrow path, which was now covered in a fresh blanket of powdery white snow. The sight ahead was enough to make even the most battle-hardened of souls quiver with fright: to the right, a dramatic ice-laden rock face rising almost vertically above their heads, all the way up to the highest point on the mountain; while on the left, a terrifying vertical drop to the depths of the valley, far below. The path ascended gradually as it curved round the icy face, leading, the king and his men anticipated, to the legendary ice caves of Prejosia. As the Eternians marched through the thick snows, Alectorious wondered if fortune would bestow upon him an audience with the great dragon, hoping all that had compelled him thus far was for reasons he had been led to believe. Whatever was to be, the king had experienced things on this journey he could have only dreamed of - and for that, he was to the gods and The Great Spirit deeply grateful. The king's quiet reflection was suddenly interrupted by the oddest sensation, with Gavastros but moments later confirming his wild intuitive impulse.

"DRAGON!!!" he screamed at the top of his lungs, jolting his companions upright.

"By the gods man, where?!" the king demanded in utter disbelief. He turned his eyes to the bright blue skies, frantically searching for signs of such a being.

"I see it - look - from out of the twin suns!" Thelosious exclaimed, pointing to a giant winged creature closing in rapidly from a distance. The Eternians were at first excited but their feelings soon turned to trepidation as they realised what it *truly* was.

"It is certainly not the great Reiactus," observed the king, noticing its bright green scaly coat, quite in contrast to the light blue Reiactus was believed to be. The massive creature was moving in at great speed, flapping its wings furiously and screeching in a most deafening roar. The Eternians realised the dragon's hostile intentions, bracing for an attack.

"This creature is no companion to us, Alectorious; listen to its screams!" Thelosious panicked. As the giant continued its approach, the king ordered his men to prepare.

"Eternians - ready to defend yourselves!" he commanded. The group of warriors promptly reacted, drawing their shining blades aloft and holding their shining blue shields in the other hand for protection. The warriors waited as tension rose and the fearsome dragon continued to rapidly close in. The giant green monster swept down, unleashing a lethal stream of white-hot flames above their position. Melting solid ice and snow, it shattered the rock like a fragile mirror. The Eternians scrambled desperately to avoid the falling debris as the mountain face suddenly began to weaken. The dragon dramatically turned as it neared the rock, trying in vain to grab hold of one of the Eternians. The beast failed as the king and his men swung their swords furiously in retaliation, just managing to cut the dragon's limbs as it swooped by. They had thwarted the creature's first.assault, but the threat was far from over as the snow on the cliff face dramatically began to give way.

"Eternians, run!" the king shouted. His men reacted instantly: the adventurers sprinted as fast as their legs and snow would allow, away from danger. As much as the wrath of the dragon, they had to avoid being caught in the oncoming avalanche. Fragments of ice and rock rained down all around as the Eternians ran further up the path in frantic search of cover. The dragon had flown back into the twin suns but quickly returned for yet another pass at the heroic band of fighters.

"Eternians, the dragon returns: be ready!" the king hysterically screamed, with his men standing by his side at the ready. The prodigy could see the creature moving directly at him but was fully determined to stand his ground. He bravely accepted the challenge as the dragon rapidly closed in and his companions looked on in disbelief.

"Gavastros, what are you doing man - get down!" Thelosious shrieked, unable to fathom *what* he was thinking. The prodigy was unmoved, fully confident *he* would emerge victorious from the titanic duel ahead. The king was speechless, praying to the gods above for protection as the dragon approached. Gavastros firmly grasped his sword as the green beast moved in at blinding speed from the east, sweeping round in a wide arc in yet an another attempt to dislodge the Eternians from the precarious mountain path. Small fragments of rock and ice continued to rain down as Gavastros held his ground, praying to the divine for protection.

"May the gods be with me," he whispered, gasping for air as he kissed the blade of his shining sword. The giant serpent arced round once more, straight into the bold Eternians' path. As the dragon honed in, Gavastros dramatically flung his sword through the air and with all of his might. The soaring blade struck the dragon clean in the chest, much to the elation of the watching Eternians. The behemoth lost all sense of direction, smashing into the mountainside with a thunderous roar, catapulting the hapless creature into the abyss, far below. The Eternians looked on in stunned silence as an avalanche of snow, ice and rock tumbled down and the dragon suffered what could well have been their *own* fate. Gavastros stood in unmoving disbelief that he had not only managed to defeat the mighty creature, but save the lives of his fellow Eternians. Thelosious approached the speechless prodigy, patting him affectionately on the shoulder in recognition of his valourous feat.

"Now, you are a *true* hero of Eternity," he said in a rare expression of generosity; Gavastros was frozen stiff in shock and utterly lost for words. The king was also, undeniably impressed by his knight's efforts, offering due praise to his loyal follower.

"They shall speak of this gallant deed for a thousand eons in The Book of Heroes, I am sure," he offered generously, congratulating his brave young companion. The Elite Guardsmen were equally ecstatic, lauding their plaudits on the prodigal Eternian knight.

"Well done, Gavastros!"

"Gavastros, the great hero!"

"Gavastros, the invincible!" came their words of approval, so impressed were they by his boundless act courage. Gavastros seemed more shocked than anything else - the whole incident had happened so fast it was like a dream - he could only imagine as to the reasons for this unexpected occurrence.

"Why ever did it attack us?" he conjectured, flabbergasted. Staring into the valley below, chunks of rock and ice continued to rain down on the lifeless carcass. Reflecting, Thelosious offered his thoughts as to the origins of the deceased creature.

"I imagine we were on its territory and deemed some kind of threat. Interestingly, it was *exactly* like the malevolent green dragons spoken of in "Tales of Eternian Heroes". I thought they had long gone from these lands but I am clearly mistaken. Perhaps it recently returned to the known lands to assist in the rise of the empire."

Gavastros was still puzzled as to the nature of the attack and as Thelosious, wondered from whence the creature had originated.

"But dragons are not meant to be hostile!" he countered disbelievingly, having always thought these large, scaly beings to be benevolent in their nature.

"Not all dragons are the peaceful creatures we would have ourselves believe, Gavastros, as much as we wish it be so." explained the king in regret.

There was a look of despondency on the prodigy's face as his long-held preconception of something he always believed to be true fizzled before his very eyes. For certain, it would not be the last that he or any other Eternians experienced of this. The king was in no mood for sentiment as he realised the need to press on - the twin suns were moving ever closer to edge of the skies - and they would wait for no man.

"My knights and fellow Eternians, the green dragon is no longer a threat: we are alive and must continue," he bluntly said, pointing up to the towering enigmatic peaks in the distance. There was only one path for the adventurers left to follow.

"Come - we cannot be far!" encouraged Alectorious, sensing the end in sight.

"The king is right: we shall be there before long, my companions!" Rhoedas agreed.

Buoyed by his tracker's encouraging words, Alectorious bellowed his orders.

"Onwards to the great Buvarious, my brave Eternians!"

ICE CAVES

Having successfully thwarted the monstrous green dragon, the king and his merry men continued their trek up the narrow mountain path, which was by now covered in a thick blanket of fresh powdery snow. One by one they trudged along as the trail wound in and out of the steep icy rock face, which was almost invisible due to the thickness of the snow. The king wondered if it would ever end as he looked to the dramatic valleys below, then to the spectacular mountain peaks glistening above in the sunlight of the late morn. Alectorious glanced out into the distance, wondering if it were true that the land of their ancient ancestors lay somewhere out there. He tried to guess what passage the ancient heroes might have taken through those seemingly endless peaks, all those eons ago, thinking it would have been the ultimate test of endurance and fortitude. It was certainly a path he wished to embark upon *if* he were to return safely from *this* intrepid adventure.

Before long the path began to open up, enabling the Eternians to walk almost side by side. It took several more twists and turns before straightening, eventually leading to a narrow plateau. Feelings of relief soon turned to disbelief as the king looked ahead: the snow had mysteriously disappeared, revealing a narrow pebbled walkway surrounded by patches of fresh green grass. The trail continued up to the mountainside before coming to a complete halt at a vertical rock face, which in turn rose dramatically up to the highest point of the Buvarious. The ground below was now completely green, with coloured wildflowers growing throughout. It was like a miniature meadow, thought Alectorious in utter astonishment.

"My king, the path ends!" Gavastros pointed in shock, as the Eternians frantically searched for an alternative route. They rushed ahead in disbelief; as much for the abrupt end in the path as the sight of grass so high in the mountains. The travellers stopped hard in their tracks upon reaching the path's conclusion, staring at the face of rock in sheer bewilderment.

"What are we to do? There is no other way up!" the king vexed, looking in trepidation to the imposing rock wall now blocking their advance. Gavastros was equally miffed.

"And this grass, all the way up here in the mountains - it makes no sense at all!" he added, shaking his head incredulously as the Elite Guards also expressed their surprise

"It certainly feels a lot warmer; how by the gods is this possible?" Lacoenious gasped in equal confusion, with Rhoedas, Aeirious and Quintos likewise disbelieving. Thelosious was by contrast unmoved as he gently caressed a beautiful purple wildflower, knowing always to expect the unexpected high in the great Buvarious.

"There are many unexplained mysteries in these mountains: powerful forces beyond our comprehension," he said, feeling the power of this magnificent abode infuse his very soul. The others looked for signs of a way around the sheer rock wall, but it was to no avail. For Gavastros, the frustration was proving too much as he lost his cool.

"It does not jolly well help us, now does it?" he snapped, kicking a small rock to the end of the path. The king was clearly unimpressed, moving to restrain the knight's wrath.

"Gavastros, calm it!" he ordered, taking a step toward him. The prodigy ignored the king's pleas, throwing his arms in the air as he further vented his feelings.

"We have come all this way into the mountains, Alectorious, and for what?" he rhetorically demanded, as he looked into the eyes of the king. The Elite Guard felt unable to argue with the prodigy but dared not voice their thoughts in front of their superiors. In frustration, Gavastros drew his replacement sword from its sheath and swung it against the face of the mountain. Amazingly, it passed through the solid wall of rock as if nothing were there at all! It was much to the astonishment of his companions but only Thelosious seemed unsurprised, with his mystical beliefs vindicated in one sweeping moment.

"The mountains have spoken," he said, smiling with a sense of deep satisfaction. The king's gaze was transfixed on the mountain face where the sword had been swung, motioning with a wave of his hand to the Eternian prodigy.

"Do… do it again, Gavastros," he urged, knowing they might have found *exactly* what they had been looking for. The prodigy duly complied, swinging his sword once more. Again, it passed effortlessly through what they had thought to be solid rock, leaving everyone in a daze. So shocked was Gavastros that he lost grip of his weapon, which flew out of his hand into what seemed to be a large cave, clanging loudly against the *true* face of the mountain. The king turned to Thelosious without a single word said, with both knowing *exactly* where they were.

"This must be it: the entrance to the caves of Prejosia!" Alectorious elated, realising it *had* to be those famed caves in which the great Reiactus was believed to dwell. There was no other rational explanation as Gavastros fought hard to articulate his thoughts.

"I… I cannot believe my eyes!" he stated, shaking his head in utter bewilderment. "However is this possible?" he asked in confusion. The others crowded round, struggling to come to terms with what they had seen. The king was unperturbed, ardent to venture forward.

"Are you ready, my companions?" he asked, as Thelosious had no question at all.

"Without a doubt, my king," he agreed, moving closer to test the "rock wall". Thelosious waved his hand as his companion had his sword: it simply passed though as if nothing were there at all. The prodigy meanwhile was struggling to contain his shock.

"Magic!" he exclaimed, finding no other plausible explanation. Thelosious thought otherwise, expressing his wise insights.

"Not magic, but a power beyond our comprehension, Gavastros. We stand upon the very edge of our reality in these mountains - of all we had ever believed to be real. This *truly* is where the worlds of men and the gods collide." The king was hardly able to contain his excitement as he drew his sword, using it to judge the size of the mysterious cave entrance. Reasoning it to be not more than a hoplite high and wide, his imagination began to run wild as to the possibilities that lay within - would it be all that he had ever dreamed?

"Quite indescribably amazing: perhaps it *is* the cave of the great one, after all!" Alectorious dreamily remarked, as a picture of a giant blue dragon appeared vividly in his mind's eye. Thelosious was in equal measure captivated by this astonishing finding.

"It would truly be a historical moment, my king," he agreed, his eyes focused.

"Oh yes, when king and dragon meet once again," responded a mesmerised Alectorious, wondering more of the wonders beheld. Visiting the abode of Reiactus, he thought in a sweeping instant: it was hard to believe that so soon, he might have *that* ultimate honour. Standing not an arm's length away, the king felt a sensation quite unlike any other.

"It certainly has an aura about it," he remarked, feeling a mysterious yet welcoming energy emanate from the cave, as if it was beckoning him to step within its unknowable depths. It was like a living, breathing being, revealing itself to only a chosen few.

"What waits beyond, I wonder?" he pondered, curious if his companions could also sense this. Thelosious was uncharacteristically straight and to the point.

"Well, there is only one way to find out - who goes first?" he asked, motioning to the rock wall. Only Gavastros seemed brave enough, needing no second invitation.

"Let I, my king!" the prodigy insisted, readying to jump through the mysterious rock.

"Go ahead, my companion," was the Eternian leader's only response, nodding him forward. The young knight momentarily paused, realising jumping though a sheer rock face defied all logic. Taking several deep breaths, Gavastros leapt into the mysterious abyss.

"Ahhhh!" he screamed in sheer terror. The others frantically tried to establish contact, believing at first that the prodigy had fallen to his peril.

"Gavastros!" Alectorious screamed. "Can you hear us?" he added, as the Elite Guard quickly gathered round the cave entrance in trepidation, fearing the worst for their hero.

"It is alright, you can come through!" the prodigy replied, chuckling heartily to himself. It was much to the relief of the king and his men who drew a collective sigh.

"Does it continue?" Alectorious asked desperately, waiting anxiously for a response. Gavastros strained his eyes, struggling to make out anything at first in the dim cavern.

"It is difficult to see but there appears to be a passageway leading straight into the mountain!" he enthused. The king promptly turned to Thelosious with eyes delirious.

"After you, my king," his companion encouraged. Alectorious paused for a moment, staring at the cave wall before stepping through. It was the most unusual sensation as half his body was stuck in the wall before he took another step forward. Moments later he found himself on the other side with Gavastros, where it was much brighter than expected. Looking back, the king, to his shock, could see his companions perfectly well: as if the wall not there at all. The prodigy was meanwhile calmly leaning against the rock with arms neatly folded, having quickly adapted to his unusual new surroundings.

"Amazing, is it not?" he remarked. The king turned to his companion, smiling.

"Indeed it is," he wholeheartedly agreed. Alectorious waved his hand where the "wall" was, observing the cave to be only a little larger than the one they had rested in earlier on the mountain path. Examining further, he saw the long passageway Gavastros had mentioned, noticing beside the entrance, similar symbols found in the other cave. The king was feverishly excited, calling to the cerebral knight on the other side.

"Thelosious, come quickly!" he shouted, knowing his companion would be able to decipher the complex pictorial symbols. Thelosious turned to the Elite Guardsmen.

"I am heading in: the rest of you wait here," he ordered, before jumping through.

"That was something," Thelosious gasped, likewise safely making it. Beckoning him to the edge of the tunnel, the king was ecstatic.

"Have a look: hieroglyphics, just like the ones we saw before - can you read them?" he impatiently asked, barely giving his companion an instant to orientate himself. Thelosious moved closer to the wall, peering curiously at the inscriptions.

"Give me a moment, I think I can do it," he said, trying his best to decipher them.

"A great many secrets lay hidden within this here ancient mountain;
Only those of noble birth, the purest of hearts and most benevolent of intentions may venture beyond.
Continue at thy peril, thou who is not worthy."

"Well, rather to the point, is it not?" the king remarked, refreshed by the directness of the message. He peered down the long, dark passageway, pondering the mysterious script.

"I wonder what would befall those unworthy..." Thelosious had no doubt at all.

"You know what this means, Alectorious - only one of us can go forth," he tellingly replied, looking to the king, who was characteristically unpretentious.

"There could be no purer soul than you, my companion," Alectorious humbly answered, looking to his cerebral companion; but Thelosious would hear nothing of it.

"You are *our king*, Alectorious; you heard yourself that it must be one of noble birth! It can be you - and none other," he insisted, responding to his intuitive senses. Gavastros was for a rare moment in his life in total agreement with Thelosious.

"He is right, my companion. If the he is there, Reiactus would wish speak *only* to you - our - *the* Eternian king," the prodigy said adamantly, pointing his finger for emphasis. Alectorious took a moment to reflect as he gazed down into the mysterious dark tunnel.

"My whole life's path has brought me to this moment: I shall embrace this challenge with all that am," the king enthused, as a surge of inspiration welled from deep within.

"I can feel Reactus' strength beckoning you," Thelosious warmly enthused, clenching his fist for emphasis as he tried to encourage his eons-long companion.

"I also!" Gavastros fervently agreed, nodding as he willed the king on.

"Then so it shall be," Alectorious promised, deciding to take on the daring challenge of venturing into the mountain caves, all alone. The king carefully checked himself, ensuring he had all that was needed to counter the perils he might face.

"I sense you shall have no need of your sword, my king; but bring it if you must," Thelosious advised, firmly believing that no danger could possibly exist within the mountain.

"I shall take it just in case - but how will I find my way back?" Alectorious worried, realising he would easily lose his way in the labyrinth of dark icy tunnels.

"Use this rope, my liege, and you will find your way," Thelosious assured, pulling a coiled rope from his pack and handing it to the king. Alectorious promptly tied it round his waist as the prodigy lit a small torch, carefully handing it to him.

"Embrace this light, my king - and you will see," he said, concerned with the wellbeing of his leader. With all that he needed, Alectorious turned to the foreboding tunnel.

"Very well, my companions; I had better make haste," he said. With a slight nervousness in his voice, he had no idea what to expect. The cerebral one could sense this.

"The gods will be with you, Alectorious: have faith they are guiding you, every step of the way," Thelosious tenderly reassured, as the king began into the mountain's icy depths.

"Good luck, my king!" Gavastros encouraged with a respectful salute.

"I shall return soon," Alectorious promised, taking one final look at his companions. As the brave Eternian leader strode into the cave, a cool breeze blew gently as if to welcome his noble presence. Alectorious felt a deep sense of calm wash over him as he took his first steps into the long, dark passageway, firmly grasping his torch in one hand and in the other, his rope. As Alectorious continued, he noticed a bluish glow emanate from the icy rock walls;

it was a shade he had never seen nor could even begin to describe; bright as were the sun lit skies yet profound - almost spiritual. As he looked closer into the mysterious blue it seemed to disappear; his eyes unable to comprehend as his mind accept this curious phenomenon.

Alectorious exuberantly continued, fascinated by the ice-laden rock formation ebbing, flowing and twisting, much like the waves of a tranquil mountain river. There were occasional pieces of rock sticking out like the spears of a hoplite, threatening as though they were most extravagant in their formation. He stopped to investigate, caressing his hand over the otherwise, surprisingly smooth icy surface of the cave wall, wondering what could have created such a fascinating place. Suddenly, the floor of the cave began to weaken as the king's foot slipped dramatically through. In a swift reflex action, he threw his torch forward, grabbing hold of the cave floor, only just managing to avert disaster. The king managed to pull himself up and forward before falling safely to his stomach. He stood up with his heart pounding as he picked up his torch and breathed deeply. Alectorious looked back in astonishment, seeing a small part of the cave floor had given way to an almost bottomless pit. He thanked the gods for sparing his life, knowing he might not be so fortunate on the next occasion. Suddenly, a voice from nowhere echoed through the long, cold icy passageway.

"Be careful, my young companion," it whispered, in a cautionary but kind tone. The king froze and looked around in shock but he saw not a soul in sight.

"Who is there? Reveal yourself at once I demand of you!" he nervously retorted, increasingly anxious as he saw no sign of life. His heart began to beat faster, wondering what manner of abode he now found himself in - was this really the place he had imagined?

"You have nothing to fear," the mysterious voice comforted in a deep, soothing tone. Alectorious relaxed once again, sensing it might be the gods themselves that spoke. These caves were as the written word had said, a truly magical place indeed.

The king continued along the dark passageway more curious than ever, with his torch illuminating the mysterious blue glow of the icy walls to spectacular effect. After some fifty spears or so, he eventually found another tunnel branch off dramatically to the left. He decided to investigate, intuitively sensing it would not go far. The king soon reached a small cave, at the centre of which was placed a most curiously fashioned statue. At first glance it appeared to be a man, but as Alectorious moved in for closer inspection, he observed some very unusual characteristics: he noticed it had much larger eyes, with a nose and ears smaller than he was accustomed to. It was unlike any man he had seen in the *known* world: the king thought it might in fact be a statue of one of the gods. Perhaps Reiactus would know the answer, he thought, taking one last look before returning to the main cave passageway. The king continued before reaching yet another turn in the mysterious tunnel. He sensed danger but boldly decided to investigate anyway. Alectorious continued to walk cautiously along the path, at the end of which shone a bright blue light. After ten spears it suddenly ended, dropping away into a bottomless cavern.

"You have not a moment to waste," whispered that deep mysterious voice, fervently willing the king on. Alectorious realised he had not long to go, hurriedly making his way back into the main tunnel. He frantically ran down the long cave passageway, desperate for answers. The king's heart started to pound, fearing he would *never* find his way out. The path began to twist and turn, once right then left, then to the right once more, passing by several more offshoots. The king intuitively decided to keep to the main passageway before eventually finding himself in another long tunnel. Seeing a great blue glow in the distance, he sensed the end was *finally* near. Alectorious ran ever faster, his heart beating rapidly as he moved deeper into the captivating blue light. Reaching the end, he dramatically stopped to catch his breath. The king looked up to find a huge, brightly cavern and was shocked by what he saw...

THE GREAT ONE

In the middle of the cavity was an unmistakable shape of a dragon from where the mysterious blue glow had emanated. Alectorious edged closer, walking around the statue with great intrigue, sensing he was on the verge of something very special indeed…

The king stood in a state of beguiled awe as he stared enchanted into the eyes of the elegant crystal dragon statue, wondering if it foretold that which he had for so many suns hoped and dreamed. Alectorious had sacrificed much by following his heart's calling into these lofty mountain peaks, risking his life and those of many courageous warriors on this noble quest. Indeed, the very existence of his nation was at stake, with every decision affecting whether in a thousand eons from now Eternians would remember this moment or be washed away by the hapless ineptitude of imperialism. Alectorious upon some suns questioned the path he had chosen to walk but knew deep down it was the only way. For if he had remained in Eternity, it would have only been a matter of moons before his great city was enveloped by the enemy hordes and become yet another province of the tyrannical Gomercian Empire. That was unless of course, allies in their struggle could be unearthed.

Alectorious began to ponder the notion of history and that its entire course could be altered in but an instant - the swing of a sword, the choice of one path over another or to venture this way or that - a single decision that had the ability to change one's life path and destiny, forever. He imagined what might have happened had he chosen not to embark on this quest; and the people, places and things he would have never encountered. He thought also of how the course of history might have been affected and the consequences for his beleaguered nation. Whatever the permutations, the king realised these decisions *had* been made and there was nothing he could do to change it. All he could do now was look to the future and make it one for the betterment of *all innocent souls* across the lands. It was a tremendous responsibility the king burdened but he was confident that, with the gods and The Great Spirit willing, he and his brave warriors would deliver freedom to Eternity *and* the peoples of the known world. All of a sudden, a familiar voice echoed from the entrance of the cavern. Alectorious was momentarily startled as he looked up.

"Congratulations, virtuous and noble king," it came. Having been so entranced by the mysterious dragon statue, Alectorious had not noticed else anyone enter. He turned around; shocked by the figure he saw standing before him.

"By Promaestious!" he gasped as he stumbled back, unable to fathom how. The curious man stepped forward and continued, unperturbed by the king's obvious surprise.

"You have shown your worthiness as the rightful ruler of Eternity; of that, there is not question or doubt. Know that few have ever trodden where you now do, which is a great honour and privilege in itself. I hereby welcome you, King Alectorious, to the Buvarious Mountains: the home of The Great One," he graciously offered. Although not explicitly stated, the king intuitively sensed he referred to the dragon, Reiactus. The king could barely articulate a response as he tried to make sense of how this could have happened.

"It is you, from the crossroads! How by the gods is this possible?" he asked, bewildered. Alectorious immediately recognised the mystic he had met earlier, wondering how he had made it this high in the mountains and indeed, the service of the great dragon: perhaps there *was* a secret passageway or entrance the king was yet unaware of.

"There is much to be explained to you, Alectorious; trust that you will know all when you are ready," the mystic intuitively answered, with a confidence hitherto unexpressed. The king could but only nod in agreement. "Please, follow me," the mystic kindly beckoned, moving closer to the deep blue glow. The king followed as his heart began to pound excitedly, knowing he was on the verge of something *very special* indeed. Alectorious could hardly believe that, after countless eons and all that had been written, he might soon have *that* cherished honour of meeting the magnificent one. Alectorious followed the mystic along the long passageway, illuminated by that deep blue permeating the caves. It became much brighter as they progressed, with the king sensing a mysterious, powerful aura with each and every step. The mystic reached the end first, turning dramatically to the right as the king's heart suddenly missed a beat. He intuitively knew this was it: he took a deep breath before moving on, unable to contain his sheer sense of delirium...

Alectorious turned the corner in what felt to be an endless moment before stepping out of the passageway and into a giant cavern. It was bigger than he had expected, with the blue glowing walls only adding to the mystique of this magnificent abode. From its depths, a large creature began to make its way dramatically into the light. The king could only watch in disbelieving awe. The creature moved forward gently as Alectorious gasped, almost falling over in shock. He took several steps back in amazement, wondering if his eyes spoke the truth. It was the most splendid regal being the king had ever seen: several fold his height, with glowing shiny blue scales and bright, golden piercing eyes. The creature's powerful talons stretched out far from its robust body, floating effortlessly above the rocky cave floor; reflective of the greatness of the being's legend and strength of inner soul. Alectorious knew it *was* Reiactus that stood before him but could not bring himself to believe it truly so.

The king was lost for words as he gazed at the magnificent being, more convinced by the moment it was indeed "The Great One". After all those suns of hardship and toil, it seemed his dream had *finally* come to realisation. The dragon shifted its massive frame closer, stopping not three spears distant. It cocked its head forward as its large golden eyes narrowed and looked at the king with intrigue. Alectorious stood motionless, allowing the mysterious being to examine him more closely. The Eternian leader was not at all frightened, feeling only a sense of calm. It was as if the dragon was trying to read his very thoughts, feelings and fears as it looked into the king's eyes - and very soul. The colossal being paused, moving back several paces before speaking in a deep, proud voice: one that could only be described as the embodiment of greatness itself.

"King Alectorious the 2nd of Eternity, I bid you a heartfelt welcome to my most humble mountain abode. It is not often I have the pleasure of visitors and indeed, *a king's* visit. I am known to your people as Reiactus: it is a great honour as it is a rare privilege to welcome you here this fine sun," the dragon offered, before taking a step back and resting, awaiting the Eternians' response. Alectorious was in a state of utter shock, having just seen his life-long dream manifest before his very eyes. The king managed to compose himself enough to respond, moving closer to the magnificent being and bowing as a sign of respect.

"Words now escape me, noble Reiactus, other than that the honour and pleasure shall *always* be mine," he offered, pausing briefly to collect his thoughts. The dragon was patient as the king continued, his eyes shining like diamonds in the brightness of the icy cave.

"Your name, your actions, you… are legendary to my people. Throughout Eternian history from the Age of Heroes hitherto, much has been written about your virtuous actions. We have spoken, venerated and even glorified the greatness of your being, which has provided us with much hope when all we could see was despair. Now more than ever before, Eternians look to your guidance as we struggle for the very existence of our nation. My men and I have toiled for many suns; overcoming countless obstacles to seek your council and the gods and The Great Spirit willing, help in our struggle against those who threaten the peace and sovereignty of not only Eternity, but all the known world."

As the king finished speaking, the dragon sat closer to the crystalline icy cave walls as if in search of appropriate response. It had been many eons since having had any direct council with the King of Eternity and indeed, Reiactus had not been expecting to again so soon. The dragon carefully chose his words; knowing whatever was said would have a profound influence on the consequent actions of the impressionable Eternian leader.

"It is greatly humbling to think one could be thought of in such high regard, Alectorious; but know in truth, my dear king, there is *nothing* that could begin to equal the brilliance of The Great Spirit and the light of magnificence it shines; for it is the all-powerful force that reaches throughout this world, as it does *all* the worlds of creation. Indeed, The Great Spirit created all in existence for the purpose of learning, growth and a deeper understanding of all things. It is to express and experience itself in all conceivable ways; those of both good and bad; light and dark, physical and non-physical. It is, was and always shall be, the greatest power in the entire universe," Reiactus succinctly explained. The king was utterly captivated, wishing to know all he possibly could.

"Reiactus, I find this something truly fascinating but how does it explain the creation of Eternians - souls - and their purpose in the world?" he asked, bracing himself for another long and eloquent answer. The blue dragon nodded in appreciation of the king's insightful question, relaxing on the rough cavernous floor to explain in more detail.

"An unimaginable number of eons ago, The Great Spirit extruded countless aspects of itself across the universe, each of which venturing out on a boundless voyage of discovery, with the ultimate aim of one sun finding their way back home to the source. These soul fragments found solace on the many worlds of creation strewn throughout existence, for the purpose of learning, growth and expanding in every conceivable way. It is upon this grandiose journey that each and every soul in this world, including *your own* travels, until they find their way back to the eternal light. Know that each and every thing in this world is an aspect of The Great Spirit, Alectorious; the rocks, trees, mountains, birds, animals *and* people... each in their own intermittent way, searching for the path home to the source of all creation: the all that is, was, or ever will be," Reiactus explained, as his bright golden eyes shone like never before. The king was rather confused however, having witnessed so much defiance of this unimaginable force of light in his twenty-eight eons of existence.

"Yet why, Reiactus, does The Great Spirit allow for all this needless suffering and pain - what good purpose could this possibly *ever* serve?" he cleverly reasoned. The dragon was very much sympathetic to the king's frustrations. He knelt, speaking close to a whisper.

"Know, Alectorious, that it is in the depths of despair that one shall find his brightest light, greatest courage and most inspiring hopes and dreams. It is in that deepest place of the soul where one shall find that inner strength to rise up against all conceivable adversity, be compelled to achieve the unachievable and reach the unimaginable. It is then that one shall *truly* appreciate their magnificent power within: the ability to change any aspect of themselves and the world around for the greater good of all," replied the enigmatic blue-scaled creature. Gasping in awe, the king was quite taken by the dragon's wise insights.

"Inspiring words, great Reiactus, and ones I shall *never* forget. It reminds me of legends that speak of your valorous actions in the first Eternian war. Could you elaborate more on this most revered era?" the king politely asked, wishing to discover more of Reiactus' enigmatic past. The dragon smiled in response, as if amused by the thought.

"Your historians have a tremendous imagination, Alectorious; creating all manner of tales, legends and mythologies to satisfy Eternians' insatiable desire for adventure and excitement. They see it as their duty to *not only* record the past, but glorify it in a way it never was to provide inspiration for those such as yourself, in moments such as now," he insightfully explained. Alectorious was disappointed with this response, probing further.

"So is *any* of it even true - did you *not exist* during the Age of Heroes, and as the legends say, save Eternity from the clutches of defeat?" he asked, as the dragon pondered. Reiactus was somewhat coy, wishing to not unduly influence the young king.

"I would say I might have greatly *helped* you, but only as any of my kind would have done. In ultimate truth, Alectorious, your heroes saved *themselves*. They fought for many suns with tremendous courage and valour, side by side with their loyal allies and companions.

They never gave in to those who threatened all that they loved, and not once questioned the unwavering belief that *they* were destined for victory. I arrived at the penultimate moment of the battle, swinging it ever so slightly in favour of Eternity and her brave allies."

It was to the great surprise of the king, who had hitherto been led to believe Reiactus played a *much* larger role in this most famous of battles. Alectorious was almost speechless.

"For all those eons I had been taught that you single-handedly saved Eternity!" he said, flabbergasted. The dragon began to speak in a more serious tone as he edged his face closer to the king's - his eyes deeply focused - the importance of his words unquestionable.

"Heroes and saviours are useful tools for those with a desire for power - people who wish to take away all your inner strength and thus, ability to affect meaningful change in the world. Be *very* wary of such troubled souls, Alectorious," Reiactus sternly warned, narrowing his piercing golden eyes. The king had no question at all as to why this was so.

"Of course: if everyone believed in a saviour, no one would ever be compelled to rise up against adversity!" the king insightfully concluded. The great one nodded - quick to corroborate the Eternian leader's intelligently discerning thoughts.

"That is very much so - and you must heed this in your *own* struggle, Alectorious," the dragon acutely advised, but the king felt truly overwhelmed by the colossal task ahead.

"But much has changed since that ancient age, Reiactus; the force we now face is *much* larger than that the heroes once did. The empire has consumed all before it, including those nations whom we once called our companions to the very edge of the known world. Eternity now stands alone, with not allies or companions to call upon and nowhere else to turn! It is why I stand before you now, Reiactus, humbly requesting your help in our most noble of struggles," the king announced, quite unsure how the great one would react. The dragon remained eerily quiet and still, sensing Alectorious had yet more to say…

REIACTUS AND THE KING

The king pushed further as he collected his thoughts and feelings, desperately hoping to convince the dragon to join Eternity's struggle against the empire. Alectorious did not wish to contemplate the possibility that he would not, believing there was now no-where else to turn.

"Great Reiactus; your legend gives my people a strength and faith I could not *even begin* to describe. If Eternians could only see you again with their very own eyes, it would ignite a belief and passion *I know would never* be extinguished. I ask; I even beg of you, return with us to Eternity and show us the magnificent soul you truly are, and together we shall turn the tide of this war *back into the light* of The Great Spirit, once and forevermore." Reiactus sighed deeply, lowering his head as if disappointed by the king's words. It was unexpected, as Alectorious had thought it would be an honour for the dragon to once more fill his role as Eternity's greatest hero. The giant blue creature closed his bright golden eyes before delving into a deep, meditative trance, searching for words to best express his thoughts, feelings and emotions. As much as Reiactus sympathised with the king's predicament, he was bound by a strict code of conduct. Since the dragon's intervention during the Age of Heroes, The Great Spirit had decreed that only when an entire civilisation was on the brink of collapse could its affairs be meddled in. Although Eternity was in considerable danger, its existence as a nation was not yet truly being threatened as it had been during *that* dramatic battle all those eons ago. The great one slowly opened his eyes, staring in a way as if to emphasise the importance of what he was about to impart. Alectorious had within his hands the ability to influence the course of history: it was this very power Reiactus wished he use most wisely. The dragon turned to the king with his piercing gold eyes.

"The strength you see in me, Alectorious, is but a reflection of what you perceive in yourself; if only you would look within to the limitless reserves of power and courage that you *all* hold, deep inside of yourselves. Eternians have long delighted in noble quests, heroic ideals and daring adventures in the pursuit of some intangible ideal, hoping you might discover a great treasure or unearth a sacred mystical knowledge that would forever transform your world. Let me impart that all you have ever sought and need know lays not a stone's throw away in the sea of your very souls. Know, believe and trust that it is only within *you* that you *can and will* find the answers to all the great mysteries of life and endless worlds of creation," the scaly blue being revealed. The king was mesmerised as he was enchanted by the dragon's divine words of wisdom. The dragon took a step back, allowing his esteemed visitor to fully absorb all he had said. Alectorious was listening intently yet was having trouble coming to terms with the dragon's cryptic way of speaking.

"Great Reiactus, I know not how I could *ever* unearth this power within of which you speak," he admitted, struggling somewhat with the intangible nature of the topic. Reiactus remained patient with the young king, knowing it went against much of what Alectorious had been taught throughout his eons living in Eternity. The dragon moved closer, resting his giant claws on the icy blue cave floor. He folded his mighty wings behind his rough scaly back, speaking in a quiet but understanding tone.

"You know so much more than you realise, Alectorious; for the power to change oneself and the world around is hidden in a secret place, deep within your soul; it is you and *only you* who can discover *and unlock* its unlimited potential. Have faith and search within; *know* that the answers to all you ever ask lie there, waiting patiently to be discovered. I see a strength in Eternity of which words escape and all description deny; you must learn to embrace this, Alectorious, if you are ever to succeed. The grace of the gods and The Great Spirit may protect you and my strength always inspire, but only alone can your divine and noble hearts of truth cross the great divide of faith to meet their ultimate destiny of greatness." Alectorious stood awestruck with limbs frozen, eyes mesmerised by the dragon's ancient words of wisdom. Reiactus continued before the king had a chance to reply, wishing he fully understand the profound importance of the message for not only Eternity, but the entire known world. As the dragon continued, Alectorious was utterly spellbound.

"You believe you are so far from achieving your dreams, Alectorious; but in truth, so very close. The scent of greatness itself now beckons you to take that one last step into the light of forever and lead Eternity *back into* the heavenly stars above. Triumph is so imminent that one can feel it in the air, whispering throughout the forests, valleys and up into these great mountains. The return to those once glorious ancient suns is so very close you cannot even imagine. *Believe Alectorious,* without question or shadow of any doubt in your mind at all that it *is but a heartbeat away*. If you could only understand this, your battle would be half won. And know always that it is *never ever* too late," the great one assured, encouraging the king to not give up on his dreams. Alectorious listened intently, imagining that ancient age of which Reiactus spoke, wondering if its' like would ever be seen again.

"You speak such tremendous words of wisdom, Reiactus, and inspire an unrelenting desire to achieve great things for this world - but it is so hard to see the light when one is overwhelmed by the shadows of darkness and despair. My nation is surrounded and we have allies no longer to call upon! It is hard to see how our enemies will *ever* be defeated," he despairingly admitted, dropping his head towards the floor. The dragon tried his best to encourage the downhearted king as he edged closer along the rocky surface of the cave.

"I know it is all you can *now* see, Alectorious; but remember, the journey of ten thousand spears begins with but a single step. When you start to believe in yourself and all that surrounds, I assure you *will* see the world change *beyond all imagination*," the mighty being assured. The king nodded in warm acknowledgement as he looked to the mysterious glowing blue walls of the cave and began to dream of those long-lost ancient suns.

"Reiactus, do you remember an age when there was not conflict, suffering nor pain - when men lived as one, in harmony with all living things? It seems almost impossible to imagine such a place ever existed!" the king dreamily remarked, drawing his eyes level with the dragon. Reiactus bowed his head deep in thought, casting his memory back to those long-forgotten eons, remembering as though it only the previous sun. The blue one gathered his feelings, searching for words to best convey his message of hope.

"Aye, I remember, Alectorious, very well. Ah yes, I remember an age now long past when man and dragon lived in such harmony together, the very mention of sword and spear was unthinkable. It was an age when every sun was an adventure of wonder and discovery to be held by all, far beyond *anything* one could possibly imagine now. Man and dragon would lie peacefully together in the bright valley meadows, listening to the sounds of forever through the bristling sacred trees and softly-flowing streams of pure life and love. They lived every moment to its fullest in unequalled bliss, with not a soul ever in need or want of anything at all. It seemed this heavenly age would last forever before the invisible winds of change dramatically swept across the lands, leaving not town, village nor soul untouched by its harrowing menace. Something inexplicable had happened that no-one could explain yet all could feel, right into the deepest depths of their souls. The world began to change; people became scared, mistrusting of their neighbours and once companions. From these feelings of fear, a desire for wealth and power over others was inevitably born.

Slowly, as man's heart grew weak and temptation strong, the Age of Harmony slowly began to slip away; the benevolent dragon went into hiding and the gods descended from their celestial paradise in the heavens to protect the vulnerable from those who misguidedly thought they were strong. And so from that happening henceforth to this very sun, the dark ones have ruled over these once-benevolent lands. They ever so mistakenly now believe that men of good hearts are at their weakest; and will seek to corrupt them to achieve their ambition to rule over the *entire* world. It is a goal they shall *never* achieve and is something they deep down know but will *never* accept. It is at this critical junction of the darkness' false confidence that men of good hearts must reach into the eternal reserves of courage and fortitude to shatter the illusions the dark ones have tried in vain to create. It is *now the moment,* Alectorious, to trust and believe like never before, and to follow the bright path of destiny that was laid out for you so many countless eons ago. *Now* you must fight with every piece of your heart and soul; and all the strength the gods and The Great Spirit allow."

Reiactus' brave words inspired the fire of desire to burn brighter within the king, who was more determined than ever to fight the empire right to the bitter end. Yet, he knew this could not be achieved by his nation alone. An emotionally charged Alectorious passionately summoned up all the words of inspiration, honour and courage he could possibly muster in one final plea for Reiactus' help, knowing without question the mighty dragon could make an enormous difference in their struggle for freedom.

"Then fight with us, great Reiactus and act upon the eternal words of wisdom of which you speak! Embrace this moment like no other and stand shoulder to shoulder with the Kingdom of Eternity! Together we shall destroy this despotic force and shatter the insidious illusions the dark ones wish us believe! We shall end this world of oppression they would have us live under and return the world to the once ways of those glorious ancient suns! I kneel before you now, with my proverbial hand on my heart and very soul in the words I speak, Reiactus, and humbly ask you to see past the rigid confines of your code that has been so utterly corrupted by Nerosis and his despotic regime."

The great one sat back against the cave wall, his wise old eyes narrowing as he went deep into thought, searching for words that would best serve the importance of his message. Alectorious patiently waited, still unable to believe he was in the presence of the great

Reactus himself. The intensity of the cave's energy increased as the dragon rose his powerful talons, as if to convey the deep importance of what he was about to impart.

"Of all the words that I speak to you, now and forevermore, remember this well: man is like a lost ship sailing into a stormy sea of affliction, where the only light shining in the proverbial darkness is a reflection of his higher self, beckoning him to come home. It is not through some magical quest over land and sea he will rediscover this place, but from going deep within to his very heart and soul. It is within *you* Alectorious, *more than anywhere else*, that you shall find the answers to *all* that you ever sought," Reiactus cryptically explained. Alectorious was greatly frustrated, feeling he had done this already.

"I ask myself moment and again, Reiactus, yet find no answers!" he protested, greatly frustrated. Reiactus' giant frame drew ever closer, his feet thundering as if an earthquake shaking the very foundations of the mountain. He lowered his head close to the Eternian king, probing further.

"Are you sure of this, young and noble Alectorious? Silence your mind and look *deep* within - let nothing of this material world interfere and your heart *will speak to you* - as the wind on a peaceful mountaintop," Reiactus promised, with a wave of his powerful talon.

The dragon remained silent, allowing the king to reflect on what was of tremendous importance to his nation's future. Alectorious lowered his head, trying hard to release all his thoughts and fears from within. He delved into the furthest depths of his soul, searching for answers to those untold questions. The king saw his life flash before his very eyes: from childhood and middlehood to the kinghood, then before he knew it, the adventure that had brought him all the way to this mysterious mountain and the great blue dragon himself. Alectorious thought of all he had encountered - the people, places and things, as many more questions without answers formed in his translucent mind - but perhaps those conversely were the answers to the questions he sought? He tried once more, concentrating as images of the many different people he had encountered flashed through his mind's eye. Reiactus looked at the king, intuitively sensing he was on the right path.

"What does your soul now whisper through your heart, Alectorious?" Reiactus gently asked. The king concentrated intently on the images, which were becoming clearer by the instant. Finally, a clear picture formed. The king immediately recognised who it was.

"The Catharians!" he elatedly said. Reactus pulled his head back with a sense of satisfaction, as if it exactly the answer he had sought from the insightful Eternian.

"I think your heart has spoken to you, Alectorious," he replied, proud of the king's efforts. Alectorious had almost completely forgotten about the forestmen, so all-consuming had his desire to find the dragon become. He had always held a curious fascination with these enigmatic nature peoples yet could never quite work out exactly why that was so.

"Although I never admitted as such, I had long believed the Catharians would be of assistance to us - is this to prove true?" he inquisitively asked. The dragon looked thoughtful as he dramatically turned the question back at the king.

"Well, do you believe *they could be*?" he asked. Alectorious pondered momentarily as Reiactus returned deeper into his cave, relaxing once more against the blue glow of the walls.

"I have *always* believed the forestmen could be powerful allies but few in Eternity ever shared my apparently controversial views. They are thought by most to be nothing more than a wild barbarous tribe - but I knew far better. I maintained my silence, hoping that one sun an opportunity to bridge the divide between our peoples would present itself. Finally, it seems it has," Alectorious proudly explained, realising he *was* heading in the right direction after all. Reiactus' shining golden eyes widened with interest as the king continued.

"At the beginning of our journey, we encountered a band of Catharians who helped us during a Gomercian ambush. They came unrequested to our assistance and showed tremendous valour in battle - especially their leader, who fought like none I have ever seen.

Their motives are yet unknown, but they clearly have no fondness of the empire. If I could have their audience once more, I know without question they would fight by our side. But even if they *do* help us, Reiactus, I fear an alliance with the forestmen would not be enough to thwart the overwhelming numbers of an imperial advance on our lands," the king admitted, looking despondently around the icy blue cave. Reiactus felt quite differently, however.

"You must open your eyes to the countless possibilities that abound, Alectorious. Many are those who can be of assistance, both seen and unseen; in the world of spirit *and* that of man," inspired the great dragon, taking a short pause of reflection. The king concentrated intently on the wise and ancient one, who became suddenly and quite inexplicitly direct.

"You must seek out your forest companions, Alectorious; for I *do* believe they wish to assist. It may not seem so at first, but they can without doubt help turn the tide of this world, *back* once and forevermore into the light. Go forth now and fulfil your bright destiny, King Alectorious, in the knowing that The Great Spirit watches over and protects you, *always,"* the magnificent blue dragon promised, with a starry glint in his eyes. The king had one answer.

"I shall heed your words of wisdom, noble Reiactus and will never forget this sun for the rest of my eons. I will be truly lost without your guidance," he expressed in appreciation, deeply saddened by the thought of bidding farewell.

"Know Alectorious, the greatest guidance is found within - *always* remember that. We will meet again, *when* your nation is ready," the dragon assured, pointing his powerful claw meaningfully at the philosophical king.

"How will I know when that is?" the Eternian leader asked, rather bewildered.

"Trust in yourself, Alectorious, *you will know*," Reactus steadfastly assured. The king nodded in understanding, readying to depart the clandestine icy abode.

"There is one more thing I must impart, Alectorious that you must promise never to forget." The king turned around, looking expectantly into the great blue one's eyes. It was something he had not expected but would forever remember. The dragon continued: his words were truly captivating as his voiced boomed out, echoing throughout the giant crystalline cavern.

"Bring light, to where there was once dark; bring love, to where there was once hate, and hope to where there was once despair. In the pursuit of all of these things, know that the gods and The Great Spirit will guide and protect you *always* in the noble pursuit of your highest truth," Reactus dramatically vowed, as his golden eyes beamed like the brightest stars in all the night sky. The king stood firmly with his eyes glazed, feeling an overwhelming sense of admiration for the truly magnificent soul standing before him.

"I shall not for the rest of my eons *ever* forget, great and noble Reiactus."

THE PEAK

After bidding farewell, the king made his way from Reiactus as quickly as his legs would allow, realising his companions would be wondering of his whereabouts. Indeed, he had been long in the mysterious blue caves and the suns would soon set into the towering peaks of the great Buvarious. With the air to drop well below freezing point through the night, there was not a moment to waste. The king weaved in and out of the icy crystalline passageways, trying his best to remember the way he had come, as the rope he had initially used went only halfway. Perhaps as importantly, he had to be careful not to fall through the fragile floor again. It seemed much easier than before, as return paths always do, with the king effortlessly winding in and out of the secretive dark passageways toward his point of origin. Before long, Alectorious arrived back at the mouth of the cave feeling greatly relieved. He found his fellow travellers unconcerned by his long absence, enjoying their wild mountainous surroundings as if he had never been away at all. It simply did not make sense.

"The king returns!" exclaimed Gavastros, throwing his arms theatrically in the air. The others quickly looked round before gathering in excitement, eager to hear of his majesty's adventures. Thelosious was simply relieved to see his old companion back in one piece, having been fearful of the dangers that lay within those dark lurking passageways.

"I am as ever relieved to see you safe and well, my king," he offered, smiling. Alectorious was confused by their indifferent responses, thinking he had been gone an age.

"Forgive me, I have been away too long," he apologised, rather bewildered. The king instinctively glanced to the blue skies above, noticing the twin suns had barely moved.

"You have hardly been away at all, my king!" a befuddled Thelosious replied. Alectorious was naturally very confused and struggled to find a logical explanation.

"That is impossible! I spoke at great length…" he began, trying to make sense of what had happened. Thelosious and Gavastros looked to each other, realising *exactly* what had. Beside themselves with excitement, they moved closer to express as such.

"So you *actually* met him… *the* great dragon?" an incredulous Thelosious asked. Gavastros displayed an equally disbelieving expression. The king's eyes brightened as the side of his mouth curled up in a wry smile, as though to reply in the affirmative. Disengaging his weapons, Alectorious was inundated with a veritable barrage of questions from his inquisitive companions. Eyes wide open and gasping, the cerebral one was first to speak.

"By the gods, this is unbelievable - whatever did he say?" he asked, astounded.

"Was he as the legends described?" the prodigy demanded, equally ecstatic.

"Was anything imparted to you?" asked Lacoenious, listening in interest with the other Elite Guardsmen. Alectorious raised his hands to quell the storm of curiosity as his men were unable to restrain themselves. With a smile and amiable chuckle, the king answered.

"Indeed, *I did* have the honour of meeting the great one; and truly an experience unlike *any* other. All I had hoped for he was, but not quite all I had expected. I *can* assure you that Reiactus is the most gracious, noble and humble being I have ever in all my suns encountered. I only wish you could have shared this immense privilege," he offered, in a naive attempt to satisfy his men's collective curiosity; but it only encouraged more questions.

"Did he speak of that which we sought; and will he assist us in our struggle?" Thelosious asked, with the others' attention impatiently transfixed. The king was elusive at first; trying to avoid directly answering anything he felt was too contentious.

"Many words of wisdom were imparted but I cannot reveal all for now," he replied elusively, as his companions were naturally disappointed. Alectorious wished not to divulge too much of his encounter, realising things had not transpired exactly as hoped. There was still a long path ahead and the king wished not to dampen his follower's impressionable spirits.

"My king, is he not willing to offer assistance in our struggle?" Thelosious pressed, hoping beyond reason it would be so. The others held their collective breaths, with it of course having been the primary reason they had ventured all this way into the mountains.

"Know that when it his moment, he will aid us once more; but for now, we must fight with whoever is willing to stand by our side," the king evasively replied. Gavastros was quick to discern the *true* meaning of Alectorious' words and was rather blunt in response.

"So he will not help us then," he sighed, dropping his head despondently. Thelosious felt this also but tried his best to be tactful, realising how difficult it must be for the king.

"Well did he offer *any* advice that might be of help?" he asked in hope. The king answered reluctantly, knowing it would not be what his companions wished to hear.

"The great one spoke in detail of the Catharian forestmen and that they could be powerful allies in our struggle, and encouraged us to strengthen our bonds with them. He also explained that alliance between our peoples was the only way to save Eternity and the known world from imperial tyranny." Thelosious was in agreement this option would need at least to be explored, realising there were few remaining. Gavastros was predictably much less enthused, having famously taken an early dislike to the leader of the forest dwellers.

"The vagabond - whatever could that foreign upstart possibly offer *our* great nation?" he spat, disgusted at the mere suggestion. Thelosious was clearly unimpressed, mercilessly scolding his vivacious companion's tactless remark.

"Mind your tongue, Gavastros!" he warned, raising his voice sternly as he narrowed his piercing eyes. Reflecting, the king's answer was significantly more diplomatic.

"I understand your personal dislike of the forestman, Gavastros; but know the fate of our nation's existence hangs precariously in the balance. *If* alliance with the Catharians can help change that - even just a little - it is an action I believe is worthwhile pursuing. I was advised by Reiactus himself on this and shall do all that I can to make it so. I need every last one of you to support me in these most desperate of suns, my companion." Gavastros was silent, knowing he was unable to argue with his king's reasoning. Alectorious delicately changed the topic, wishing the young prodigy not to be unduly embarrassed.

"The only question is, can we make it to the bottom of the mountain before the setting of the suns?" he asked, realising their journey up had taken much longer than at first anticipated. Rhoedas was quick to allay any fears, having already explored the area while the king was exploring the Prejosian caves.

"Fear not, my liege; for in your absence I discovered an alternative way. There is a rock-face nearby we can walk through, just as we had the cave entrance. I followed for a considerable number of spears: it winds down below the path we first came up and back to the forests," he explained, pointing toward a nearby, outwardly solid wall of rock and ice.

"Excellent work, Rhoedas; do you think we can we make it there before nightfall?"

"If we make haste, we should do," the tracker enthused. Alectorious breathed a sigh of relief, naturally wishing to avoid being stuck in the perilous mountains after sunset.

"But where shall we dorm, *even if* we make it this night?" Thelosious asked, knowing it too far to return to The Valley of the Gods. Rhoedas was confident, knowing the lands well.

"Worry not of that - we can build a shelter in the forests or seek refuge in nearby caves," he promised. The king did not hesitate, knowing they did not have long.

"Then we depart immediately - Eternians!" he ordered. With that, all gathered their belongings for the journey back down the mountain.

The seven adventurers embarked the hidden path Rhoedas had found, managing it with considerably less difficulty than their troublesome ascent. The snow falls had long ceased and the trail was covered in a blanket of thick white powder, and the skies above were now a clear, bright blue. With the path clearly visible, the Eternians took every step in their determined stride. It was with an ambition unlike the king had ever felt, in the deep knowing he was *finally* taking hold of his destiny. Soon they reached a break in the path, prompting the group to stop in their tracks.

"Wait! To where does this lead?" asked the king, pointing to an untracked narrow path that seemed to wind further up into the heights of the great Buvarious.

"That is the strangest thing, my lord; I had not noticed it before! I would imagine it leads to the summit of the Buvarious." The king was silent for a moment as he looked to the cerebral Thelosious, who knew exactly what his companion was thinking.

"We had better make it fast, Alectorious," he said, knowing any attempts to dissuade him would prove futile. The king smiled with a light chuckle as he turned to the tracker.

"Can we me make it up and back, Rhoedos?" he asked. The Elite Guardsman knew it was more of an order than a question, but nonetheless replied in the affirmative.

"We should, my liege; the return path, from what we can gather, takes a very direct route back down to the valley." The king nodded with smile as he looked to his men.

"Eternians; to the roof of the known world we venture!" Cheers of elation rang out from his men but Gavastros was unusually silent, perhaps by virtue of the fact he was still troubled by his experiences earlier in their mountain adventure.

"Are you ready, Gavastros?" asked the king, sensing all was not well.

"For Eternity, my king - always," he answered, knowing Alectorious was not at all convinced. The king let it slip, sensing the prodigy would be fine.

"Just the way," he acknowledged, patting his companion firmly on the shoulder.

The Eternians soon embarked on the mysterious snowy path, which wound gradually round the face of the mountain, presumably to the highest point in the great Buvarious. With every step they took, the path narrowed to the point that there was enough space to place only one foot after another. The adventurers kept their backs to the wall as they went, using their open palms on the smooth face of the rock to steady the way, while taking intermittent glances out to the spectacular views before them. As the Eternians drew nearer the top, the sense of anticipation became ever greater within the king, in the realisation a life-long dream would in mere moments come to fruition: to stand upon the roof of the known world. Each step seemed like an eternity as excitement rapidly grew, and the king hoped it would fulfil his lofty expectations of all he had dreamed it would be. As the moments passed, a smooth snowy plateau became acutely visible but twenty spears away. The king stalled, as if in disbelief, perhaps even denial of what his eyes told him. Thelosious duly expressed his concerns.

"Is all well my lord?" he questioned, unable to see what might possibly be wrong.

"I cannot believe we are here; but paces away, my companion."

"Then take the opportunity now, my king, before it disappears forever." Thelosious encouraged. There could not have been a better piece of advice the king had ever heard. He waited not a moment more and took his final steps forward onto the summit of the Great Buvarious Mountains. As he did, Thelosious signalled the others to hold back, knowing his companion needed some precious moments alone. The king stood in the centre of the small summit, which was a circular area not more than three spears in diameter. On the east side, the rock tapered up to form a pointed top reaching to about seven spears. Below that was a natural rock seat, which appeared from a distance like a large throne. The king did not at first make the connection as he simply stood in the centre of the summit, breathing in and out slowly with eyes closed, connecting to this moment that would never come again; expressing his appreciation to The Great Spirit for this divine opportunity. He slowly opened his eyes and looked out to the endless fields of mountains stretched out before his eyes, with their snowy peaks like a thousand beacons of hope to this troubled known world. With that thought, the king realised how much this epic journey had changed him and how he was seeing meaning and magnificence in the seemingly most trivial of things, compelling him to delve ever deeper both within and outside of himself in pursuit of the meaning of life, the universe and more specifically, why he had been brought into this world so full that it was of trickery, deception and despair. Perhaps beyond those mountains was a land that knew not those things, and how he wished to venture there if it were so; but on reflection, that was all the more reason for him to stay and fight with every fibre of his being for all that was right, good and true. He could only hope that the gods and The Great Spirit would, as he assumed they already were, supporting and protecting he and his knights on this most noble of quests. With that thought, the king turned an eye to the future, hoping beyond the brightest of all hopes that it would surpass a thousand expectations. He knew that within his heart, and if he were to follow it to his destined path, all that he dreamed would come to fruition – and so much more than that. As the king looked round, he noticed his men watching anxiously.

"This summit was not made for I alone, my companions; please come hither!" he insisted, motioning Thelosious, Gavastros and the Elite Guardsmen to follow him. The others needed no second invitation as they gleefully stepped onto the small plateau. They enjoyed the moment like there was no morrow, taking deep breaths of fresh air as they absorbed the experience into their being and enjoyed the stunning vista that the near cloudless sky offered. Others tried to spot recognisable landmarks or tried to guess what manner of civilisations might lie beyond, while some playfully took turns on the natural rock throne, pretending for just a moment they were the king of all the known world. The king was paradoxically the only one of group not to do so, which only reflected the humble nature of his being.

"If only we could somehow freeze this moment forever, Alectorious; what a memory it would be," imagined Thelosious, as he greatly enjoyed the uplifting energies of the summit, lamenting the fact they would so soon have to depart.

"Perhaps it will one sun be possible, my companion; only the gods know how. But fear not, for the memory of this, and all of our adventures will live, if we so wish it, forever in the depths of our souls." These wise words brought a measure of calm to Thelosious and the nearby Gavastros, who knew the king spoke only the truth.

"LOOK, MY LORD!!!" shrieked Gavastros hysterically as he pointed to the skies. The king and the others looked up in collective disbelief of what they were seeing.

"It could not be…" Thelosious remarked, disbelieving.

"It be he, my companion," the king assured with a warm glowing smile.

"REIACTUS!" Thelosious squealed, simply unable to contain his excitement. The others looked on with eyes utterly transfixed and without whispering a word, as if they wished not to miss a moment of what they were witnessing. The great blue one looked even more magnificent in full flight thought the king, as his bright blue scaly coat and golden eyes glimmered in the light of the setting twin suns. There could not have been a more magnificent being in all existence, imagined Alectorious, as the dragon swooped round the summit in a wide arc. He made several loops of the peak before flying at great speed into the twin suns. Then, without the Eternians at first realising, he turned back towards them. On this occasion he flew straight over their heads, only emphasising the dragon's massive wingspan, which must have been at least twenty full spears. The blue dragon then flew dramatically vertical before doing a perfect loop. Once he again he went vertical before he came to an abrupt stop in the middle of the sky. Suddenly his body plummeted at frightening speed, as the king and his men watched on in trepidation. As Reiactus appeared to re-gain control, a warm smile appeared on the face of the king, having known it was the dragon's plan all along. Reiactus dove down into the valley of the gods and pulled up suddenly at the last moment, travelling at great speed up to the summit of the Great Buvarious. The dragon appeared as if out of nowhere directly above their heads, before landing perfectly on the protruding rock rising up from the throne with his might talons. The dragon then opened his wings to full span and bellowed the most impressive roar one could have ever imagined. It was not in any way at all frightening to the Eternians as they watched in mesmerised wonderment, simply content to bear witness to a being of such divine magnificence in his prime. Before the Eternians could take another breath, the dragon leapt up and took off at great speed, first towards the twin suns before turning dramatically up into the heavens, accelerating so fast that he disappeared in a flash to stars above. There were words to neither express nor describe how the Eternians felt; for never could they have imagined they would witness such a thing. The king was first to speak, in fitting reflection of the collective sense of awe felt by all.

"There are simply not words to express, my companions." he said in fitting acknowledgement. All must have been in agreement, as indeed, without another word spoken, the Eternians looked out to where they had last seen the great dragon in the bright blue sky, wondering what manner of divine place he had ventured. With a tremendous sense of sadness, but an equal measure of fulfilment, the Eternians departed the roof of the known world, content they had made a memory that would last them a thousand lifespans and more.

As the Eternians continued back down the path, it took some moments for anyone to speak a word. It was as if they did not wish to spoil the magnificent grandeur they had been witness to, but the king realised that, as magnificent an experience it had been, they simply had keep going; to move on and make life all it could be from this moment on.

"We had best make haste, my companions, the suns will not wait for us!" the king insisted, taking a rather more light-hearted approached than he had hitherto. Thelosious read his companion well and offered his due words of support.

"Do they ever, my king?" he humoured, as the king played along.

"Well, certainly not for me, at least," he laughed, as the others joined in.

"But the gods will, Alectorious," Thelosious promised.

"I hope so, my companion," the king expressed, with a faint smile.

"I know it so, Alectorious," his life-long companion assured. With that, the Eternians continued down the path in complete silence, thinking of all the wonders the future might bring, feeling inspired as they were by the indescribable magnificence of "The Great One".

As the twin suns began to set, the skies became a myriad of spectacular colours, with the snow-capped mountains emanating a mysterious orange-purple hue. It was unmatched by anything in the known world and a rare privilege they would *always* cherish.

About halfway down the snowy mountain path, the Eternians stopped to rest before the final stretch into the forests. Taking up position against the rough, rocky walls, the king gazed out in amazement to the kaleidoscope of colours reaching across the skies.

"Truly amazing, is it not, Thelosious?" he said, as though staring into the heavens themselves. His companion was similarly taken, gazing in beguilement to the twin suns edging into the distant peaks. It was a sight unparalleled by anything he had ever seen.

"The gods truly bless us," agreed the cerebral knight, gasping in a dazed awe.

"I wonder though if they shall bless us also in the morrow," Alectorious wistfully hoped. Thelosious was thoughtful, offering his wise insights to this.

"We cannot control the will of gods, my king; only our reactions to the challenges they bestow upon our noble path. If we aspire to be all that we can be, I have no question the higher powers that be shall stand by our side, each and every step of the way."

"I only pray you speak the truth, Thelosious," Alectorious acknowledged, nodding. Rhoedas was visibly agitated as he looked to the twin stars above with great concern.

"We had best continue, my king, for the suns are setting fast upon us," he starkly warned. Alectorious had to strain to pull his eyes away, realising the need to push on.

"Very well; Eternians, onwards to the forests!" he ordered. The adventurers continued on the winding snow-covered mountain path as fast as was possible, with their legs now showing clear signs of fatigue. Fortunately, the Eternians arrived at the crossroads just as the suns passed into the distant mountains - it was much to the relief of all. They knew however that they would have to quickly find refuge for the cold wintery night ahead.

"It will be dark before long, my king - what now?" Thelosious asked, noticing the dramatic reduction in light. The king turned instinctively to the tracker but a spear away.

"Rhoedas - can we return to The Valley of the Gods? It is not far and we need to fetch the horses anyway." Rhoedas was not so confident, offering an alternative solution.

"It would most certainly be dark before our arrival, my king. I think it far wiser to make camp here: there are plenty of branches to make shelters on the forest floor," the tracker advised, as the king realised there was no other viable option available.

"Very well, we shall rest for the night in the forests; for without doubt, the nature spirits will watch over and protect us," he confidently proclaimed. The Eternians went quickly to work: they made their way into the nearby snow-covered forest, gathering all the fallen braches they could find before piling them into a thick bundle. The travellers placed them in several triangular formations before tying the branches together with the sinewy-like rope they had used in the mountains. Over that, they placed a lightweight but strong cloth they had been carrying for such eventualities, which would serve to block the elements of wind and cold. Afterwards, they cleared the ground of snow before positioning the triangular shapes upright as walls of several little forest huts. Finally, they piled snow around the outside to act as further insulation for the cold air that would inevitably seep in through the night. It was a tried and tested technique for many an Eternian traveller in the winter months, and would serve them well throughout the freezing night ahead. Before long they had erected three such shelters, with everyone exhausted from the sun's exertions and ready for a good night's rest. Gathered in the little improvised huts, Alectorious and Thelosious enjoyed their well-earned rest as the prodigy busied himself outside, making a small campfire for warmth in the long mountain night. Thelosious made himself comfortable on the forest floor, spreading his blanket out as best he could on the patch of ground cleared of snow.

"I wonder what the future holds for us and our nation, Alectorious, I truly do," he quietly reflected. Laying down his weary head, the Eternian knight tried to make himself as comfortable as was possible on the rough surface. The king was barely able to manage a response, so exhausted was he from the sun's exertions.

"Only Athesia and the gods above could possibly know, my companion; whatever it is to be, know it will be a bright," he assured, before resting his head on a makeshift pillow. "The future is as the great mystery of life, Thelosious: we shall never know until we reach out and experience it with all that we can be," he added, leaving his companion deep in thought. Alectorious slowly closed his eyes and drifted away, sailing peacefully into the endless world of dreams.

IN SEARCH OF THE FORESTMAN

The Eternians awoke at the crack of dawn to the singing of countless birds perched high in the trees above, with all ready to embark on the path home. There was an excitement not felt since first setting out on their grandiose quest, with the realisation they were *finally* returning to where it had all begun. It seemed an age since last setting eyes on their beloved Eternal city, with its magnificent boulevards, splendid gardens and not to mention the breathtakingly beautiful castle. The travellers looked forward to enjoying the many distinct scents and fragrances as much as they did Eternity's indistinguishably bright and colourful atmosphere. There was nowhere in the known world to compare to their cherished city; for it was truly unique in every imaginable way.

The Elite Guardsmen Chamelious, Segaerious and Mykos had meanwhile returned from the Valley of the Gods with the horses, well-rested and ready for the journey home. The Eternian steeds seemed in particularly good spirits, stamping their hooves impatiently as if in need of a nice long gallop through the forests. There had not been much for the equines to do in the valley other than lay around the lush grassy fields all sun long, so it would certainly be a welcome change for them to be back on the path again. As the group of knights assembled, the king had important words to impart.

"Eternians, listen! Our journey into the mountains has proven successful beyond question but there is one more thing we must do. Our struggle against the empire has raged longer than any could have imagined, and if we wish to see its end, Eternity must stand as one with all who oppose its tyrannical rule. We shall therefore travel to the lands of Catharia in search of the one named Sandros, in a bid to forge an alliance between our two peoples. If there are any amongst you who oppose, bespoken now," Alectorious announced, but all remained silent. While Gavastros disagreed, even *he* knew Eternity would struggle to overcome the empire all on their own.

"Then so it shall be - prepare to depart!" the king added, as his men hastily gathered their belongings into their saddlebags before mounting their steeds. Alectorious drew his horse nearby Rhoedas, who was closely examining the path ahead on the map. There was a single road leading all the way to Catharia, which they would undoubtedly take.

"Rhoedas; how long will it be to the forest lands?" the king asked, peering curiously at the old weathered parchment. The tracker focused his eyes intently as he fittingly answered.

"If this path is as direct as the map suggests, it should be before the twin suns set."

"Excellent!" Alectorious turned to address his awaiting men. "Warriors of Eternity - hear me now! You have done well to make it thus far on our most noble of quests; further than any Eternian in living memory. We have achieved much together, and witnessed countess wondrous things that we shall never forget for the rest of our suns. In as much as I have relished the challenges of our journey, it must, as all good things come to an end. It is therefore I announce our return home!" the king declared. A chorus of cheers rang out amongst his loyal followers, with some having felt it would never end. "Eternians, forward!" Alectorious dramatically ordered. Casting his arm ahead, the entire force took off on their mighty steeds like a bolt of lightning from the heavens.

There was a sense of relief amongst the Eternians as they made their way briskly along the forested trail, with a deep-seated feeling that despite being a great distance from home they would safely make it back. The horses soon broke into a full gallop along the seemingly endless tree-lined path as a strong wind blew on the backs of the brave adventurers - a perfect elixir for the trials of their gruelling journey. The return ride was quite in contrast to the perilous expedition *into* the great Buvarious; the path was certainly much wider and smoother as it gracefully transported the Eternians from the majestic heights of the mountains to their far-away city home. The trees surrounding offered a protective canopy from the elements, which could at any moment threaten to rain down upon them.

After almost a full sun's ride along the forested path, Alectorious sensed a distinct change in in the air; a feeling quite different from anything he had experienced on the journey thus far. Looking into the distance, the king *was convinced* it was because they were nearing the forest lands. Alectorious suddenly noticed an old man walking along the side of the path, who seemed blissfully unaware of the approaching riders.

"Thelosious, up ahead!" the king whispered, turning to his noble companion.

"I see him, my king - seems harmless enough - perhaps he can help us?"

"We approach - but with caution," warned the king, before delivering his orders. "Thelosious, Gavastros - ride ahead with me. The rest of you remain behind - twenty spears distance!" he barked. His men acted in prompt compliance. Alectorious rode ahead with his trusted knights, who tried their best not to cause alarm. As they approached, the man turned and looked at the Eternians with a kind of vague ambivalence. It was as if he was used to seeing groups of heavily-armed warriors, sensing they meant no harm.

"Greetings, my companion!" announced the king, raising his right hand. Approaching on his mighty steed, Sephalos, the man was quite surprised upon realising who it was.

"By The Great Spirit, I have not seen your kind for many eons indeed," he chirpily said, squinting to see properly. "What could I possibly do for you, good sirs?" he asked. Drawing his horse to a halt, Alectorious examined the stranger in detail. Dressed in light-brown earth colours, it was a clear sign he hailed from the lands of forest dweller.

"We search for the one named Sandros - do you know of him?" the king bluntly asked. The man was initially silent as he turned and looked deep into the forests. Thelosious suspected something, probing further. "We believe he hails from these lands, if this is indeed

Catharia…" he said, as Gavastros checked for movement in the surrounding forests. The man seemed to be debating with himself whether or not to reveal anything as he carefully inspected the heavily-armed Eternian knights.

"Catharia it is… well, the outer limits at least..." he began, hesitating before revealing more. "As for the one named Sandros; he's well known in these parts, sure. Carved quite a reputation, standing up to the empire and all; commands a lot of respect here, you know. Wait a moment - are you not King Alectorious… *the* King Alectorious of Eternity? You look exactly as I imagined him to be - without question you are Eternian - and most certainly look to be a king," the stranger realised in astonished disbelief.

"You would not be wrong, my companion," responded a bemused Alectorious, as the man dramatically changed his tone.

"Well it's an honour, your majesty! I never thought I'd meet a king, but there you go - The Great Spirit certainly works in the most mysterious of ways," he casually replied. Although impressed, the man was not overawed too much by the king's presence. It was hardly surprising, as Catharians considered all to be equal in the eyes of the creator.

"The honour is truly, all mine," Alectorious diplomatically offered, bowing slightly.

"You know, once long ago, Catharians and Eternians were great allies; I truly hope we see those suns again," he said, looking dreamily into the mystical forests surrounding.

"That is *exactly* what we wish to achieve - we believe Sandros and his companions could be of great help in the fight to free the known world of the Gomercian Empire - something that affects every last soul in these lands...." Alectorious warned, as the man mulled over the king's words. He was seemingly, greatly sympathetic to the Eternians' plight.

"Well in that case, I think I *can* help you. You seem to be a reasonable, honest and sincere king - not at all as I had expected. Now… if you follow this road, well beyond the two rivers, you'll arrive at a small village named Eskaldia - that's where I understand Sandros calls home - for now at least. I can't promise you anything, mind, but I *did* see him there, hmm… it must have been not two suns ago. It was quite odd… almost like he was waiting for someone… or something to happen. Quite unCatharian I must say but you know - there are some who say he was born of The Great Spirit or in some far-off mysterious land. Anyway, you had better hurry before it too late!" he divulged, as the king's eyes dilated.

"Thank you, my companion; we shall travel at the speed of the gods. You have been a tremendous help, and I wish The Great Spirit be with you." The man was humble.

"I was most happy to be of assistance, king. I truly hope you *do* find Sandros *and* form your alliance. It is the only way for Catharia and indeed, world to survive beyond the coming winter. I have heard all manner of horrible stories about the Gomericans: I can't bear the thought of them coming to *these* lands." he squeamed. The king was in total agreement.

"Neither I." he admitted, continuing. "If I may say so, you seem rather more favourable of Eternity than I had expected a Catharian to be - are there many others of your disposition?" he asked, curious as to how Eternity was seen by their closest neighbors. The man was frank in response as he looked to the enchanting treetops high above.

"Well, it's certainly not as it used to be: my ancestors would have said Eternians to be blasphemous heathens who thought far too highly of themselves, and cared nothing for the forests and animal worlds. I, as many others, always knew this *not to be so*. Eternians are people just as we Catharians, with the same thoughts, feelings and fears *we all* experience in life; most humble creations of The Great Spirit that we are. Wherever you go it's the same, I suppose - you'll find people of all kinds, both virtuous and unkind. Those you see eye to eye with and those that you don't," he wisely remarked. Thelosious was in particular admiration of this refreshingly simple, yet profound insight.

"All so very true," he remarked with an agreeable nod. The Catharian continued undiminished.

"Things have changed a lot since then - there still *is* that element of resentment around but young Catharians are now more curious than anything else - keen to know more of their proud, enigmatic neighbors. Perhaps as you are too, eh? You know, we *do* share a lot of history and culture, although both sides will never *openly* admit this. I feel it won't be long before we are all finally forced to confront the past," explained the man. It immediately reminded the king of conversations with Skolastros in The Valley of the Gods and those stories of Eternity's origins in the Age of Heroes. Alectorious was encouraged by what he had heard, with no idea perceptions had changed so much in his own lifespan. His nation had for long been cut off from their forest companions so there was no way of gauging what their feelings toward Eternity now were. The king realised simple, direct communication could have long ago eliminated the any misunderstandings that existed between their peoples. It was furthermore, quite amazing that despite their relative proximity, there were no formal relations between the two nations: something the king intended to change - very soon.

"Thank you once again for your wise, insightful words - we must now be on our way. I warn you to be aware, my companion - we were ambushed in the forests not a few suns ago by imperial forces," Alectorious revealed. The man was bemused by the king's assertions.

"Ha-ha! I thank you for concern but worry not of me; I know these forests better than any Gomercian *ever* will!" he assured with a dismissive chuckle. The king nodded, realising the folly of his statement.

"I thank you still..." he began, as the Catharian intuitively revealed his name.

"My name is Aeilious," he answered, politely smiling to the Eternian visitors.

"It was a pleasure, Aeilious; I bid you farewell," the king offered with a regal salute.

"Goodbye to *you*, King of Eternity," said Aeilious, before returning to his peaceful walk. With that, Alectorious pulled Sephalos' reigns, making his way back onto the tranquil forested path in search of the mysterious forestman.

THE HIDDEN VILLAGE

The Eternians rode briskly past the two rivers described by Aeilious to an area long known to be inhabited by the Catharian forest dwellers. They found little sign of life at first, other than the occasional small animal scurrying across the forest floor or chirping birds flying between the branches of the tall, thick-trunked trees. Alectorious had expected to find a large bustling settlement, yet there were no visible signs of any village or even people at all! At first glance, it was nothing but a vast forested area of enormous trees, with most of them reaching to heights of some ten hoplites. The soft forest floor was blanketed by countless fallen leaves - a clear indication the winter was fast approaching.

At closer examination of the forest canopy, the king noticed several suspended walkways connecting the larger trees and a number of small huts built around their trunks but well concealed by the thick branches - an impressive sight indeed. Alectorious was quite in awe of these ingenious creations, with his first impression being a sense of regret that he was unable to call such an enchanting place his own…

"Look - above in the trees, my companions!" Alectorious remarked. The knights and Elite Guard glanced up at once as their jaws dropped in equal amazement.

"Oh, I see it, alright," Thelosious concurred, gazing in fascination at the network of walkways and huts strewn across the forest ceiling. Lacoenious was also clearly awestruck.

"Very impressive; it is no wonder they have never been invaded," he remarked in astonishment. Meanwhile, the prodigy was busily scanning for signs of life.

"Catharians nowhere to be seen, though," he observed, oblivious to the marvels of creation surrounding.

"They cannot be far," sensed Rhoedas, whose instinctive nature was strong.

As if on cue, two burly men clad in earth-coloured clothing sprung out suddenly from the trees to the east. Further in the distance, yet more armed figures could be seen emerging from the forest: heavily armed and seemingly hostile. They made their way swiftly to the stationary Eternians, who readied themselves for confrontation. The Elite guard instinctively reached for their weapons but Thelosious was quick to signal restraint.

"Steady men - hold your swords fast - I believe they mean only to talk…" he whispered, intuitively sensing no genuine threat was at first posed. The Eternian guardsmen simultaneously loosened their grip, remaining wary however of the threatening group of warriors forming in the distant cluster of trees. The first two men moved aggressively at the Eternians and stopped not paces distant, demanding immediate answers.

"Who goes there - this is sovereign Catharian land!" demanded the larger of the two in a stern, rasping voice. Gavastros needed no second invitation, responding incredulously.

"By the gods, you do not recognise us? We are none other than the Knights of Eternity!!" he said, with more than a dash of his characteristic hubris.

"Gavastros, please!" the king quickly interceded. He stepped forward, offering a considerably more diplomatic reply than his overzealous companion. Alectorious bowed respectfully and tipped his helmet slightly forward before speaking to the man.

"Greetings, most noble Catharian; I am King Alectorious of Eternity and these here are my most loyal knights and guardsmen," he said, motioning to his surrounding followers. "We but humbly request safe passage through your lands," he added, before taking a step back. The Catharian was rather taken aback by the king's disposition, somewhat lightening his tone. The man looked the heavily-armed Elite Guard up and down, understandably questioning their purpose deep within forest lands.

"What business could Eternians possibly 'ave here? Catharia 'as no quarrel with you!" The man was quite suspicious of the Eternians' intentions, whose standing army was considerably larger than anything Catharia could realistically hope to assemble. The Eternian city had an uneasy relationship with the forest peoples; there was a degree of mutual tolerance for each other's nation, culture and customs, but lack of formal diplomatic relations between the two had led in recent eons to strong feelings of mistrust and indeed misunderstanding. Catharians had for long been wary of their powerful neighbours, fearing they would one sun be absorbed into a greater kingdom of Eternity. It was a feeling that had grown considerably since the rise of the empire, fuelled by the expectation of Eternians' desire to protect their nation's borders. These concerns were understandable perhaps, considering the forestmen's inability to effectively defend their lands from a full-frontal imperial assault. For now, Catharia survived mainly by virtue of Gomercian superstition, with it thought their lands were cursed by mysterious forest spirits that would swiftly vanquish any invaders to the haunting realms of the Netherworld. It would not be long however, before this ageing belief was found out by the ruthlessly ambitious Gomercian generals - something of which Alectorious was *quite* aware.

Catharians had always been a people close to the land and worshipped the natural world in all of its forms, believing the earthly elements and vast animal kingdom provided all the sustenance they required. Eternity by contrast had developed from a small hill-top settlement seven-hundred eons ago into a highly civilised, technologically advanced society: a city now home to some seventy-thousand souls. Eternians were also great innovators, having pioneered such inventions as the drawbridge, trebuchet and turreted castle walls. Meanwhile in the village, the man still seemed very much unconvinced as the king did all he could to reassure him of Eternity's peaceful intentions. Alectorious chose his words carefully.

"I assure you, we seek no trouble; our only quarrel is as yourselves with Nerosis and the Gomercian Empire. We wish merely to speak with the one named Sandros and shall peacefully be on our way," he requested, politely as he could. The Catharian nervously looked to his companion, at first hesitating before responding.

"And why exactly would you desire to speak to 'im?" the man suspiciously asked.

"To but thank him for his noble deeds unto us - I understand he is of these parts - do you know of him, or his whereabouts perhaps?" the king probed. The two men looked at each other bewildered, as if unsure how to answer. It was abundantly clear they knew *something* but were unwilling to divulge any further details. The smaller of them nodded to the larger, finally breaking his silence with an albeit rather bungled response.

"Sandros… oh 'im, long gone from here 'e 'as, deep into the forests, many suns ago it was…" he answered, nodding in a fashion as though to convince himself of his own words. The other, smaller man made a feeble attempt to support his companion's rather unconvincing claims.

"Oh yes, disappeared 'e 'as, many moons ago in fact; probably deep in the mountains by now… nooo chance you'll *ever* find 'im," he agreed, trying in vain to act straight-faced.

"Absolut 'ly; no chance at all…" assured the larger man once again, voraciously shaking his head. It was a poor attempt at hiding the truth but perhaps to be expected. The king realised how valued a warrior Sandros must be to Catharia, especially if they were to come under sudden attack; and it was equally understandable why they wished to hide him. Whatever the men's claims, the king knew deep down that Sandros *was* somewhere nearby.

"I assure you, we have no intention whatsoever of harming him," Alectorious promised, hoping it might ease their obvious nerves. "In truth, Sandros saved many Eternian lives - he is a hero to my men - and to me. I simply wish to offer my thanks," he added, sure that was enough to convince them, but the men steadfastly continued to deny all knowledge of Sandros' current whereabouts.

"I'm sorry, we can't 'elp you!" replied the man, as if to suggest *he did* in fact know something. Gavastros was becoming particularly impatient as he tightly gripped the hilt of his sword. Thelosious sternly shook his head, again signalling for restraint. The king finally decided to speak his mind, feeling a more direct approach was needed.

"You know, I think you *do* know where he is, so why will you not say?" he demanded, with an uncharacteristic forthrightness. Before they had a chance to conjure a response, a young boy appeared dramatically from the trees, running straight to the gathered men. He was some eons from being able to wield a sword, thus considered of little threat.

"Oh my - knights, real knights - I have always dreamed of meeting *real* knights! Are you *the* Knights of Eternity?" he asked excitedly. Pacing around the gathered Eternians, the boy admired their blue-gold armour with its elegant engravings and shiny smooth surface.

"That we are, my young companion," the king proudly answered, but in a kind-hearted tone, much as one would to a child of that age. Unusually, the two men did little to stop the boy, Thelosious sensing he was perhaps the son of someone important in the village.

"Amazing; Sandros told me *all* about you!" he remarked, having not been aware of the conversation until this point - or had he? The king looked to Thelosious and Gavastros with a mischievous smile as his suspicions were immediately vindicated. The two Catharian men's faces froze, trying to force the boy away.

"Sprachias back 'ome with you, 'tis for your own good - this is men's business!" the bigger Catharian said. The vivacious young boy was seemingly quite undeterred by his much larger compatriot, continuing as he added to the man's already great embarrassment.

"Sandros said you would come here one sun - I never realised it be so soon!" he continued in awe, with the king taking his opportunity to probe.

"Do you know Sandros, child?" he asked, as the smaller Catharian put his head in his hands. The boy concurred enthusiastically.

"Of course I do - *Everyone* around here knows Sandros - he's a hero in Catharia! In fact, he's sitting right over there, just by the river. Follow me - I'll take you to him if you'd like!" offered the chirpy small lad, quite happy to be of assistance to the knights he apparently so revered. Alectorious turned to the two men, humiliated as they were frustrated by the boy's unwanted intrusion. It was odd they had done virtually nothing to stop his unwitting attempts to lead the visitors to Sandros. It was quite a sight to see: but a small boy silence two heavily-armed men. Finally giving in, the larger of Catharians realised he could no longer conceal Sandros' presence.

"Make it quick, Eternian, and be on your way," he barked resentfully, motioning to the king. "Only you: the rest of your men must wait here," he uncouthly added. Alectorious was only too pleased to comply, having tracked Sandros much sooner than expected.

"Very well - Thelosious, Gavastros - do as the good man wishes and await here my return," he said. Nodding in compliance, Thelosious was relieved it had not escalated further.

"Understood sire, we shall not move; please, be as long as you wish," he assured. The king turned to the two burly "guardsmen", offering his humble gratitude.

"I thank you, my Catharian companions. My knights shall cause you no trouble - you have my kingly word on this. I shall speak with Sandros and immediately be on my way," he promised, before turning to the nearby riverside. The boy was already several paces ahead, excitedly beckoning the king towards the riverside.

"Quickly, before he goes!" he yelped. Alectorious followed, thinking curiously. It seemed all too convenient that Sandros just happened to be here *exactly* at the moment he wished him to be - perhaps it was by sheer coincidence - or it *was* fate, after all? Maybe the gods had even arranged it somehow, as they often do many events in life from their lofty abode in the heavens. Whatever the case, the king would soon find out the reasons Sandros was here. As Alectorious approached, the sounds of the river and birds in the surrounding trees were soft and peaceful, growing ever so slightly louder as he made his way to the water's edge. Alectorious knelt and removed his helmet before placing his hands in the trickling ice-cool waters, splashing his face to refresh from the long sun's ride. The king intuitively looked up and along the clear flowing river's edge, quite unable to believe what he saw: sure enough it was Sandros, sitting quietly as he leaned peacefully against a tree, enjoying the serenely elegant waters and delicate sounds of nature. The young lad approached Sandros, who placed something unrecognisable into the boy's hand before the child scurried back into the forests.

Alectorious made his way up the river, unbeknownst to the enigmatic Catharian and quite unsure what to expect. The previous encounter had been brief and given very little away of either man but Alectorious hoped this sun would be markedly different. As the king approached, Sandros moved closer to the river's edge and stared deeply into the mystical stream of transparent blue liquid. He swirled his hand around the crystal-clear waters, feeling the essence of life itself flow throughout his body and soul, seemingly unaware of the king's presence. Alectorious then knelt close by as Sandros casually turned to face him. The forestman was unphased: he turned back again and looked deep into the water as if the king were not even there at all, silent as he collected his thoughts and feelings.

"The great river of the forests, such a peaceful journey it follows; like watching life itself passing before your very eyes… it twists and turns… ebbs and flows… slowly but surely finding its way to that ever-elusive path of destiny," the enigmatic Catharian remarked, expressing his hitherto unseen philosophical side. The king listened with intrigue, sensing Sandros had yet more of this hidden wisdom to impart. "It moves so gracefully; through any obstacle one is to place before its path… all the things it must overcome…. you can try to block it… but it always… somehow… seems to find a way. Such is the path of life, is it not, King Alectorious?" Sandros asked, almost rhetorically. The king simply nodded, mesmerised as he looked similarly into the crystal-clear blue waters flowing gently by. There was not a word he could disagree with: it was truly the perfect analogy. Sandros continued as Alectorious listened with great intent. "I've been fascinated by this idea all my life, ever since I was a small boy. Does it interest you also, Alectorious - do you *also* believe that like a river, life can find a way through all obstacles placed before it?" asked Sandros, turning meaningfully. The king was quite moved by these pensive insights, likewise requiring some moments to conjure an appropriate reply. It was certainly a departure from the heated nature of their previous meeting, which had not exactly reflected the better part of the Catharians' personality. It only served to deepen Alectorious' curiosity in the mysterious forest dweller.

"As a young child I would often be taken to the River Glasovia, close to the walls of Eternity. I would make small boats out of wood and parchment, sailing them downstream to rougher waters. Such memorable suns were they; I would do *anything* to bring them back," the king nostalgically recalled, as he cast his mind back to those long-past innocent eons.

"So now, Alectorious, the mythical ship of Eternity, sailing into rough waters; but will it find its way, as does always the river?" asked Sandros, turning evocatively to the king.

"Only the gods and The Great Spirit could possibly know our destiny, Sandros," he wistfully acknowledged, sifting his hand briefly through the soothing, fresh trickling waters.

"Perhaps they do… or perhaps… they do not. I believe only *you* and the nation of Eternity can ultimately determine this… Alectorious," the forest dweller reasoned. The king was surprised by this sudden proclamation by the forestman.

"You do not believe in destiny?" he asked, bewildered as he squinted his eyes.

"Oh yes indeed, very much so; but in the end, Alectorious, it is up to us to fulfil what has been preordained by The Great Spirit to be. Destiny is merely written: it is only one's actions that can bring it to realisation," responded Sandros, with his meaning much clearer.

"With that, I cannot argue, Sandros," the king conceded, impressed with the Catharians' deep clarity of thought. "I wonder, though; *will* Eternity find its way through these proverbial rough waters?" Alectorious prophetically asked. Sandros became quiet, looking reflectively into the thick forests surrounding the tranquil river.

"If she stands united with all who oppose her enemies... my answer would be aye... but if she continues to stand alone... I fear the hand of fate may not be so generous..." he starkly replied. In that moment, the king saw his opportunity.

"That is *exactly* the reason I sit before you, Sandros - I have realised we - Eternity, can no longer do so, and need all the help we can possibly find in fighting this insidious force that threatens not only ourselves, but the *entire* known world, *including* Catharia." he revealed, before sitting on a nearby rock facing the river. Sandros nodded in acknowledgement but was silent at first. He peered into the flowing river, listening to the sounds of trickling waters that had always so enchanted his enquiring soul. After a few moments of contemplation, Sandros broke his silence, and with a distinct change of tact.

"I must apologise for my actions before; it was very much out of character," he suddenly admitted, alluding to the initial meeting with Alectorious and his knights in the forests. It was a stark break from his previous statement as the king countered.

"I believe it is *I* who should apologise... for my knight's behaviour... it was *he* if any, who was out of order - Gavastros is his name..." explained the king, somewhat embarrassed.

"I know, I heard," Sandros bluntly replied, with a slight hint of resentment.

"In the heat of the moment, things are said that we never truly mean..." Alectorious reasoned, in a half-hearted attempt to defend the young prodigy.

"Yes, the heat of battle - the test of a *true* warrior - one who can keep his head cool and heart strong through the most testing of circumstances - *that's what truly* wins people's hearts and minds, as much as it does battles; *even* wars," added Sandros. The king was again, greatly impressed by the forestman's wise insights.

"Prophetic indeed," he freely admitted. "You really need not apologise. If anything, I should be thanking *you,* Sandros; you saved *my* life, without question. If it was not for your courageous actions, I would most certainly not be sitting here now," the king admitted. Secretly, Sandros warmly appreciated this sentiment, answering graciously.

"I did what any would have done - help a soul in distress," he outwardly insisted. Turning again to the gently flowing river, the forestman wished for no glory from his actions.

"There are not many who would have risked themselves like that, Sandros."

"Perhaps not," the forestman said, losing himself again in the ebbing waters.

"Well in any event, there are some *rather* pressing concerns I must discuss with you before my return to Eternity. Come, shall we walk?" the king asked. Standing, he invited Sandros to accompany him for a brief walk along the meandering riverside. He accepted, and the two men began along the narrow upstream path. Alectorious continued, but in a far more serious tone than before. "As you probably know, Eternity is under threat from a force unseen in many generations: it has swept through the known world to the very gates of my city. As you might *also* realise, it is not only *my nation*: the lands of Catharia are also in great danger. It will only be a matter of suns before the Gomercians come here; to these forests, your village and this very river, even. In one foul swoop, they will take away *all* you have ever loved and held dear," he explained, hoping it might sway the brave warrior's opinion. Sandros seemed remarkably unphased, adamant the empire posed no immediate threat to either himself or the forest lands of Catharia.

"There is nothing for them here, Alectorious: not castles, gold or jewels! Nerosis is well known for his superstitions and truly believes these forests to be cursed!" he pointedly countered. The king would not give in, illustrating the reality of Catharia's predicament.

"And how long will that last, Sandros - how long will it be before he realises this is *not* so? You saw them on the mountain trails - it is not that far from here!" Sandros was silent as he turned to look at the surrounding forests. Alectorious continued, with his voice tensing. "And if you think there is nothing for him here, you are greatly mistaken Sandros," he added.

"Then what *is* there for them in the forests?" the Catharian asked, while secretly knowing. The king answered in no uncertain terms, placing the forestman on the defensive.

"Land: vast stretches of forest to hide their massive legions. Here, Nerosis will be close to the one place he longs for more than any other to hold within his imperial grip: the nation of Eternity. If he were to gain a foothold here in Catharian lands, it would make invasion of my city *very* difficult to prevent: it is the only explanation for his forces having been so close." Sandros listened intently, but was ultimately dismissive of the king's fears.

"Catharians will defend these lands to their very last breaths: they will *never* allow them to be taken. The Gomercians don't understand these forests and the sacred importance they hold," he resolutely maintained, confident any incursion would easily be thwarted.

"Nerosis cares nothing of that, Sandros! All *he* understands is that he commands an army *vastly* superior in number to Catharia or Eternity. We *cannot* allow him to come this far," the king warned, emphasising the catastrophic consequences of inaction. The Catharian was discerning, sensing an ulterior motive within the Eternian leader.

"We, you say - is that the reason you have come here - for my service, and sword in your army?" Sandros bluntly asked, knowing already the purpose of the king's visit. The forest warrior hid his feelings well but decided to hear the king out first. Alectorious unapologetically continued, believing Sandros could hold the key to great change. He sensed a power within the forestman unlike anything he had ever encountered. But perhaps that was merely a reflection of what he saw within himself? Alectorious continued undiminished.

"I have seen you in combat, Sandros, and the potential you have to make a difference in this world. Never in all my suns have I seen such bravery, swordsmanship and willingness to risk oneself for a cause that is not his own." Sandros was quick to dismiss these lofty assertions, having seen it as merely his duty to serve the greater good of the world.

"I showed no more than any other warrior who risks all on the field," he replied, as the king was further taken by his unassuming nature.

"And such humbleness," Alectorious added, continuing. "Men like you can inspire an entire nation, Sandros - change the tide of a battle - even history. They have been immortalised as legends, forever remembered in the great books of heroes," the king further encouraged. Sandros was bemused as he was indifferent to such high praise from a king.

"I helped you defeat an inexperienced patrol, *not* an army! This blinding love of mythology and legends makes you see things, and people that aren't really there. You want to believe in a hero that can singlehandedly defeat the empire and save all the known world! It was never meant to be the way, Alectorious. Can you not see what this is all about - what The Great Spirit is trying to tell you?" he inquired. The king shook his head bewilderment.

"It's because that person doesn't really exist!" he dramatically revealed. The king tried hard to hide his look of disappointment as Sandros enthrallingly continued.

"We have to find the hero within each and every one of ourselves, Alectorious - not in some mythical forest warrior or dragon, high up in the mountains! It's the only way you can ever hope to win this war and save the known world from this tyranny." It was quite the revelation for the king to swallow, having all his life been led to believe that one soul above all others would rise up to and vanquish the empire from these once benevolent lands. The king had long believed it to be Reiactus, but alas, had discovered it would not be so. He was then sure it could only be Sandros; but now the forestman seemed to be in denial. In spite of all this, the king was still confident the Catharian could do much to assist.

"Perhaps we all *will* one sun find that hero within, Sandros, but there will *always* be great warriors. I think that you *can* still make an enormous difference in this struggle. In fact, I think you *want to help*," insisted the perceptive king, intuitively sensing, for reasons unbeknownst it had been Sandros' plan all along. The forestman was again illusive.

"Perhaps I could and wish to, but would Eternians willingly accept *me*; one who dwells in the forests to stand amongst them? I speak, think and act not as you do," he mused. Alectorious remained calm and steadfast, replying in equal kind.

"Their king receives you - there is no need of any higher recognition than this. I promise, the people of Eternity *will* accept you," Alectorious replied, sensing a deep-seeded desire within Sandros to join their ranks. Why, he could not explain, but would find out in due course. The forestman looked deep into the cascading blue waters of the river, then to the treetops above in search of words of inspiration.

"The force we shall face is greater than anything that has come before, Alectorious, I can assure you: the Gomercians *will not* be defeated by hiding behind your great city walls. Eternity's defences are the strongest in the known world and for now, are safe. However, the empire is watching *very carefully*, waiting for the perfect moment to strike. It may be not now, the morrow or twenty suns henceforth, but strike they eventually will - and with all of their might. Nerosis will surround you with his vast armies and not leave until Eternity submits to his oppressive rule," Sandros chillingly predicted. It was as much a warning as a seeming admission of his desire to help the Eternian cause. Alectorious was greatly sobered by this stark realisation, taking a few breaths to come to his senses.

"Well, what would you have us do then, Sandros?" he despairingly asked, having seemingly exhausted all possibilities for a counter-offensive with his commanders.

"Something audacious; risky, even dangerous you may say, but something Nerosis would *never* think of in all his wildest of dreams. It is for that very reason it *will* succeed..."

Sandros assured, as the king's eyes excitedly lit up. He intuitively sensed Sandros was onto something and desperately wished to know more. The very thought of defeating the Gomercians was almost too good to be true as Alectorious pushed further.

"Then travel with me to Eternity, Sandros, and show us what you are *truly capable of.* Together, we shall rid the known world of the Gomercians and restore peace, once and forevermore to these lands," the king encouraged, hoping he had done enough. Sandros relaxed as his mood markedly changed.

"On a whim, king of Eternity; would you put all your faith in a mysterious man of the forests?" he quipped with a playful chuckle. Alectorious calmed, smiling in good humour.

"On the contrary, forestman, it was *you* who risked your life for a complete stranger!"

"That I did," conceded Sandros, as the king's expression became suddenly serious.

"Truthfully, I would never do *anything* on a whim. I have and *always will* follow my instinct, Sandros, and it says I should trust you now. There is something about you I feel but cannot see - I sense you know a lot more than you will admit - I know not what it is but you are quite unlike your fellow countrymen," he disclosed, unable to place his finger on it.

"Indeed there is much, Alectorious, and all will eventually be revealed."

"Only when you are ready, Sandros," the king replied, wishing not to pry too much.

"So, what would you have me do?" asked the forest warrior, in an apparent offer to help the Eternians. The king smiled in satisfaction, knowing it would be the beginning of a powerful alliance. He answered calmly, knowing there were no promises.

"Three suns from now, there will be a tournament in celebration of the autumn's end and coming winter. The finest warriors in all Eternity will gather to compete for the prestigious title of the city's greatest swordsman. It will be a chance to test yourself against the finest warriors in the land, and an opportunity that may never come again. If you *do* choose to participate, I believe you have every chance of being victorious. You will be an honoured guest in the king's residence and be afforded all the honours as such; *if* of course, you would be only so willing as to agree. What say you of this offer I bestow upon you, Sandros?" the king expectantly asked. Seeing that burning fire of desire ignite deep within the forest warrior's eyes, Alectorious immediately knew the answer. It was an offer too great for Sandros to resist: his chance to prove himself against the very best had finally arrived after all those eons of waiting.

"The finest warriors in all Eternity, you say; a most enticing offer. I fear however, that your people will see me as but a vagabond foreigner, no matter what my actions of valour on the field." The king was quick to dismiss his concerns, reiterating his earlier promise.

"Remember, you shall be there by virtue of the *king's* invitation, and a most honoured guest. You *will* be accepted, Sandros: of that, you have my kingly word."

"But how will I travel beyond your city walls, into Eternity?" asked the forestman, in a final acceptance perhaps of the king's alluring offer. Alectorious promptly responded, with his eyes beaming in sheer delight.

"Take the north entrance and inform the guards you are Sandros of Catharia on the request of the king himself. I shall advise them of your arrival in advance. Take this coin; for it is the mark of the Eternian King," Alectorious proudly answered, placing an elaborate golden piece in the forestman's palm. Sandros looked up, with a telling look in his eyes.

"Then so it will be, Alectorious: three suns from now, we shall meet again in the glorious City of Eternity," he promised. The king had heard all that he needed. He stood, before beginning along the winding, clear blue river to his companions waiting in the village. Alectorious dramatically turned around before looking the forestman directly in the eye.

"Three suns from now, Sandros; and this world will change, once and forevermore."

Made in the USA
Middletown, DE
18 May 2021